'...a well-structured and accomplished character-driven work...a flowing, subtle and rewarding read.' *Australian Bookseller and Publisher*

'Rhyll McMaster tosses us in at the deep end...enlivened by a genuine mystery, a slender but powerful narrative thread... It's a masterstroke ...she makes this novel so much more than a simple story: in the clever patterns of imagery, the brilliant descriptions, the narrative structure and the understanding...that a good novel has something to say about the world.' Kerryn Goldsworthy in *The Australian*.

'McMaster is interested in the fragility of identity and the dynamics of personal power. This superb first novel is beautifully written but not for the faint-hearted...in a class of its own.' Christina Hill, *Australian Book Review*.

'...In tracing Sooky's progress from a traumatized suburban childhood to the beginnings of a successful international career as an artist, McMaster charts the emotional complexities of dependence, loyalty, cruelty and betrayal...' Kerryn Goldsworthy, *The Australian Literary Review*

'rich, darkly funny and disturbing.' Rachel Slater, *Australian Women's Book Review*

'*Feather Man* is boldly original and self-assured. The narrative voice is darkly witty, but beguilingly honest. Nothing is sugar-coated here...' *The Courier-Mail*

'...an exhilarating and absorbing work of prose...' Catherine Freyne, Producer, *The Book Show*, ABC Radio National.

'...men will loom over Sooky in one way or another, demanding to know whose girl she is. Sooky is...observant and clever and at times wonderfully funny.' Michelle Griffin, *The Age*

'Rhyll McMaster has struck gold with her debut novel of betrayal and loss... This is a stunning, dark story with tight, controlled prose. Unforgettable.*****' *Goodreading Magazine*

FEATHER MAN
by Rhyll McMaster

MARION BOYARS
LONDON · NEW YORK

Published in Great Britain and the United States in 2008 by

MARION BOYARS PUBLISHERS LTD
24 Lacy Road London SW15 1NL

www.marionboyars.co.uk

Printed in 2008
10 9 8 7 6 5 4 3 2 1

First published in Australia in 2007 by Brandl & Schlesinger, NSW,
Australia

Copyright © Rhyll McMaster 2007

A CIP catalogue record for this book is available from the British Library.
A CIP catalog record for this book is available from the Library of
Congress.

ISBN 0-7145-3148-0
13 digit ISBN 978-0-7145-3148-9

Set in Goudy Old Style 11/14 pt
Printed in England by J. H. Haynes & Co. Ltd., Sparkford

ACKNOWLEDGEMENTS

I wish to thank Rodney Hall for his generosity and for his skill in helping me refine the early structure of my novel; Peter Porter for his kind encouragement and defining critical commentary; and my editor, Diana Giese, for her invaluable and erudite assistance in the final shaping of my work.

Acknowledgement is made to the following copyright holders for quotations from lyrics:

'Five Minutes More,' by Sammy Cahn and Jule Styne, Cahn Music Company, c/- WB Music Corporation, and Morley Music Co., c/- MPL Communications Inc; 'It's Only A Paper Moon,' by Billy Rose, E.Y. Harburg, Harold Arlen, Anne-Rachel Music Corporation, c/- Warner/Chappell Music Inc., Glocca Morra Music Corporation c/- Next Decade Music and S A Music Company; 'She Wears My Ring,' by Boudleaux Bryant and Felice Bryant, House of Bryant Publications, Sony ATV; Tennessee Waltz by Patricia Lynn Rothberg, The Bogart Trip, c/- Patricia L. Rothberg, APRA.

Every effort has been made to contact copyright holders, but should any have been overlooked, we would be pleased to hear from them.

Contents

Redmond

Paul

The nymph, Lyce, made Daphnis swear eternal fidelity to her; otherwise, he would go blind. Intoxicated by the princess Chimaera, Daphnis broke his vow and at once lost his sight. He killed himself one day by falling from the top of a cliff.

Lionel

Out of the Blue

The day before had been a day of rain and once again Lionel and I were busy in the chook yard. The summer rain started in the late afternoon. One rumble of thunder and it poured. The spears of rain fell straight down, no wind, curtain after curtain of water, as if the stage manager had overdone the effect.

The smell of damp chooks thickened the air as Lionel worked to clean up their yard. I didn't like the smell. It was so strong that I retched behind my hand. It was the same heavy smell their dead bodies gave out when Lionel dunked them in hot water in the downstairs concrete tub.

'Softens their quills,' said Lionel. 'Then they pull out nice and easy.'

He put his whole hand up their bum holes and pulled out their innards. He showed me their crops, still full of undigested grain, their tiny red hearts and brown livers and something I couldn't identify, ribbed and hard and orange in colour. I watched, unable to turn my eyes away, as he chopped their heads off on the block in the back yard, leaving a mash of blood and neck feathers. Their heads fell to the ground, their eyelids closed and whitening, their combs fading.

On top of the smell of wet feathers was the stench of liquefied chook shit. I could bear it when it was dry, but when wet it had a slimy, gutter smell of gizzards. The yard turned to liquid mud mixed with runny shit and Lionel used a shovel to clear out the bigger pot-holes, slinging scoops of stinking gravy through the wire fence.

He worked hard, his faded white and yellowing Chesty Bond singlet spotted with manure, a bead of sweat forming at intervals and running off the end of his beaked nose. The humid air pressed down on the back of my neck, a burning clamp. Rivulets of sweat ran down my back and into the crack of my buttocks.

I stood at the doorway and watched him work. I scribbled on my note-pad what I saw through one of the six-sided holes in the wire fence, reluctant to enter this Ypres of mud and sodden birds. He worked without speaking, his lips pressed back against his china teeth. Sometimes he let out a thin whistle of exertion. He propped his chin on his shovel handle, and wiped his forehead with the back of his arm.

'Taking a breather.'

He pin-pointed me with his right eye, framed in a net-hole. 'Come in and help.'

'No, I don't want to.'

'What's the matter with you? Come and help Lionel.'

'No, I don't want to get dirty.'

I shifted position. Now I saw both his eyes calculating. I tried to keep my distance from him, but the more I evaded and retreated the more he advanced. All of a sudden he was up close, so close I saw the freckles on his shoulders, a pattern of tawny confetti.

'Don't you say no to me.'

He hoisted his shorts up, put his hands on his hips and stared.

'Come on, I'll give you a piggy-back and you can get the eggs for me. I'll lift you over. You won't get dirty. Hop on.'

He bent his back and braced his hands on his knees so that the skin pushed over his knee caps in loose puppy-fat folds. He gestured for me to get on.

I thought of those times of contented indulgence when he piggy-backed me round the yard so I didn't get bindi-eyes in my feet. It was a world free of adults up on his back. I raised my arms and brushed the soft, fishbone foliage of the giant poinciana. I grabbed a handful of leaves and shredded the leaflets off their stalks so they fell in tropical snowflakes as he jogged around.

I thought of my father shouting 'Look out!' as he carried me on his shoulders. He ducked under the Hills Hoist and raced down the side path at break-neck speed, the dog bouncing ahead and turning her muzzle to smile, one ear askew and turned back on itself.

I always trusted Lionel and my father to look after me, even though I knew it was my job to watch out for myself, up there in my aerial kingdom. The best part was when I got lifted down, my entire body weight held for a moment, suspended in that stopped world between earth and sky, safe within the bookends of their hands.

'Lift me up, lift me up,' I pleaded to my father, wanting again that ineffable sensation of weightlessness.

Now Lionel waited. His finger pointed up his curved back. He had a curious lump on the middle of his back, near the spine. I got on, tucking my spiral-bound note-pad into my waistband. He had taken off his singlet so my bare legs stuck to his skin and I felt my body heat front up to his clammy coolness. He stepped up the yard under my weight. I saw his sandalled feet land on the scraped stepping-stones.

We entered the relative dryness of the nesting boxes, but he didn't stop to let me gather the eggs. Instead, he swung me off his back, stooped again and laid me down in the space under the ladder that gave access to the higher perches. There was a bit of straw there under the over-hang of the boxes, a few pinnacles of chook poop and some dry dirt.

My hands still gripped his shoulders. I felt the bat wings of hair that ran across his back. He pushed his face close to mine. I looked at his eyes. They were remarkable, glassy, with yellow rays, but now they had a white glare in them, as if I was looking up close into the tunnel of a turned-on torch.

'Whose girl are you?' He gave my shoulders a shake.

'I'm nobody's girl. I'm me.'

He straddled me on his hands and knees. His face showed a mixture of threatening authority and displeasure, but now the threat held a blaze of excitement that didn't seem to have anything to do with me.

I wanted my mother to come down the back yard and call for me. I wanted her voice to intervene and fetch me back to what I knew. Even though I'd get into trouble, I wanted her to find me. She must have been down at the shops or reading a book or having a cool shower, for she did not come to rescue me.

He sat up on his haunches and undid the buttons on his baggy khaki shorts. It was dark in there between his legs. He didn't have underpants on the way my father would have. He forced my left hand to touch him.

'Feel that. Nice. Tickle my willy.'

'No, I don't want to.'

He let go my hand and bent over me again. His face came close with its lit-up eyes. He slobbered on my mouth and nibbled my lips with his teeth, a deranged rabbit. He sucked my nose so I couldn't breathe. He stopped and I hoped he had finished. I couldn't stop him. In the end, I always did as I was told.

My mother's timid politeness was my rickety refuge. If I did as he said, he would go back to being Lionel the magistrate. The universe would right itself; sense and grown-up sensibility would prevail. But it didn't, not this time. Instead he shoved my shirt up my chest and kissed me on the stomach.

'I don't want you to do that.' My voice sounded hollow.

'Why not? It's nice.'

He strung out the word 'nice' in a slur. I had never heard him speak like this. What was this thing that had climbed out of the Lionel I knew, this hairy tarantula? One of my father's phrases came into my head. 'Grin and bear it.' I couldn't grin but I hoped I could let this macabre story play itself out.

'Nice,' he said again and moved his head down. At the same time he pulled my Elizabethan bloomers down round my ankles.

'Here, give me those silly scribblings,' he said, and he threw my note-pad out of my line of vision.

He bent and slobbered between my legs and my heart beat in tiny, unaccustomed patterns. I saw a pair of chook's legs walk by my head. Even the chooks acted as if everything was normal. The wire of the chook fence to one side of me looked as usual. The bit of sky over one of Lionel's shoulders was a disinterested blue. But my thighs looked unusual, the way Lionel had jacked them up and spread them apart. I wasn't used to seeing them that way. They looked pale and nude, the inside of frogs' legs, as if they were too unripe to be like that.

Lionel fiddled one hand around between his legs where he wanted me to touch him. Now his hand moved in rapid jerks. He stopped and spat on his finger. He grabbed me round the neck with his other hand, his thumb and fingers under my jaw, and squeezed. He didn't cut off my air but I felt a sense of pressure and dizziness. He pressed and dug with his spat-upon finger in that area my mother called my bottom, pushing until his finger went right in.

I ached inside, the raw ache you get when you press your eyeballs hard. He groaned. His mouth hung open. He took his finger out and lay on top of me. Now I couldn't breathe or move or call out for my mother as he took his hand from round my neck and pushed under my chin so my head went back as far as it would go. He tried to poke something in where his finger had been. I was dry and stinging down there. He gave up. I felt something bulky on the skin of my stomach and then he lurched up and down, his head thrown back, making more groaning noises, this time mixed with grunts of exertion. After a while he stopped. Then he got off me and started doing up the buttons of his shorts.

I stood up, cracking my forehead on one of the nesting boxes, disturbing a chook who might all that time have been laying an egg. She clucked in that astounded way chooks have of showing their displeasure. I walked past Lionel and kept walking, brushing myself clean as I went.

Lionel called after me, 'Hey girlie,' as if to a stranger. His voice coaxed, conciliatory, but I kept on walking until I reached the drain that divided our yards. Something shifted position out to the right. I kept my neck stiff. I didn't look. I ran to our back door.

I had strange sensations in my knees as if they might turn to fluid and give way under my weight. The top half of our Dutch door was open as usual, but I knew by the silence and emptiness that there was no-one inside. I shut the bottom half and then in a rush snibbed the top half shut. My fingers were putty as I turned the brown key in the lock.

I walked up the hallway past the brown hall cupboards to my bedroom and stared at it. Everything the same. Figured wallpaper the same. Chenille bedspread covering the made up bed, the same. There was the lump at the bottom that was the dog.

If my mother was in a rush she made the bed with the dog in it. I lay down on the quilt, too tired to pull it back. The dog moved under the covers. My feet were cold. I rubbed them together but it didn't help. I moved them down to the faint water-bottle warmth of the dog lump. There was grit under my waistband and as I passed my hand across my stomach I felt something slimy.

I fell asleep. When I woke up my mother was standing over me, grinding her teeth.

'What have you been doing to yourself? You're lying on your quilt!' Her voice rose as the list of crimes escalated. 'You're filthy dirty. How dare you come into the house covered in filth?'

'Look!' She slapped at my back. 'You've got dirt all over you. Don't you ever think about how hard I work to keep this place clean? You're always making a mess. Now I'll have to wash this quilt. Get off it. This instant! I don't run a house for guttersnipes. You dirty girl!'

She pushed at me as I got up. She stripped the quilt off in one sharp movement. The pillow tumbled out of the tuck-over and landed on the floor.

'And get that dog out of your bed. How many times have I told you not to let animals in your bed? You'll get worms. I've told you that. No-one listens to me in this house. You just go your own sweet way.'

She glared at me. 'What's that graze on your forehead? You silly girl. You'll get an infection going around like that. Go on, go and change and put those dirty things in the clothes-basket. And wash your hands,' she called after me.

I welcomed getting into trouble, her lack of sympathy. It was a return to normal. I knew if I was careful and kept out of her way, I would get through. I would be all right. If I just kept quiet about this, one of my mother's constant exhortations, it would go away.

I knew I had made one decision. If I was all on my own, I was never going back to Lionel, ever again.

I did get an infection but not on my forehead. My private parts stung and then itched. Small lumps formed on the raw skin inside. I stood in the shower with the water scalding hot and held a steaming flannel to myself as a poultice. I locked the bathroom door. I sat in the shower recess with a flannel blocking the drain till the hot water ran out. The room filled with steam and I imagined myself in the Land of Polar Bears from *The Enchanted Wood*, even though I was too old to read such baby stories.

And I got a dose of worms, that bane of my life. My mother answered my entreaties at bed-time, when the worms were at their most active. She made me prop up my bottom and searched for signs of them with a torch. She made a *tsk, tsk* noise and adjusted her glasses with one finger.

'Have you wiped your bottom properly? The eggs live under your nails. That's why you have to wash your hands. I've told you and told you.' Then a final salvo. 'And don't touch yourself down there!'

She had various strategies against the worms. She put sticky tape over my bum hole, the way you catch flies on fly-paper. That didn't work. Nor did smearing my behind with Vaseline. I hated the greasy feel it made, as if I had dirtied myself. Once I saw a worm she caught and held out to me in triumph on the end of a cotton-wool-swathed matchstick. It was the glassy white of rice noodles with a pointy tail that whipped round, frenzied, as if it didn't like the light.

I saw why it itched so much. I imagined hundreds of them inside me and it maddened me as I scratched and scratched until I was sore. One night I felt them making the trek across the little bridge of skin and I squashed them through my pyjamas in horror.

I hoped Lionel had got some of my worm eggs lodged under his horny fingernails. I put my hands under my chin and prayed that he would forget to wash his hands. I wished he would get the biggest dose of writhing worms that I could bring to life in my imagination.

That is how it ended, that heavy summer day. But it had begun some time before.

# 2 Fate

Lionel often sang a little ditty: *Long may live my lovely Hetty / Always young and always pretty*... Sometimes he hummed it under his breath. The point of his tongue sat between his lips as he worked. His tidy bench lay waiting.

Down under the house was Lionel's kingdom, behind the long wooden slats. He was a sultan with a turban. I thought of his hands as the roc's claws in *Sinbad the Sailor*. Lionel wore leather sandals with an instep strap, closed, in at the heel. They looked feminine, his sandals, except where his big toe emerged with its coarse toe-nail poking out the front hole, a hairless mouse with a celluloid shield.

I believe my mother played a part in what happened that day. I know she kept reeling me faster and faster towards the master bobbin that was Lionel, and I felt helpless to stop the process. I suppose I was a pest of a child and perhaps all she wanted was a bit of peace. Surely I was safe next door, being looked after by Lionel and Dolly.

She must have wondered, the many times she pegged my clothes on the line, 'Is this all there is?' She might have hated the dead weight of my unending presence. I must have been a torment to her, her one late hatchling, demanding, arrogant, loyal only to my father. Yet even before what I called to myself the Great Gap, there were things I could not speak of, even to him. My mother frightened me with her power to shame me in front of my father, to expose me to his ridicule or disapprobation. My mother's chivvying made my brain rattle, a tin boiling in a saucepan.

So it was that the roc that was Lionel plotted his course and made one more lazy turn before he headed in for the kill.

'Lionel asked where you were today. Don't be rude, go in and see him. Lionel's like a grandfather to you. Don't let him down.'

She pauses and I can see straight into her head where the circuits blare full strength.

'Go on, go in and see Lionel and Dolly. They're both missing you.'

My mother sits in front of her sewing machine in the hallway, wedged between the telephone table and the edge of the bookcases. Another pause to negotiate a hard curve in her sewing. She once ran her machine over the tip of her finger and broke a needle.

'Lionel says you haven't been to see him. Don't be naughty. Go and see him. He's under the house waiting for you. Go on.'

'I don't want to. Not today.'

I fix my gaze on the books on the shelf above my mother's head. Lamb's *Essays*, a book called *Rebecca* by the exotic Daphne du Maurier, a row of condensed *Reader's Digest* volumes. There is a paperback with a lurid cover showing a young woman under a tree. She's got no shoes on. She gazes up at a man with his shirt open. It's called *Call Me When the Cross Turns Over*. I haven't read it yet but I'm going to. I reach up and start tearing a small piece out of its paper jacket.

'Why not?'

My mother's eyes are sharp and suspicious.

'Don't tear that or I'll smack.'

She frowns in the yellow light, her brown permed hair horizontal today. She does not like sewing. It gives her a migraine. But she knows she must profess an easy skill with it. She lives her hateful lie and bears her headaches.

Her fingers fumble the material as if devoid of sensation and she stopstarts the machine in frantic rushes. She is making me another romper suit, bloomer pants with elastic at waist and legs and a sleeveless top with buttons down the front. This set is in a figured, light green material with broad vertical lines, a bit like I imagine Elizabethan wallpaper. I love my romper suits and pretend I am Sir Walter Raleigh out of Arthur Mee's *Encyclopaedia*.

She is so inept I think she will never finish. She stops to clutch her hair with both hands. 'I'll blow my top if this doesn't come out right.'

'Why don't you want to go?' she continues, relentless. 'Don't just stand there. Answer me.'

'I just don't feel like it.'

I stare at the oblong globe of the sewing machine light. I can see the bright entrails of the filament inside. The gold curlicue design around the S of Singer stands out against the machine's black enamel.

'Oh for heaven's sake, go on.' She grinds her teeth sideways.

'You've got nothing else to do. Go and help Lionel. You're standing in my light.'

She stamps her foot on the accelerator pedal that has taken over from the metal knee rod that sometimes, if she is in a good mood, she lets me press. The cloth flies through the machine's mechanism, accumulating a line of perfect, spaced stitches.

So I wander, reluctant, out to the back terrace. I cross the fence line marked by the cement drain and the line of ti-trees that smell of lemons. Excitement tinges my reluctance. Lionel transfixes me with his prowess in the practical world, with his ability to be absorbed by his hobbies. He is the master of time. Lionel does things when Lionel wants to, and stops when he wants to stop.

I know to look for Lionel under the house where he ladles pollard and mash for his chooks. The pollard clings to the strong hairs on his arms. If he's not doing that he is at his work bench making another shadow box. He never makes one for me although he makes several for himself and Dolly. My mother says they are all the rage. It amazes me that grown-ups have them when it seems to me they are meant for children. Why else would I love them so much?

The one I like best contains a series of sleeping Mexicans, their sombreros tipped over their eyes as they rest by bright green cacti.

Lionel greets me the same way each time.

'How's my little fairy today? How's my girl?' He hugs me and holds me to his body.

'Whose girl are you?' He grips my wrists in crossover and pulls me backwards into him. I say, 'Yours' at the same time as he says, 'You're mine.'

Then he makes me kiss him. In the early years I kissed him on the cheek, in the crease where his jowls had started to hang. Some time later I kissed him on the mouth, his lips fierce, his eyes hot in that second before I closed my eyes.

This is new kissing, his teeth pressing, urgent, into my lips, unlike mother kissing or father kissing or the occasional aunt kissing. Then all returns to normal and I am left feeling alarmed and silly with embarrassment. Some days he has a red lump on his lip and he says, 'Softly, softly, catchee monkey. Give me a butterfly kiss,' and I tickle his lips with my eyelashes. When the red lump breaks to a brown scab I must kiss him on the lips once more, with the cornflake of the scab an added texture.

He gets on with his whittling and I watch as he holds a tiny screw in place with his dry square fingers with their yellow curved nails. A pool of light moves with him. His face is a square that sometimes shifts to a rectangle. With his hunched shoulders he appears very powerful. Everything about him is big and authoritative. I imagine him hurling the cement slab stepping-stones in his chook yard with the fury of Moses.

I do not see the petulant under-lip, and nor do I judge the petty fussiness. Lionel is an addictive presence.

For me, this world of 1958 is normal.

I remember the first time I saw Lionel. It was a tableau out of a Biblical text, opened at Arab Lands. He stood on a wooden ladder gripping an outsize pair of wooden-handled shears, trimming the hook-thorned bougainvillaea that grew in an imposing magenta ball on a boundary post between his place and ours.

For us, it was moving day. I was cross that we were leaving our first house that I thought was perfect. I suspected that this old man was a troublemaker or, even worse, what my mother called common. I thought he looked proprietorial with his great ladder stuck on our ground. I noted his leather sandals, his baggy khaki shorts and his putty-coloured skin. I thought he looked aloof and menacing, nothing like my father, who looked as fathers should, well-proportioned, tanned, casual but not dapper.

I thought men should wear sports coats or dark city suits and black shoes. They should roll up the sleeves of their white cotton shirts to show their sinewy arms. Lionel broke all the rules. His shoes and suits were brown, his shirts yellowed nylon and see-through, a sin so grave in my mother's eyes that to this day I find myself judging men's characters by their shirts.

To make it worse, he drove the wrong type of car, a two-tone Holden with a kewpie doll dangling from the mirror. He caught the bus to work and only drove the car at weekends after interminable sessions of washing and rattle-fixing had taken place.

Lionel had a bony nose and in hot weather a drip formed on the end of it in a foreign, unsatisfactory way. It should have been straight and middling, the way my father's was.

When we arrived, I believed I should ignore him for ever. I treated the thought of him with disdain and a sort of arrogant anger.

We moved suburbs in the year I was six. I was just starting out at primary school. I walked there by myself after the first day when my mother escorted me, an official or warrant officer delivering a prisoner.

On my walk, I observed a set of obsessive rituals. When I turned the corner after climbing the first hill, I took off my shoes and white ankle socks. At the entrance to the Catholic school was a small shelf of shale rock that made me think of a concert platform. I imagined a grand piano and a Beethoven figure playing music like the concertos on my father's records, and I bent to clean this tiny world with my toes. I pretended to dawdle, examining the sole of my foot.

Once an older girl in uniform came out. I saw a black-and-white nun coming behind her down the palm-lined drive. The girl stood with her school shoes obliterating my secret platform. She glared down at me and said, smooth as ice cream: 'You dirty little guttersnipe.'

At the bus intersection, Mowbray Road ran off to the left. It headed into the dry bush and the housing estates with their fibro houses. I went straight up the hill past the house on the corner with the cactus garden. I jumped the crack in the footpath so that I wouldn't die. A girl lived there who had 'done it' with a boy. Her name was Glenda and they said she'd be sent to a Home if she wasn't careful. She had sun-blonde hair and long brown legs and I thought she looked like me. I crossed my fingers behind my back to break any association with her.

'Dirty slut,' I whispered.

One of the girls at school said she was a bike. I wasn't allowed to ride a bike. If I asked my father questions about such things, he tantalised me. 'It's a wigwam for a goose's bridle.' I thought Glenda's bike might be one of those.

The school street was long and open, but at the front gates another street ran down to the left to the tuck shop. This was a far more frightening street with an out-of-bounds feel to it, since it dwindled past clumps of gum and wattle and disappeared off into scrub. An Alsatian dog guarded the tuck shop steps and urinated on the potato sack that served as a doormat. I never saw it do it, but everyone knew. I held my breath to stop the acrid smell from contaminating me. The smell was brown and I associated it with flypaper and the name Smith. Inside the shop there was the type of dark that hid serious dirt. The shop had wooden floor-boards and half-empty varnished shelves.

Other children bought pies and pasties but I was not allowed. Instead, on those days when I was courageous enough to push to the front, I selected black-striped Humbugs from the lolly jars, and Licorice Allsorts. The Humbugs were the same as Grandpa had in a glass jar by his bedside. The sandwich of colours in the Allsorts, interspersed with black licorice divisions, was thick, vibrant. They were in the same colour combinations as my mother's zinnias with their furry pastel limes and pinks.

'You go any further down that street than the tuck shop,' said my mother 'and I'll tell your father. And go straight back inside the school gates when you've finished.'

She always added a rejoinder, as if I'd answered her back.

I was never to set foot in the dense scrub that ringed the school, because bad men, who did things to little girls, lurked there. I didn't know what things they were, but the thought of an encounter terrified me. The thought of getting into trouble made me cringe even more. I knew that whatever form this encounter took the man would be angry. He would blame me and then he would kill me.

Any man who didn't dress the same as my father was suspect. I extended my suspicions to all men except my uncles. Old women I assumed to be witches who had stepped out of Hansel and Gretel and were out to do me harm. Somehow I mixed up my mother in this feeling. I had an early, sharp memory of her rushing towards me down a hallway, murder in her eyes.

The world as depicted by my mother was an alarming place. My parents, my only arbiters and reference points, seemed to bulge and swell out of shape, to loom and shrink, disquieting, unreliable, inconstant when they should have been solid.

Despite their supervision, they often managed to leave me unattended. When Lionel found me hanging about he did not return me in good order to my parents, nor take precious care of me all winter until spring came, as the fairy tales suggested. Instead, he picked me up, examined me and whittled at my shape with his penknife. When he found I was hard wood he dropped me on the ground half-formed.

I feel obliged by my shapeless sense of panic to re-invent myself. My face in the mirror is a shock: photographs depict me as a criminal in a mug shot. Perhaps this was Lionel's malign gift to me, the shadow in the shadow box he never made. He made me feel as if I was a fake girl, apart from everyone with my heavy secret. I could not join in with the other children, effortless. I was the guilty party who dared not let my guard down. I knew I would be exposed in the next instant.

Lionel robbed me of naturalness. He severed me from the right to grow up easily. He took from me the expectation of good things, and contentment. He stole the mundane, unexamined happiness of ordinary life. He took these with such greed, such self-indulgence and he took them, with a staggering lack of compassion, from a child.

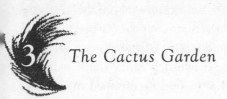

3 The Cactus Garden

I can't remember when Lionel first won me over. I think he must have worked at it, fiddling until the tight little knot that I was came undone. It may have been the cactus garden that made me vulnerable to his advances. I suppose I was live bait in a small tin and it was just a matter of time and propinquity before he threaded me on the hook.

The cactus garden was a gift from my father. It was my intact place, perfect and ordered, in manageable dimensions. I was its overseer who forbade entry or added to it, judicious. It was a desert cemetery where I could go to contemplate my father's erratic absences.

If my father promised solidity and continuity, he heralded disappearance, implausibility. He faded out when I needed him and re-emerged, disconcerting me, when I could have done without him.

'You're a tricky so and so,' my mother once burst out. 'You couldn't lie straight in bed if you tried.'

Unrepentant, my father smirked, 'I'm the Cheshire cat's grin, Darl.'

At first the cactus garden pleased me more than anything my father had given me. More than my gold bangle he cut off my arm so that I complied with the dress rules of my new private school. The cactus garden was more precious than the opal ring I got when I was six, that I thought had talismanic powers to ward off evil.

But nothing saved me from becoming a casualty the day Lionel asked my name.

'Hullo.' His voice behind me was shocking, unexpected.

'What are you doing, girlie?'

I sensed he was on his side of the dividing drain, but only just.

'Nothing.'

There was a dissatisfied silence. I knew this would not be enough.

'Playing with my cactus garden.'

I could not look up, but I made my voice cold. I was too old to play at anything and we did not talk to the neighbours. I brushed sand off the round mirror that made a pool beside the miniature painted china temples and bridges, the sampans and pagodas.

'What's that you've got there?'

His large foot was right beside me. He had sneaked up on me, breaking through the membrane of the bubble I glided in. His foot in its peep-toed sandal pointed to the old-man cactus, my pride, my most noteworthy plant, with its white hair. No-one knew what it was but my father and me.

I heard myself whisper, 'Grandfather Cactus.'

I shocked myself. Something was happening because of this leg I could see that disappeared up into the dark recesses of his wide shorts. I knew that if he let me, I could have fitted with ease in there and climbed into worlds as endless and fantastic as the ones that swung past at the top of the Faraway Tree. More than anything I wanted to ascend into magic and step off into weightless suspension. I wanted a place where everything was pretty in blues and silver, where objects glided with the tranquillity of the fish in our goldfish pond. I wanted excitement that was observable but from which I was detached; a dream afternoon where gold glinted against moss green, like the bits of tin in the creeks where my father took us for Sunday picnics. I wanted to be where nothing belonged to words and actions or held solid significance and nothing happened that I couldn't disengage from, read and re-read and put down beside the bed, disarmed.

'What's your name?'

He shouldn't have asked, because my mother said I shouldn't tell strange men my name. Lionel had rules of his own though.

'Well, what's your name? Cat got your tongue?'

I laughed. I had never heard that before. I knew he owned a big white cat with a sun-spotted nose that his wife painted with Gentian Violet. I had seen her do it gingerly, with gloves on, while Lionel held the cat upside down by all four legs. When she took the gloves off, big, pig-pink washing up gloves, I saw her fingertips were pale prunes, creased and dry the way mine were if I stayed too long in the bath.

His tone was bossy, I decided, as if he were one of the big boys at school. There was a subtle difference between Lionel and my father, who had an adult aura even when he played baby games with me.

I wasn't going to tell Lionel my real name. I gave him my nickname, and even then I was reluctant. Not so much because of my mother's strictures but because I believed that intimacies such as names were a form of sentimentalism that only common people practised, Catholics or dowdy Baptists. Dad said we were Presbyterian but he also said God didn't exist. I was the only one in my class who could spell atheist.

I knew no-one used my real name because I, too, didn't really exist.

Dad called my mother Darl, but he called my aunts Darl as well. Sometimes, absent minded, he called me Darl, which thrilled me with its casual, grown-up elegance, its sophisticated lack of attachment. When he was in a good mood he called me his popsy.

'Sooky!'

Lionel sounded angry. Dad said he called me Sooky because I was a girl. Now this interloper stared at me, challenging with his changing, yellowish eyes. He looked familiar up close. Then I saw he was the same as the red setter that sometimes trotted loose-limbed, loose-skinned and always onto something, down our street.

'How did you get a silly name like that?'

'Don't know.'

'You don't know?'

My answer enraged him. He chanted:

Polly put the kettle on
Polly put the kettle on
Polly put the kettle on
We'll all have tea.

Time flew round me in elliptical rings, a forsaken moth. He put his hands on his hips and mocked me:

Sooky take it off again
Sooky take it off again
Sooky take it off again
They've all gone away.

I considered re-entering my bubble but he said: 'You'd better come and help me feed the chooks.'

This was an irresistible offer. I had been watching him in his chook yard for weeks. Every evening when he came home from work in his brown city suit he disappeared inside and I heard him talking with his wife. Then he emerged on the back landing in his old shorts and singlet and stood for a moment in the late afternoon light, staring out over the spread of the poinciana that dominated his backyard.

Then he trotted downstairs, sometimes with the buckles of his sandals undone and clinking with the sound of tinny bells. He disappeared under the house to re-emerge with an old Milo container in his hand. He took it up to the waiting birds massing in their run, calling 'Chook, chook, chook' in a high voice. He threw the contents over the wire fence. Then he stood and watched.

'What with?'

I felt safe with knowledge. I always needed to find out as much as I could. I tried to eavesdrop on as many of my parents' conversations as possible. I believed the more I heard of the adult world the more it would make sense. I knew they kept things from me just to tease me.

'Pollard and mash.'

His voice said ordinary words and yet his eyes conveyed a strange overtone, a complicity in something I could not read.

'What's that?'

'Come and see,' and he reached down, insolent as a rooster, and took me by the hand that only my father ever held.

4 The Water Tank

My father moved down the corridor every morning after his shower, freshly-ironed shirt flapping, clutching underwear to his genitals, the neat cheeks of his pale, tight bottom just visible as he passed me. Concerned though he was for the proprieties in a female household, he must have felt his behind was not a sexual object. I knew I had filed away that glimpse of his unprotected haunches.

I liked to look at my father's legs. They were sinewy, tanned and covered in golden, curly hairs. Most of all I loved his forearms, the paler inside sections with their raised, blue blood vessels. They were the most male thing I knew. I grouped them with men's muscles as something apart from the heavy female influence that pervaded our suburban existence.

This femaleness, which was my mother's presence, was insistent and nagging but never impressive. It was not the essence that was in control. It did not predominate but hung back. I never imagined that I added anything to it. I did not even see myself as female. I was merely an organism pushing up to the surface of a pond, like a mosquito wriggler in our rain-water tank.

On hot days I lowered myself through the tank's man-hole and trod water. Breathless from aquatic claustrophobia in that dank vessel where I dared not touch the sides, I was triumphant at having found a place where parents could not follow. They thought I lived with them but my real abode was in that galvanised container. I was detached, as muffled voices called my name. No need to answer. I stared at the slime-encrusted rungs and floated.

The musculature of my father's bottom was the same as the flensed haunches of the hare that my cousin had shot and skinned one August holidays when he took me on an early morning shoot. He woke me in the frost and I hopped in the back of the old jalopy with its dark drums and metal tool box, inanely grinning kelpies and tangle of rabbit traps.

He held the dead animal by its long ears, still attached to its narrow, intelligent head, so like my father's, its light red flesh glistening in the fractured morning light.

There was a New Zealander staying with my cousin and his wife. A tall, blond man, he could run barefoot across the thistly, black-soil paddocks and never feel a thing, so toughened were the soles of his feet from walking on coral at low tide. He never acknowledged me. Not once did he look down in my direction. All his communications existed in an air-space higher than mine. I thought him a mythic creature and never really expected him to see me. But being so low down in the order of visibility, I had an open line for staring.

It was silent after the shots exploded, as if they had knocked over not only the hare, but Nature itself. A bird tried out a twitter and the bowl of black earth in which we stood looked once again ordinary and settled, as if no living thing wanted to admit what had occurred. My cousin looked in his bag and he and his friend talked in low, rumbly, satisfied voices.

We drove through another paddock until we hit the banks of the Condamine. My cousin shot some wood duck that had settled in a mass of penny-royal. The mounds of scrambling vegetation smelt so overpowering they made me sleepy.

'Don't you nod off,' he said, 'or I might shoot you too.'

Teasing me, he wiped my cheek with the hare's bloody, dismembered paw.

'Jugged hare.' My cousin rubbed his belly in appreciation and looked sideways at me.

'Why do you put it in a jug?' I saw the milk jug on the kitchen table with a raw hare sitting in it. They laughed at me and didn't answer. My mother said my cousin had a roguish eye. On the way back they sang in unison over the rattling of metal:

Give me five minutes more
Only five minutes more
Give me five minutes more
In your arms.

Adults told me everything made sense in the end, but I could see it didn't. I souvenired the paw and when I came home put it out on the tank-stand ledge, the way my cousin had told me, to make sure I'd cleaned out the maggots.

They lived in the paw for a long time. They thrived on bone and skin. The paw smelled of hare fur, a dense stench quite unlike the live cat fur that it resembled, but whose light, dusty smell it lacked. When I transferred it to my dressing table, its choking odour filled my bedroom. My mother threw it out when the maggots started a wobbly migration across the laminated top.

I wanted to use the paw as a powder-puff, like women in Regency times, dipping my hare's foot in orris root. Most of my information on such things came from the *Children's Encyclopaedia* or another leather-covered book called the *Household Medicinal* that sat on the top shelf of the china cupboard in the kitchen hall-way. It had diagrams of the human body and coloured illustrations with instructions for the laying out of the dead. I cajoled my mother into being the dummy, tying up her jaw with one of Dad's big handkerchiefs and putting pennies on her closed eyes. She drew the line at having her orifices stuffed with cotton wool.

My mother would have nothing to do with the powder puff idea. Nor would she let me use the face powder that she kept on a shelf inside the built-in clothes' cupboard my father had made out of red cedar. It excited him when he found the wood stacked and languishing under Lionel's house. Lionel preferred to use plywood.

'Crikey, you wouldn't credit it. Silly bugger doesn't know what he's got. Wouldn't know how to use it if he tried.'

'Don't swear Darl,' my mother pleaded, casting her eyes sideways and nodding her head backwards in my direction.

My father believed in the veracity of fact, science and logic. He believed in the truth of truth, but then he must have felt the foundations listing. Uncertainty of outcome rolled, a sneaky wave under the rickety jetty on which he stood fishing.

'You can go to Hell,' my mother told him, with more and more regularity. 'Go on then. Go. Don't let me stop you.' At first I stood side by side with her in the face of this oncoming threat. We pegged out our malice and our rage in deep lateral lines. We wished him failure and discredit because he wanted to go away, to defect, to be happy elsewhere at the expense of our misery. Yet at the same time as I reviled him, I thought his wish to leave was but another aspect of his superior right to freedom from the usual and the ordinary.

'He wouldn't dare.' My mother sounded certain. I believed my parents would stand opposed in their opposite kitchen corners forever. Nothing about them was ever likely to change.

Just in case she had got it wrong, I started to imagine the loss of what comforted me, the space where he used to be, the silence in the lounge where his music once played. I imagined the inane chatter of my mother's radio and her staccato-voiced resentments taking over.

I saw it in dog-image: the wolf-hound departing and in his place a Pomeranian bitch yapping, uncontrollable.

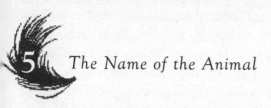

5   The Name of the Animal

The first and most important thing to mention about Redmond is his burnished hair. It is the colour my father brings up out of mahogany, as he polishes in small oily circles. The fox coat. Deep and rich, active, alien. Not a colour our family has. We are blond or brown, muted, Australian, washed-out. We have the sort of hair that goes to the beach or the shops and blends in with everything else. When my mother, feeling the tug of Dad's imminent departure, dyes her hair seaweed red, it is the sign of a woman about to drown.

Redmond keeps his hair clipped short but it is so thick it becomes more noticeable. I watch him as he practices his golf putts in the backyard. He is tall with wide shoulders and an easy elasticity. He is home with Lionel and Dolly from being somewhere called Cloncurry, where he is in advertising. I know no-one who does that and presume his hair is complicit in this activity. I imagine Cloncurry to be tumeric yellow, the same colour as the prawn dish my mother makes once a week from the Keens' Curry tin.

He hits a ball just as I step over the boundary line between our yards and it whacks me square in the eye. I stand still and wait for what will happen next. My mother is forever telling me: 'You never pay attention to the important things' and now I pay no attention to my eye. How can he be their son when he is so grown up? Although I am old enough to work it out by now, I still have a secret difficulty with the concept of aunts and uncles, nephews and nieces. A son in his twenties doesn't fit.

The sons I know are my age.

'You're a silly duffer,' my father says often and I feel the shame of my strangeness surge through the tunnels of my bones.

Now there is a lot of running around. Redmond holds my shoulder and looks into my eye.

'Gee, Sweetheart.'

But Lionel takes me up in his arms and deposits me back on our terrace where my mother, ineffectual as usual, fusses. She has nothing to apply to this wound, my swelling black eye, but I don't care. The only thing that interests me is the feel of Redmond's hand on my shoulder, the brevity of that contact before Lionel claims me yet again. My father likes to say that Redmond is an accident about to happen but whenever I catch sight of him I get short of breath and my head prickles with excitement.

The grown-ups have decided that I can call Lionel's wife by her first name, Dolly, and I notice in all the commotion that Dolly stands outside the action, a peg doll. Everything in my world is connected by signs and portents. Dad says Lionel's a royal beast and he's king of the kids. Redmond's name is already perfect because of his hair, and Dolly gets her name because she is pale and dry, wooden and blank, a peg before the doll face gets drawn on.

I notice that my mother and Lionel talk together like conspirators. She sends him glances. My mother flirts in a bemused, captured way. She is the same as our dog in the way she cringes and wriggles. With Dolly she is more stand-offish and then I think of her as a cat, in the way she pretends not to be attending. I am sure she feels superior. Dolly, however, has her own secrets. The two women seem intent on a silent battle. I never listen to their conversations. I judge them to be unexciting, about bodily matters.

I listen to what my father says, and Lionel's sentences stand out in my mind in bas-relief. The men's words come out of somewhere strange and significant and I pay attention and watch everything they do.

I never notice that my father is mad. Much later in the composition of my mother's life, with its ubiquitous conflicts, climaxes and many endings, it is apparent that he is strange beyond repair. Yet he has to orchestrate an official nervous breakdown before anyone mentions it. Before the craziness takes hold, his oddity is an acknowledged part of his charm. 'He's pixillated,' my mother says, as if it's something to admire.

He is a father who has taken the freedom to be different. He invents hobbies for himself that keep him down under the house late at night.

He and Lionel work with wood, but whereas Lionel makes do with ply and shadow boxes, Dad works with cedar, making cabinets with dovetailing and French polishing. I think the two men despise each other in a polite way that hardly ever shows on the surface.

Dad often sneers at Lionel in private. 'Never yet liked a bloke who uses 2-ply.'

'Keep your voice down,' my mother hisses, 'please, Darl.'

Lionel always had a plan. Lionel befriended me, and his friendship was assiduous. It had soft tentacles that closed round me so I didn't notice. He couched it in a manner they taught me to respect. At first he was a grandfather with a grandfather's strictures, a benevolent grandfather's distance. In slow time that changed.

My parents had taught me that I must behave in front of adults.

'Be a good girl and do as you're told.'

'And don't tell fibs.'

When they gave Lionel the green light he moved, confident, through the intersection. Smoothly he pulled into the kerb to pick me up. What was happening in his world of Lionel the unconscious animal? Did he think of me as anything more than a small round button to press because it was there, available, on the circuit of his desire?

The opera of Lionel's life opens with his shaving ritual. But first there is the overture of the early morning cup of tea. Lionel stands in his kitchen.

Their house has a vague smell of dry and antiseptic. Lionel's discarded, torn-up singlets lie, yellow and scabby, in the sink cupboard. There is an overlay of the smell of cat saliva.

It is dark enough to switch the light on but he leaves it off. It is 5.45am proper Eastern Standard Time. It is serene and quiet. A grey pearliness subdues the hot tropical Brisbane light. The word promise unfurls across the top of the picture. Piece by piece the objects in the kitchen change and strengthen. We must hasten with our task before the light of ordinary day robs our tableau of magic.

Lionel takes a wrapped pound of butter out of the fridge to soften. It is most important it be spreadable, because now he cuts the white loaf of bread into the thinnest imaginable slices. Thin but not so thin that the slice disintegrates. I watch but he won't let me help. He is the master in charge of this production. He must do it to perfection.

Lionel busies himself, elbows out to keep me at bay. He boils the kettle and makes tea in the teapot and covers it with a tea cosy. He holds a bread slice up to the light coming in the kitchen window. His discoloured fingernails curve. His hands are hard and thick with yellow calluses.

'Look at that. Thin enough to see through.'

I smile up at him. I am as pleased as he is. There are two slices now spread with butter and cut in half. They sit on a blue Willow pattern plate that Lionel lets me carry into the bedroom. He takes a tray laden with two cups of tea and another plate of bread and butter. I follow him through the dining room. I look up as I walk under the wooden rail that divides it from the living room. We go through into the side foyer that precedes the bedroom, bathroom and spare room that was once Redmond's.

The foyer is an air lock before we reach the engine room. We have nothing like it in our house. A Dutch rail at picture-hanging height runs round each room, and the covered verandah on two sides has deep window sills and heavy wooden blinds that roll down in a clatter of chains.

This is happiness, as good as I will ever know it. As Lionel and I march in to wake up Dolly I notice that his khaki shorts are completely flat at the back. He has no bottom and this, too, is compelling.

Without your love
It's a honky-tonk parade

Lionel, how I loved you. I was a file waiting for pages to be inserted. I was wide open to attachment. I was a plate of medium in a laboratory ready for someone to seed me with the bacteria of love. Anything might have stuck. Healthy, unhealthy, fungoid, parasitic. I couldn't discern between them. A dog, a parent, the man next door, it didn't matter, as long as something took root, divided and sub-divided and grew into a shape to fill the empty petri dish.

But Lionel was mistletoe growing up the side of my sapling soul, robbing me of energy. At first I did not feel it. Parasites, to prolong their own lives take a long time to kill their hosts, insidious.

I should have known better. Any well-brought-up child would have avoided catastrophe because the well-brought-up don't enter the domain of indecency. But I had no foothold in experience. I did not recognise the face glaring in the watery ravine.

My private agony was that I might be the only one who did not know better. I might be clinically deficient, the same as the idiot boy who lived down at the Junction. Everyone else would have got out of trouble, swum to shore. It must be my fault.

'Keep quiet. Don't make a fuss,' my mother intoned in my head.

Lionel guessed how I would think. He knew my reactions by heart, this man who attended to details then traded on them without mercy.

They say evolution is a mechanism for building better adaptations to changing local environments. It happens over eons, but I had my own small evolutionary mechanism at work, searching for a niche where I could grow. Was it with my father or was it with Lionel, ever-hunting, always gathering, fossicking?

My father sometimes read me a bedtime story that began: *There was a camel that lived in the middle of a Howling Desert...* That is all I can remember because the image of the howling desert was so flagrant, so evocative and awful that I could think no further. And I felt for no apparent outward reason that I was that camel in its howling wilderness with the sand stinging its legs, frenzied and unable to pick my direction.

My father complained in a joking way that he was in a household surrounded by women and that if I had been a boy he would have called me Jock. So I attempted to fashion myself into a tomboy, but despite my assiduous companionship my father never took my boyishness seriously.

He let me watch but didn't invite me to participate. He got cranky with me if I attempted to use his tools. If I stood next to him and ran my thumb across the shark's teeth of his biggest saw he'd round on me: 'For Christ's sake, don't fool around with that. Leave it alone.'

One Christmas I badgered my parents for a cap pistol until they gave in. The way it opened to reveal the roll of caps with dots like the fern spores I had seen in my grandmother's garden was perfection. The sharp crack as it went off and smell of gunpowder made me feel in charge of everything. But it was inferior metal, as crumbly and aerated as Violet Crumble Bars and the trigger soon broke.

I knew if I had been a boy they would have given me a proper gun.

'I don't know what I'm going to do with you.' My mother slammed the Electrolux back into the broom closet. The door waited a second and then re-opened on its broken hinge. 'I'm at my wit's end,' she said. So she didn't do anything. Nor did she teach me. My one attempt at knitting ended when she couldn't remember how to cast on. She didn't have time for me. She was too busy fussing and worrying.

She had pet phrases that scurried round with her, conspiring rats with their teeth drawn.

'You have no idea.' Sometimes she added 'my girl' for extra effect. A favourite phrase was 'I've never been appreciated in this house.'

'Do as you're told' came with the slam of a kitchen drawer.

In a pensive mood when I tried to approach her she would mutter 'I wonder...' and let it trail off. She often followed up with 'No, never mind.'

If she said, 'Well, I've probably just missed out' she was referring to the bus time-table or to a quiz question on the ever-loud radio. I watched her lips thin out. 'You're irritating me to death.'

Where was the hidey-hole where I could grow to fruition? I began to think that Lionel could nurture me, as he fed the chooks and let me hang round him. He didn't mind if I asked him questions while he worked at his jig-saw or opened little pots of paint to daub dots on the cacti in the Mexican panoramas in his shadow boxes.

I enjoyed by proxy all of my father's pursuits. We weren't allowed to call them hobbies. He had a deep interest in marine life, as if fish were the arbiters of some vacuum he wanted to enter. Their blank equanimity fascinated him. He went through a phase where fishing was his most serious enterprise. He let me go with him as long as I didn't talk. I spent hours sitting on rock shelves at Coolangatta or the sand at Palm Beach, watching as my father stood knee-deep with his long bamboo rod pointing out to sea.

If I complained he said: 'Give it a rest. Don't be a blinking nuisance. I'll leave you at home next time' and I went silent. When he caught something, usually bream or flathead, he poked them in through the hole in his cane fishing basket and I listened as they heaved and flapped. Then they, too, fell quiet.

He taught me how to tie on sinkers. He didn't let me handle the hooks but I memorised the loops and knots and the way his short fingernail pushed the last knot tight. The best part was using the yabby pump to catch yabbies for bait down on the estuarine sand flats at Tallebudgera. We put them in a billy of salt-water and threaded them live on the hook. When I asked him if it hurt them, he said 'No, they don't feel a thing' – and grinned.

I stared into the silver sides of the billy. The reflected light shone right through the bodies of the yabbies. I thought it would be much better if people were see-through. They would be more understandable if all their vital organs were apparent.

When we went out fishing at dusk, I watched his outline until it got dark and he and I disappeared together. Nothing left but the spangles of phosphorescence along the shoreline and the stars bristling.

My father kept a tank of sea water in the spare room, with sea horses and sea anemones. Each afternoon after school I went in there to touch the sea anemones to make them retract. Their tentacles were sticky as they tried to eat my flesh. When they closed up I rubbed their blobby, glutinous bodies with my fingertip. When the male sea horse hatched babies in its pouch my father stared through the glass in profound silence. He said: 'They mate for life.' He liked the idea of horses and flowers underwater. He searched for the ridiculous or the out-of-place, the askew, the left-handed, like himself. I never knew if I was seeing things through his eyes or mine. He looked at those sea horses with so much incomprehension.

I knew what he had missed when I floated in the ocean. Alert to changes, I understood momentary balance, fallible stability. I knew the apprehension and enticement of letting the swell carry me. All these feelings left me when I was back on the sand.

Dad's other, more active pursuit was dissection. The spare room became an autopsy chamber full of the smell of chloroform as he snuffed out guinea pigs, sliced them open and pinned them down on small slabs of beeswax. He made the slabs by melting chunks of wax and pouring it into our aluminium ice block trays. It was as if he was conducting a tentative study of death. The smell of the guinea pigs' fur over-rode even the smell of chloroform. It was sweet and musty, a vegetarian exhalation.

He began dissecting frogs. He excited a particular nerve in the just-dead frogs' legs and made them kick. Up and down they paddled in the dry air, trying to escape to some resurrecting pond. Their small, exposed hearts were still capable of beating. He looked at me to see my reaction and laughed at my disquiet. He had a peculiar way of laughing, a manic snicker high in his nose that I tried to emulate.

My mother's only entree into the life of science was to feed the fish, though she did take on one self-appointed duty. She made tiny slip-over jackets for the live frogs, to keep them warm while they awaited their demise. It was the only sewing task she appeared to be any good at and she did it with a warmth of feeling that was lacking when she made my clothes.

My father was a consummate hypochondriac, as if the actual living of his life was a risky venture. At night he stood with a medicine glass in his hand, measuring out pink liquid. My mother agitated behind us. 'Just take it, and be done with it, Darl. For heaven's sake.'

He ignored her and said to me: 'See how the meniscus dips in the middle?' He liked to add a bit more to make up for its concavity. When his sinuses blocked he buried his head under a towel over a steaming bowl of water laced with Vicks Vaporub or eucalyptus oil, and inhaled. After an interval of noisy sniffing he invited me into his tent. Claustrophobia struck at me. I had a deep fear of imminent danger, an irrational belief that he might push my face one inch further, into the boiling water.

'Let's do it.' His eyes jumped with points of light. 'Just for fun.' There was no end to the possible terrible outcomes of his games. They always teetered on the edge of something overcharged, electric.

My mother said he'd always had too many amps. She'd had her misgivings at the start and even tried to return her engagement ring, without success. Not long after she had married, she returned home, convinced that something was wrong. But her mother sent her back, telling her: 'You've made your bed, now lie in it.' Was this abandonment the wellspring of her resentment? Was this when she killed her heart?

In me, my father had an audience who idolised him, who thought he epitomised assured and brilliant normality. Did he, like Turgenev's hero Bazarov, dissect frogs to 'build his knowledge and centre his life'? I believe he went through the motions without heart, with a cold distance from life.

My life with Lionel and my life at home took on the lineations of a superspeeded evolutionary transformation as I tried to alter my fate. Proper normality, the only one I knew, existed on the home side of that semi-permeable border marked by the line of ti-trees.

I led a double life. In Lionel's habitat, a skewed and aberrant existence began to play itself out. On his side of the line Lionel kept a secret and I had to guess what it was. Lionel had picked me, he said, because I was special. I knew if I did everything he said, if I never took my eyes off him, he would let me in on it. Lionel's promise was too enticing to do without.

Lionel was the boss. As the mechanism ratcheted between the two opposing slots I saw who was in control. I was shunted this way and that, in charge of nothing. I held my multiplying scratching apprehensions inside myself.

Stiff Dolly is propped against the head-board when we two come into the bedroom. Her nylon nightie and bed-jacket are a nylon grey. She is dry as the husks Lionel blows off the birdseed for his one-eyed canary. She never says much to me but her tone when she talks to my mother is slow, lifeless, hollow. We dance round her, full of energy, pink and warm from our recent encounters in the kitchen.

Lionel lets me sit on his bed. They have separate beds. It is yet another grown-up mystery that sometimes parental beds get pushed together and at other times they are on opposite sides of the room. This bed-manoeuvring occurs on odd occasions for no reason. Some mornings Lionel plays a game, laying me out on his bed and tickling my ribs until I squeal. I understand straight away that he does this for his pleasure, not mine. His hands often end up in strange places. Sometimes he ends by pushing me down on the bed, lifting my top and blowing raspberries on my bare stomach. I don't like it very much. I am too old for such baby games. Nor do I like doing it in front of Dolly. She never says anything, but she looks stony and disapproving. Her face hardly moves a muscle but the corners of her eyes enlarge from time to time, a spooked horse.

Refreshed from ministering to the lifeless form that is Dolly, Lionel sends me downstairs to search for the Sunday paper. It is good when the paper boy throws it into the middle of the trimmed lawn, surrounded by its mortared edging of shale rock slabs. More often it lands in the gutter in the green slime, or next to a dry, white dog-dropping on the footpath, or in the spidery fernery under the front steps. I race up the front stairs with it, feeling athletic in my role of helpful dog, although the one time I hold it in my teeth, Lionel doesn't like it.

'Don't do that. Here, give it to me properly, you silly girl.'

The paper has a defining smell, a damp and acrid inkiness. In a world governed by taste and smell, this one rules off the early morning and heralds the heat and Sunday torpor to come.

Each Sunday Lionel cleans his lace-up shoes. He rubs them with a toothbrush, his square face absorbed. The knot in my stomach goes away when his hot eyes are concentrating on something else. He prepares their surfaces with his square hands, with his hard nails. He spreads the polish on in busy circles, shiny and tight. Then he uses a hard rag before the soft rag. He finishes up by putting them into the bars of sunlight that slant underneath his house.

'That helps the polish soak in, see.'

Last of all, the soft cloth brought forth. Such love of ceremony. I thought he did it all for me, his audience of one. His brown lace-up shoes burnished to a high gloss. Then I hold myself tight, because it is time for a dandle on his knee.

My meals are taken at home. Some tastes are an abomination to me. I hate beans and peas and cabbage. My mother dishes them up at our table with monotonous regularity. She watches me as I swirl the defiling objects round my plate.

'Here, have my chop.'

She never gives me her food with clean decision, but hovers her offering over my plate. The chop levitates, fussing above my pile of mashed potato that is the only food I like. She tries to hide my portion of vegetables. She mashes pumpkin in with the potato. I consider that is marginally acceptable. Her most winsome trick, which she forgets never works, is to put peas and warm potato in a wrapped lettuce leaf.

'There's a surprise packet for you. Now eat up.'

She enrages me with this naked subterfuge. The combination of warm potato, cold lettuce and bright green, pungent peas embedded in the gluey potato is disgusting. She is a bad cook. For her, food is tyranny. I like meat in a tender, picky sort of way, but a diet of steak and salad, chops and salad, with a roast chook at weekends disappoints my father's palate. I side with him. As Dad gets more critical he starts his habit of pushing away his overloaded plate.

'Aargh, Darl' (it rhymes with snarl) 'you've given me too much.'

Exasperated anger makes his voice resonate and Mum bends over him, timorous, stricken. Why doesn't she ever say 'If you don't like it, don't eat it!' She never rebels against her fractious culinary clients, almost as if she expects litigation to ensue if she falls down in her duty to please. I want to yell 'Cowardy custard!' at her, but I'd get into trouble.

I have no guide to action other than my mother. Both of us crouch with our eyes to the peep-hole into the male world. She is never game to write her own scenario. She lacks something innate, and is timid and oppressed. She never finds the strength to 'put a stop to it', to anything, though she often threatens to do just that, in an unspecified way. The small, strangled root in her heart never grows. Struggling in the shade, her natural intuition is pot-bound. She doesn't help me grow up.

The atmosphere at the dining table is thick with suppressed tension as I avoid eating despised vegetables. Meanwhile my father compounds the torture by teasing me with his superior knowledge on almost any subject. This isn't hard, given his seniority. His teasing is merciless. I leave the table howling, my stomach churning, to sit out under the lemon tree with the dog. She turns her muzzle up to me, expectant, while Mum clatters dishes in the kitchen sink and Dad retires to the lavatory with the evening paper.

If I disturb my mother in the kitchen after a meal I find her gnawing at our chop bones or eating left-over pieces of fat and gristle. 'Waste not, want not' she says, caught out. She doles out such meagre amounts for herself at the table. She purses her lips so that small cracks show around her mouth, 'It's not ladylike to take a lot.'

If I take a second helping of food that I like, she shames me. 'Your eyes are bigger than your stomach. Leave some for others,' she tells me, as if a host of mewling children inhabits our dining room.

After one too many of these statements Dad lifts his head, a sharp grin on his face, 'Try not to be pusillanimous, will you Darl?' She never takes enough. But she is always ravenous.

The dog is the only welcoming recipient of my mother's food, wolfing down chop fat and green vegetables with élan – though she too draws the line at 'surprise packets'.

When Dad goes away to one of his many conferences, Mum and I enter the world of the TV dinner taken on our laps. Stir-fries have come into vogue, and fried rice. Sometimes we have tripe and onions in white sauce with parsley showing against the sauce's creamy texture, the snippets of tripe patterned on one side like air-cell blankets. Culinary life at least becomes easier and more companionable when my father is away, and the dining room comes to look more and more like a crypt where the absent body of my father lies buried under the glass tabletop.

All those onslaughts on my temperament set up an irritation, an allergy to pressure. I think I suffered people-burnout at an early age. I watch with surprise as others bounce back, take it on the chin, have equilibrium, roll with the punches, are ebullient, operate with happy pragmatism. I am not that way. It is as if my fabric is a gluey substance that accretes attack, the way sand grains stick round the soft edges of a sea-anemone's interior. I wave my tentacles in search of sustenance then withdraw at the touch of a questing finger. I lie quiet at the bottom of my ocean, doggo as a stingray at low tide, minding my own pure, oceanic business as the surge of water passes over.

I still feel that tidal susurration, almost a taste of saline in my mouth. I like the early mornings, the 6am hiatus before life starts its scrunching and rumbling, before smells pervade, before the anger of lives intervenes, that clear, clean envelope of atmosphere where trees shine and sway, expectant, and the sky is the colour of my mother's pale blue Wedgwood ashtray.

I was the maiden cast in white stone who picked her way through the glassy slivers and intersecting planes of light, the sharp greens. Dew lay on the grass. Snails glided as if on horizontal escalators. The cat, with tail erect, was the only intruder. I loved it, that early weather.

My beset mother, her antennae waving in distraction, makes attempts to satisfy her ungracious husband and her ungrateful daughter. 'What's wrong?' she asks, her lips pursed into creases of compunction. She can't pronounce her 'r's' when they followed 'w's', so it comes out as 'What's wrong?'

My father's efforts to torment her about her shortcomings redouble but I am resistant to her few sympathetic ministrations. How can someone who can't pronounce words be of any aid to me? She fails to be useful. 'Tentative' is her password and it operates no doors. She isn't good at anything and comes, after repeated, fussy efforts, to take on the useless and fading persona of the glimmering mantle I saw once on a backwards-swimming squid.

No-one ever said wise things to me. It might have helped. But they left me to work things out on my own. My rights were unrecognised. It seemed to be the natural order of things that I was all alone.

'You don't say much, do you?' Lionel speaks to the mirror above the basin.

'Nuh.'

'Don't say nuh, say no.'

'No.'

I sit on the folded-up bath-mat on the edge of the bath. Lionel is careful of my comfort while he shaves, and this gladdens my heart. I can think of nothing more engaging than watching him as he manoeuvres his razor across the skin folds. He is solicitous as he holds his nose up with one finger to shave the hairs on his top lip. When the razor slices through the lather leaving a pink path behind it, my feet tingle. He wipes away the foam left high on his cheekbones. He uses a cut-throat razor that he strops on a special leather sharpener. The blade of the razor has curlicues indented into its silver surface, and he shows me where it says *Made in Sheffield*.

'Smooth as a baby's bottom.'

'What?'

'Don't say 'what' – it's rude. Say "I beg your pardon."'

'I beg your pardon.'

'Smooth as a baby's bottom. Here, have a feel.'

He extends his face to my hand, chin jutting. In his old singlet with his geometric face and big chin, he is Chesty Bond. His face feels nude. I think the shaving scenario is ridiculous but know better than to say so.

Sometimes I laugh, and he says: 'What's tickling you?'

'Nothing.'

'Nothing, eh?' and he takes the opportunity to grab me round my ribs and tickle me. It is exhausting pretending that I like it. When he's finished he draws me back to himself and cradles me in his arms with just enough urgency for me to feel unsettled. After a minute I struggle free. One morning he says 'Killjoy' when I jump away. I don't understand, but I sense his displeasure. Sometimes he calls me 'Sourpuss' and I don't want to be one of those either. If he wants to send me into a silent frenzy he has only to say:

'You're spoilt.'

I never see Dolly get out of bed. She never once comes into the bathroom to watch Lionel shave. She misses out on the best part of the day, time after time. The ritual plays itself out with Dolly backstage and when it finishes I go home for my cornflakes.

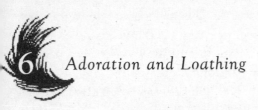

6   Adoration and Loathing

At the height of my parents' cohesion as a couple, they held cocktail parties. The extended family of aunts and uncles retreated to their niches, and an influx of bright, new people surged instead into our lives. At one of these a new woman turned up, whose helmet of Doris Day hair and easy modernity thrust my mother into the shadows.

'Call me Davina, my love.' Her smile scintillated as I hung round the kitchen watching her. She was big in amateur dramatics and I adored the way she pirouetted her hands about. She stands armed in memory, red rubber gloves on, as she helps wash up the crystal at the tail end of one of those stilted occasions. The remarkable thing was that she had brought the gloves with her. The contrast was extreme: between my mother's stiff, square, garden-stained hands and this woman's elegant, pampered ones, as they emerged white and unscathed from their red coverings.

After that, my mother attempted to erase the damage done to her hands by years of neglect. They never improved: her thumb and forefinger sported deep black cuts and her caramel nail polish was the wrong choice. How could she be so inept? I despised almost everything about her. She never stood up to my dislike. She gave me no courage to override my father's subversive condemnation of her personality.

Les and Joan were their oldest, best friends. They came to most of the cocktail parties and sometimes Joan called in on my mother, a brief visit, for she was a busy woman. As she stepped through the door she always said:

'I've only got a minute.'

They were groomsman and bridesmaid at my parents' wedding. They stood in a row in the wedding photograph that sat atop my parents' built-in, cedar-pink clothes cupboard, overshadowing my mother and father with looks of triumphant importance. They were successful, middle-class. He was a dentist. She worked in the surgery as his receptionist. They made so much money they wrapped it in newspaper and hid it in the freezer. They had a house down the coast with a cabin cruiser and one girl my age, a goody-goody called Kirsty, whom I loathed. Pushed together one night at one of her parents' parties, she took me into the bathroom.

'I have cystitis.' She stared at me. 'So I have to be very careful when I wee.'

I think my loathing of her was my first free thought not dictated by anyone, and impervious to remonstrance.

7 *Straw into Gold*

This morning I am up at dawn, somehow full of hope. As I creep through the curtain-shrouded lounge room, last night's cocktail party dregs lie abandoned. The party turned into a late night bash that ended with a doorstep smooch between Les and my mother and Joan and my father. I heard them being quiet and sneaked out into the hallway to have a look. Les was kissing my mother on the mouth. They were swaying back and forth. Dad was hugging Joan with his hands way down on her bottom.

The lounge room smells of cigar stubs. I find some wet peanuts and eat them. There is a half-glass of beer on a side table and I drink that down. It is warm and bitter. Another half-glass has a cigarette stub in it. I find a green olive, the kind with a stone in it, not the sort with the tunnel and the piece of red something stuck inside. The cat comes out of the fireplace where it has been sleeping in the warm ash, looking only somewhat catlike, her fur a frowsty grey. I open the dining room French doors and step onto the terrace. I can feel the day breaking out of its egg and sliding onto the pan of bubbly events.

I am making a list of wishes that I know will get fulfilled. My parents are still asleep. I can sense their furry party breaths filling their bedroom, but now, out here in the yard, the trees are crisp. Up in the not-yet-Reckitt's-blue sky the leaves shine and sway, glinting in the thin yellow sunlight that fingers its way across the terrace. The goldfish plop in the pond. I dangle my fingers just under the water and the fish take turns investigating these large pink worms. They suck on the end of my fingers with their Gladstone bag mouths.

Next door, even Lionel is not up yet. I can't visualise what he is doing. Is he asleep beside Dolly? That doesn't seem right. I imagine he is in a night cupboard where he stands waiting when he isn't being his day self.

I walk out onto the grass in the sloping backyard and bend down. There is much to look at in this close-up world. The heavy dew lies in tiny round crystal balls on the clover. A grasshopper with a green spike extending from its head springs out of nowhere onto my hand. Its mandibles graze my skin. I can feel it eating me. It seems friendly in a detached way that suits me. I am queen and king of this region and nothing can harm me. I run inside and find a piece of shopping list paper in the kitchen drawer and the stub of a pencil my mother uses.

I consider using my Waterford pen, but it is in the old rosewood writing-box my great-uncle gave me and I must not arouse my sleeping parents. Besides, it leaks and this morning I feel pristine. The thought of ink on my writing finger disturbs me.

Outside again I scribble something down. I do a quick drawing of the grasshopper's leg, the saw-like serrations, the hook at the end, in case the words aren't enough. A feeling like a bowel pain surges through me. I am in a glass bubble. I can see its curve as I bump and drift, with a curved outline of a window etched into its oily sides. Then I am out again. I fold the piece of paper and tuck it into my waistband. I must show Lionel my writing.

8 Place of Birth

My father was born in Charters Towers. He was the only boy at the local kindergarten. His blond, curly hair was allowed to stay long and girlish and when he was small his mother tied a pillow to his head because he fell down all the time.

There was nothing strange in any of this for me. The family owned at one time five large properties, which in Western Queensland they call stations. They speak of some magnificence, not borne out by their physical presence except in the sense of the number of square miles they covered. I used to imagine that, because they called one station Moscow they lived on a wild tundra with the properties connected by private train that ploughed through snow, chuffing, ominous. They were well-sinkers and built a woolscour. 'Not farmers. Graziers,' my mother insisted.

My father gave my mother a large yellow sapphire for her engagement ring. They dug it out of that ground. Its crown setting jutted out from her finger, a brilliant indictment.

That country looks like badlands. It is lorded over by roaming emus, deranged soubrettes, feathers tipping in slight breezes, their eyes at once insane and judicious. A country where white people are precarious and defensive. It is a place to traverse in a good season and then get out to something softer. There are no landmarks. The calamitous circle of the horizon is the only boundary. Nothing to tell you who you are. It is a place where your soul gets cooked to stone, your heart withers into leather, your sense of yourself turns to a watermark on sand.

My mother caught herself up in the myth of its grandeur. She would later admit that by the time she married my father the family properties had gone bankrupt. They moved into town, Brisbane, where all good sold-up graziers go.

My father hated the country. It was an effort to get him beyond the outer suburbs. He had a sensible fear of the outback, with its flammable wooden houses, explosive kerosene fridges, generator electricity, white ants and snakes. We lived on twenty-three perches in a double-cavity brick and stucco house in Manderley Road, just off a main intersection. Nothing there a white ant could get its teeth into.

This is where my father brought me to consider my fate. This was where he left me, in my own badlands.

# 9 Sanctuary

In my grandmother's house, I feel loved and protected. She is a benign trundling monument. I believe she has castors on her feet, she moves so smoothly, all in one columnar piece.

I stay with her when my mother becomes sick. No-one tells me what the sickness is but my mother goes to hospital and comes home with nothing and they say it's just as well. She's too old; Nature Knows Best.

'What a shame, what a disappointment for him,' they whisper, meaning my father.

Someone says: 'It would have been good for that kiddie. She's such a spoilt thing.'

My grandmother lets me brush her hair while she has her afternoon rest. Her hair is white and cream, cut in a soft bob. She won't lift her head from the puffy down pillows for me to brush at the back, though she will move it from side to side. Other than that she is available.

She keeps her reading glasses in a moss-green case that snaps shut with a sudden click. I note that sound and also the sound of her turning the pages of her book. Afternoon sunlight filters through the Japanese bamboo and chilli pepper screen that grows outside the spare room. 'Do what you like,' she says. 'Within reason.'

She lets me help her shell peas on the green-tiled kitchen table, but never makes me eat them. I dry the white plates in the steamy scullery that smells of gas and decaying steel wool. When I have dried a plate back and front, Grandpa puts it away in the kitchen dresser.

Grandma only ever reads me one storybook, *The Three Billy Goats Gruff*. My grandmother intones the sound of the little goat's hooves on the bridge in her calm singsong: *trip-trap, trip-trap*. When I tell her I wish she would read me something else, for the troll makes my heart pump with a disabling panic, she says: 'It'll do for the time being.' She surveys me, a smile in her eyes. 'You have to try for pastures green, you know. Never mind the monsters. They're always lurking under bridges.' And she thumps her chest with her fist.

Grandpa takes me for slow walks and introduces me to the neighbours, who shake my hand. Grandpa wears a knitted vest. He is egg-shaped and smaller than Grandma. He is a large-size kewpie doll, the way he stands with his feet close together, his stomach protruding under his vest, his eyes placid yet surprised. He has a fob watch that he consults and then makes disappear in one fluid movement, using one hand.

'Where's it gone?' he asks, looking foolish for my pleasure.

Grandpa's front gate has a metal plaque that reads *Please close this Irwinbilt iron gate.* When we go out together he waits each time while I read it. Each time, to my incomprehension, he says, 'That Irwin builds a sturdy gate.'

Grandma's clothes line stretches right across the vast yard in two wire strands, supported at intervals by wooden clothes props. I watch the white sheets billow in the hot wind. They crack at unexpected intervals. The laundry at the back of the house smells of Sunlight soap and the wet wood smell of the long birch tongs she uses to fish boiled clothes out of the copper.

They have old, bald grass, cut short. There's a row of fruiting fig trees down the side fence, tortured with age but still bearing. I climb their reptilian branches and stay up there until the angular, relentless march of the Spit-in-your-eye bugs dislodges me. The fig leaves look made by hand, they're so regular. Their sandpaper texture is startling. I admire the clean way they break off the twigs. Their smell conjoins with Grandpa's visits to the outside lavatory.

I believe that what I felt at my grandmother's house, despite the shadow thrown by the troll, was serenity. Protection, mild indulgence, serenity.

10 Dryness and Precision

I practise my running writing and try to perfect my signature. Dryness and precision obsess me. The compulsion to repeat, to make precise, to polish. Repetition, replication. Something in my nature demands I perform, in exactly the same way again and again, compelling, self-designated tasks. I have to align everything. I hate the awkwardness of the letters I form.

Lionel polishes his Holden with the squeaking chamois. 'You can write a letter to Redmond in the mother country, but you mustn't make any mistakes. I'll help you.' I know he will want to hold my writing hand as he stands behind me, so I say: 'I'm not good enough yet.'

I long to be able to write with fluency and character the way my father does. Night after night I watch as he corrects examination papers from the Technical College where he teaches linesmen not to electrocute themselves. He is scathing in his condemnation of their inadequacies (and by inference mine) and I feel shamed for them when he puts a large red 'O' in their margins. His sneering frightens me.

'The little twerp. He's a dead 'un,' and I visualise yet another would-be linesman toppling from his theoretical pole.

There are drawings of power lines and power poles and sometimes electro-mathematical formulae. He says it is physics. I think they are art works and long to be calligraphic.

My body is changing, becoming unacceptably moist. I wipe myself inside and out. I cannot bear the thought of drops of urine escaping to dampen my underwear. At the same time I become terrified of electricity and Dad fosters my fears. He takes unnecessary risks, or so my mother says, changing light bulbs without turning off the switch. He makes sparks fly out of power points. When he solders his own sinkers, blue lights flash out of the end of the solder iron. He wears no protective goggles. He has a rubber grounding mat that he stands on in his workshop when he uses electrical equipment, and he teases me by saying there is no room on it for me.

'Look out,' he yells as he turns on his machines and I run outside in a panic and leap onto the cement edge of the flower bed to get away from the murderous ground.

He is the magician safely afloat on his rubber island while I flounder, ignorant. Wetness conducts electricity, that much I know. It frightens me. The conjunction of water, electricity and my father is a dangerous triangle encasing me.

Thunderstorms are my mother's black dog. When February comes, the humid oppression intensifies and her mood darkens. Roiling cumulus clouds bank up in the west, starting white as the inside of sheep's fleece, then turning thick, black and purple. Light turns bruise green and a stillness falls. Small birds race tweetering for cover. A wind rushes in as if to fill a vacuum, the trees bend before it, and the venetian blinds rattle. Mum rushes to close the windows. She jousts with the cords, grabbing the heavy chintz curtains to her bosom. She leaves it too late to switch off power points, hesitating undecided in front of them before she heads for the bedroom clutching the dachshund. At the first thunder, under the bed the two of them go, the dog shivering.

To my surprise I am never afraid of storms. They excite me with their undiscerning power, their rambunctiousness. Thunder is deep music. My father tells me that it is the sound of the god Thor throwing his hammer. That's the name on my mother's washing machine, next to a silver logo of a fist holding a mallet and a lightning bolt. I ask Dad what else Thor does up there and he gives his wild grin and says that Thor vanquishes women.

I delight in peering under the bed at my mother and the dog, coaxing them to come out and watch the fun. Lightning is the silver of physics. It snakes and crackles across the sky and I watch it find its mark somewhere over the city skyline. I count the seconds before the thunder booms out; that is how many miles away it is. A whip-crack overhead means it's close and my mother issues a muffled command for me to join her and the dog as they cower under the bedsprings.

Sometimes, just for the experience, I crawl under there. It's almost as good as lying on my back on the grass, sky-gazing. I stare into the dusty spirals of the springs, inches from my face, next to the licking dog and my trapped mother.

'You shouldn't be near all this metal, Mum.'

She moves, restless; 'I'm not budging,' and the confusion in her eyes affords me sweet delight.

I take charge in a storm. I become my father. Power in my father's hands bespeaks misuse. The power of the storm is greater, uncontrolled and unleashed, but it's not crazy, it's pure chaos. It isn't directed at me. It is independent, disinterested.

Storms wash the air cool. I imagine the dog urine running off the grass, with body dust, clothes fluff, mites that live in mats, cat-sick, all cascading down the drains. I divert the brown flow in the gutters with my bare feet. Once a boy down the road makes me a tiny paper boat. I imagine it sailing down the drain at the bottom of our street and off to the sea like in *Scuffy The Tugboat*. At the last minute a hand that might be my father's plucks it from annihilation.

Trees sink towards the ground under their hood of water. The house, the yard, the suburb, the city, life itself goes into hiatus during and just after a storm. My mother's power gets suspended in the space under the bed; my father is out checking lines or sub-stations. I am the still point. I reign in the void.

I want to believe that I can grow from this: bigger and better, older and stronger. But it happens in fits and starts, in side shoots, not in the imagined way straight up the beanpole. Growing comes at me through fears, shame, disruption, black water, deaths. What gratification I have in change gets ironed out the next instant by the pain of loss. I get rid of, repeat, regain lost ground, feel empty, disconsolate and that I never will refill. When I complain of sharp sensations in my arms and legs, my mother is dismissive.

'They're just growing pains. Nothing to make a fuss about. You must be super-sensitive. Have you written to Redmond yet?' Her voice is querulous and I know Lionel has been badgering her.

'I don't feel like it.'

'You'll never get anywhere if you don't try,' she nags.

I notice few surfaces are soft. Except for the cat, in one way or another almost everything is sharp, and hurts.

Goethe had a theory of negative space, the shape of which defines our unfurling. What is not there becomes our dimensions. Our genetic code might unfold in response to that emptiness. The storm became my symbol of emptiness. The storm was where I grew, where I felt my power, where I learned to let it happen. In the storm, in my imagination, I let all of it go: my small life, item by item. In the storm's wake I delivered up to fate all I had: the cat, the dog, my parents, Lionel, the boy at the end of the street who rode scooters with me, my gold bangle, even my grandmother's sanctuary. Then I saw what remained. At the end I knew I could not do without one last thing. That was the house of thought in my head.

I want to be perfect and in particular I want to be unwrinkled. The story of *Saggy Baggy The Elephant* disturbs me. He is unacceptable. Not for me the redeeming moral at the end where he finds other elephants and comes to accept his sags and bags. I am Saggy Baggy and I don't want anyone to know. My socks are a special torment. I fold the tops and pull them straight, but they settle into inevitable wrinkles round my ankles. I have my father trim my fingernails short. Their shape dissatisfies me and I bite them into submission. Straight lines and desiccation. I want to live in a paper world, written in my father's left hand.

Lionel, on the contrary, wants me wet. He has taken to touching me between my legs, outside my underwear but inside my bloomer pants.

'Hot,' he says, then withdraws his hand and smells his fingers.

I can't tell my mother. I know enough not to speak of it. I can't tell on him. I'm honourable, shaped by playground lore and caught in a vice. In Lionel's workshop, Lionel's iron vice.

11   *Obedience*

I can hardly bear to unpick these stitches. Just like my mother with her Quik-Unpick, opening the wounded cloth, catching the frazzled material in her hurry, botching holes in the fabric. The cut stitches sit up, perfect whiting bones.

'Damn and blast.' She adjusts her light blue plastic glasses with an impatient thrust of her forefinger. She looks ugly. She looms with disgruntlement. She makes the task mean. 'It's my own damn fault. I should have followed the pattern. They had instructions. Bloody, bloody hell.'

Lionel and Dolly are not pleased. They have joined forces in their condemnation. At the first expression of myself in my beautiful poem, the grasshopper grazing on the skin of my hand, its temporary friendship, they stamp and crush in unison.

'It doesn't rhyme. Poems have to rhyme.'

'No they don't.'

'Don't be a silly-billy,' says Dolly. 'Of course they do.'

'Don't be cheeky to Dolly. What's this silly drawing? Where's the rest of it?'

'It's all there.'

'Well I can't see it. Come downstairs with me,' commands Lionel. 'We'll leave Dolly alone. She has a headache. She can't put up with dunces like you.'

He takes me down, erased, obedient, to his workbench. He grabs me and gives me a kiss that mangles my teeth against my lips. I feel his horsy false teeth dislodge. 'Whose girl are you?'

I leave a silence that enlarges, a balloon filling with exhaled air. For the first time I feel defiance, but he smears it out of existence by sliding his hand down into my bloomers. This time he travels in between my underpants and the skin of my stomach. Has he made a mistake? He seems sure. His hardnailed finger slides inside me. I wait, transfixed. My mother told me not to let anyone touch my bottom. What if he has slid round to that other aperture by mistake? I get so embarrassed for him in his clumsiness that I feel wooden.

Lionel acts as if he owns my body. All of a sudden it is no longer mine. I am only allowed to wear it when he gives permission. My internal secrets are his; he reads my inner diary with impunity. While his hand fiddles inside me, taking over, I have one thought that rides above my outrage and defeat, which hangs on, stubborn, a last red flower on the poinciana. I run inside my head and stand at bay. He cannot follow there; he can't get in. I push the door in my head shut and lean against it, out of breath. Down where his interest fixes, his finger stops. He pushes me away. 'You're dry.' He is dismissive.

A shamed giggle escapes from me. Lionel returns to his workbench. He looks cranky and aloof, displeased with me. I have been naughty and he must punish me. He won't acknowledge me standing, lame, in the bars of sunlight. Tears of fright and loneliness well in my eyes. I can't bear it when he acts as if I have offended him. He is all I have, my boon companion. I ask him a question but he will not answer. I sidle up to him, but he has turned into a wall. He is adamant. I must please him again before he will answer me. It is my fault. His sulky silence sends me away. He has locked me out of myself. When I move I feel disengaged from my limbs as if the rubber bands holding me together have all of a sudden perished.

12 The Three of Us

Her name was Rosie. One day Redmond turned up again with her in tow. Then I entered by default a soap opera that was at the same time someone's real life. Off to one side, unimportant by their standards, inconspicuous, but centre-stage by mine. No-one told me anything, but I was down there with the cat and the dog in the best vantage point, underfoot, slinking, observing. At the same time, when I thought of Lionel, I was filled with the rage and fear of an animal being backed into a corner.

I was ripe for Rosie's wantonness, ready to embrace her and it with my skinny arms, needing to sight freedom, to fall in love with it.

Redmond had been on an overseas working holiday, for twelve months. Once my father had taken my mother down to a conference in Melbourne, but that was it. They brought back with them tales of a place called The Buttery that turned out to be a bar in some select club, perhaps the Melbourne Club. Redmond had brought back Rosie. She was Irish, with the first peaches and cream complexion I had ever seen, used as I was to weathered and tan. She liked to sun bake in a halter top and shorts. She was short, shaped like a Coke bottle my father said, endearing, pink all over as if she had just stepped from the bath.

Her shortness and easy camaraderie made me feel as if she were a same-age friend.

'Rosie says we're girlfriends,' I tell my mother.

'The cheek of it. She's old enough to be your mother. You make sure you be polite. And don't go pestering them all the time.'

Rosie doesn't feel anything like my mother. She doesn't sound like her, either. Her Irish intonations are adorable.

Everyone loved her at first, even Mum. Dolly seemed a bit aloof but it was hard to get Dolly to behave in any other way.

'She's put out over the London wedding bizo.'

My mother eyes the hissing pressure cooker. She has poured herself a shandy and has taken the first sip without waiting for my father.

'That Redmond's always done exactly what he wanted. He gets away with murder. Of course he's the apple of his father's eye.'

I repeat the phrase to myself. It sounds so good I want to write it down and draw a juicy russet apple with Lionel's eye in the centre.

'It was a bit mean of them,' my mother announces, not looking at me. She doesn't really want to talk to me but she's got no-one else. 'He could have thought more of his mother. How she'd feel. I know what I'd think about them doing a thing like that.'

I listen to her entangle herself. 'You've got to be fair all round. After all...'

I think there's nothing to follow when she checks the time on the kitchen clock with a quick lift of her head, and takes another guilty sip of her shandy – but there is. '...They've got some lovely photos to show, even if it was in a registry office.'

She gives a big sniff and lights a cigarette. 'She's always grizzling about something, Dolly. I mean, I'd fall over backwards if I ever caught her with a smile on her face.'

As if that clinches the argument. I try to imagine Dolly cracking the rigor mortis of her face with a wide smile, but nothing happens.

'She should be satisfied with what she's got.'

My mother pushes up the bounce of her newly-permed hair with the back of her hand.

'If you ask me, I wouldn't be surprised if those two had to get married in a hurry.'

She exhales a gladiatorial plume of smoke. I see there are some straight bits of her hair sticking out underneath the line of stiff curls.

'Why would they?'

'Why would they what?' my mother hedges.

'Get married in a hurry.'

'I wasn't talking to you. Go and make your bed.'

Dolly seemed pleased enough with her son's enchantment. The neighbourhood was abuzz over this acceptable though foreign trophy Redmond had managed to haul into his net and Lionel and I were talking again.

The early summer grass rocketed skywards. Lionel was out with his hand mower pushing and pulling, making clean whirring noises surge out of the blades. He still kissed and fondled me as a greeting but he reserved the light in his eye for Rosie.

Rosie smoked and wore a bandanna tied round her neck. When she dressed up she wore gauzy scarves tied in a perky knot. She spent her whole time smoking and reading novels, lying on a reed mat in the hot shade of the poinciana. After school I would join her, sitting on the raised, lizardy roots and, if she wanted me to, I would get her a cold drink of cordial with ice-blocks in it. She thanked me and looked so languid I would have kept up a running courier system of frosty glasses if she had demanded it.

Before he left for work each day Lionel had taken to storing beer glasses in the ice-box for her, so melting was her Irish appeal.

'She's a china doll, isn't she?' he confided to me.

I agreed, thinking of my china doll called Rosebud, pleased that he had picked just the right description for my secret paramour. We adored her together and bowed to her every desire.

Redmond, too, fussed about her. He was anxious around her as if she might whip out her paw and scratch him if he made a wrong move. I liked to calculate her moods when he was around. She was supine but in charge, without twitching a muscle. He pounded up and down the back stairs in search of something she wanted. He needed me to help, all the time.

'Give us a hand, kiddo,' he says and I go up with him to their room and help him carry things down. He lets me touch the cut glass-bottles and the amber necklace on Rosie's dresser. 'Put them back in the same spot and it'll be our secret, Sweetie.'

Sometimes we just stand in the doorway together and look at the room as if we are taking a quick photograph. Once he puts two dabs of her perfume on me, one behind each ear, and kisses me on my nose. 'Elizabeth Arden's Blue Grass.' He smiles at me. 'Picked it up in Singapore.'

We were proud of her possessions. I loved him for looking after her. I loved the secret of them being together with me included, allowed to watch, kept warm and alive. I felt daring, slithery and fresh as if I'd just broken out into a new skin.

I started to ignore Lionel.

Rosie had a round, glossy-red, aluminium, rotating, apple-shaped ashtray. She carried it with her and stubbed out her pink and blue Sobranie cigarettes at its core, then pushed the plunger and made the butts disappear into its maw. She let me press the plunger if she was in the throes of painting her nails.

Nail painting was acceptable. Even my mother brought out her pinkish-caramel polish and applied it to her garden-stained nails in an apologetic fashion. Rosie went one better and painted her toenails as well, using a flagrant red. She did it with such insouciance. She made the world stop when she painted her nails.

I liked it best when Redmond rubbed suntan oil on her skin. 'Not too hard and not down there, Darlin',' she moans, holding her paperback novel against errant sunrays that spear through the poinciana branches.

'Sorry Sweetie.' He looks distracted, as if pretending she hasn't caught him out doing something he shouldn't. I smile at Rosie and she gleams at me through her eyelashes. The sun shines on the oil-smeared bottle, and the kiwi bird's curved beak on it, its meek, feathered bottom completing a perfect crescent.

I don't remember any rain after Rosie came to live next door. There must have been a drought. In the dry heat my grandfather cactus grew a flower that opened at night with a sugary perfume. I took Redmond to see it, carrying my father's heavy torch. The grass had frizzled up but the bindi-eyes brandished their tiny darts with renewed vigour. I could rely on Redmond to help pick them out of the soles of my feet and piggy-back me to Lionel's back steps.

When Redmond came home from work I would see him walk down the hill with his coat slung over one shoulder. He would wave at me in my cactus vantage point before turning to kiss hullo to Rosie. She would be waiting on the front lawn. When he bent over her I saw a stain of sweat down the back of his shirt, in a long vee between his wide shoulder blades.

Each afternoon, as I waited for Redmond to stride into sight, I held the warm body of the dog between my feet, lifted up her ear as if it were a letter box lid and whispered: 'This is the happiest day of my life.'

Soon the fights started. They began around the time that Lionel took Rosie to the Saturday afternoon pictures down at the Junction, one weekend when Redmond had to go away. My parents didn't allow me to go to the pictures because my mother said they were all guttersnipes. My father was against the idea, too. 'Silly rubbish. You don't want to grow up an ignoramus.' Neither was I allowed to read comics. I had to be content with subterfuge speed readings at my friend Margot's place. Margot's mother was my teacher at school and didn't seem to have anything against comics. She also taught us how to make damper so I received double value at Margot's scrambly house. When my mother found out they lived in the housing estate she no longer let me go there.

The fights grew out of that Saturday afternoon at the flicks. Rosie got up from her mat, hissed something at Redmond, and slammed into the house.

One day a bit later, out of the blue, she said 'Stuff your bloody drinks' and threw her book at him.

I didn't know what was going on. I began to worry that Rosie might be spoiled. My mother started telling my father things she didn't want me to hear. Dolly looked grim. At night, if I stood in the spare room with the window open, I could hear tirades of high-pitched argument coming from Redmond's bedroom.

'...coward!' Rosie shouts one night. I push as hard as I can on the sticky metal window sash and it gives a fraction, emitting a dull squeak. I hold my breath. 'You won't even stand up for your own wife, will you, Redmond? Will you?' Rosie's voice hangs clear in the night air. It's like watching the television with my eyes closed.

'You're a charlatan, Redmond. A charming, bloody hollow log... you and your fraud of a father.'

'Don't you talk like that about my Pop,' Redmond says, all of a sudden, in a loud voice. Then silence. I hear them walking across the boards of the verandah. Then they are in the kitchen, opening a cupboard, throwing something into the sink. I duck my head down below the window frame.

'And what's he up to with that poor little poppet?' Rosie's voice is only feet away from me, across the drain and the line of ti-trees.

'You've got eyes in your head!'

I wait for Redmond to say something. A chair scrapes on the floor. A cramp starts in my right foot. I watch my toes splay out all by themselves. No more voices, but a momentary lull as in a telethon, when the panel members look at each other and then all peer out to the side. After a while the light goes out in the kitchen, then moments later in the bedroom.

The wooden slats on the side verandah room stay closed at weekends. Redmond doesn't wave to me any more, or let me stand with him in their bedroom, or say 'Hi there, Sweetie' if he sees me idling in my cactus garden waiting for attention.

More often, if I leap across the dividing drain to see Rosie he says: 'She's having a lie-down.'

The bindi-eyes sting worse than ever and I have to pick them out by myself.

One dreadful day, full of screams and imprecations, he tells me to leave Rosie alone.

'Beat it, kiddo,' he snarls in his best American accent.

I hated him that day. He had spoilt everything, leaving me out, breaking our unspoken pact. Me and Rosie and Redmond.

At school you got into trouble if you changed sides. That was breaking the rules. I knew Lionel had seen me digging my toes in, ready to leap. I was going to get into trouble again, jumping too soon, found out before I had calculated a landing spot. Redmond hadn't stuck up for me. He hadn't waited to catch me in his arms.

I knew if I could see Rosie I would fix things up. She would be happy again with me around. I would play being her servant. She would continue to be our living treasure. Redmond wouldn't stay cranky. We would make him behave nicely to us. My life would become female and halcyon once more.

13 Apassionata

While I could still fit in comfort on my father's lap, music was the only pleasurable physical contact I could legitimately expect to have. Music was passion larger than me. It was solace and balance.

Music had begun to waver and die as I grew older and my father more remote. It was never the same once I could not couple it with his shirt front and his whisky breath, his nicotine-stained fingers, his male breathing pattern. Breathing in and out with my father was my gourmet's secret.

Music soothed us both. Music, from the speakers he had built for himself in the lounge room, sacrosanct in the tattered tapestry warmth of his lounge chair, where even the cat did not dare sit. We were replete. His music, the ordinary classical repertoire of an ordinary, middle class man was not my mother's. She suffered it from afar in the kitchen.

As he became wilder and more disordered, the music got louder and more chaotic. I began to sit across from him in my own chair or lie humped over the upturned leather pouffe he had brought back from the Suez.

My great-aunt, who was still alive, had been a nurse in the Great War. She told me that pouffes were dirty things stuffed with soiled bandages. 'Those filthy Arabs,' she said. 'The way they widdled next to the trains and in the streets.' It was open-ended condemnation.

The whisky glass became my father's constant companion. He began to go off to work white-faced, the whisky bottle glinting in the glass cupboard in the kitchen hallway, down to its halfway mark. If my mother pleaded 'Turn it down Darl, just a fraction,' he sometimes complied. When she took to chanting 'Darl, turn that music down,' her lips pursed and furious through the diamond glass of the lounge room doors, Dad laughed his high, snickering laugh. A mad light snapped on in his golden eyes and he walked to the rosewood cabinet and turned it up. Just a fraction.

As time passed, opinion in our house began to change about what was going on next door. I heard my mother say Rosie was a common little bint. But I didn't think so. She was my lovely, living heroine, my passport to a freedom I could not yet decipher. She was decisiveness and derring-do, courage in the line of fire, everything my mother and Dolly were not. She didn't stay around long enough for me to make out what war she was fighting, but at least I understood that not only my great-aunt had been to the Front. Other women could step out with their weapons loaded and aimed.

The last thing I heard Rosie say, through the wooden louvres of Redmond's bedroom windows, was: 'You can both go to buggery, you and your rotten father.' It was the first shiver of regret that I ever felt pass through me.

Before Rosie finally disappeared, it became very quiet. My mother spoke to my father in a lowered voice, and they both stopped talking when I walked in.

'What are you talking about?'

'Nothing.'

'You can't be talking about nothing. You must be talking about something. Tell me.'

'Nothing for your ears.' My mother looked across at my father.

'A wigwam for a goose's bridle,' Dad grinned.

One afternoon I heard Dolly talking to my mother. 'That Rosie used poor Redmond as a ticket out. She packed her suitcases and called a taxi. She's gone to live in a flatette in Yeronga.'

'Yeronga?' My mother seemed gratified. 'What a cheek! Did she take anything she shouldn't have? I don't suppose you really knew where she came from.'

'Fancy calling a taxi. At that hour of the night,' Dolly whimpered.

I thought it was the perfect place for my Rosie, mystical, sophisticated, independent. A week later, a silent Dolly handed my mother a pair of seersucker shorts and a halter top and my mother gave them to me at the tip of her fingers. It was as if Rosie had left me her skin if not her body. Though I failed to fill them out, I wore them till they were rags.

After church on Sunday Redmond went to Wagga with his burnished hair, and he forgot to say goodbye.

14 The Russian Woman

After Rosie's defection Lionel came out of his corner fighting. He had worked out his moves. Now he had a ruse and a set of decoys. They weren't ducks. They were chooks, and one young White Russian woman walking down the street.

White Russian émigrés had infiltrated our neighbourhood. They didn't look too foreign except in winter, when they tended to wear greatcoats and round fur hats. Dad said they were ratbags but I think their politics must have been pretty close to ours. 'They're White because they're not Red,' Dad said. I thought this was one of his funny jokes.

Lionel worked for a law firm somewhere in town. 'He's only an articled clerk,' my mother sniffed in her disparaging voice. I thought that must have something to do with wearing spectacles. Once, with my mother, I saw Lionel outside the Magistrate's Court in a grey cloth dust-coat. He must have reached retirement soon after that, for he began to be at home all the time. Although he appeared to have a strict roster of daily events, he made time to hang out of the front verandah windows, the heavy wooden blinds rolled up on their chains, to watch who walked down the street.

Saturday morning was his favourite time. We stood together, resting our elbows on the wide window ledge. There were lots of dogs padding past in our street. Once I saw an Alsatian go by with a guinea pig in its mouth as if it were carrying a parcel. Little kids on tricycles made concentric circles on the footpath until they struck the gutter. Boys whizzed by on bikes.

The Russian woman walked by from left to right, entering and exiting a hot painting. The street was always hot, made hotter by the cement divide with its white wooden railing that bifurcated our street, just past Lionel's place.

Lionel notices the Russian woman first and begins to discuss her attributes. There is a subtle difference from his talk about 'our Rosie'. This one is all his. I begin to know the repugnant feeling of comparison.

'Here comes my girlfriend. Look at her neat bottom.' He licks his dry lips and picks with the side of his thumbnail at a torn quick on his index finger. I am silent. 'Look at her legs, will you, in those high heels?' I look.

Lionel speaks to me as if I am his male companion. He strips me of the small tendrils of sexual awareness that have begun to emerge out of the top of my head, a summer pumpkin vine. He suggests I join with him in his lasciviousness, oblivious to the hormonal lioness crouching inside me, waiting to spring into being. Mine was such a tiny sexual identity it did not take him long to damage it. I resent his assumption that I don't mind being treated as a boy or a neuter. He hurts me by thinking I don't notice.

But I do not have the courage to complain. I can't even put into words how I feel. It would be shocking to voice my feelings. I have no rights of complaint. I feel disquiet and the discomfort of manipulation. This is a game I don't want to join.

At the same time I watch the Russkie with as much interest as he, but for different reasons. What is it about her that he likes, apart from her legs and her unmentionable bum? I need to find out, so I can copy it. At school everybody copies everyone else. I can change to suit him, quick as a chameleon. Then I will do for Lionel, one fine day, what she does.

Without your love... It's a melody played in a penny arcade...

I want Lionel's approbation, his satisfaction. I want to please him again. He is all I have now. I want him to be proud of me. I want to have all his attention. I want to be indispensable to him and special. I want to be the apple of his eye. I want to get to the point where the tables turn and I make Lionel do my will, the bearskin stripped from him, the prince in the cloth of gold exposed. In my heart I know it will happen if one morning I can make Lionel laugh.

# 15 Symbiosis

My mother and father were two mirrors looking at each other. They both stood with their left foot resting on their right instep. Which one had the habit first? Which species infiltrated the other? Those might be the wrong questions. Perhaps the gesture existed only in duality. What happens when one mirror looks at another mirror? It sounds like a joke in a Christmas cracker. Does mirror one see into mirror two, or are they both blinded by the blankness of their own reflected image?

Here is another question in the Hall of Mirrors. Does the other care for us or only make deals? If the deal falls through or tips over in our favour, to their detriment, then is the deal off?

The evolutionary mechanism tells us that we must view all others as a threat to our environment, that position in a structure confers power. We must occupy the available space. The substance does not matter; all-important is the form. Position, position, position. Occupy the space or the other will steal your light, rob you of sustenance, drink your well dry, eat your children.

Better then in this risky environment that you have no partner. Put the other into service for you: the subservient Victorian female companion, the beholden Filipino wife, the unpaid Aboriginal stockman and his house-girl daughter, the unacknowledged child bride. A place for everything and everything in its place.

Power always wins, but power must have resistance to exist. Never forget the hard shiny surface of the other. Never forget that Spinoza noticed that substance wills itself to persist. Notice also that fungi and algae make lichen in symbiosis. And never forget the persistence of the rock in a hard place.

16 Six Battery Chickens

What is it about even numbers? My father buys six white laying chickens and has them strung out in a galvanised iron laying cage in the back yard. Each has a coloured plastic band placed on its leg for identification. Bluey, Greenie, Whitey, Blackie, Reddie, Pinkey I call them. With a charcoal stick from the barbecue I do a drawing of their feet lined up, and colour in the bands.

When they lay an egg in that punitive and sterile environment, it rolls into a trough at the front. They have a feeding dish they can reach by sticking their heads through the bars, and each has a small water container hanging on the inside. It is my job to fill these every afternoon after school. I always talk to each chook in turn so as not to show favouritism. But they are a boring lot, stupid in their captivity. Each one has its beak tip cut off so it can't even peck its neighbour. Nothing to do. They can stand up or sit down but they can't turn around.

It is quite acceptable for my father to incarcerate his chooks. He prides himself on his scientific animal husbandry. The birds repay this treatment by having no character. I do not even mind when the non-layers have their heads chopped off by Lionel's tomahawk. The fall of the blade severs no connection. Serves them right.

By contrast, Lionel houses his chooks in a spacious yard down the back, abutting the wooden fence covered in cats-claw vine and morning glory. Each of his chooks has its own elusive character. Lionel calls them by name, but collectively they are his 'girls.' When Lionel takes Dolly to visit Redmond in Wagga, they pay me sixpence a day to look after them. I would do it for nothing, though I love the shiny sixpences and pile them in neat stacks on my bedroom dresser.

Lionel is fond of his 'girls' and only ever kills the roosters. I don't feel the same affinity with the roosters that I have with the hens.

Feather-dusters, Lionel calls them. Their spiralling tail feathers are replicas of my mother's feather-duster. When she is out at golf I take it from the broom cupboard. It hangs next to a wide leatherwork belt my aunt made, that has an interlocking silver buckle. I stroke my hand down the parabola of shiny colours.

The chook yard is half-covered over at one end with wooden planks and old tin, to form a bonnet. From his back steps you can see right into it. Inside this enclave Lionel has constructed laying boxes out of fruit crates lined with straw, perches made from old broom handles and a wide ladder for them to climb to the perches. I climb it to collect eggs from the top boxes and if I make intimate chook noises the chooks never peck my hand. They like to perch as evening falls and in that half-hour before darkness I watch them mass on the man-made branches, ruffling out their feathers and closing their hooded eyes. If I make a sudden move some of them open one eye and close it again, a shutter made of skin. There is one Black Orpington, her thick legs covered in scales, which goes to roost first.

Lionel has placed sections of broken concrete footpath as stepping stones through the bare soil of the yard. The chooks scratch, assiduous, between them, creating pockets of erosion in which black-horned beetles live. Millipedes trundle between the sections on their thousand articulating legs, and red-backs breed beneath them.

Every couple of months Lionel lifts and stacks the pavers. He shovels archaeological layers of chook droppings into the wheelbarrow and dumps it on the compost heap on top of the spiny bougainvillaea canes. Then he rakes the yard level and re-lays them. In between times he dislodges the pinnacles of chook shit with a large bamboo rake. The chook poo has a heavy, mushroomy smell. The pinnacles start black at the base and end in brilliant, coagulated white. I wonder if I can use it as paint in my sketch-book.

I spend hours down in the chook yard communing with them. I learn their habits and language. One day I show a hen my opal ring through the wire wall, and prompt as a bundy-puncher she pecks at its iridescence, dislodging a significant proportion of the stone. I sit back on my heels in shock. She's not supposed to do that. The chook looks at me, expectant, with her beady eye. I look back at her, stupefied. 'Crazy chook. You're silly as a two-bob watch.'

What will my father say? He gave me the ring and I know it is precious, that he expects me to look after it with my life. I take it off my finger. I can't tell him what has happened so I walk to the back fence where I can look down into the neighbours' rambly garden behind the garage. It is a mess of suspended cats-claw vine that has scrambled up into his mango trees. I throw the ring into the viney mattress and go looking for my father.

'My finger got thinner and thinner and it just fell off.' I have a vision of Hansel and Gretel, poking thin sticks instead of plump fingers through the cage bars for the witch to feel. I cry in front of him. I think I am good at lying, though I don't know if he believes me. I am a known confabulator. When my father catches me in a fabrication, he always sounds exasperated. 'What are you doing, repeating these fairy stories? You can't make things up all your life. Grow up.'

My parents tried to break me of the habit of lying. They threatened me with the tale of the boy who cried wolf. But imagination just kept forming words which popped out of my mouth. That day my father said very little, and didn't challenge me. It was the first loss and grief I can recall in my life.

17 Dead Cat

I want to tell Dolly about our new cat. The importance attached to telling might invest the creature with more emotional significance than it presently carries. Our old cat has died, but not in front of me. Mum took it to the vet with some feline complaint and never brought it back. Neat as an ant she has hi-jacked my feelings with her *fait accompli*.

'Don't make such a fuss.' My mother's voice is sharp as she glances at my aggrieved face. 'We can always get another one.' So we do. Out at a desolate cattery at Kuraby I choose my next playmate. We bring it home wrapped in a towel in case it sicks up. My mother paints butter on its paws so it won't stray.

I interrupt my mother and Dolly talking out on the terrace. 'Our cat's a she. When she gets older we'll have her neutered. But she has to come on heat first.' Dad has told me the details.

Dolly shifts, restive, but nods her head. She looks morose but at the same

time self-important. She stands close to my mother, who sits on the banana lounge, smoking. Something sombre and secret is in the air.

'So when she's had her operation she'll be an "it".' I keep my voice bright. Dolly's eyes widen.

'A she - it.' I am still working it out. I go the next inevitable step. 'A shit.'

It's one of my cleverest jokes.

'Shame on you, swearing in front of your mother.' Dolly purses her lips into a chook's bum of outrage. 'In her bereavement.'

I stare at my mother for an explanation.

'Grandma died.' She looks away. 'Last week.' She is reluctant to give me details, to let me in on grown-up emotions.

My heart gives a hurtful squeeze inside my chest. 'Why didn't you tell me?'

She has told Dolly before me. Dolly, a mere neighbour. Dolly, who is not family. Dolly, who doesn't know the unbearable, silky texture of Grandma's hair, her solid, amused profile as she lies reading on her pillows. Neither of them understands my loss is the more profound. I have lost benevolence. I have lost being wordlessly understood.

Guilt plays across my mother's face. She stares out across the terrace at nothing. She stubs her cigarette out on the concrete, then gives me a brief glance. 'I didn't think you'd be interested.' Dolly turns, making a satisfied huffing noise and stalks away.

'You should have told me. Why didn't you tell me?' I stare at the top of my mother's head. I know I will choke on my tears waiting for her answer. My mother will never grant me true feelings. I give her a savage hit on the shoulder as I go past and run to my bedroom. She does not tell my father of my rude behaviour, and in this matter she never retaliates.

18 *Round One*

Phrases my father used drift in my mind as so much flotsam. 'It's a foregone conclusion,' he would say with satisfaction. It was a foregone conclusion that Lionel would win the first round. He was too powerful for me. After that day when I found out what Lionel's promise was made of, there was a lull. Then he lashed back at me with his weapon of choice: reproof.

Here is a secret straight from the horse's mouth, in that place where the iron bit lies across the tongue. The torturer does not enjoy torture. He does not lie awake at night sluicing in the juices of punishment. He does not dream of pliers and electric cables. Pleasant visions of burnt and nail-less bodies do not assail his senses. These are his means to an end, nothing more. What he dreams about is submission. That is what matters.

The torturer says: 'This is my kind of power. This, which gives me my name.'

My mother told me that Lionel was a POW. She said: 'They call them the Walking Dead.'

They imprisoned him in Burma, starved him till his knees stood out like knobs and his teeth dropped out. They said he was a living skeleton. When he came back home I imagined his legs emerging from his roomy shorts, disengaged chicken bones. They weren't the only things disengaged. He never talked about his War experiences and yet I sensed that he had suffered deep humiliation at the hand of arbitrary power. He saw tyranny brandishing its irons, he felt tyranny infiltrating his brain, and he brought tyranny back with him in secret, stuffed into a body cavity.

Tyranny says: 'All otherness is gone, you know that now, don't you? You are without obligation, absolved of relations. You know you must believe in this if you want to be the young man you were before I took your life away from you, before I removed the spark plug of your sexual desire, before I left you with intent bereft of joy, before I counted your teeth into the metal pan one by one. There is only totalitarian rule if you want to be yourself once more.'

Should a case be made out for Lionel, that he was a zombie held in a trance by writhing spirits? That one day, if we waited long enough, the real Lionel would re-emerge from his carcass, unharmed by his sojourn in the land of the dead? That he would unwind himself from the python's grip? I know I kept looking into Lionel's eyes hoping to see the glaze clear away, hoping to find Lionel breathing inside, waving to me in loving recognition.

Did Dolly know what had happened to him, or was she a zombie too? Anything is possible in this probable world.

Hearing of other people's happy childhoods, that the best days of their lives were at school, that they slid into adulthood as if into a pond full of burbling frogs, makes me feel lopsided. I have to pretend to emotions of ease and lightness of heart, because I don't feel any of them. I have no true emotions that flow like Saxa salt, no normal reactions such as instant grief. I do not feel my heart breaking, nor hear another's crack at the moment it gets dropped. Everything is on hold for me, everything gets watched. It is as if I have an inbuilt delay mechanism that gives me time to manufacture an ersatz response.

I can only assume from watching others that the emotions they display are happening to them. Then from a theoretical position I can pretend to similar feelings. It is always an intellectual exercise, through which I can believe they aren't putting it on, through which I can appear to be reacting in a normal way.

It is very lonely out here by myself in the land of the unfelt. I often search for that blankness in another, hoping to find a companion in my desolate landscape. I do not wish to live out here. I do not reside by choice in the country of perversity, cradling my beggar's bowl and spoon. One day I might hit upon a mythic rite, the performance of which will free me from exile. Right now, my one tool is the tin spoon of anger. I recognise it and when I feel it, it affords me the most intense sensation. It is the one genuine emotion to which I can lay claim.

It is not as if I don't remember when things were different, before my banishment from ease and happiness. That I can recall a time when I was cocooned by my father's tenderness only makes me more bereft. My father took my hand in his big hand and together we explored a valley of plenty. Apples plopped from trees and they were golden apples, and even though I stooped to pick them up, unlike Atalanta I still won every race. My father and I were inseparable companions. I looked up at his profile in admiration and in his care I could dare any adventure.

In the year following the coronation of Queen Elizabeth II, I have my last tomboy adventure. I suppose Elizabeth has her last one too, coming back from safari in Africa to her stultifying crown and a tour of the colonies. I sit on my father's shoulders as he stands in the crowd in Brunswick Street, The Valley, as her motorcade goes past. My father thinks I am too shy to wave my flag on a stick but that isn't it. I never understand the pleasures of group solidarity. If they are all waving, I look the other way.

We go out to a friend of my father's in New Farm near the river to see the Royal Yacht. The friend has an old wooden house that falls in three levels from the street. Its front door is a back door and once inside you have to descend a flight of dark steps that go down to the kitchen. Another flight goes up to the three daughters' open bedroom in the loft. There are no dividing walls up there, but they each have curtained alcoves and dormer windows.

Their names are Natalie, Ingrid and Tamsin, in descending order. Tamsin is ordinary, a small brat, but the other two are beautiful and gallant. They eat olives and oysters and their father, a short, muscled, beaming man, gives me pickled whitebait to try. Natalie is an aloof fourteen but with the glaze of something younger still in her eyes.

We have a barbecue out on an elevated platform of grass that opens out from the rows of French doors at the back of the house. The back, really the front, has a view over mangroves to the Brisbane River. All this topsyturvyness is exhilarating. This family is my first taste of bohemia.

A Chinese fish kite flies from a pole, its mouth gulping the air. The adults stand around drinking beer. They take turns to look at the

Queen's yacht through binoculars. I have a turn just at the moment when she emerges to stroll the deck with Prince Philip. I notice her feet in peep-toed shoes and that she is pigeon-toed as she walks. I affect the Queen's walk for a long time afterwards.

When we grow tired of the adults' company, Natalie says we should go down to the mangroves and wade out to the yacht. The adults are hogging the binoculars, but if we go, we might even get invited on board. Natalie takes us down a flight of steep garden steps and through a pointy wooden gate. We have to help Tamsin down the last three steps and I know she will be trouble. We are barefoot. No self-respecting child wears shoes in the Brisbane summer.

It is a steamy, cobalt blue summer afternoon, softened by the ominous bruise of a thunderstorm brewing in the west. We walk into the line of mangroves. Down here there is no sight of the yacht at all, just the waterline at low tide a quarter of a mile out. Off to the right, visible above the tops of the lower trees and through ragged gaps, we see the shiny metal spaceships that are the gasworks storage tanks. They have silver ladders attached to their sides that go up and up until they get tiny. The tanks are outlandish: huge and toy-like at the same time.

Down under our unprotected feet the mud is hard and caked, with the occasional crab hole from which issues, in irregular rhythm, a sly underground click. It is quite easy to walk at first between the trunks of the addled mangroves, but as we get further out, their roots, sticking up through the softening mud, become more numerous and harder to dodge. Soon we are balancing on an entire network of sharp rootlets growing just below the surface, a bed of nails. Tamsin starts to whinge and Natalie has to carry her on her hip. Natalie pats her bottom and murmurs encouragement: 'It's okay Tam-Bam.' I think Tamsin should walk.

We break out into open space. The Brisbane River is straight in front of us, its deadly edge just a few feet away. It is deep and wide with a strong current. In the far left distance we can just make out the Royal Yacht.

'Blast. Nowhere near it.' Natalie looks undecided.

We reconnoitre. Behind us is the torture of the mangrove roots, and in front the barrier of the river. We decide the best way to go is to the right, towards the gas tanks and the main road, with a detour up the ladders on the way past. The idea frightens me but I agree. The shininess of Natalie's leadership lures me on.

'You're being a hopeless baby,' I say to Tamsin.

'No she's not,' says Natalie. 'She's only five.'

We move back to the harder ground at the edge of the mangroves and make our way towards the open flats bordering the gasworks. The acrid, badeggy smell of gas becomes stronger.

'Don't light a match,' Ingrid giggles.

Now we have come to another impasse. Between us and the silver ladders is an expanse of black mud. We try out our feet in it and sink down above our ankles. The sky is lowering now, the light gloomy, a held-off sense of storm in the air. It gets icily cool. Old drums and coils of broken wire rope litter the ground. Ingrid runs back to get a couple of wooden planks and she and Natalie lay them in an untidy footwalk, one in front of the other, while a reluctant Tamsin and I hold hands. The idea is to uproot the plank behind and place it in front as we go. Natalie ventures out first and stands at the end of the farthest plank. I look at Ingrid and she smiles down at me. I can see she has drawn a smoky, smudged line with kohl pencil on her upper eyelids. She turns and walks out, and in response to that inclusive smile I follow. Then we beckon for Tamsin to join us.

'Watch the nails,' cautions Natalie in her casual voice. Halfway across, Tamsin falls off.

We have no leverage point to pull her out without falling off the plank ourselves. The mud is viscous quicksand. It sucks our feet down. Now it is raining and a film of tidal water is spreading across the flats.

Tamsin starts a howling litany: 'I want to go home.'

We haul her between us, and by scrunching on our bottoms get to firmer ground. But not before I wet my pants, my warm urine seeping into the glaucous cold of the mud between my thighs. When we get back to the house, covered in gas-smelling mud, blue and red with cold, we have a hot bath together.

I like to remember that day and the way I felt: proud, confident, secure. It was my last day of feeling that my own providence watched over me. That was the last time I felt my face to be unshielded and open. We had been to the verge of real danger. So excessive were our actions that we didn't even get into trouble from our parents, though my mother roused on me when we got home, and I vomited up the vinegary whitebait I had eaten.

When Fate gets bored with one game she wants to play another. Fate tired of my father and me in our idyll. She picked me up by the scruff of the neck, a mother cat with her errant kitten, determination in her eyes, and deposited me in Lionel's demonic playpen. 'Here's some fun,' she said. 'Watch this.'

It was only then that my father glanced down at me and saw he had made a mistake, that I was a mere girl. I used to think that his abstraction meant that he didn't notice I had been abducted. But I came to see he had abandoned me, just as surely as if he had thrown me from the car on one of those night drives up Mount Coot-tha, to see the city lights.

'You're a nuisance,' he said as I got older.

'You're a big girl now. Go and do something.' When it got to the point where he snarled 'Go away and play trains,' I knew I had to give up claiming his attention. He challenged me to follow him, wading out further and deeper, his mesmerised sea creature. He knew self-preservation would send me back. Only then, like Atalanta, did I lose the race, as he forced me to marry my destiny.

19 Take the Blame

At school I listen to the big boys fighting at lunch time. 'Take the blame,' the biggest bully demands. He drags some smaller boy forward with his arms pinned and the rest of them hit him around the head for a while until he cries and runs.

Having someone take the blame is important. Girls do it to each other to a certain degree, with less violence. They use the weapon of scapegoating or condemn with silent abuse, sending the victim to Coventry, an appropriate place given the civil war that rages in the playground.

School is a prison where you are sure to have one awful thing happen to you every day. Big boys beat up younger boys. Disgruntled, middle-sized boys tease and threaten the girls. The boys like to hang around outside the girls' toilet, pointing derisive fingers and trying to pull down our pants or undo the bows on our dresses. I cannot understand why they are so angry at us, and try smiling at them – but it never works. Attempts at contact only make them gang up on me.

When a girl gets ganged up on, the other girls stand at a distance in a huddle, meek guinea-pigs, and watch. They never come to help. They understand something I don't want to understand: that there is a process with rules and regulations that I refuse to follow. Some girls have big brothers who save them. I have no-one, and nor can I tell my parents. After all, they have sent me here to suffer and fend for myself.

'Did you have a good day at school?' My mother wears an expectant, empty smile and I know she doesn't want me to complain.

There is one boy called Gregor who draws aircraft in the margins of his books. He lets me see over his hunched arm what he is drawing. He only ever has a stub of pencil. I hold his stained, brown schoolboy fingers that look so useful, as the planes emerge from the paper. He smiles straight into my eyes as I look into the cubby-hole of his arms, and we both get into trouble. He gets the cane on his brown hand and I have to stand exposed in front of the class for the rest of the lesson. The girls flick looks at me as if I am a pariah.

Lionel acts just like the big boys. He is the perpetrator. He should have sprouted tar and chook feathers after that day when everything changed, but he makes me take the blame. Now I have no reprieve from the tension of being attacked, either at school or at home. Lionel is clever. He works through Dolly and my mother.

As I wander lonely as a cloud, proscribed now to our backyard, I see Dolly on the other side of the drain pegging out her washing. Both my mother and Dolly have clothes' baskets on wheels that they trundle the few yards to the rotary hoist. Whereas my mother's is metal and wire in pale blue with rust spots, Dolly's is wooden with small wheels of the type used on boys' billycarts. I have always wanted a billycart. I know I could sit, my feet on the cross bar, my hands on the rope and steer my cart down the steep hill with as much dexterity as any boy up the road. But they won't let me have one.

'Why not?'

'Because you're a girl,' my father grins. Are boys as desperate to play with dolls as I am to own a billycart? I don't think so, but I want to know why.

I think Lionel made the clothes' basket for Dolly. What if, instead, he had made her a billycart? What if the world of proscription had overturned and we had found Dolly one bright afternoon zinging down the road waving and yelling 'Bugger the lot of you' as she went by? But she continues to do as she is told. She is glum, pegging in cautious circles, tied to the spider web of her rotary hoist. She is a study in dead-ends, her flat hair held in snail curls by bobby pins, her circle of existence digging in like ingrown toenails.

Balancing on the drain I call out 'Hullo Dolly' to her silent back. She continues pegging out her clothes using wooden pegs, Lionel's underwear and hers in complicit affiliation. My mother has graduated to plastic pegs. Dolly acts as if she doesn't hear me. There is nothing you can do with a silent back. I hop off the drain and go away.

I don't see much of Lionel. He keeps under the house. I see his shadow moving sometimes behind the wooden slats. One afternoon I see him go to feed his chooks, tin in hand, his shoulders hunched, looking straight ahead. He has a sulky, distant expression on his face. I call out to him, conciliatory, eager to establish contact. All will be forgiven; that's the right thing to do. 'Forgive and forget,' as my mother says.

I want to get back what I have lost. But Lionel, too, ignores me, as if I don't exist. It looks as if I have to find the key to turn in the lock of Lionel's truculence and outrage. What have I done? The tables have turned and I find it difficult to keep in my mind how things happened that blue day after rain.

One day Dolly comes over to our house again. She and my mother used to have regular terrace talks but then they stopped. There she is, looking down her nose, talking. There is quite a distance between them. She stops talking as I sidle up.

'Hullo, Dolly.'

She purses her lips and doesn't answer. She gives my mother a significant look and walks away. My mother turns too and I can tell by the way she swings her rump that she is angry. She walks into the kitchen slamming the Dutch door behind her. I follow her in.

'Why have you been upsetting Dolly and Lionel? I didn't teach you to act like this. Lionel says you're a stuck-up little thing. You won't say hullo to him. You're rude to Dolly. You never go and visit them. What's wrong with you? You're just a spoilt little brat.'

'I'm not. Nothing. I didn't.'

'What do you mean, nothing? Causing trouble like this. You're a general nuisance. You make it very hard for me.'

'I just don't want to go over there any more.'

'Why not? Has something happened?' My mother stares at me. She has her school query look on her face, but without the smile.

'Nothing's happened. I just don't want to go over there any more.' My excuse sounds lame. 'I'm too old for breakfasts.'

'I give up. You're a naughty, naughty girl. You'll get a reputation for being a snob, you know. You don't realize how important it is to get on with the neighbours.' Her final jibe is loaded with anger. 'Who do you think you are, Lady Muck?' – and I know someone has said this to her.

'I'm not. I don't care.' We break away from each other, two exhausted wrestlers.

But Lionel hasn't finished there. The game is not over. He takes to calling in on my mother on some pretext, using the front door. He knows my mother and I have a habit of arriving at the door together, in competition to field the visitor. Any interruption is welcome: the baker, Mr Jones the greengrocer, the Electrolux man. Mum speaks to them through the half open door. Sometimes she lets them in, especially the Electrolux man who tips dust on her lounge room carpet and sucks it up again, in demonstration.

When Lionel starts coming to the front door, Mum is coy, as if she is flirting with him or as if he frightens her. The first time it happens I stand behind her. I see Lionel's face past her shoulder. He speaks to her and looks at me. His eyes are hot and full of hunger, a roaming mongrel's. I move away and lie down in my room. I hear Mum close the door and then she is standing in the doorway.

'Lionel found your note-book. Look!' and she throws it on the end of my bed.

'Wasn't that nice of him to bother picking it up? I hope you're grateful.'

He has plenty of opportunities for his forays because my father is never home on time. So Lionel stalks me. I think at first, in my panic, that he is even going to tell my mother what happened. I feel dirty. I squeeze my eyes shut: 'So long as he doesn't tell.' I know I couldn't bear the shame if my father found out. I know I couldn't stand the humiliation and suspicious cross-examination if my mother knew.

Whenever Lionel comes to the door, I cross my fingers. Instead of forgetting, the longer I live with it the worse it gets, my guilty secret. It hampers everything. I have first to check out where Lionel is. One day, coming home from school, I see him walking towards me. It makes my stomach ache to watch his body coming closer. He stares at me, threat in his eyes, before we pass and walk by each other. I learn his footsteps and hide in my room when he comes up the front steps. I keep out of the back yard. I moon about the house.

I develop a pain in my heart. It sits to the left of my breastbone. It is a chook that pecks with a metal beak. I press my hand to it. I tell my mother.

'Don't be silly. Little girls like you don't get heart pains. You're imagining things.' She lays out my school clothes on the end of my bed: shirt, skirt, singlet, white panties, socks, in a marshalled row. She picks what I am to wear. I know they won't sit right. The inside chook scratches and pecks, delivers a suggestive bolt of pain.

'But it hurts.'

'Tripe and nonsense. Go out and play. Get some fresh air.'

'Don't feel a thing,' suggests my head voice. It whispers: 'What's the use? Make up something better. You can if you want to. Then I promise I'll stop. Make it all up.'

'You're getting moody,' my mother tells me. Dad takes to calling me Sadsack. It has a nasty edge to it.

Maintenance at our place starts to break down. One humid Saturday I lie on my bed reading. Mum is in the kitchen. I hear the Thor washing machine clunk as it comes to the end of its spin cycle. In that quiet frame from which mechanical noise has exited, my mother lets free a long, surprised 'Aaaah.' 'Ooooh,' she cries, a second later, as if someone has grabbed her. I run down the hall to investigate. She stands with her right hand on the washing machine knob as if she can't let go. Her left arm extends halfway to the electrical switch. Stuck, a desperate heroine in the frame of an old movie. I don't know what knowledge makes me grab a tea towel and knock the switch off with the back of my swathed fist. She comes loose, moaning and cold.

'Are you alright, Mum?'

She looks so strange. She is struck dumb. She felt something run up her arm, her wet hand an immediate conductor. My father blames a fault in the machine, but he installed the circuit when the mighty Thor moved up from the downstairs laundry where it had sat next to his workbench, down in his domain.

Luck or my mother's will to hang on to life holds this time around. It is only a mild shock in the electrical sense.

When my father is at home he does mad, upsetting things as if on purpose. He is jagged and on edge, as unpredictable as lightning. He tries to melt some solder in a kitchen saucepan, puts it down red-hot on the Formica bench, burns a hole in it and sets fire to the kitchen curtains. The kitchen corner sports a black burn until he repaints it months later. Then it boasts a large red fire extinguisher.

Mum mutters: 'How can I make dinner with this thing in the way? Botch jobs. It's just terrible what I have to put up with.'

The kitchen becomes an extension of Dad's workroom, his province extending by the day. It is as if the floorboards have erupted and Dad has shot up through an opening, brandishing a lightning bolt. He never gets around to re-lining the bench. When he is home on time he is always on the phone, talking cryptically. When he isn't home, my mother is either on the phone to one of her girlfriends or waiting for his call. Mum's friends seldom ring her back. 'He'll be home late,' she says. 'Don't exasperate me. Stop your whining.'

I notice one tiny rebellion. She starts cooking food my father does not like.

Dad starts to spend a lot of money on his hobbies. 'Money we don't have.' My mother won't look at him, but she is in confrontation mode all the same.

'You're wearing your dark look, Darl.' He gives her a speculative glance from his yellow eyes.

Large power tools appear in his workshop, usurping his old woodenhandled drills, his chisels and mallet, his hissing planes that issued forth fragile curls of golden shavings. His handiwork begins to show split corners and cranky screws where dovetailing had lived before. It's as if he wants to enrage my mother by making desks and occasional tables that have broken spirits. The house fills with ugly objects that say: 'I don't love you any more. Take that.'

My mother makes me her confidante, her whinging post. As if I'm interested. I don't want to be on her side. My whole life feels swamped. I can't see myself rowing through the huge stretch of water between here and growing up. I try to imagine passing the marker buoys of ten, eleven and twelve. Each year is lower in the water than the last with the weight of its extra, indecisive digit. Christmas Day's plum pudding is a giant sinker dragging me under.

Christmas holidays are heavy with heat. I know nothing will happen for six weeks.

'I'm bored to death,' I accuse my mother.

All she says is: 'Well, I've got something to do... every minute of the day.'

No-one sends us Christmas cards now. Dad and I used to thread them on cotton and festoon them across the fireplace. The house sounds hollow on New Year's Eve.

'Why don't we go somewhere?' I whine at my mother. 'We never do anything. No-one ever comes here.'

As I lie under my mosquito net I hear car horns tooting and shouts of 'Happy New Year' from dark back yards. No raucous party at our place with Dad singing *Auld Lang Syne* in a Scottish accent. Tears well in my eyes and I let them drip into the hot pillow. They smell salty.

Adults are complicit in keeping good things from me. Excitement is elsewhere. Happy events happen in other people's houses. Other people stroll through Sundays contented. Other families enjoy each other's company. They aren't driven mad with misery by the sound of the races droning on radio or the deadly clunk of cricket balls and the commentators' voices.

Unhappiness builds its framework within me. I dare not sleep during the day for fear I will miss out on something that is going on, going on without me, leaving me out. Anxiety for a better life sees me staying up late at night, the last to go to bed, lest at the last minute I should miss out on the offer of some simple pleasure.

I am always missing out. It is my catch-cry. Once, when my father teases me to the point of madness I yell, 'Don't you know I exist?'

'Where's that voice coming from?' he sneers.

Hunger for inclusion leaves me alone and panicking. I learn early the trick of standing outside myself until it becomes my only tactic. I learn the bad habit of never living in the moment, because the next moment – or someone else's moment – might be better. Anyone else's moment comes to look more grand and full than any I could manufacture. I teach myself false truths: that only others have a right to happiness. I become suspicious of my own existence and in secret revere other people's shining lives. That's the truth of it.

I can't wait to be an age with 'teen' on the end of it. Then they can't say I'm not old enough. I long to be important. I want to break away to talk about myself.

My mother and father fight in a curious way. My mother stands in her corner of the kitchen and he in his, whisky glass on the bench in reach of his hand, bottle at the ready, the contents steadily reducing. My mother could be lying on the lino floor, pegged out with pins, so nailed to the spot is she, so incapable of avoiding dissection. She can't start tea until my father says he is ready, so there she stands. He decides her fate at his leisure. She can't match him whisky for whisky because she has no head for it. He pours her a shandy and the next morning, getting ready for school, I find the half-empty bottle of warm, stale beer standing on the kitchen bench next to the burn mark.

Most of the time she stares at the floor and he stands and smirks, with his smile getting crazier and drunker. I hear them arguing, but if I walk in they stop.

When I hear my father cackle: 'You've got to see the funny side of it, Darl. Where's your sense of humour?' I know it's time for my mother to give up and retreat to her bedroom to read one of her capacious paperbacks. Once or twice in the night I hear them making love. It never takes very long. I hear my father's footsteps creak across the floorboards as he goes back to his own bed.

Then for days at a time my mother does not speak to him.

'Argh Darl,' he snarls. 'Give it a rest, will you Darl.'

'Don't touch me.' She shrugs off his hand, as she sits on the terrace, glaring at nothing.

My father slides me a look as he sees me watching from the dining room doors.

'*Noli me tangere*,' he chortles.

My mother is impaled on her situation, as if she is one of Dad's yabbies he uses for bait.

One night the woman I had seen once with my father, sitting in our car, comes for dinner on her own. 'Apparently she thinks she's somebody,' my mother hisses under her breath as she pulls the roast out of the oven. 'Just because she plays second violin in the Brisbane Symphony Orchestra.' She gives the fizzing pressure cooker a dangerous bang. 'Second rate, more like it.'

My mother is stiff as if with grief as she returns to the dining room, her store of small talk suspended. Dad acts in a coaxing way but looks angry or rebellious, as if Mum is his mother.

I stand on one foot in the dark hallway. My mother goes past me muttering, 'It's not right.' I could believe we live in a madhouse with rubber walls, so erratic is everyone's behaviour, the unspoken feelings turning our baked potatoes to wood, lumping the gravy.

I do not like Miss Whatsername, who is cool and superior. She casts a glance my mother's way with a surprised and supercilious look on her pert face. I think she looks like a pumpkin. Her turned-up nose is disdainful, even if in truth she might feel something quite different. My mother stalks back and forth from the kitchen under some terrible duress. It is the worst meal she has ever cooked. I know she is suffering tonight as my father lays bare her lack of importance. What is she worth? Very little. What has she ever done to boast about? She can't even win at golf.

Later, while my father drives 'the Violin' home, I dare to stand in the doorway of my parents' bedroom. My mother has propped herself up in bed in her old quilted nylon dressing gown, her glasses on the end of her nose. She is reading.

'You ought to be in bed.'

'I can't sleep.'

She looks at me, resentment in her eyes, the way she looks at my father. Then it fades and she says: 'Go and make us a hot milk with vanilla. Not too many drops – it's alcoholic.'

It is such a nice offer. I wait for those few times when my mother seems to enjoy my company. I race to the kitchen and heat the milk in the aluminium saucepan. I reach up to the bottle of vanilla essence on the top shelf of the pantry cupboard and count in six drops. The drops spread small stains on the milk, giving off their chocolaty aroma. I carry the glasses up the hallway on the silver tray.

'You shouldn't have used that. That's my precious tray.' My heart gives a thud of misgiving so that my hand jerks. I hold the tray handles tight. She purses her lips, disgruntled, then sighs, 'Oh well, never mind this time.'

I sit on the edge of her bed. Everything is delicious: the room lit by the lamp, the hot glass of milk in my hands, the nylon curtains seductive as they mask the venetian blinds. Cosy with my mother. We will talk. About good things. I might show her some of my drawings. I will tell her all the things I do in my head.

She clears her throat. 'When you grow up, you'll know what it's like. Promise me you won't be jealous. It's no good for you. Ruins your life.' She drinks her milk, snaps it onto the silver tray. 'Finish your milk and get to bed. Leave the glasses in the kitchen sink. And put that tray back where it came from.'

Now the room looks cold. There is a box of pink tissues by her bed and another box of tablets. My father's bed on the other side of the room looks clinical and unused. I go to my own bed wondering what's so wrong with jealousy.

20 *Waking in the Night*

When was it I realised I was no longer a child? It had something to do with the concept of time. All of a sudden time was anxious, doom laden. Dreamy hiatus receded. Time cut itself into strips. It was a timetable but it wasn't mine.

I was quite old before I learnt to tell the time. I had difficulty with one whole side of the clock. I recognised the concept of 'past' easily enough. *It is past twelve o'clock*, as the nursery rhyme says. But 'to' was harder. *Not yet one o'clock*. How can something be *not yet*? Climbing up the clock gave me the sensation of stumbling backwards with my eyes shut. Something was happening or it had just happened, but how could I understand what had not yet occurred, was about to be? I lived in ignorance of the text of future time. It was an unreadable book which did not tally.

I had to learn by heart, in my untimed world, that summer followed spring and then came autumn, winter and spring again. The Brisbane climate did not help, with its blurred seasons of hot and humid, followed by cooler, then hot again. The only times that stood out were the August winds and the February thunderstorms.

I watched my mother tally the runes. She was good at fatalistic foreboding, that morose dimension where fault-finding walks the beat, where punishers and persecutors threaten in their grey officious dust-coats. But foreboding is not the same as being able to understand the shape of the future.

My father had his own timetable and he proceeded to implement it. It began with the vaccinations.

At about this time, as his behaviour became frenzied and difficult to fathom, I began to have a recurring nightmare. I had always been afraid of the dark. I knotted up with tension when faced with the need to sleep. I dreaded the sensation of unconsciousness overtaking me, sending me to that place where menace loomed. Those citizens of foreboding that visited my mother at night also found their way down the hall to me. But I loved sleep. Sleep should have protected me. Instead, it kept its distance.

One dream was of my bedroom cupboard falling forward. It never did, but its doors sometimes swung open. It was not the fear of being crushed but fear of who might fall out of those yawning doors. Another dream was of footsteps creaking up the hallway. I would wake, my body rigid. My heart would pump, jumping in my chest, a trapped frog. I hated my heart because its action would betray my position to the enemy.

One night I dreamt I saw my father standing in the doorway of my bedroom. I opened my eyes with an enormous effort of will, against the weight of unconsciousness. Though my body was immobilised I knew if I stared at him I could compel him not to bring me pain. When he finally turned away, I knew his presence had not been a dream, but real.

This night war, waged by a general, paralysed the insurgents with panic. I demanded that my parents leave the hall light on, but my mother always switched it off when she went to bed. She always promised she wouldn't and she always broke her promise. Both my parents laughed at my terror and teased me about being afraid of the dark.

'Don't be such a goomp.' My father knows the word enrages me. He grins in derision.

'Don't be so silly,' my mother chimes in.

I developed a phobia about getting into bed. I checked the cupboards and deep drawers and under the bed while it was still daylight, to make sure no-one lurked. But by nightfall I knew they had got in again.

My father developed a safety phobia of his own. He had made himself a waddy out of black bean wood, dense and murderous. It was in the shape of a miniature baseball bat and he slept with it under his pillow. I liked to play with it in daylight hours, hitting tennis balls to the cat. But when night fell, the image of it under my father's pillow assailed me.

'Who are you going to hit, Darl, the milkman? my mother scoffs.

My father sneers back, 'You don't know what you're talking about,

Darl – as usual.' So my mother retreats and makes up his bed every morning with the waddy tucked under his pillow.

One weekend my father decides to change the locks on the front door. The door is cumbersome and made out of silky oak. Beads of resin extrude from the wood and it swells in wet weather so we have to push it shut that final inch, with some force. Solid, a Bluebeard's Castle door with a sound brass lock. So I am surprised to find my father gouging out a slot for a new lock with one of his old chisels.

'You're making an awful mess, Darl,' my mother whines. 'Do you have to? Da-arl.'

But my father just snaps at her: 'Get to buggery', which makes both of us scuttle to the kitchen.

It was not long after when my father made a unilateral decision. We should all have smallpox vaccinations. He didn't have to, because he'd had his when he was a travelling post-graduate. My mother and I in our timidity accepted this dictum. It was not as if we were going anywhere where smallpox raged but, unable to defy him, we had our jabs.

I hear my mother on the phone to one of her golfing friends.

'The GP thought we must be off to China, but he stuck us anyway. We've suffered the tortures of the damned.'

Mum has to wear her arm in a sling. She sits in the lounge room for two nights, propped up, crying with the pain. No friends visit. It is the first time I feel sorry for my mother. Her image separates out, though it soon blurs again. My hot and throbbing arm keeps me awake until she gives me a sleeping tablet, against her better judgment. It has the opposite effect from sedation and I lie alert, thrashing in my bag of pain.

My recurring nightmare is clear as an MGM movie. I stand in the kitchen, my mother behind me. The Dutch door is open. It is early evening. A man comes rushing up the side path in a contained frenzy. I can see him coming as if I am a roving camera's eye. He is lean and tanned. His hair is white in contrast and he carries a reaping hook, similar to the one my father borrows from Lionel to slash the long grass along the back fence. He looks purposeful and in a hurry, as if he is hunting something, but in another way he also looks hunted. As if on a split screen I recognise my father, but his name in the dream is

Jim Glitter. His bright blue eyes are most noticeable and they crackle with madness.

I rush in my dream to close the door before he gets up the path. My mother is stock-still behind me as, frantic, I turn the key in the lock and lean my weight against the door frame. I am not heavy enough. This nightmare returns night after night.

21 Ink Dog

'Everything's going to rack and ruin,' says my mother, locked into her standard domestic nightmare. If she'd had a tuneful voice she might have sung *Unchain My Heart*, wanting to be set free. But brute forces were the only things being unchained in our house. I could see what she'd been worrying about when the fish tank cracked open.

'Put the dog to bed, will you?' my mother calls.

'Please,' I say under my breath. I coax the reluctant Sparkles with winsome noises and clicking fingers down to her cubby-hole under the house. She makes a run for it at the last moment and I have to chase her. I gather her wriggling body up in my arms, resting my lips on her silken ear as I carry her to her dungeon. She hates being put in there under the floorboards of the spare room, locked in for the night with her welcoming fleas and her sad doggy smell. She probably wonders if I will ever let her out. When I shut the barred door against her I spend minutes saying a contrite goodnight. I wonder if her heart thumps in her chest. 'Close your eyes,' I croon. I know it's better not to see the dark. Some nights she is inconsolable and howls until Mum stamps her feet on the spare room boards to get her to stop.

One night she stamps too hard. A sharp crack sounds and the glass front of the monolithic marine aquarium develops a rapid running thread. It spreads and widens. Then the contents gush out, all fifty gallons of it. It carries with it sea-horses, weed and coral, and the black and white striped fish called Humbugs that flit in and out among the sea anemones' tentacles.

My mother, in an unusual effort of renovation, dyed the old carpet with Quink blue ink. She was proud of her cost-saving innovation until Dad saw it. 'You're bloody cuckoo, Darl,' was all he said.

The sea water mixes with the ink to produce a soggy blue swamp. It smells of sea creatures in extremis. The fish flop in the mire, the sea-horses on their cardboard sides looking surprised as ever. Mum thrashes around to retrieve them as I hold out a bucket, but there is no sea water left for them and the chlorine in the tap water soon kills them.

Fate brings my father home early. He stands in the doorway surveying the scene.

'I told you this would happen, Darl,' my mother cries, as if her fears made any difference.

My father turns away from the mess in his city suit and leaves her to clean it up. The next morning when I let the dog out she emerges with a guilty look on her face, ears down, tail drooped. An awful smell comes out with her, of wet and stinking doggy blanket and marine disaster. The ink has dyed her tan coat blue.

 **22** *Tennessee Waltz*

When my father left our house, he took music with him. I lost Beethoven's Seventh, though I didn't know its name, as well as his Piano Concerto Number Three. Smetana went missing. Dvorak faded. There was an eerie silence. As with unequal Siamese twins when the surgeon cuts them apart, the heart of music remained embedded in my father's side.

My father did not leave in one smooth movement. After all, he had half a lifetime to dispose of, and it was awkward fitting it into the rubbish bin in one go. He conducted his campaign in fits and starts. If he made us smaller and smaller, then he could push us down to fit. Just a matter of exerting the right pressure.

   I began to pick up talk of an overseas trip. He was going to Brussels and Vienna. Something to do with the Symphony Orchestra. What had he ever had to do with the Orchestra? Then I remembered Miss Whatsername. I knew with certainty she had no rights to anything, especially to my father, but what I thought didn't count.

   I thought I was old enough to try out an alliance with Dolly. I felt adroit as I turned one of our infrequent conversations to 'the Violin'. But Dolly just sniffed. She reared her head back and looked down at me from an acute angle.

   'You've got your opinions now, haven't you, Miss?' she chastised me before she turned her back.

   My mother was to go on the trip, too. After she had suffered more vaccinations. I don't know what was to happen to me. I don't think I even figured in the scenario. It was as if I was the changeling my father always said I was, left to rot under the cabbage where I had first turned up.

   My father's offer to my mother was a false one, one that he hoped she would baulk at – and of course she did. Not because of the threat of another round of vaccinations, although she used that as her reason. She was the third party and she knew it. I knew it too. By now I could see something of what was going on between my parents. My mother's mulish face and my father's derisive laugh told me all I needed to know.

My parents begin one of their muted arguments in the kitchen.

'It's a catalogue of disasters in this bloody house,' my mother whines.

'Argy bargy, argy bargy,' my father taunts. 'Is that a withering look, Darl? Where's your sense of humour?'

'You're not going to make me,' my mother says. 'You'd better watch out!' I know what follows. 'Or there'll be trouble.' A pot and the frying pan (I can tell the difference) clatter. The saucepan cupboard slams shut.

'Make up your mind, Darl,' Dad sneers. 'Stop beating round the bush.' He sniggers. 'Don't hesitate. Are you going to throw it or not?'

I hear my father walk up the hall and open the front door. There is that second of struggle as the door sticks the last inch. I hear him scuff the frayed and rucked piece of carpet with his shoe. Mum comes rushing after him as if chasing the course of fate, and the dog rushes with her.

'You'd better do something, Darl,' she yells. 'I'm sick and tired of this. You must be having a nervous breakdown.'

The dog barks in confusion at my father. By this time he is halfway down the steep brick stairs. From my bedroom doorway I am just in time to see my mother trip on the rucked carpet and the scuttling dog, and fall down the steps after him.

My mother got a black swelling on the side of her eye and a bad concussion and tore the tendons in her foot. She was clearly tiring under the onslaught of chaos. So was I. We had even begun to gang up together, forming a temporary unacknowledged friendship of sorts, the kind formed under the baton of shared terrorism. Once more I became her confidante by default, since her golfing friends kept away.

Dad had taken to calling her Typhoid Mary.

'Christ! What did you do to these curried prawns, Darl? Leave them out of the fridge for a week? You've bloody well given me food poisoning.'

Other than that, Dad thrived.

'It's all true.' My mother placed the big black handpiece of the phone back in its cradle, with jangling finality. She had been on the phone for days. 'Nancy saw them in town together. Him and his popsy.' Her bandaged ankle stuck out in front of her. She breathed in. 'If you can take a breath you're still alive... I suppose,' she added.

'What am I going to do?' she asked the hallway air.

I, who had begun to follow the tortuous workings of the plot, said nothing.

'That', as my father would have said had he been present, 'is the whole point, Darl. You're not supposed to do anything.'

My mother rubbed her right eye, which ever since the fall had caused her trouble. 'I'll have to see about it,' she said, 'it's always blurry.'

'What?' she whispered.

I shook my head. She kept thinking I had spoken, but didn't respond if I spoke behind her.

'It's just unheard-of,' she said in her laryngitis voice. 'That's the limit. Well, I'm not having any more injections and I'm not going. That's final.'

Her voice faded on the last word.

'You're going deaf is what you're going, Mum,' I tested, behind her back.

'What?'

'Don't say what, say sorry.' I giggled. I chanted under my breath, 'Blind, deaf and dumb.'

'What?' she whispered. 'Don't mumble.'

The night he left, everything was out of synch. That morning he hadn't driven me to my posh girls' school as usual, across town in South Brisbane. He had exhumed his leather port from the hallway cupboard the night before, dusted it and examined it for spiders.

Mum on her crutches didn't help him get it down. He took down his stack of old 78 records from the shelf above the ports and broke each one over his knee.

'You're breaking my heart,' my mother said.

I stared at his hands as he did it, his spatulate fingers, the blond hairs on his knuckles. The records mounted up in a jagged tower, the brown paper sleeves with their cut-out circles dispatched to their own pile.

When we remember the dead we recall only parts of them, the distinct traits, the characteristic bits. I recall his hands with such clarity. They were apart from him, with their suppressed tension, their angry energy, their lack of compunction. I felt his power overtaking me, felt my inability to stop anything at all from happening. I felt the finality as the bottom dropped away from my heart, a sole coming away from a shoe. I was watching someone do deliberate damage.

The night he left, Mum stood halfway down the chilly hallway in her dressing gown, holding the gap together with one hand, hanging on her crutches. I ran after him to the front door, still in my school uniform. He stopped on the second top step and grinned up at me. I wanted to tell him something before it was too late, but a line from my school Shakespeare came into my head and stopped me: 'What? My foot my tutor!'

He looked past my grey-stockinged legs in an exasperated way. There was nothing to see behind me but darkness. He had his drinking look on his face.

As if to a stranger, he said as he moved off: 'Bye Darl. See you in the spring.'

That, it seemed, was that. Something had come to an end or come apart. My mother, though made to feel she was wrong about everything, was sometimes right. It had always been a question of maintenance.

Dad went to Europe and did not come home – or not to our place. He didn't remember to send me anything for my birthday the first year he was away, but the second year a parcel came from Japan. It was a tea-towel and on it was a line drawing of a Japanese man and woman, entwined in calligraphy.

'It's a geisha.' My mother looked pleased. 'It's art. You know – they do the tea ceremony...'

'As if I didn't know,' I interrupted her.

She flirted the tea-towel out in front of her, self-important.

'We could get it framed for you.' She pursed her lips in concentration and laid it on the bed, tweaking it with her hand. Already I felt as if it were hers. She stared at it harder. Her satisfied look fell off her face.

'It's rude.' She sounded astonished. 'Well, this is the limit. You're not having it,' and she marched off with it, her back stiff with outrage.

When Dad and 'the Violin' got back, they moved up the coast to Caloundra. He ran an avocado farm for a while, but I think it failed. Whenever I asked my mother what Dad was doing she would snap: 'Fishing, I suppose,' and give a hard sniff. I wasn't to ask questions. 'Don't bring it up. Go and do your homework. You'll never matriculate at this rate.'

My mother looked at me as if I was in the wrong house. 'Thank God I've got my BHP shares, that's all I can say.'

One weekend, a former work colleague of Dad's called Stephen was at the door looking embarrassed. Dad had delegated him to collect his remaining records. Mum handed them over with her snooty look on her face, but without a murmur of dissent. After all, they had meant nothing to her but loud noise and irritation. I did not want him to take them, but I had no say in it.

It was the last assault, but it did not hurt the way the broken 78's had hurt. That loss had reduced me to a size that fitted into my father's forgetting. Shriven of *Gallop* and the lugubrious Ramsbottom family in *Albert and The Lion*. No more *Silent Night* sung by the Vienna Boys' Choir: *Stille Nacht, heilige Nacht*. No more Mum marching in to turn off the cabaret songs sung in German. 'You can't play those filthy things in front of your daughter!' – and Dad looking gleeful. Dad had a translation he kept in his desk and he taught me one line. I think he did it out of devilry to spite my mother: *You gave yourself to me in the undergrowth, first this way, then that.* No more black and white image of His Master's Voice, the mournful dog on his haunches next to the gramophone, spinning round and round on the turntable.

He smashed my favourite song that night he left. It had been one of his favourites, too – or so I had thought. It was the one he would put on at the tail end of a cocktail party. Once he let me stand on his feet and hold on to his forearms and lean back. We waltzed to its tune, in this awkward but supportive fashion, round and round the lounge room.

I knew all the words. If forgetting is forgiving then memory casts me into implacable metal:

I re-mem-ber the night and the TEN-NES-SEE WALTZ
Now I know just how much I have lost
Yes I lost my- lit-tle dar-lin'- the night they- were- play-ing
The beau-ti-ful TEN-NES-SEE WALTZ...

Peter

23 Interregnum

Ask me what I believe. I'll tell you. I believe nothing ever gets lost. Nothing gets left behind. Nothing ever disintegrates. I believe in species limitation – in particular, human limitation. I believe in observation. To comprehend what we observe we must stare at the image. The image, either dead or alive, remains vital. If you stare at the image hard enough it will tell you all there is to know.

Ask me what I don't believe. Go on. I do not believe in the divine, nor in unconditional love, though I do believe they are ideas we want to believe in. I believe one more, very important thing. The observer skews the experiment.

My mother has become vague. Ever since my father's departure she has taken on a sullen and suspicious air. For her, good intentions don't exist and so good things do not come her way. She falls out with almost everyone. The greengrocer's fruit is inferior, and she tells him so. Little wonder he drives past our house. Mum watches him down the street as he deals, jovial, with the Browns and Joneses. The Electrolux man receives no more invitations to suck up dirt and sell her accessories. The neighbours on the other side cut down her lasiandra.

'I'll never forgive them.' She screws her cigarette butt into the articulating jaw of the skull ashtray I gave her one Mother's Day.

Lionel and Dolly keep to themselves. Lionel has got rid of all his chooks after a visit from the Health Inspector. 'Knocked them all on the head, every last one,' my mother says in disgust. 'And burnt them with their feathers on, the dirty so-and-so. No wonder I've got sinus.'

There is no sign of Redmond. My mother has no news of him, though Lionel and Dolly go on mysterious trips away from time to time. Then she has to feed their ailing, cancerous cat. 'Well, I had to offer. She'd never ask me for a favour,' my mother pronounces. I know she misses her gossip sessions with Dolly, however stilted they might have become.

My mother still plays golf. She finds it hard to get a partner. Now she has to employ handymen to cut the lawn and fix broken appliances. She is bitter. 'They cost more but they're just as useless as your father.'

I imagine my father and Miss Whatsername live a different, more important existence. I imagine that contentment fills him, that he has no further need for his scientific pursuits. He is away free. 'Leading the life of Riley,' according to my mother. Yet he must have continued to dissect some form of animal life, because just before my final exams he tries, though he fails, to put a stop to himself, one ordinary day. He places a bag soaked in chloroform over his head. That must have been one of the most profound inhalations he ever took.

His failure to kill himself draws a bitter comment from my mother: 'Promises, promises,' is all she says.

She and I form no lasting rapprochement after the novelty of TV dinners fades. We have nothing to talk about now that Dad is not there to incite her. I ignore her presence.

'You go your own sweet way, don't you?' She glares at me and I know she adds to herself: 'Just like your father.'

She has little effective authority over me. No-one does. It is sweet, this interval of my last year at school.

I deserted the listing ship as much as I could. I spent most of my time at my girlfriend Christine's rackety house. My mother was moribund. Christine was alive. It wasn't hard to choose.

I knew all my mother's cautions by heart. She had already instituted her strictures about men before I had even approached the slippery riverbank of 'going out with boys'. Her remonstrations about not letting anyone touch me 'down there' I had taken as a matter of sanitation, one of the reasons she had failed to save me from Lionel. She foresaw attack but never provided me with any defence.

Rights did not come into it. I had no real autonomy. She told me what to do and made me do it, so that the flow-on effects of my behaviour would not disturb the adult world. She didn't speak to me or wait for my response. She never held my face between her hands and looked in my eyes. She just exhorted me.

I lost something indefinable when my father 'left us in the lurch.' Whenever my mother repeated that doleful phrase I thought of the line from the song: *There was I, waiting at the church, waiting at the church...* I imagined my father as the black and white bridegroom atop a wedding cake. I watched him jumping off in slow animation, leaving the white bride standing. She howled in a clockwork voice: 'Darl? Where-are-you-go-ing?'

It was as if my father took an airy framework away with him, a superstructure of many levels, the steel outline of an ocean-going liner. This structure might not have matched his actions but it was in dry dock nonetheless, a blueprint to refer to that was not the close domestic, kitchen and bathroom strictures of my mother.

When I was still young enough for picnics, my father used to take us to a spot high in the hinterland behind the Gold Coast. There, at the end of a red soil track was a waterhole, deep in the black basalt rock. There were just enough footholds to scramble in and out, and an overhanging rock to jump off. It was deep, bottomless my father said. My mother hated it. She sat back on the bank in the buffalo grass and looked miserable.

My father watched as I went in and clung for a second to the side. When I floated out, dog-paddling, I would look up and see my father's face grinning down at me out of the blue sky. It was not always reassuring, that grin, but I had no reason to believe that he would not save me if I got into difficulties.

I had to keep moving, for even on the hottest days the water was icy. It was so black, that water, that my body disappeared into it as if it had bitten me away at the neck.

I thought being a teenager was a shallow creek, quite different and apart from the silent waterhole from which I had scrambled. It was hallucinatory freedom. I floated face-down thinking I could discern quite well enough the bottom of the river. I did not think growing- up mattered. I never thought I was in danger of drowning.

24 Christine

Sing it. *Da da, daa, da dar* (to the tune of *Strangers in the Night*)...

I can never bring myself to look into the eyes of boys. I fear what they might find out. Christine loves them. She is so brash. She stands in front of her mirror and looks at herself. I am sure she says to herself (like I imagine Marilyn Monroe does): 'I can make my face do anything I want.' She takes herself in sections. Like those mismatched books of Incredible Creatures, Christine turns the disjointed pages of herself, and the top half never goes with the bottom.

In front of the mirror in her bedroom she arranges her hair. I lie on her bed and watch. The mirror is a cheap cheval, not tall enough to show all of her at once, so she has to squat to see the top of her head. She backcombs her frizzy black hair into a bird's nest. Then she bunches it on top of her head with a rubber band. She reaches into the mess of bottles of gluggy Elizabeth Arden foundation, glitzy *diamante* hair clips, blunt eyeliner pencils and cakes of spit-smelling mascara that clog her dressing table. She finds a packet of thin bobby pins and proceeds to savage her curls down into a precarious topknot.

She skewers a few stray, artful curls into place. She sprays it into shellacked hardness with evil-smelling Cedel hairspray. The smell is toxic yet exciting, speaking of forays at the local bowling alley into the world of boys. I do it too, with less success, my unmanageable, chlorine-green, straight hair defying the strength of hairspray and teasing. I look and feel unsatisfactory. I keep seeing the real, frightening and unacceptable me behind the image in the mirror. I know I cannot cover up what has happened – or only by subterfuge. What I want to hide is indefinable. But it lurks in my body.

I know I will let it out, tainted, the minute a boy touches me. I am not wholesome like the other girls who gather down at the school oval behind the camphor laurel trees to tell their boy secrets. 'Did you do it with him?' 'Did you go all the way?' they ask each other, and whether they have or not, this is all in the natural run of things. I will be a pariah if I let go my secret, so I have no entry into their circle. Already I have a reputation at school for keeping away from boys.

'You don't like boys, do you?' demands brisk Wendy, the prefect, a calculating look in her eyes. Later she falls pregnant and has to get married. I look away, profess wide experience and a sexual allure that I must keep under control.

'It's too dangerous me going out with boys. I've given up on them,' I state, but it doesn't wash. They think I've 'done it' and because I won't discuss the details, I'm not following form. I get ostracised from the popular group and move down a rung or two, to the social failures. My heart chook pecks at a sliver of flesh. 'Get on your perch,' I tell it. 'Nothing's happened.'

Christine belongs to no particular group. She is a messenger who flits between, unconstrained and as vagrant as rooster feathers. I draw a sketch of her with mercurial wings attached to her sandals and a winged helmet with a spike on top, and one afternoon at the bus stop I give it to her.

'That's me,' she says, delighted, as if I've handed her a mirror. 'You can really draw.' She looks again. 'I don't like beanies, but.' She throws her arm around me, forgiving. Then she folds the paper into a tight wad, bends down and puts it into her shoe.

I paint a watercolour of a girl who holds a hen. She cowers under the shadow of a man, her face upturned. The hen's yellow beak is sharp as a spike or spur. It has a beady, broody look. I don't show it to anyone, though a thought urges me: 'Go on, tell someone.'

Christine has one of the first American teenage magazines. In amongst the Ten-O-Six ads are pages and pages of teenage models. Their T-zones exude no grease; their complexions are pimple-free. They have self-confident smiles and perfect hair and no doubt in their eyes. Christine has a variant of that look. She has no doubt in her eyes either, though her appearance is rather more home-grown and ratty.

'I don't know why you go out with that girl. She looks like a widgie. You'll get a reputation,' my mother warns.

'I don't care.' She is too late. I have got what I wanted. Christine has adopted me.

'Don't Care was made to care. Don't Care was hung.' My mother turns her back and marches off down the hallway. 'Don't Care was put to bed with mustard on her tongue.'

Christine dons a black skivvy, rims her eyes with black eyeliner pencil, applies the rancid mascara. Next she smears foundation across her cheeks, chin, forehead and nose in a freckle-defying mask. It stops at the edges of her face with a beige line. She wipes her hands on her quilt in a careless action. She stands up straight and her head disappears out of the mirror. She looks down. She has on aquamarine Bermuda shorts, skin-tight, which come to just above her knees. She is very skinny, so her upper thighs are concave, making her look bandy legged. She rummages under her bed and comes out with a pair of scuffed high-heeled sandals. They, too, are aquamarine, but only just. She puts them on without undoing the buckles. She stands back a bit, bumping into the bed. Then she hops up on the bed to get a better look at the shoes. Her sectional picture pleases.

'Mum's friend Betty – you know the one,' she chatters, 'says I could be a model.'

She looks nothing like the composite models I yearn to be. She is Daffy Duck, a cartoon creature dressed up to be a person. She is not stupid; there are just a lot of things she does not worry about. Like sewing lessons at school. While I labour from one seam to another searching for precision, Christine has her foot down hard on the pedal. She holds up the shorts she is making, then tries them on. She is the first to finish. One side of the shorts Miss Allen helped her with; the other side is Christine's independent handiwork. She tries them on in front of us and falls over. She has sewn her side of the shorts flat so there is no possibility of getting a leg in, even Christine's skinny one. Her nickname at school is The Happy Hooligan.

We go out down the Friday night road with hoons roaring by, to the Bowling Alley at Greenslopes. A car slides to an idle beside us.

'Want a lift?' I risk a look at the car occupants. The one asking the question has his greasy head stuck out the window. He has a smile on his face. Behind him, the back seat seems full of what my mother would call 'bodgies'.

'Between the legs,' sneers another from the interior of the souped-up car. The smile on the face of the one out the window metamorphoses into a leer.

Christine pulls me on.

'Keep walking,' she hisses. 'Fast.' She dashes across the road against the lights, with me following, loitering to defy the revving bullies. 'Come on!' she yells. The car screeches round the corner and disappears into the fluorescent distance.

Everything in the vicinity of the Bowling Alley is fluorescent, neon-lit. A sign showing a bowling ball knocking down the dollies repeats its staccato pattern above the entrance.

Bowling alleys are new, turning Greenslopes from a place of dead-end appliance stores and greengroceries into the hub of existence. It is, as my mother would say, not a nice place to be at night, and beyond the lit-up area the suburban streets are reproving, menacing. 'You'll come to no good,' they mutter. Television sets in front rooms flicker their green lights, their black and white images. People are still proud of their sets and do not draw the curtains. We can see them sitting inside, dogs around a fire, mesmerised. Conjugal, transmitted harmony. Fake Beatrix Potter people, plaster figures in dolls' houses.

I feel the suffocation of the suburbs, like a blanket thrown over my head. Christine doesn't seem to notice.

I don't want to notice, but I do. I can never concentrate on the main story because of the sub-text. Now Christine is walking me past the bouncers at the door. They are the big boys from my old primary school. She says 'Hi' to them. They know her brother so they ease their legs and look monolithic and pleased as she passes. They look at me uncomprehendingly. I am a private school girl now and I am out of place. Stuck-up, that's what I am. I long to join a group, any group. I want them to recognise me, but like Saggy Baggy, I have not yet found my métier. I don't know where or what it is, so I tag along with Christine.

I like Christine. Why wouldn't I? She is my real life at one remove, like the concept of second cousins that my mother speaks of, that elastic extension of relationship boundaries. I expect one day to have my own life, but I'm in no hurry. I am hungry for the 'pictures' I was never allowed to go to. Christine is a film in the making, in

Technicolor. She manufactures episodes for my delight. I am the figure on the left, just in camera. You can make out my right shoulder and the side of my face.

25 Interruption

Right at this moment, Dolly, after an unexamined and unrecognised illness, dies. She leaves this world as stagnant and expressionless as when she enters it. *Myasthenia gravis* gets her in the end, immures her in bed, helpless. Her life wastes away. She has wasted her life. One or the other. Like Aristotle Onassis she spends her last days with her drooping eyelids propped open with tape.

I like to imagine she chooses her disease, that staring into Lionel's breakfast face day after day has become intolerable. Hence the eyelids that want only to close. Lionel wins that round too, by taping them open again.

'Here I am, your tending monster,' he tells her. 'I haven't left you.'

I used to think that Dolly was transfixed because she had been set the task of sorting right from wrong, her pruney fingers busy, busy all night long, as she picked grit out of the peas, an ageing, overlooked Cinderella. Now I think she might have been encased by what she saw, the worm inside the stick-insect's camouflaged cocoon, too horrified by wickedness and falsehood to do more than poke out one tiny section of her nub head as she nibbled her way across the maelstrom of the world.

Poor Dolly: blank, faceless character, made of wood.

Redmond comes home in a new red sports car.

'I hope he's not going to the funeral in that,' inhales my mother.

He takes it with care up the cobblestone driveway and manoeuvres it into place underneath the house, beside Lionel's Holden. I see Lionel's horny hand shut the wooden slats of the garage doors.

They are quiet for two days before the funeral. Although I have never seen live hamsters I have read about them in English children's books and I imagine Lionel and Redmond spinning round and round, happy and busy on their exercise wheel in the hamster cage of their house.

I would like Lionel to stay transfixed in his hamster guise forever, but I am hoping to see Redmond in the back yard. I have my commiseration speech ready. But they do not emerge. Neither my mother nor I have been invited to Dolly's funeral. My mother is offended.

'They're a dark lot. He's always been one to hold a grudge.' She casts me a meaningful, reproving look.

I still can't bring myself to tell on Lionel. My mother's possible reactions have the power to frighten me, even now. She might blame me for being a dirty little girl. What if she says: 'You must have led him on' – or worse: 'You're mad, just like your father. It's all in your head.' She might demand the story detail by detail, then look at me in disbelief and say: 'But he was a POW.'

What am I, set against that? A guttersnipe who tells fibs. Worst of all, she might tell me: 'For heaven's sake, what a fuss you've been making all this time about nothing much. You silly girl.' This snarl-up is lodged behind my heart and I will not untangle it under my mother's unsympathetic gaze.

Sunday morning, and Redmond and Lionel tinker with their cars down under the house. I can hear spanners knocking against metal. I tiptoe across the brown wooden floorboards of the spare room. Even with the carpet ripped up years ago, the room still smells of low tide, a rusty iron smell of algae.

Redmond's voice says: 'Hey Pop.' One of them slams shut a car bonnet.

'Take a look at this, Pop.'

Redmond's voice is rich and warm, brimming with life. Lionel murmurs a sentence and then he says: 'Go ahead, son.' Redmond starts up the engine of his car, a vibrant roar, then cuts it off.

It is the first Monday morning of my final mid-term school holidays. My mother and I stand and watch from her bedroom window as a taxi pulls up outside Lionel's place. My mother has been stationed there since breakfast in a pointed show of respect. That no one but me can see it does not concern her – or perhaps that is the point. Redmond and Lionel walk together down the driveway. They are both dressed in dark suits, Redmond's mahogany head of hair next to Lionel's rusted grey.

'Two peas in a pod, aren't they?' my mother muses. She holds down the Venetian blinds with one finger, to get a better view.

Redmond opens the taxi door for Lionel and ushers him in with a supportive hand under his elbow. Lionel looks frail, his shoulders shrivelled and hunched.

'I'm all churned up,' my mother announces. 'Well, at least I tried to do the right thing.' She looks smug. 'Even if they didn't.'

Redmond helps Lionel get his left foot into the taxi. 'He's in the prime of life.' She makes it sound like a curse.

'Who? Lionel?' I ask, to stir her up.

'Don't make jokes at a funeral.' She gives me a haughty look.

'We're not at a funeral. We weren't invited, remember? We're just stickybeaking out the window.'

'Oh, you're impossible.'

'Doesn't look to me like he's got a girlfriend,' she ventures her next opinion, undeterred. 'Or not one that he could bring.'

I look down at Redmond as he gets into the other side of the taxi.

'He ought to be settling down by now. He must have got divorced, surely.' She sounds resentful at her lack of knowledge of the details. An ache starts behind my ribs. She brightens with purpose. She lets go the blinds and they come together with a metallic snap. She turns to me. 'I'll get you to take some flowers over, later on.'

My eyes sting with a rush of tears, as if a bank of clouds has rolled up from my heart to lodge behind my eyes. I round on my mother.

'I'm going over to Christine's, so do it yourself.' To her astonished face I say: 'Big fat frauds. I bet they're not even sorry she's dead.'

I don't bother with a challenging look as I push past her out of the room.

26 The World of Boys

Christine and I never play bowls at the bowling alley. That is not why we are there. We are there to pick up boys. We hang around the juke box. I am so self-conscious it is an effort to walk naturally, let alone press the right buttons. Christine is in charge and I watch as the machine selects the silver records and puts them in place. Possibility shimmers as the arm drops the record into the right slot. I feel sophisticated just watching it happen.

Christine has started chatting to some boys who invite us to have a bowl. I don't know how to chat. What do I say? All the wrong conversations jostle in my head, the sub-text as ever confusing me. I've tuned myself to two or three stations at once. I am so intent on pulling them apart that I can't recall if I have said anything at all. I remain silent and avoid their eyes.

Johnny O'Keefe's *Shout* is playing. When he sings it on Bandstand he looks sweaty, sexy and maniacal and quite a lot older than most of the callow youths who are making it to rapid pop stardom. Boys my own age don't interest me. I keep seeing them as jumped-up kindergarten babies swinging from jungle bars. I would rather have a Johnny O'Keefe or a Redmond. They are men. Redmond shines and glitters, a rotating image. Boys are bits and pieces of a puzzle. They make no sense. I have no idea what boys think. I don't believe they think at all, which is another reason I can't talk to them.

Christine, wobbling on her high heels, throws a ball wide into the gutter. She is talking about cars and footie. The cars I know are my father's Humber Super-Snipe and my uncle's Vauxhall. I discard the image of Redmond's red sports car nestled close to Lionel's two-tone Holden. None of these seem to fit this conversation.

'Would you like a go?'

The taller boy whose name could be Brian stands next to me,

proffering a large black bowling ball. The smaller boy now has his arm around Christine, helping her to throw. It ends up in the gutter again.

'OK.' I throw the ball, knocking down most of the dollies.

'Wow,' whistles Brian or Steve. But I sense I have spoiled his fun. He would much rather have put his arm round me and guided my hand.

'Play the game,' whispers the hidden chorus of girls at school, but something stubborn in me hates organised sport.

Christine has taught me all I know. Once, on a bus to Swansea, she taught me how to smoke and do the drawback. 'Breathe in and say "I saw a train going through a tunnel and it went *Whoooo*", then blow out.' She watches me while I practise.

She's keen to show me how to kiss boys, getting her brother to cooperate one drowsy Sunday when his girlfriend is home doing her ironing. Whenever I usually see his girlfriend she is lying on his bed on top of the quilt, on her side, with her head propped up, her hair in large spiky rollers. She is an awkward clothed version of a picture in my school art book of Cranach's *Reclining Water Nymph*.

The kissing practice is a most matter-of-fact and technical exercise. I do not join in and neither of them suggests I should. Lionel pops into my head and stands there, his shoulders hunched.

'Stop looking,' I tell him.

'What did you just say?' Christine gives me a curious look. 'You're funny sometimes.' Her brother looks as if he doesn't trust me.

Then she teaches me how to dance. Although I am diligent in going to the Boatshed on the Brisbane River to learn the Quickstep, the Foxtrot and The Pride of Erin, I learn nothing, except that I attract the duds. A butcher's apprentice who smells of meat asks me to dance. I forget to smile and he looks wary and offended. He offends me with his red, sweaty hands and his prickly blue suit. Most of the time I sit on the sidelines. I say *wallflower* to myself and hate every other girl who is sitting out. I think there is a good reason for every one of them to be rejected – except for me. One Saturday I am the only one left on the sidelines. I go to the toilet.

Once, I dance with a man of my desires, a dark-haired University student. I don't see him coming across the room until he asks me to dance. He has black, irresolute eyes. He does not look as if he owns either a surf board or a souped-up car. He asks my name. I hate saying my real name: they always get it wrong, so I have to repeat it.

I wish I had a name like Barbara or Carole or Linda, not one that makes me stand out from the crowd, and not one that attracts silly jokes.

'You've got a very special name – it's classical,' my mother reproves me, on the defensive. 'Classical Greek.' She looks momentarily doubtful. 'Or Roman. It means fidelity. Anyway, your father chose it.'

'How would you like a name that makes you sound like a bug?' I retort.

Since my father's defection I have decided to discard my nickname, but I have no good alternative to fall back on. I hesitate and stutter. Now I feel nameless.

I want the brooding University student for myself. I want to put him up on the mantelpiece at home and stare at him in solitude. The feel of his hand on my back is tender and suggestive, but I can't sink into it.

Instead I say: 'I hate dancing, don't you?'

He looks down at me, stupefied. He does not hate dancing. I am the misfit here. We finish the dance in silence and the next dance he asks a pretty girl with dark hair who glides round with him. Months later I see his engagement photo in *The Courier-Mail*. Her name is Jennifer; his name is Ross. I despise him, but cut out his photo, screwing up the fiancée. I keep him in my wallet.

Christine teaches me to rock'n'roll. We practice the limbo under her mother's broomstick, and she tries to teach me a music hall number where you wiggle your knees and cross your hands over and back. I can never manage it. Christine is skinny and knobbly and double-jointed.

I quite like rock'n'roll. It means I don't have to touch my partner. It also means that girls, if they have the nerve, can get up and dance in the crowd by themselves.

In return, because I am learning French at school and Christine is doing the secretarial course, I teach her French phrases. I cannot get far beyond *Oui, Bonjour, Bonsoir* and *Comment allez vous?* I teach her

Quel heure est-il? In the middle of doing something she will ask: *Quel time est-il?* She likes *Je suis Christine* but it is just a joke between us. She would never use it in her real world. She knows not to frighten boys by being clever.

I do not like boys who like me because I am a girl. Don't they know I can swim better than they can, ride a horse bareback, stand on my head, walk on stilts? Why are they consistent in preferring girly and stupid things I am not good at? The 1960's are tiring me out.

I wish to find the mate for my soul. I will settle for someone with a bigger problem than I have. I am ripe for a tormented rebel or a drug-addicted recalcitrant, but they are hard to find in Greenslopes. Anyone practical, easygoing, uncomplicated or friendly does not interest me. Gloom, ambivalence, the unresolved: that's what I want. An exotic mix of my own concoction of cleverness and lassitude is what will attract me. And they must have broad shoulders and brown skin. No chicken chests for me.

My search distracts me.

I am pretty sure this one's name is Steve. He is conferring with his sidekick, who is definitely Greg. I get the useless information correct. Christine will get Greg and I will settle for Steve.

Steve looks not unlike a greyhound with a crew cut. There is something about him that is consoling, ordinary. He wears cord trousers and riding boots, jackaroo gear. They want to drive us home and we both know they want to go the long way. We agree.

'Don't go getting into any cars,' warned Christine's mother as we clattered down the back steps. We pretended not to hear her so technically we are not disobeying her now.

I like Christine's mother. She is cosy and crumpled. She looks relaxed. Christine tells me she is suffering from necro-something. I suggest necrophilia but Christine doesn't get the joke. She never bothers with big words. It turns out she has narcolepsy and on a trip to Sydney with them I see she is growing sleepy as we walk through Wynyard station. She lies down on the tiles. Christine's father is an aeronautical mechanic. He has a rumbling laugh and a clipped moustache. He bends his stocky frame and hauls her mother up. 'Not right at this minute, love,' he laughs. No-one seems to mind.

Now I get into the front seat next to the greyhound. Christine and

Greg are still chatting in the back, with occasional bouts of silence. After a while, they have some disagreement and Greg spends the rest of the ride leaning forward, ostensibly conferring with our driver. We reach the outer suburbs fast and soon we are speeding down red dirt roads in a section of Sunnybank that is still orchards. The headlights pick out dropsical custard apples hanging from their trees.

In the headlights now I can see a female figure walking along the side of the road. Steve sees her too and applies the brakes.

'Geez, what's that sheila doin' out here?' asks Greg. It unsettles us. It is late at night and the roadside is empty of houses. We come up alongside her and our driver winds down his window and sticks his head out. 'Need a lift?'

'Lucky it's not between the legs,' intones the voice in my head.

There is a *whumphing* sound and a male figure tries to smash my greyhound's head in with an iron pipe. Steve is in gear and careening off as another *whump* sounds on the bonnet.

'Shee-it! Jesus Christ,' howls Greg. Nothing as exciting as this has ever happened to him.

'Didja see that. Shiiit! Hey matey, whaddya reckon? A set-up, hey?'

I must be in shock because I am still trying to work out Steve's name and Greg is not helping.

Greg is still fulminating. 'Geez, hey. What a bitch! Didja see her? What a hooer!'

They appear to lay the blame on the girl for tricking them. They admire the aim of the male assailant. 'Geez, he almost got me.' My greyhound shakes his shoulders. 'I would've been a gonner. I've got a plate in me head. Here,' and he guides my hand to the side of his crew cut where I am to feel the metal plate. I can feel nothing but a small indentation and the silky bristle of his hair.

'You'd better take us home,' says Christine.

I keep silent, but I feel warm inside. I have a question welling up inside me, 'How did you get that metal plate?' Because I am still unsure about his name, I can't ask. Nevertheless, I start to like him. Recklessness under fire.

I like riding in cars with nowhere special to go. It makes me think of rides with my father. When I was still small, he took me for car trips late at nigh, to put me to sleep. 'Hop in the back,' he'd say and

I curled up on the leather seat, lulled by motion as the car rushed humming through cold air. I liked the feeling of being cocooned, of being outside time, never-ending. I didn't think about what was going through his mind on those long car trips. The familiarity of the amber lights at the Five Ways, blinking on and off, filled me with a weight of sadness. The streets were deserted. The last scene before home was the ice factory at Stones Corner, gleaming, an underwater Antarctic refrigerator. When we pulled up again in the driveway there was a moment's stillness. I looked at the back of Dad's head, then he'd say into the silence: 'Home aginny gin' and I would start to cry.

We pull up in Christine's driveway. It must be quite late, past midnight. The street is silent. All the houses are dark. A dog barks and the sound echoes down the street. Christine and Greg get out and sit on her low, stucco fence.

'What's your name?' asks Reckless.

I tell him. 'Sooky'.

'That's a nickname, isn't it? What's your real name?'

'It's stupid. You don't really want to know, do you?'

'Tell me.' He touches the side of my face. The gesture surprises me, so I spell it.

'That's a bit different.' His voice is polite. 'It's like I've got an auntie called Moira.' Helpful, he spells it out for me.

'That sounds fateful.'

He looks at me, uneasily. He doesn't understand the reference. I read too much and know too much and make boys unhappy.

'She lives in Ipswich,' he says.

My private voice replies, 'So what.'

'Where do you live? You don't live here do you?'

'No.' I tell him where I live.

'I'll drive you home.'

'No, it's OK.'

He has his arm round the back of the seat. Now he leans across the gear stick and kisses me. It is a nice kiss, but I hold my breath. 'See you next time I'm down.'

I duck my head and smile, but that stubborn feeling of fidelity to an image I can't make out is on me again. I picture myself in a fibro house in a country town. Pittsworth or even worse, Ipswich. All I can see is stunning heat, withered paspalum and lost jackaroos. A crisp-jacketed grasshopper sways on a stem. I start to draw it in my head as he reaches across and opens the door for me, and as I get out a relieved Greg leaps in.

When Christine and I look into our near futures we can see nothing but getting a boy friend, going steady and, if a miracle happens, getting married. Christine has her bottom drawer half-filled. She has a pair of white sheets in a cellophane packet at the bottom. Some beer coasters, a set of four raffia place mats, doilies, and a crocheted Afghan rug come next. Two wooden salad servers, and a pair of stove mitts in the shape of kookaburras, that she likes to play with, sit on top. Stuffed down the side is a pair of broken sunglasses that shouldn't be there.

I tell her about dowries that I have read about in Georgette Heyer novels.

'Yeah, sounds like a good idea, but Dad couldn't afford one. Not on his pay packet anyway. Mum fell asleep on the job and they asked her not to come back.'

We do not know we are Baby Boomers, not yet. They haven't fully invented us. But we know we want everything in a hurry and marriage appears to be the key to everything. When asked what we want to be when we grow up, we have no idea.

'I'll get a job.' Christine sounds matter-of-fact. 'But then I'll stay home and have kids.' She has picked out a name for her first child. 'It'll be a girl and I'll call her China.'

I cannot visualise anything so concrete for myself, though for a moment I think of Redmond.

We sit in her kitchen. It is so late now that even I am bleary-eyed. The Kookaburra emblem on the old-fashioned gas stove slides in and out of focus. The kitchen smells of leaking gas and something sour in the drains. There is a small window on the western wall with a tin hood over it. The lino, in green and black squares, is pock-marked from Christine's metaltipped high heels. She tiptoes across to the bench to make tea. She sets it out on the Formica kitchen table, complete with knitted tea-cosy and starts to make the Saos.

It is as if Christine has invented Saos. I love everything about them: the way they come out of the packet so crisp and square, the sound of the paper tearing, their dry, calming smell. We have four each. Two have butter and Vegemite on them and two have butter and tomato with pepper and salt.

We don't talk much. Tiredness has hit us. In between the Vegemite and the tomato we lay our heads on the table and talk sideways.

'I'd better go home.'

'You can stay the night if you want.'

'No, I'd better go.'

Christine often asks me to stay the night, but I don't want to lie giggling with her in her lumpy bed or get up the next day and see a morning version of Christine. Christine only exists for me at night. Even though my mother will be waiting up, an accusing look on her face, I think of the luxurious solitude of my own bed. I will lie there and think over every line and angle of my Christine night. I will draw the Saos and Christine's scuffed aquamarine high heels. I will draw her legs, up to and including the knees. In retrospect it will make me feel happy.

At this point, Lionel dies too. Not straight away, but soon enough. Nothing to feed on. But he doesn't really die for me. He's a Jack-in-the-box hanging around in my head. He's still in my life, active as ever, pacing back and forth behind slat after wooden slat. He calls his chooks and shaves his face each morning. His face is the most persistent part. I can see the pink of his aftershave skin tones. The eyes are hot but not real. He stands inside his ageless face, waiting to pounce.

On Sundays he washes his car, tinkers with the infernal rattle and motors out to the Styx. He has not driven across yet, deterred by the thought of chassis rust. He is the busiest, most meticulous dead man I know.

27 Taking Notice

I have begun to understand that while I am incessant in my observation of others, I might myself be observed; I might figure as a character in their lives. Does someone sit thinking of me? Am I the end product of their quest?

It is hard for me to believe that I promote desire. Not that I think of myself as ineffectual. ('Far from it,' my father's voice jokes.) It's just that I sometimes feel as if I'm not here.

I used to believe I wandered through life examining but unnoticed, a passionate ghost. I might be real somewhere inside myself. Scientific surmise. The public version of me, whatever it is, is a fluctuating fabrication, a double image. I retain the function of intervention in one-way mode. I will control you, but try to steer me and your hand will go straight through. When someone takes me for a real live image it startles me that they can't tell the difference. Their mistake.

Everyone else appears to believe in their threatening, overtaking reality. It is enticing, their confidence in their corporeality. It may be a matter of conviction, a question of faith: 'Believe in yourself.'

I was right the first time. Dad always ended an argument with those words.

We're all made up.

I have just left school when Redmond comes home from Wagga. My mother elicits the information that he is moving back to Brisbane for good. With his parents neat in their underground chambers he is selling their house. An ugly red and orange For Sale sign goes up on the footpath. Redmond comes and goes, in a hurry. He looks light-hearted. I am the only one left sufferingfrom Lionel's Jack-in-the-box propensities. Sometimes Redmond calls out 'Hiya Sweetheart' to me as he gets into his sports car. I walk past, stiff with self-consciousness, giving him a tiny smile. I don't want to get too close in case he smells the Clearasil I've put on the pimple on my cheek. He looks glossy and handsome but so far out of my teenage league that I feel embarrassed even day-dreaming about him.

'Wait for me, Redmond,' I print on the board inside my skull. I print it in mirror writing, so even I can't crack the preposterous message.

Two weeks later he disappears.

'Where's Redmond living now?' I ask my mother in my most casual voice.

She gives me a look and says loftily: 'Haven't a clue. Why would you want to know, may I ask?'

'Oh, for heaven's sake.' I make myself sound superior, 'I'm just making conversation.'

It takes me three months to find a job, each knock-back verifying my unreality. I pretend an interest in advertising. I can draw, I am literate and I am sure I can sell a product. After all, it is only a stretch of the imagination. None of my prospective employers likes my new folio of ghosting images nor my attitude, because they believe they are selling something real. Every time I open my mouth I say the wrong thing. I do not go to Art School although my mother canvasses the idea. I meet any suggestion from my mother with rejection.

'You won't be told, will you?' She looks at me and grinds her teeth from side to side.

I appear for an interview at the University. I do not expect to get the job of Secretarial Assistant to a one-breasted, aging woman academic – but I do. I cannot believe she wants to employ me. She looks at me as if I appear normal. 'You can start on Monday,' she tells me.

I have few skills, although I can type. The job suits me. I have my own office adjacent to hers at the back of the Biological Sciences laboratory. I walk through the lab every day. I like the beakers and Bunsen burners and chemical smells, the red rubber tubing. I like sending away for a new external saline insert for my boss after her breast bursts when she goes up in a light plane.

I like the white coated lab attendant, whose name is Harry. He is no threat because he is engaged to the Senior Secretarial Assistant, Dorothy. He has a pet magpie that sits on his shoulder and carols in the mornings. The magpie looks at its image reflected in Harry's eyeball, its murderous beak not quite touching the white of his eye.

In between typing discursive letters and academic papers, I draw. Noone interrupts me. I have plenty of time to stare out my window and think. The light is good. It is an old building and we are on the ground floor. I draw the newly-hatched cockroaches that emerge from my manual typewriter when I type w. The post-graduate students are older men from suspect countries: India, Botswana, Indonesia. They are courteous, sometimes playful and pretend not to notice the charcoal dust and my bulky folder of drawings.

I am too preoccupied to move from home. I can't imagine myself in a flat, so I do nothing about it. If I could visualise it I would do it. Nothing comes to mind. What's more pressing and numbing is, I can't visualise myself. The only bits that ever seem real are my legs and my feet.

I like the long bus trip across town to the University, crossing the river at the Grey Street bridge, watching the seagulls and pigeons fly along the river. I change buses at Toowong. I often miss the connection because I am doing a series of drawings from the wooden overhead bridge, showing the train lines intersecting at Toowong Station.

Most days I am late for work, but I somehow avoid censure. I operate outside the pale. The drawback is that the others in the general typing pool treat me at morning tea with silent dislike. I solve that by not having any. Nothing touches me. Then they do not typify me as stuck-up any more, just remote. The post-graduate student who was a Patrol Officer in New Guinea and enjoys jollying along strange indigenous people says: 'Give me a smile. Go on, it won't hurt.' He chucks me under the chin.

I compose drawings on the bus home and hold the lines in my head until I can transfer them to paper. Sometimes I overshoot my stop. I spend most of my wages on paper, inks, pens, charcoal, pencils and now that I am introducing colour, on gouache and oil pastels. I have found some beeswax left over from Dad's autopsy displays. I melt and mix it with the pastels. I will use anything in combination to get the right effect. I am not sure that I know what I am doing. I show no-one. I lock my bedroom door against my mother's intrusions and take the key to work. She does not see that I have also begun to paint on the wallpaper in my room.

In the tight sealed compartment of my mind where I keep the Redmond who loved Rosie and by extension, me, I write myself a new note. 'Come back and get me, Redmond. I'm waiting.' I don't know why, but I am certain that we have an inescapable connection, even though, at the same moment, I don't believe he would waste any time on me. He is too smart, too fast, to even want to know me. He is nothing like Lionel, who lives in a separate box of his own making. I will not think about Lionel and Redmond in the same thought.

I wonder where Redmond lives. My mother still hasn't found out, but I've heard her on the phone trying all her connections. When I see him in Toowong talking to a woman outside an art gallery, I chide him in my mind for avoiding the inevitable. I close my eyes and will him towards me. 'Come to me,' I say out loud. I sing the refrain from *Bali Hai* under my breath, and smirk at myself.

Lionel pops out of his box, his jowls hanging. 'Stop kidding yourself,' my inside voice berates me. 'You're making it up. To Redmond, you're just the brat next door. He'd laugh if he knew you had a crush on him.' I picture him, an older woman hanging on his arm.

One lunch hour, I sit on the grass outside the Biological Sciences building. I scratch at a sketch of electricity poles, intent on the way the wires sag. I am trying to decide how to make the blue of the ceramic insulators when a medical student who is the University football hero sits down next to me. He has a stocky body and a Slavic face. He has had his two front teeth knocked out in a game and the false ones make his mouth altered and vulnerable. He has broad hands that swing in front of him and a rolling walk. He is not how I imagine a football hero to be. He speaks in simple sentimentalities that embarrass me.

'I've been watching you for months. I've only just got up the courage to speak to you. Hullo.'

'Hullo yourself.'

He won't be put off by my silences or by my staring into space. He just keeps talking and smiling at me until I agree to our first date. We go to the pictures at the Regent and see an Elvis Presley movie called G.I. *Blues*. He holds my hand for the first time as we go up the Regent's grand staircase. We stand around in the foyer and I think how the festooned red velvet curtains are posh and tacky at the same time.

Peter is quite a respectable date. Other couples stare at us. I don't know anything about the football world but suppose that is why they recognise him. Despite his obvious social attributes I feel uneasy, bored and irritated.

I think it is a case of mistaken identity. When he takes me out to see a Uni Theatre production of A Midsummer Night's Dream I expect him to leap out of his seat when the flower juice drops into the lovers' eyes, and point his finger in accusation.

What does he see in me? It intrigues and flatters me, in a way that I despise in myself, that someone so popular should pick me. We are so unsuited it is criminal. But I keep going out with him because I have nothing better to do. I can find no good reason, or the words to reject him.

I meet his parents, who are earnest and cautious. They dote on me because they believe I, too, adore their son.

He has a sister called Tamara who treats me like a little sister. I expect to find their Russian Orthodoxy fascinating but the only Russian thing about them is a silver samovar and a yard planted out to vegetables, front and back. It occurs to me they would know the Russian woman who sashayed, disruptive, down my street.

I am cruel to Peter when I see how besotted he is. It is not my fault that he feels this way. I let him take me out to Romano's, the most expensive Italian restaurant in Brisbane. When he picks me up he has a corsage for me and a bunch of flowers for my mother. My mother is infatuated with him. I leave the corsage in the car.

I order Lobster Thermidore and won't let him touch my breasts when he kisses me goodnight. He is bouncy and rough, a seal presenting me with wet fish. Each time he slides up to me, joy in his sorrowful eyes, I reject him.

Months into this grudging relationship he is still unflagging in his pursuit. I agree to watch him playing football but go home before the end. I tell him I am sick with sunstroke and he brings me more flowers attached to a purple, furry troglodyte doll that is some sort of good luck charm. His simplicity frightens me.

He calls me Baby and Honey Heart and on more formal occasions uses my real name. He holds my hand walking down the street.

His arms are disproportionate and our hands never sit right. He is amenable to most things. That is part of the problem. I am a jump ahead of him. He likes talking information but surmise is not his forte. He smiles at me when I go off on a riff of conjecture and says: 'I wouldn't know about that.'

He is fond, benign. He condones my whims. They engage him. His indulgent attitude infuriates me. I suspect he thinks girls have their day in the sun, glorious creatures, then they turn into wives and mothers of children, get a bit broader, more sedate. Just now I can kick up my heels. The wild has its place. He believes I will learn my own dignity. It is an astonishing assumption and I take exception to it. I turn on him, savage.

'Don't tell me what I feel. How do you know what I think? Don't tell me what I'm going to be! You wouldn't have a clue. You don't own me!' The demon inside me wriggles, ferocious, and would clap its hands if it had more room to move. I want to say 'Fuck off!' I am just getting used to it (girls don't swear) and he cringes with such authenticity when I use common swear words that I can't bring myself to say it.

He is proud of me when he introduces me into his circle of friends. They have just finished engineering degrees or are still doing Medicine. One is an anthropologist in the making. Most of them have become engaged and some are married. I hear him talking Russian in the kitchen to one couple who live in a high-rise apartment in Petrie Terrace above the Brisbane River. It is obvious that he is talking about me, the way their cautious faces turn towards and accept me.

The sound of Russian is exotic, but he will not teach me any. He is at his most gruff and defensive, unsure that I am not making fun of his difference. He does not appreciate my romantic fancies with his language. To him it is a pragmatic inconsequence. He is a buffo Australian. The language of his parents is a private matter.

I find his friends not so much sedate as sedated. When they're not at a football match they move and talk in slow motion. I want to scream at them or stick them with hot metal chicken skewers.

There is a set menu for their dinner parties that goes round and round. They make carpet-bag steak with insidious oysters concealed inside. They all have fondue sets complete with long forks. There are *pirozhki* for starters. Hungarian goulash with sour cream is a constant and bouillabaisse if they're feeling rich and someone's been fishing. And always a large salad with salad dressing.

Salad dressing is sophisticated, marking us off from our mothers' salads of undressed lettuce, tomato, grated carrot, wet tinned asparagus and bleeding beetroot. On the Night of Bouillabaisse I get an attack of diarrhoea from the rich food. The toilet in the friends' tiny flat leads straight onto the dining room so they hear every explosive emission. I stay in there a long time, so that the smell will die down. When I emerge they lower their eyelids.

Peter says in a loud voice: 'You OK, Honey Heart?'

'I'm fine.' I kick his foot under the table. When he is considerate I feel mean and tight, but I can't help myself.

His friends never talk about anything that interests me. It's not as if I know what interests me – but it is nothing they have to offer. Peter tells them I draw. I feel exposed, embarrassed. I needn't be, for they express polite surprise.

But what I might do doesn't really interest them.

One couple already has a baby. They expect me to tiptoe into its room and look at it sleeping. I see Peter looking at me as I bend over the blurry form.

'No, don't pull the blanket back, I can see him.' Then I wonder if it is a *him*. Peter looks disappointed and the mother offended. 'That's Caroline.'

Peter draws the blanket back from the sleeping baby and touches her clenched fist with his large footballer's hand. That is one thing I like about him. I start to think about drawing his hands and forearms, the way the blue blood vessels stand out in robust cords. His silky brown skin. His skin is much finer-grained than mine. I plan an anatomical drawing because now I see in vivid detail, as I close my eyes to concentrate, the light glinting at the point of the scalpel. I might use colour, just for the blood vessels.

Peter is saying something. Grudgingly, I answer: 'What?'

'It doesn't matter Honey Heart. You go back to sleep.'

His friends drink inordinate amounts of Chianti in raffia bottles. Peter drinks very little, because he is in training. His friends encourage his semiabstinence. He carries the standard for them. He is a local hero and there is a lot at stake. There is unspoken anxiety about me. They hope I will treat him right and not put him off form.

I am derisive. 'What do your friends think, that I'll sap your strength?'

We have not made love and although I would say no if he suggested it, it maddens me that he hasn't insisted. He avoids going out the night before a big match, and I make sure that he knows I have noticed.

'Did you know boxers don't like to lose seminal fluid before a bout? They think it will weaken them,' I tell him. I put an inquiring look on my face and pretend a clinical interest. 'Are footballers the same?'

'Don't be like that, Honey Heart.'

I can never stir him into retaliation. He deflects the cutting comments that I have modelled on Bette Davis in *All About Eve*. It is impossible to engage in witty repartee with someone who does not respond, but stands waiting for the moment to recede. If goaded beyond even his endurance he will say, as if soothing a recalcitrant horse: 'Now quieten down.'

He locks me into battle with myself. I hate his steadiness, his compromising rationality. I don't fit into his world. The taste of red wine at the houses of his friends makes me think of tinned blood. I am awake and alert as the parties bog down into slurring, amiable argument about who's got the best hi-fi system or most reliable car, or discursive accounts of football matches. They are pleased with themselves, set already in a pattern they believe will last them all their lives. Cars, babies, mortgages (I don't bother to find out what a mortgage is, but it sounds like something to do with death), careers in business. They will live in the same suburbs, the same houses, cities, states, the same marriages for ever and ever. Nothing will ever happen to them, and for that they will be grateful. No bumps or obstacles.

They are already responsible.

It is so safe, this idea of life. I could let them tell me who I am. I could be a comfortable cow led by the nose with a silver chain, calf trailing. If only I did not react to the thought of the hypodermic full of anaesthetic being inserted into my erratic, impatient heart. I will not descend into these bathtub banalities. Like Scuffy the Tugboat, *I was meant for bigger things.*

Life and art are inextricable, we all know that: *'Perhaps you would not be cross if you went sailing', said the man with the polka dot tie...*

Peter asks me to go to Sydney with him for a weekend's sailing. He has mates who are crew on the *New Endeavour*. The glamour of this invitation to the Smart Set mollifies my mother and at the same time horrifies her: the impropriety of going away for a weekend with a man! That decides me. I tell Peter I'll go. He is pushing the boundaries for me. I feel suddenly more benign towards him.

I quote Scuffy inside my head, buoyant: *'At last Scuffy sailed into a big city. Here the river widened, and all about were docks and wharves. Scuffy said, 'This is the life for me.'*

Peter takes my hand and plants it on his thigh. I leave it there until it begins to seem detached from me, then I take it back. My relationship with my body is still tenuous. I am confident about my hands if I don't think about them. Then they have an alarming predilection to look like my mother's. Even when I make love to myself, which I do with sneaky regularity, I feel as if something is overtaking me. It is as if I am not in charge. The thought of making love with a stranger with invisible motives disconcerts me even more. I put this in a box with an unreadable label. What will I call it? To call it sex is hardly descriptive.

'Oh, oh!' cried Scuffy when he saw the sea. 'There is no beginning and there is no end to the sea.'

They have moored the *New Endeavour* at an inner bend of the harbour near Balmain. His friends here are similar to the Brisbane set, though racier. They are fond of Peter and are casual about accepting me. I thought we would put to sea in the big ship. Instead we board a large yacht with lots of beer and a few serious sailors in charge. Each time we change tack I have to duck my head as the boom swings over. There is a lot of letting in and out of ropes and leaping about, and the women say girlish things and look pleased in a lolling way. They wear stripey tops and bikini bottoms and apply suntan oil to their legs.

I can't make out what they are talking about because Peter has both arms round my neck from behind and his head is blocking up one ear. All I can hear is the rustle of his breath and his skin scraping mine. My bet is that they are talking about diets. The Grapefruit Diet is the in-thing. Already I have drawn the segments my mother gives me for breakfast. She is a diet cheat and piles on sugar. I draw the sugar granules that turn amber when they fuse with the juice. It is a difficult colour to get right.

The wind is in the other ear, so I forget about trying to hear their conversations and concentrate on whether or not I feel seasick. I have a beer and not long after, all I can think about is my full bladder, pressed in by my tight white hipster pants.

I never feel comfortable in my clothes. Sometimes I wish for the airy freedom of my romper suits, even when this makes me think of Lionel. We are still a generation constricted by our clothes, just like our mothers. My mother, as she ballooned from plump to extra-large, wore corsets that started at the thighs, contorted upwards across her belly with a large-toothed zip and were attached by hooks to her brassiere. This had circular stitching around the cups and when she bent over and fed her breasts into them, then stood straight, pink cones stuck out from her chest. The rolls of fat were still there but they no longer wobbled.

In senior school we all wore step-ins, light elastic corsets which stretched from waist to thighs. Little girls wore suspender belts. Our stomachs had to be as flat as radiator grilles. If you bounced you should consider yourself cheap. Sitting all day in school on wooden seats in the Brisbane heat, the step-ins pressed into our bottoms, leaving an itchy imprint. When I got home from school I would strip them off and give a vigorous scratch.

The other supposed benefit was that they were effective chastity belts.

Even now that I have discarded my step-ins, I still feel constrained inside my body. Someone has sized it up and fitted it out. It does not feel like me. Someone has taught me dissatisfaction with it and disgruntlement with it: shame and suspicion. Who was that? Who planted this enormous doubt in my head? Which of them shall I blame? Mother, father, Lionel, my school headmistress, Robert Menzies? He's ubiquitous enough, with his portrait in every hall and doctor's waiting room alongside the Queen's, she of the hems weighed down with lead in case a breeze should excite her skirts. Arbiters of conformity, who says they are right? What about me, told to fit in, bunched into shape, frozen, starved, eviscerated, encased, leached of colour, told to wear bone or oatmeal: *you can never go wrong with bone?* Is every female in Brisbane on a diet? I want to find someone who will laugh with me and agree that of course wearing gloves in the sub-tropics is silly. I want someone to say: 'It doesn't matter. None of it matters.'

I must find someone who will discover the source of my discomfort, the pea under the pile of mattresses that distorts the couch on which the princess lies. He will burrow his hand to the centre of all that striped ticking, those glowing layers of ruby eiderdowns, draw it out and say: 'Yes, here it is. You were right all along. A small green pea. It's a wonder you felt it, but here it is.'

Peter gives me a sloppy tongue kiss, a seal of ownership in front of everyone. Not that they are attending. They're doing it themselves. All except the helmsman are snogging away. The helmsman says 'You beauty' to noone in particular.

I need to go to the toilet. They call it the head. Once inside, I wonder how long I can stay locked away. I have had too much beer. The tiny compartment smells of engine exhaust, boat oil and bilge water. I have a slight familiar ache in my stomach and discover I am getting my period. I put my head in my hands and bend forward, but closing my eyes makes me feel worse. Inside my head, it is black, dizzy, starry. Oily circles meander across my plane of inner vision.

I can hear my mother saying 'You need to have your head read.'

I repeat the phrase over and over to myself, morose. Why can't I ever let things alone? 'Relax,' I say to myself. 'I will be nice.' I take a deep breath of engine fumes, pull up my pants, unlock my odorous cubby hole and start up the ladder to the top deck.

We go back to somebody's parents' place in Woollahra. They are away. It is a three-storey mansion built in the twenties, with recent architectural inserts. It overlooks the water. We leave our bags in a downstairs bedroom. There is a print of Chagall's Lovers on the wall. I am so relieved to be off the boat that I let Peter kiss me. He tastes of beer although he hasn't drunk much. He has a plan. It is so obvious and he is so determined that I laugh out loud.

'What are you doing?'

He tackles me with his feet and the weight of his body, and sends me backwards onto the bed.

'Don't laugh at me.' He cups my face between his hands. 'My little

Christmas fairy.'

How's my little fairy today, says Lionel. I pull Peter's hands away and hold him at bay, by his wrists.

'Do you love me, just a little bit?' he asks. 'The way I love you?'

'No.'

I stare into his eyes. It is a mistake. I think: 'He is too human, too apparent.' I want to rub at the edges and make him more idealised. I want to draw over the page of his life set out so plainly for me. I do not want to live within the warm bear-hug of his arms. I do not want a future where I show an interest in pediatrics and go to AMA dinners up on Gregory Terrace. I do not want to make dinner for him and wait up when he is late or out on call, and have him say: 'Sorry Honey Heart, sorry Baby – I'll make it up to you.'

I do not trust him to see how what is inside me has to be wild and unobserved, not spoken about. He won't know he is doing it. He will overwhelm me with practicalities and domesticities and three weeks' holiday a year at the Gold Coast. I will shrivel up and I'll start to say: 'No, it doesn't matter. I've got you: that's enough.' I will become poisonous and controlling as I live his life for him because my own is dead. I'll begin to nag him about new curtains and the state of the carpet. He will buy me a new car at five-year intervals and I'll chivvy him about the colour. He will say: 'Nothing's ever perfect.' Then he will say: 'I've never stopped you from doing anything you want.' But he will stop being encouraging and more often look grim. And one day he will go out without a word and I will see him dancing with a girl with dark hair who loves to hold him tight and knows why she is there.

'I can make you love me though, can't I?' He looks defiant.

'No you can't.' I look away from him, keep my face bright and get up from the bed. 'Didn't I tell you? I only fall in love if it's a leap year.' I feel as if I'm acting in someone else's drama. None of this is real. It is too crass. I refuse to feel sad or hateful. I have a right not to feel anything if that's what I want.

We go out to dinner at a Russian restaurant in Kings Cross. We are in an upstairs room, empty except for our party, and we sit at a long wooden table. I have a glass of wine and eat something with sour cream on it. Outside the window I can see the lights of Sydney blinking blue and red neon signals and see the swoosh of car headlights as they go down towards Rushcutters Bay.

Peter keeps looking at me as if he is checking that I'm still there. I have had more to drink tonight than ever before and I congratulate myself on how well I am handling it. As the wine takes effect I smile at him and let the conversation blur out at the edges. I am adept at saying very little at dinner parties. I have discovered that if I stare fixedly at the dominant speaker he takes it for encouragement and I look as if I am taking part in the conversation. I hardly ever get caught out.

Now Peter is on his feet. I wait for a Russian toast, something about good food and fine company perhaps, or a sentence with a serious sailing metaphor. My mind has already slipped out of gear when I hear my name '...and in the company of friends I wish to ask you to be my wife. Say yes, Honey Heart.'

I stare at him. Is this some awful Russian custom? I feel a blush of outrage start behind my ears and at the edges of my face, until my entire face burns. I consider my options. My brain has turned into an icebox while outside all else is malleable, hot and fleshy. I can say *no* and humiliate him in front of his friends and now the restauranteur who has appeared at the top of the stairs as if he knew this was going to happen. Then what will I do? Call a cab? Where will I go? Will they gang up on me and say: 'Don't be silly, of course you must accept his offer' and prevent me from leaving?

Or I can say *yes*. What will happen if I say *yes*? It is possible that I might live happily ever after. But Peter's eyes are the eyes of a real animal, not one which lives in a fairy tale. Has this all been my fault? Did I lead him on to expect this outcome? I should have stopped going out with him ages ago. None of this is fair. I feel as if I'm at a teenage party where spin-the-bottle is playing and I must kiss the boy or risk condemnation from all. I want to blow up like a helium balloon and sail out the window, with them looking after me, shouting: 'Come back, you must come back!' No way out, not yet. It looks like I am going to turn into someone's nightmare.

I say *yes*.

Peter pulls me to my feet. I think: 'Now I have to kiss the boy.' But he takes my hand and slides a two-banded ring on to my engagement finger. Clasped hands hold a tiny ruby heart. It looks at once trinket-like and endearing. I can see that it is old, the gold bands worn thin: someone's heirloom.

I never liked the ending of *Scuffy the Tugboat*: *Just as the little red-painted tugboat sailed past the last piece of land, a hand reached out and picked him up... Scuffy is home now with the man with the polka dot tie and his little boy. He sails from one end of the bathtub to the other...*

There is, as well, the tale from a Norwegian wood. They say that the nymph, Huldra, sometimes appeared to the woodcutters, but as they approached her *she turned her back – and vanished. Once Huldra turned her smiling face away, there was nothing.* Huldra's back was invisible.

How can I interpret this tale of my engagement? Does anyone know what I am going to do next, having imagined the look on my face as I let the ring slide onto my finger? When will I give it back? Because, naturally, that is what I am going to do. I am going to be let off this engagement. I am already engaged, inaccessible, the dial tone not operating. The Fates will take pity and claim me back before I am hacked into little bits in this world. They will excuse the short-term damage I might do.

When someone wins an argument they don't necessarily win the other party's agreement. My father won every argument he set up for me to lose, but he lost a small piece of my devotion each time. Peter thought main force would win me round. He thought he knew best how to bring my emotions to heel. I could credit him with thinking that I was hesitant because he had not shown me what his intentions were. Now that he had, of course I would agree to the rest of the contract, this entangling, this exchange, for goods and services, of the invisible.

Instead, I turn my smiling face away and leave him with nothing. I have no back, only a front, with a rictus smile. A cut-out cardboard figure glued beneath a paper moon.

We make love in the Woollahra bedroom. It is my first assisted orgasm. It feels awkward, though not because I don't know what to do. I keep thinking of the literature of love that I have read. But I have read the wrong books. I would have been better off studying for my Senior certificate rather than reading Mary McCarthy's *The*

Group, secreted in my biology folder to fool my mother. Poor Dotty in the book, having an awkward time of it with her cold lover, who afterwards tells her to get a pessary – and she thinks he is referring to a pig. Another novel, Australian this time, sticks in my head. This one has a heroine on a hilltop who farts in the middle of love-making and spoils her chances.

Poor benighted souls, hand-picked for haplessness. They make love and evade contentment; they are sad and ill-matched. One holds something in reserve and strings the other out to dry. One imagines the face of another, in place of the one under or over them.

Peter's stomach and mine make a burping sound as they rub together. I know it is inexcusable to laugh. I am not attending to what is going on. My mind is darting all over the place, a mouse plague in a feed bin that I saw once on my cousin's farm. I can smell the rubber of Peter's condom and imagine smoke coming from it as the friction increases. He is too warm and I fail to ignite. The here and now is nothing to me, although the orgasm is enjoyable in an aching, mechanical way.

I feel sadder and sadder, just like Dotty in *The Group*. I think 'Is this it? Lying here, lost in the interpretation? Can this sustain me for the rest of my days, till arthritis and heart disease do us part?'

I want more. I will not settle for the bear in *Snow White and Rose Red* who may or may not turn into a prince. That is his business, not mine. Let him extricate himself from his bearskin. My task is to cover my back from his raking claws. I turn my face towards the evanescent, the fugitive object over there, on reserve for special people. I am determined to get it.

28 Blood

I wake and sit up in the morning sunshine. I feel violent. I can feel the blood well out as if a plastic bag has broken inside me. It trickles down my thigh. I rummage in the bedclothes for my panties and use them as a wad. I look down at Peter's boxy back. It looks so personal, so intimate. I can't bring myself to touch it.

'Peter?'

He sleeps on. What apparition is he chasing in his morning dreams? Probably me.

'Shit and fuck!' The words are loud in the quiet room, but the thought of bleeding all over the bed clothes is worse than the thought of activating him.

'Peter!' I touch his back in the way a stranger taps someone on the shoulder. He reacts, opening his eyes and rolling over.

For one second he looks at me, revealed as himself. Then he says, 'Hullo Honey Babe,' smiling out of his grey-green eyes.

We have matching eyes on which he likes to comment. His colour combinations are his best feature. I like his brown hair that looks and feels like a horse's winter coat. I make a quick scan of his torso and decide that I never want to draw naked bodies. The trouble is that he is too many animals rolled into one. His genitals, for instance, spoil the line. They are cunjevoi innards, cut open for bait, though the colours are interesting, a mottled purple-blue-red. On the other hand, it's as if a star-struck squid has splashed down overnight into the crevice of his legs.

He reaches up and takes hold of the breast nearest to him. 'What are you doing up there, Honey Heart. Come over here.'

'Leave me alone.' I know I am being petulant. 'I'm bleeding to death. I haven't got any tampons.'

He rolls out of bed and starts putting on his trousers. 'I'll go and get you some. Wait there. Won't be long. Back in a tick.'

When he's in a hurry, his gait turns into an ursine roll. His arms hang far too short. I stand up on the bed to check where mine come to. As I thought, half-way down my thighs. I am re-adjusting my bloody underwear pad when he pops his head back in, stares at me in surprise and throws a toilet roll onto the bed.

I have disconcerted him. Perhaps I can disgust him. 'Oh, for Heaven's sake. I can't go round with bits of toilet paper stuck up me.'

'No, no, I'll go and get you the right things. Back in a jiffy. I'll nick down and get the papers while I'm at it.' He walks back into the room as I plump down onto the bed. 'Give me a morning kiss.'

'*Give me a morning kiss, Mum*,' I mimic in a slow drone. 'What is this, an episode of *Dad and Dave*?'

'Sarcasm is the lowest form of wit,' I can hear my father saying. But he used it all the time, just the same. Peter gives me a big kiss, ignoring my crankiness, his sorrowful eyes warm with purpose.

Left alone, I forget his details. I have him in outline, but I will never reconcile myself to his mass, his density, his chemical body. I have noticed this before. Each time I see him it is as if for the first time, a continuing shock to my system as he materialises in front of me. If he is the bear then I refuse to believe he is a prince in disguise. His common warmth presses up against the glass of my perfectionism, my critical coldness.

Even if he was a prince among Ursidae he would still say in the end: *...and you shall become my wife. Your sister Rose Red and your mother must come and live in the palace of my father, who is a King. We will make plans for the future and now we must go back to the cottage to tell Mother the wonderful news.*

'Bloody hell,' I say aloud into the dead space of the room. 'Bloody palace, bloody Mother.' I try out a few more epithets to make myself feel better.

'Bloody, bloody, shit, shit. I bet the palace is cavity brick. Fuck.'

I thought this trip to Sydney would offer something that I didn't know about and could not imagine, a reprieve from the inertia of the Brisbane suburbs. It was a liberation fantasy. But Peter has offered me nothing new, only tantalised me, then scooped me up before I can reach the sea. It is as if I had never left. We will go back home and he will place me with tender care in the bathtub where I will bob until I sink under the weight of soap scum. We will tell my mother the good news and she will live happily ever after.

'Like hell!' I am my father's daughter.

Redmond

29 The Prize

My mother was famous for saying: 'I'm absolutely certain.' Dad, with a barb in his voice, would add: 'It's her intuition.' Then she'd get it dead wrong.

We hardly talk going home. Peter is wary of my bad mood. I make the most of it. I hope he's worried about being engaged to a neurotic, hormonal tragedy. I dread arriving. The motion of the car does not lull me as usual. Instead I feel peevish and fretful. I keep imagining how it will be, getting out of the car, greeting my mother: her false surprise, her true delight. I feel tired, smothered and ugly.

A pile of newspapers lies between us on the seat. Peter stares ahead in concentration. 'There's an art prize in there.'

'Where?'

'*Sunday Mail*. You ought to go in for it.'

'What for?'

'You might win. You would win.'

'Fat chance.' I stare out the window.

As we coast down the home hill, I feel sick. Peter breaks into song: *She wears my ring...* He glances at me and squeezes my hand. *To show the world ,that she belongs to me*, he warbles. It's a second or two before I realise my mother's car is not in the driveway.

'Mum's out at golf. Don't come up.' I gather my gear into my arms. 'I feel like I'm going to throw up. I just want to go to bed.'

Peter fusses, conscientious, getting out of the car, coming round to my door, opening it, contrite, as if my bad manners are his fault. 'Got everything?' I reach out to take the newspaper. He does not seem to notice. I try to shove past him. 'See you soon, Honey Heart. Look after yourself for me. I love you.'

I don't respond. He gives me a careful hug as if I have had an operation.

I drag myself up the front steps. I can hear the dog barking inside, frenzied. The door sticks as usual and the dog falls back. She has developed cataracts that have turned her brown eyes a milky blue, but she still recognises my smell. I unlock my room, fall on the bed and stare at my engagement ring. I take it off and hide it in the zipped pocket of my bag. The cat has followed me in and sits staring up at me, her eyes intense and empty as car headlights. Cats leave a space.

'What the eye doesn't see, the heart doesn't grieve over,' I tell her. 'She won't know it from me.' I give the cat a dark stare. She curls round, one small hammy leg in the air and her eyes closed, licking her bottom with industrious concentration.

My mother's intuition is out of action. But she is certain that something is going on. She prods and probes but she finds out nothing. I keep Peter and my mother apart. I tell him that she's not very happy about the engagement (I'm so young). I say he must give her time to think about it, and that he should leave her alone for the moment. She'll get over it. I insinuate to my mother that Peter's Sydney friends are out of my league and thus hers: a fast lot. Pseudologia fantastica. Suspicion hangs in the air but the two parties are nicely on hold.

I have entered the art prize with a portrait of Christine titled *Incredible Creature*. She is in sections, the way I have always seen her. Mismatched, lots of attention on her knees. I feel my intuition racing. Something is pressing in.

I leave things to the last minute. I get my mother to help me take my painting to the gallery at Toowong. This is a sop for her, because she has missed out on the engagement jackpot. She believes she is the organiser of my fate. She is full of intentions for me. As we walk in, my mother fussing, with one hand holding a corner of the painting (she paid for the framing), Redmond comes out of the office.

Down low, in what my father called 'your vitals', I feel a distinct thump. My mother hisses: 'I knew he worked somewhere.' Her intuition again. 'He's a dealer. He's out of advertising now.'

'Stop hissing at me.'

'Go up and say Hello. Go on – it can't hurt. I'll hold your painting.' She smiles at no-one in particular and (I can't believe it) gives me a push in the exact same way she pushed me into the classroom on my first day of school. Though I resent her interference and want nothing more than to smack her in the face, a force now pulls me forward.

I walk towards Redmond's back. He has his hand on the shoulder of the dark-haired, vivid woman I have seen him with outside the gallery. He looks sideways at her, consulting. They turn and go back into the stacks of shelved paintings adjacent to the office. I stand in the narrow doorway. He looks up. He sees me. It gratifies me when he says straight away: 'Hullo Sweetheart.' His voice is warm, as if he has never been away from me. Up so close he looks taller. The woman gives me a careful look. Redmond says something. The woman looks amused. She watches what is going on behind me.

'So you've got an entry, have you Doll? Is this your mother?'

I turn, reluctant, to see my mother lugging the painting across the floor. Redmond moves to help her.

'Well, well.' My mother is overjoyed. 'One thing leads to another. How are you, Redmond?'

'Very well – and you?' His voice resonates with colours. The woman pulls the brown paper off my painting. I stare at Redmond.

'Pamela looks after everything.' He gives the woman's shoulders a sideways hug. 'She's my little organizer.'

'Partner, Doll,' warns Pamela. She examines my painting. She exchanges a glance with Redmond. He looks surprised.

Pamela says: 'Just leave it here. It'll be right. I'll get you an invite.' She disappears into the office. Redmond looks at his watch. 'I'll see you later, Pammy,' he calls after her.

He looks down at me. His eyes are so intimate, so grown-up with their black depths, that I forget to breathe. 'I'll give you a call, Sweetheart.'

I can smell his sports coat. It exudes intoxication like a well-appointed lair. Then he goes. He leaves me with my mother.

Pamela is now on the phone. She signals me with her free hand, passes me an invitation and then turns her back on me.

Out in the hot air of the street I see Redmond getting into his red sports car. I look away. I cannot bear to watch him if he is unattached to me. He must not exist in another space. I will only be alive in his presence. Then, Lionel does not talk to me. He has receded or rather has gone underground, disappearing through the floorboards, a Rumpelstiltskin.

I do not think of love, thinking of Redmond. Rather, excitement gets in the way of love. Redmond is my dynamic. I do not think in the long-term but in the headstrong demand of the moment.

On the afternoon of the opening I meet Peter after work. I stand under the cloisters looking out over the quadrangle. It is July now and getting cold. I have on a burgundy woollen pants suit and matching court shoes with no socks. The white of my ankles shows. I have had my fringe cut and feel very Cleopatra in a blond sort of way. I have kohl eye makeup on, just like Elizabeth Taylor. I have applied liberal dots of Blue Grass perfume at strategic spots: wrist, elbow crease, behind my knees, cleavage, back of the neck.

'Pulse points,' I hear Christine say. 'Or where you might get kissed. Don't put it on your nipples.'

I am going straight to the gallery without going home. I have not told Peter the show is on, even though the invitation says '...and friend', but I have informed my mother that Peter is the friend so she can't come. She is too timid and afraid of the proprieties to barge in.

I am planning to stand Peter up. I feel steady, a premeditating assailant. A couple of plovers swoop in to land in the dusk of the quadrangle. Their shrieking is jittery and hostile. I watch them stalk around and then I see Peter rolling across the grass towards me, lumping his bulging briefcase. He takes a swipe at a plover as it runs at him. He looks stern and a little forlorn. Things aren't going right for Peter. He does not like to be on hold. He is at his genial best when he is in charge.

'You're looking very beautiful.' He sounds reluctant. 'I thought we'd just go to the pictures.' He puts his briefcase down and kisses me. I am so wooden I stand on his foot in the brief scuffle. I don't want my body to touch his.

'I can't.' I hold my breath. He looks so forbidding that I start to wheedle. 'I've got something on. It's very important to me.'

'What?'

'It's this opening. At a gallery.' I want to exclude him. I want to lock the door in his face and never let him in. 'It's that competition. I probably won't win but I've got to go. Only me,' I hear myself gabbling.

'Invitation only.'

I have run out of breath. I heave air into my chest where it feels dry and rasping. 'I don't think we should go out anymore.' My heart starts to thump, out of my control. The hen in my chest wakes up and flaps its wings, startled.

'Go *out!*' His voice is disbelieving. How could he not know? 'We're engaged, for shit's sake!'

'I know, I know,' I try to sound placating. I don't know where to go from here. I will have to make it up, because I feel nothing but an urgency to get away from him, to have done with him, to falsify the document of my life so far. He is supernumerary to my needs. He is a nothing and he doesn't know it. I want him to switch over as I am about to do and not feel the pain. Can't he be a cardboard figure like me? Why does he have to be so bloody human all the time? It's not my fault.

I didn't promise you a bloody rose garden, I say to myself. More likely a briar patch at the bottom of my tower that will scratch his eyes out and send him blind to stagger in the wilderness for years. I will never kiss him better. The witch who cut off Rapunzel's long plait and let the prince climb to his doom must have taken me over.

As I say, it is not my fault.

I shift tactics. 'I'm no good for you. We're not good for each other. It will never work.'

He has not noticed that I am not wearing his ring. I rifle through my bag and bring it out. I try to give it to him. He looks down at my hand as if I am presenting him with something poisonous, and takes a furious swipe at it. Not wanting to drop it, not wanting to enact the scene where we both stumble through the grass looking for it, I hang on tight. My right fist stings from the impact of his blow, then goes numb.

'Lucky for me you weren't still holding your briefcase.' I make my voice cold. 'That's my painting hand.'

He looks at me. I have never achieved such a look on his face before: tragic, wounded. His lower lip trembles. He starts to cry silent tears. He contorts his mouth in an effort to stop himself.

I haven't seen anyone cry since primary school. It is such a curious phenomenon that I can't bear to look. I push my hands under my fringe and cover my eyes. I know I have to do what I am doing. I am absolutely certain. This is necessity – but I don't necessarily like the effect.

A frantic fear twists me. Fear of dwindling into domesticity with this nice boy, this perfectly acceptable young man, nothing wrong with him, with his perfectly pleasant life held out to me. His blind, bland innocence of his effect on me, his trundling satisfaction with what he has to offer. He will never comprehend how he will diminish me, how I will waste away, deprived of possibilities.

I will not succumb. He will not catch me. I will chop off his head if I have to. He comes up to me and drags my hands away from my face, holding me by my wrists. He is grim and earnest but not pleading. Now he thinks he is on a winner.

'Say you hate me. Go on. If you can say it, I'll go.'

I can smell Blue Grass, released by the warmth of his big hands. Its scent makes me reckless, as if I have caught a whiff of freedom.

Inside his eyes I can see trust. But my boat is bucketing out to sea, slipping past the man with the outstretched hand, ignoring the consternation on his face. I don't care what's out there. I just have to go. Necessity defies reason, and the tug of the heart. Necessity guarantees nothing, only risk. But the decision makes itself. Remorse won't catch me in its grip. I pull my hands down. No more contact, ever. I think: 'How curious. We will not touch again for the rest of our lives.'

'I hate you.' I make my voice wooden, an actress in a dubbed film.

I watch him long enough to make sure of the impact, then I walk away down the colonnade. Everything belongs to the moment, smooth, inexorable and, as if in consort with cosmic harmony, I catch the last bus to Toowong.

Say, it's only a paper moon
Sailing over a cardboard sea

The first face I recognise in the gallery, in the crowd of art students, is Christine's painted one, up on the wall. The art students avoid my painting. There is a space in front of Christine's knees as if a ship has just left her dock. The students hang together in animated cliques, some of them holding wine glasses as if they are practising growing up. They eye me, covert, as I come in, the outsider. Dressed alike in black on black, some of them even wear French berets. Standard art school dress. I knew this would be a trial, that I would know no-one. My hands start to tremble but I stare the faces down.

I walk up to my painting of Christine and a paper plaque tells me that I have won. It is an acquisitive prize worth $400.

Pamela is busy in the crowd, talking to a group of much older people. When she sees me she walks up, brisk. 'Well, Doll, you must be pleased. I must say, it's a good portrait. Who taught you?'

'I taught myself.' I feel myself stiffen. 'I'm not an art student.'

She smiles at me as if she's worked everything out. 'I can see that. Listen Doll, come and meet this nice man over here. He's going to put you in a book. *Young Australian Art* – something like that. Here, have a wine. Something to hold onto.' She grabs a glass as she passes a drinks table. She has beautiful hands, long, boneless, tapering, with dark red nails. On one arm she wears a fat, tubular silver bangle. It gives me a twinge of envy and regret in memory of my thin, childish gold bangle.

I meet the publisher. He wears a collarless Nehru jacket and speaks with an English private-school accent. He is not unctuous but he holds my elbow as he talks. So tall that he stoops, he is a man in charge. He has a young woman in tow, whose dark hair is in a Hiawatha plait down her back. There is an older couple whose names I do not catch. The publisher mentions something about angels and treats the older couple with jovial deference. I don't care about his book. But I feel my star rising. They won't swamp me.

I catch sight of Redmond. He comes up to us and puts his hands on my shoulders. 'What did I tell you, Clive? Isn't she a beauty? My little protégé.'

His words shiver through me. Some action of the waves is tapping and surging beneath my keel but already the boundless ocean that is Redmond has buoyed me up. While one part of me promises itself that it will watch the currents, the other drifts on the swell, hypnotised by the image of landfall, a long, long way ahead under the horizon line.

At last I am riding on something I trust to carry me with it. Redmond is the monstrous curve of the world, the generous bed of the seas. As well he is flotsam whose true shape is hard to identify as it floats, tantalising, in the foam of the whitecaps.

He needs nothing because he has it all. At water level he is a man who can do things, make promises happen. I will give him a gift: myself. He will understand everything about me without my speaking. He will read me in my eyes. He is my devoted friend who knows that my imagining demands absolute concentration. He will harbour my innocence. His tenderness will be just for me. He will be my everything. When I'm with him I shall always sing in tune.

We shall not think of Lionel in his grave. We shall ignore the Brisbane clay baking him to a crust. Redmond will not want to speak of Rosie, her coke bottle outlines immured forever in her Yeronga flatette. He will have me and he will get back for me what I have lost.

Redmond likes a crowd. Redmond needs a crowd because he likes to work the room. This concept is something I decide I do not have to worry about. I think: 'They will see my work. That's enough.'

As the opening thins out, Redmond takes a large group of us to a nightclub. It's really a trumped-up pub and the same things happen in it, except it has strobe lights and a small band playing on a shallow stage. Redmond keeps close to me, settles me at a table and gives me a glass of champagne. He kisses me on the top of my head. Then he table-hops. I am happy where I am. I watch everything, and from time to time bend forward to hear what Clive and his girlfriend are saying to me. The place is noisy, so they give up after a while, with benevolent smiles. The girlfriend, who is only a little older than I am, seems friendly and as if she is sending me a message, but I suspect I am making that up.

Everyone here is busy fulfilling themselves, ardent, facing success. There are no dark secrets, no damp dungeons. No one blocks the light jingling blood-stained keys.

Redmond comes back. 'Dance?' He lifts an eyebrow.

There is a small space in front of the stage with desultory partners drifting to the cheesy music. I can't identify it. It is neither rock'n'roll nor the Pride of Erin.

Redmond is an enigmatic partner. He hardly touches me, pushing me out and twirling me round under his arm in distant intimacy. He is at his best across a table when his voice warms up and his black eyes make a covenant.

He is what my mother would call 'a party animal'. I can see his friends feel clever around Redmond. His crowd is the loudest. Other groups turn their heads to watch, as if hypnotised, as Redmond makes his way round the room. I watch him, voluble at one table, vibrant at another. He does not stop in one place for long. A woman catches at his arm as he goes by. Her face lights up as he pauses and bends his head to hear what she has to say.

After a measurable amount of time has passed, he comes up and announces that he should take me home. I am a school girl about to get delivered up to the family by a kind uncle. But when we get into his sports car he makes the turn to Auchenflower. We arrive at an old-style wooden house on stilts, with dual wooden stairs leading up to an expansive verandah.

Redmond says nothing as he ushers me in, and I have nothing to say either. What can I say? 'Aha, so you are going to make love to me after all. You have inveigled me into your lair, sirrah and I will go no further.'

I stomp up the steps after him. We walk down a long hallway and into a sparsely-furnished lounge room. There are a few chairs and a blow-up mattress over by the wall and an old heater, the sort with a cone coil. When I investigate the kitchen, the sink is full of dishes and a broken wine glass. There is a rucksack in one corner and a Formica kitchen table. There is one wooden chair painted red and one plastic-covered chair with the springs showing through. There is nothing on the walls.

I watch Redmond, my enchanter. He takes my hand and leads me to his bedroom. He does not switch on the light. Pushed against the windows is an unmade three-quarter bed. The streetlight shines in yellow rays across an unzipped sleeping bag that acts as a quilt. There are some dusty suitcases underneath the bed, and a metal tube with the lid off. What does it have in it?

He is not at his best as we get into bed. Perhaps it is the wine. I have drunk enough to make me feel that I can do anything and not worry about the consequences. He may have drunk too much.

Redmond sits on the bed, draws me to him and kisses me. He is a natural. It is a stirring kiss. But it ends too soon. It is almost as if he won't enjoy it or that it is distasteful. I worry that I might have bad breath. He takes off his shoes but leaves his socks on. Being winter they do not smell too much, although there is a slight mushroom odour in the cold air. Suddenly it comes to me. The tube reminds me of the casing for rabbit fumigant pellets that my cousin used. I want to ask Redmond why he has such a thing under his bed, but I stop myself. Now he undoes his zip and pulls me on top of him.

'Take your pants off, Sweetheart.'

I think: 'Shouldn't you be doing that, peeling them off in slow, languorous movements?'

The moment has a flavour of clinical deadness. He has taken off his trousers and his shirt and I see he wears a string singlet. *Oh, Redmond*, I grieve.

Below the dreadful singlet, in the light from the street, I can see his erection. That looks funny too, a polyp or sea worm waving around in the current. I admonish myself: *It is not really waving.* I can never harness my mind to the task. His socks, which are still on, distract me.

I am immune to people going in and out of focus, changing shape and size. At one minute Redmond is potent, supernaturally strong, his blue five o'clock shadow glowing. At the next it's as if he is a wizened elf with his straggly beard caught between two rocks.

Redmond says: 'Come and sit on me.' I have peeled down to my bra and panties but I feel too awkward to take any more off. He should be doing it for me. I climb on and straddle him and think of riding my cousin's horse into the Condamine.

'You're on the pill, aren't you?'

'Not yet.' I feel my face get hot.

He reaches down, half unseating me and comes up with the metal tube in his hand. He shakes out a tablet. 'Lie on your back.'

When I do, he pushes the rabbit fumigant into me with his finger. It starts to foam. He pulls me back onto him.

'Tickle my balls.'

I am listening to the 'Snap, crackle, pop' as the tablet effervesces inside me, but I reach behind and give them a desultory tickle. Nothing much is happening for me, so I lean down to kiss him. He is reluctant and keeps his eyes open all the way down until we are staring at each other. There is something immutable in his eyes. Behind the facade of attention is a black stone obelisk. I draw back, feeling as if I have by mistake crossed some boundary to a place where I am not welcome.

Redmond tugs at my white Cottontails so I take them off. He grabs my hips and sits me on his erection. That, at least, is exciting and he slips into me. We start lovemaking and just as I am getting close to orgasm, he groans and stops. No more movement. I wait for him to encourage me, but he lies there looking blank and uneasy.

'Hey, Sweetheart, did you come? I'm too sensitive for you to sit there too long.'

'You didn't quite get me, if that's what you mean.'

My words fall into a sudden hollow. I roll off and he lets me lie on his arm.

'It's called coming, Sweetie. That's your department. I've never had any trouble with my sexuality.' He sounds huffy.

I want to cry. I feel exposed, out of my depth, bobbing with my chin just out of the water. Are there things I don't know yet? Are there predatory creatures in this sea that are only now emerging out of the black depths? Is this sophisticated sex, cool and clinical, every man for himself? It must be. I will have to get good at it. Is this the love that will keep me afloat only if I do not apply the stranglehold of panic?

I shall will myself to float, detached. I shall appear serene. I shall keep swimming with Redmond, whatever happens. He will not leave me behind, to be picked off in the shallows.

It is late. It must be near two in the morning. We get up and Redmond makes tea. The light coming in the kitchen window has changed to a predawn grey. Redmond says I can stay if I want, but as with Christine, all I want to do is go to my familiar bed. He says he will drive me home. As he makes the tea he is so sophisticated that I find a new calm. With Redmond I will have detachment from the banal.

He goes out of the room and I can hear him lifting up objects on the hall table. He comes back in, feeling in his trouser pockets. 'I can't find my car keys.' He is the soulful illusionist who has missed his trick. He runs his hands through his hair, distracted, then rubs his face. Now that he has his clothes back on he looks tousled and handsome.

'I'll have to call you a cab.'

'That's OK. It doesn't matter.' I use my coolest voice. I know he is lying. Anyway, I don't want him to drive me home. I just want to be by myself and think.

Soon he walks me down to the waiting taxi. He opens the door and I get in. He does not move to kiss me but gives me a salute as the cab moves off. He should have white gloves on his conjurer's hands. The cab driver ogles me in the rear vision mirror. I give him my address and refuse to talk.

As we cross the river and pass Paul's ice-cream factory, a rosy glow suffuses the skyline. I remember how my father used to watch me learn to swim. Every summer morning in the five-thirty dark he drove me down to the baths at South Brisbane for a lesson with the best coach in Queensland.

I have a hard ache behind my breastbone that wants to travel up my throat. I swallow and think of nothing, and it almost goes away.

30 Bluebeard's Wives

I did not hear from Redmond for five months. I saw him a few times in the near distance as I passed through Toowong on my way to work. It was beneath my dignity to ring him. Or rather I could not think of a good enough pretext on which to call which would save my dignity.

I began a painting of my parents. I called it *Two Little Fishes in Fish Shaped Dishes*. It depicted my mother and father standing in their habitual kitchen corners. From the waist down they were fish and their tails curled into sardine tins. I made much of the rolled-back tins and the metal keys. Their eyes were huge and shallow. Their glassy stares were not for each other. My father's eyes were beginning to dry out and his mouth was half-open in a gasping attitude. He held a glass of golden whisky in one hand, and his other elbow was propped up on the kitchen bench. By contrast, my mother's eyes were still wet but her tail was patchy, the opalescence dimming.

I began by painting thin washes of acrylic. Each dried quickly. After I had developed a satisfactory ground to work into, I smeared wax medium onto the canvas. I began to find the forms with oil stick, mixing the oily pigment into the wax with my fingers. I applied some ground-up pumice to a small area around my father's eyes to make them appear dry and gritty. The mix created a watery shine, transparent and deep. I started to develop the knack of dimensional layering, pushing the paint with my fingers.

I found a roll of fine flywire in my father's workshop. I cut a piece and sewed it on an area of background with fishing twine, making the knots my father had used when fishing had been his passion. I said out loud in my empty bedroom: 'I've taken your gear, Dad. What do you think about that?'

The hatching of the flywire created a sense of imminence, as if the sea had come right up to the kitchen windows, the waterline visible and with a storm brewing out over the Pacific. It threatened to overtake my parents in their domestic vacuum.

It was my first large painting. I had spent some of my prize money on canvas and even paid to have it stretched by one of Pamela's minions. I decided not to have this work put in a frame so painted right round the edges. I hung it on my bedroom wall and extended the waterline onto the wallpaper.

I knew I would see Redmond again. I just had to wait.

I started on a series of small paintings of marine life. First the translucent yabbies turning somersaults in their contained sea inside the silver billy-can. Then one of soldier crabs as they emerged at low tide on the Tallebudgera flats. I got the milky, ceramic blue of the soldier crabs just right. It was almost the same blue as the electricity insulators I had tried to paint. For a moment I re-ran the film clip of Peter.

'Child's play,' I said to the empty room, dismissing him. 'I'm in the big league now.'

'Did you call me?' my mother sang in her dog-calling voice. She hung about in the hallway outside my locked room. I had let her in since I had won my prize. I knew she would now be more likely to condone the devastation of the room, the painted and smudged wallpaper, in the name of successful art.

'Incidentally,' my mother has snuck up on me and hovers in the doorway, 'I hear he drinks a lot. And they say he's had a lot of girlfriends.'

'Who are you talking about?'

'You know who.'

This was, for her, strong interference. She surprised me. I believed, divorced or not, she thought Redmond was a good catch.

'Bloody old golf biddies.'

'I'll ignore that remark.'

'Go right ahead.' I thought she would stop then, but she returned to the attack.

'I don't know why you don't go out with that nice fellow Peter any more,' she whined. 'You're just throwing your chances away.'

'Mind your own beeswax.'

'Mark my words.' She wagged her finger at me and I thought of a chicken bone. 'They were always a moody lot. The whole family. I hope you don't live to regret it.'

I paid no attention to her.

The waiting game. All things come to those who wait. The dissatisfied will triumph. The needy will go to the front of the queue. All the same, my father's sardonic voice hung, incorporeal, in the air. 'Had a nibble?' he enquired. A moment later. 'Nuh, looks like a snag.'

I had been to the Toowong Gallery once or twice, on the pretext of getting advice on stretching canvas, once to talk about Clive's book. Each time Pamela had greeted me and there had been no sign of Redmond. Pamela was friendly in a breezy way as if she cared about nothing, as if the concourse of relationships was a passing parade. Underneath her casual manner she was intense, but I couldn't work out where her passion lay. She was efficient and ambitious for the gallery and had a good eye for the up-and-coming.

'Fostering talent, Doll. Nothing pays better.'

It was the under-layers I couldn't see.

'Drinkies?' She proffered a plastic cup. It was ten on a Saturday morning. Perhaps her intensity was from alcohol. 'Or do you wait until the sun is over the yardarm?' Her eyes looked amused.

'I might wait, thanks Pammy.'

She seemed to like my work. 'You ought to be thinking of your first show, Doll. What have you got? Got enough for the big room? Got to move it and shake it, Doll. Don't wait to be asked in this game.'

I mumbled that I had some things. I had started a portrait of her from photographs I had taken as she moved round the gallery. I liked working from photos. I liked the way the camera caught people in flagrante delicto, surprised by life.

I had filled the gap that was Redmond's absence with work. I couldn't get away from it. The ideas rushed in, tidal ripples up a beach, one after another. 'Immersed, that's what I am,' I told myself. I felt strong and energetic, the best I had ever felt. My usual sensation of emptiness had left me. Sometimes I even chatted to my mother without getting bored. When I was home I never left my room for long. This waiting at the same time made me feel that I was full of violence which only work could discharge.

The painting I liked most from that period was one of my father's hands, his nicotine-stained fingers, his short nails as they pushed the knot tight on the dangling fish hook. Squatting on the sand, he was there only from the waist down, his khaki shorts pushing against the golden hairs on his thighs. I drew my legs as I stood beside the cane fishing basket, watching and waiting. They were transparent. Behind us the sea had crept up, showing a thin line of sneaking foam.

Pamela came round to our house near the end of that time to see what I had. She breezed past my mother who contorted herself with a combination of wary frostiness and obsequiousness.

Pamela laughed at her portrait, and surveyed the rest of the paintings.

'Well, we'll get you started, eh Doll? You cut corners, but it works. Bring them in and we'll set you up for a solo. Big room, I think. You have been working, haven't you?' And she marched out.

I knew all about empty waiting, impaled on other people's promises. This was different. This was a gap where potential steadied itself. One day, soon, Redmond would glance, surprised, as I broke free from my papery shell. Soon, as I hovered on my drying wings, he would stop to notice the unfolding transformation. Then he would say, as he extended one finger of his hand: 'I must have you, you beautiful, delicate thing.' And that would be that.

In any season the colour red does not suit Brisbane. In winter, bloodrust poinsettias, with their dirty cream centres, look as if bird droppings have landed in them. In early December the colours of heat emblazon the already scorched city. Orange-red poincianas blare, parched and dusty. In wilted front gardens nothing stands up except dry red gerberas.

I had been doing some half-hearted Christmas shopping on my way home from checking with Pammy at the gallery. I knew my mother expected a Christmas present, even though she told me: 'Don't bother about me this year. Save your pennies.' I expected a present too, but not from her.

The shop windows in Queen Street were garish with Christmas decorations. Santa and his sleigh reared in a promising arc, with

Rudolf's red nose a pulsating neon stop sign. People hesitated at the entrance to Allen & Stark, where the air-conditioning gushed out a frigid blast. An unfriendly Santa, sweating and scratchy in his woolly suit was having a cigarette in a doorway next to Coles. When I crossed the intersection at North Quay, I had to avoid patches of road tar and blobs of chewing gum that had melted.

When I got home I tipped the cat off the quilt and lay on my hot bed. It felt as if I was grilling. The room was empty now of paintings. I tried not to think about my show, opening tomorrow, about what might happen. The combination of possibilities buzzed round me. I knew Redmond would have to be there. I knew it would happen the way I wanted, as if by magic.

I was picking chewing gum off the sole of my high-heeled shoe when I heard the phone ring in the hallway. My mother answered it. Then her steps came up the hall to my door. 'It's for you.'

Her voice was sepulchral through the keyhole. I waited for her to go away, then came out. I knew she would have a miffed look on her face. I knew she would listen at the servery door.

'Hullo, who's that?' I knew who it was.

'Hi there, Sweetheart. How've you been?' I could almost breathe in his voice. It was so pungent, redolent of the Redmond who lived in my head.

'Busy,' I said gamely.

'What are you doing tonight? Can you meet me at the Regatta? There'll be a crowd of us there. We'll do something later.'

As if there had been no five months of silence.

'Sure,' I hoped I sounded blasé.

On the airy instant I accepted everything. My stomach lurched as if I was on the ferris wheel at the Ekka. I saw Redmond dressed in a cool suit of silver tinsel. I saw his face, his eyes, his foxy hair. I subtracted everything that did not fit the picture: his thin hands, his imperviousness that lurked in the shadows, that breath of burning coldness. I was left with what I liked. His rangy dissatisfaction, his practical awareness, his edgy, charming bonhomie. He was the other half of me, the completed, assured reflection in the mirror.

Yes, it's only a canvas sky
Hanging over a muslin tree...

This sensation I felt seemed to come from the inside and spread out towards Redmond, my perfect, illusory object. An inexorable amoeba engulfing a shadowy phagocyte. Almost nothing to do with him. Almost as if it could have been any other. But it wasn't. He was particular, identified, sought-after. No-one else would do. I was heading straight towards his beckoning hand, eyes wide open.

I think now that this feeling was hope of recognition, hope transformed into certainty, oblivious to the odds. I was addicted to my desire that the oceanic be personalised, given over to someone who I believed would deal out whatever I wanted. Free attention, on-call desire, benign, generous – because he who desires you in return is as besotted as you are.

I dismissed the shadow of Peter, who may have felt the same about me. This sensation was for special people like me and Redmond, and anyway, it struck at random. Nothing to do with me. I was after unity, the annihilation of all discord.

'You've fallen hard,' admires the voice of Christine from her hot bedroom under the creaking tin roof. But I ignore her too.

I borrowed money from my mother, who looked dubious. Then I took a taxi right across town to get there on time.

There was a crowd at the pub. Some journalists Redmond knew, Pamela, Clive, his girlfriend, some University people and the art group. I didn't try to talk to them. I couldn't really take them in except for Pamela, who said over her shoulder: 'Hullo, Doll. Have a drink.' Clive's girlfriend smiled at me. I discovered she was called Sweetie. They introduced me to Jason Somebody who was an artist. He had curly blond hair, wore a cape (or was it a mantle?) and an air of mystical importance.

Redmond kissed me on the lips and I saw Pamela watching us from across the room. He looked unattainable in his handsomeness, a prize I had received by mistake. The planes of his face, the lines of his mouth mesmerised me. I felt warm and cosseted, charged-up and apprehensive all at once. I wondered if he had seen my pictures that Pammy had hung the day before. I couldn't ask him. Tomorrow it would open. I had not seen the completed hanging myself, wanting the shock to hit me as I walked into my first solo exhibition. Redmond said nothing, but there was plenty of time when we could be alone later. My sense of something having started was strong.

Clive put his arm around the back of my chair, not quite touching my shoulders. 'Big day for you both tomorrow. We'll be there, won't we Sweetie?'

Sweetie nodded and smiled at me with her large, hurt, trapped eyes.

Clive beamed at me. 'He'll go far, that Jason. Fire in his belly.'

I looked at him. Why was he talking about bloody Jason? It was going to be *my* day. I didn't care if Jason dropped off the edge of the world using his cape as a parachute. Pamela had shown me some of his paintings that she had in the stacks: landscapes in the Romantic manner with hazy red cliffs. He was a bad Antipodean Turner. There were also dolly-bird nudes of his current girlfriend.

I smiled at Clive who appeared to want to jolly me along. I saw Pamela looking across at me again.

Clive and Redmond went off to the bar and Sweetie put her drink on the table, leant over her knees and spoke in a low voice.

'You're not going to marry Redmond, are you?'

'No, of course not. I hardly know him. Well, I used to know him ages ago, when I was a kid.' I couldn't explain any more. It was getting too complicated.

Sweetie stared at me, interested. 'That's OK then. I just thought I should warn you... I don't want to interfere. I don't really mean warn. I don't know what I mean. I'm just being silly. Clive's always telling me I carry on about nothing.' She smiled, shamefaced. 'The men are in charge, aren't they? I don't know what I'm talking about.' She smeared her wet glass mark with her finger.

'But what if I did? What's wrong with him?'

'Nothing's wrong with him. He's gorgeous. Clive thinks the world of him.' She wiped her finger on the edge of her dress. 'He's a real sexpot, isn't he?' She smiled up at me. 'It's just that... I don't know – he's used to getting his own way or something. He got hurt once and it really changed him, Clive reckons.'

'Yes, Rosie, you mean. I used to live next door.'

'Oh,' said Sweetie on an ascending note.

I felt my face getting hot. This was not the image of me I wanted, the hanger-on, the little kid. Sweetie seemed nice but I thought she might tell Clive everything. And I knew it was probably going to be important to impress Clive.

Now Sweetie was backtracking. 'I'm not saying he's selfish or anything... don't take any notice of me. You'd know what Redmond's like, then. You don't need me to tell you. Anyway, Clive says I'm hysterical.'

She moved away as Pamela changed seats and sat beside me. I could see Redmond across the room talking to a University type who was leaning forward and poking him in the chest as he spoke.

Pamela turned to me, 'Listen Doll, you'd better know. You're in the smaller room. Not my idea. Not my idea at all. I want you to know that. Whatever else, I like your work. You're good.'

'What do you mean, the smaller room? I'm having a solo, aren't I?' I felt a creeping sensation in my calf muscles.

'Well, Doll, it was decided you mightn't be able to carry the space on your own.' Pamela was watching me. 'So we gave Jason the big room. Look Doll, you might be disappointed, but just between you and me, you'll steal the show. You're way ahead of him, Doll. You're exceptional, in my opinion, but some people have a hard time handling heavy stuff. You're very intense, Doll. Wouldn't hurt sometimes to lighten up a bit and learn some footwork.'

'Who decided? Was it Clive?'

Pamela looked disappointed. 'It was a Gallery decision.'

She shook out a cigarette and offered me one. I took it, my hands shivering, and she lit up for both of us. I dragged back on it and felt better. I took a large swallow of my gin and tonic and then another. Pamela went off to work the room. My hands stopped shaking. I placed my empty glass down next to Sweetie's smear mark. No-one was coming near me. Redmond had parked me at a table while everyone else was now standing in groups.

The drinking session went round and round. The academic still had Redmond caught up with him. I didn't have the nerve to walk over to join them. As each minute passed I felt more paralysed. Clive came back with another gin and tonic.

'Good girl.' He patted me on the shoulder.

They left me alone. Some of the crowd gave me sidelong glances.

Finally Redmond came over with the Professor, who swayed over me holding an opened bottle of champagne at a dangerous angle.

'Sweetheart, this is Henry. Henry's going out to the public sector, so he's celebrating.' Redmond, behind Henry, winked at me.

I thought, *Don't wink at me Redmond, as if I'm an acquaintance.*

'Henry's a friend of the arts.'

'Hi.' I gave him my most unimpassioned smile. Henry looked offended but sat down next to me, put his swollen hand on my knee and ogled my breasts.

'How's it going, girlie. You're very succinct. Got a kiss for your Uncle Henry?'

'No, I'm not your niece.'

'Oho!' thundered Henry. 'What've we got here, Red, a femmo?'

Redmond laughed the suggestion away.

Fuck it, why should I have to lighten up? I vowed to myself. *Not to this creep, not ever.* 'Can I have some champagne?'

'You surely can, my dear,' slurred Uncle Henry. 'Here we go.' And he picked up someone's used glass that had held red wine and sloshed champagne into it. It turned a rather nice pink.

'And a cigarette.' This time he tilted himself from the waist in a courtly gesture and lit one for me. I blew a stream of smoke over his left shoulder, as close to his ear as I could get it.

'I didn't know you smoked.' Redmond said.

'Sure do.' This time I gave Uncle Henry my warmest smile. 'I do everything.'

Henry patted my knee. 'Good girl. You've got a good one here, Red. You look after her. Right?'

Redmond's smile at him was stilted, but then he turned his gaze on me. There was an immense landscape of intimate promise in Redmond's black eyes. I drank some more champagne. Uncle Henry was drab social material, but with Redmond next to me again the situation had to improve.

Now Redmond was staring across the room again. He reminded me of a roan stallion, headstrong. It was hard to hold his attention for long. He fixed his interest on the open gate, the last fence.

Pamela came over and put her hand on his arm, a small signal between them. Then she took him away. I tried not to mind. They were business partners, after all. I felt dizzy. Henry was leaning forward gloating over my breasts as if they were a plate of liver put in front of a hungry dog.

I made a decision. I stood up.

'Well, I must be off to the loo.' I drank down the rest of my champagne and gave the glass to Henry, who took it, dumb. I stared at him and felt my rage rising.

'But look, why don't you have a feel, since you're so keen.' I took his free hand and plunged it down the scoop neck of my black top. He was holding tight to the glass so I fished his hand out for him and walked away, threading through the tables. I smiled as I passed through the staring crowd. I had always wanted to be one of them, but it was too late to worry now. Down the steps I went, hanging onto the railing to steady myself. At the lower level the fresh air hit me. I felt overpowering nausea. I just had time to lock myself into the toilet cubicle and get the seat up before I vomited.

I stayed there for a long time with my eyes closed. I thought I might faint. Inside my head the black swirled round and round in concert with the contents of my stomach. Every so often I vomited some more until I was dry retching. I tried standing up but fell back to my knees. In the distance I could hear someone speaking my name.

'You OK, Doll?'

'Go away.'

'Open up, Hon,' Sweetie's voice wheedled, 'and we'll get you out of there.'

'I can't.' I started to cry. I could hear my weak sobs and felt ashamed.

'Stupid. I can't stand up, stupid.' I giggled. Somehow it all seemed silly and I wondered why I had done any of it: getting drunk, being rude to Uncle Henry, bothering to get upset about anything at all. Let them have it their way.

'You're all shits,' I called out through the swirls in my head.

'Don't be like that, Doll.'

I heard Pammy conferring, then there was the sound of metal on metal and the door swung open. Pamela and Sweetie hauled me to my feet. Before I closed my eyes again I saw that Sweetie, holding a ten-cent piece, looked concerned, Pamela ironic. They each got under a shoulder and frog-marched me to the door. Outside, I opened my eyes for a fraction of a second and saw Redmond's feet and his trouser bottoms. They were grim, the way I imagined a policeman's feet would look apprehending a criminal.

It's all my fault, a voice moaned in my ear. *I'm the one to blame.* But the voice didn't belong to me. It was my mother's. I closed my eyes. In the dark, I felt calm.

They dragged me outside. Redmond opened the car door and they deposited me face down on the back seat. I heard Redmond's voice. 'Thanks, girls. I'll be right.'

You'll be right? I thought, aggrieved. *Think about yourself, why don't you.* Redmond slammed the door and we moved off. I started crying, thinking of my father and our night drives, so unlike this one.

'Gee Sweetheart.' Redmond spoke from the front seat. He half-turned and patted me on the shoulder. The car swerved and my heart lurched, remembering him saying those same words when he hit me with his golf ball.

'Can it, will you? I hate a crying drunk.'

31 *Exhibiting Symptoms*

'I blame myself.' My mother took responsibility for her fate, her genetics, my father's disregard, her stupidity and vulnerability. 'It's my own fault,' she repeated, over and over, when it was obvious that some of the fault was not hers at all.

Did she derive perverse pleasure from such expansive owning-up? Was this all she could own? It's easy enough to believe you are the sole cause of your own distress. None of us is as different from our mothers as we might think. The same symptoms persist.

I stayed the night at Redmond's. I missed my single bed.

'Don't do that to me again.' Redmond is now wearing a pair of faded jeans and a T-shirt that is too short. 'That was pretty embarrassing, in front of my friends.' He makes a comical face. 'Don't make me feel I can't take you out in public.'

'Don't be ridiculous.' I just manage to get the words out. I am sitting on the red kitchen chair, wrapped in his dressing gown. The gown is a terrible colour, grey with coin spots. The morning sun, angled through the window, is already strong enough to ricochet off the sink and dazzle my eyes. 'They're certainly not my friends. Especially not that creep Henry.'

'You'll have to clean up your act, Sweetheart.' Now he sounds less indulgent. 'Henry's an important man to know. He has an interest in the gallery. So has Clive.' He leans at me, his shoulders hunched.

This is a different Redmond. I start to feel frightened. Nice Redmond, charming Redmond begins to seem a phantom. Perhaps I have been stupid. This is a grown-up world after all.

'Henry has contacts. He'll put in a good word for me when I go overseas.' His words settle at my feet, blank and busy pigeons.

'Go overseas?'

'Yes. In a couple of months. To London.' He crosses his arms. 'I was thinking of asking you to come with me.' He stretches his lips back and presses his thumbnail in between his front teeth. When he sulks, with that touch of danger, he looks remote and glamorous.

I am silent. I can't bear him to be angry with me. How long has he been planning this move? He scratches his stomach and stares into the sink. I can see the whorls of hair round his belly-button. I think of having sex with him, good sex this time. My resolve to stand up for myself no longer seems such a good idea.

'I couldn't go, anyway. What would I do for money?'

I get up and walk over to him. I have brushed my teeth with his toothbrush and feel sure I don't smell of sick. Standing on tiptoes to look in his high shaving mirror I think I don't look too bad once I have rubbed the mascara smudges off with spit. Now I attempt to wind my arms round his neck in the best movie tradition. He stands there, reluctant to respond, so that I hang off him like a leech. I look up into his eyes and he stares back, his pupils contracting. I feel an urgency to warm him up, cuddle away his coolness, hold him in my arms, kiss his eyelids.

'I'm sorry. It's just that it upset me when I found out Clive had relegated me to the small room. I won't do that again.'

His eyes change. I proffer my mouth for a kiss. I can see his pupils expanding as he bends his head. Are his eyes black or dark blue? They are a colour I can't name, as if they aren't a colour at all.

When he kisses with purpose I think of it as a spermatozoid kiss. A wave of wrigglers surge down my body and land, tiny arrowheads, just above my pubic bone. I feel a distinct thud as they connect.

We make love in an armchair in the lounge room, a strategic position for him but not much good for me. I can't get any traction with the chair arms in the way. I long for his bed, for a room where the sun is shut out, where we can lie in coiled and tender luxury. Making love with Redmond is turning out to be a magician's promise. I might have to train myself to orgasm just by looking at him.

There is something, so far, about sex with Redmond, which is edgy and unsure, as if we are doomed to be uneasy strangers in bed. The trouble is, that although he is dutiful about foreplay, he doesn't seem to equate it with pleasure. An automatic touch with no feel to it, a means to an end.

'Do you like that, what I'm doing?' he enquires. He sounds dispassionate. I say, 'Yes' and then he stops as if there is no further need.

He grills me afterwards. 'Did you come?' When I say no, he sulks, so I say: 'It's OK, though. It's nice.' More silence that I rush to fill. 'I'm sure I will next time.'

I smile at him and he looks relieved of an awkward burden. I am learning fast.

Afterwards he becomes expansive and talks about what he wants to do. I stare at his profile as he daydreams about himself and I think: *You are so beautiful you are like a contagious disease, Redmond.*

He has myriad short term plans. He does not mention his long-range plans. London is prominent in his talk, and a job in the Victoria and Albert Museum. Also the contacts he will make.

We sit apart. He looks relaxed now, satiated. He does not seem to want to cuddle me. More than a physical space lies between us. I get up and try to lie over him, draped from head to foot, but he says: 'Don't smother me, Sweetheart, it's too hot'. He shrugs me off.

I crave warmth from him, but begin to settle for what I can get. What do I know? What will I ever have that is better than racy and cool? This is maybe how the adult world operates. Sex like same-day dry cleaning. Deposit in the morning and pick up at night in a plastic bag, with a whiff of chemicals the only after-effect. Clinical but clean, the job done.

We go, that evening, to my opening. If I feel anything, I feel subdued. This crowd I now move in impresses my mother. It shows on her face. She looks so out of place she embarrasses me. I feel superior to her. I have begun to see that nothing is how it looks, that all sorts of sub-plots and dramas are in play. I will have to rely on Redmond to be my guide.

I sense an undercurrent of tension and reserve from the gallery inner circle, but receive praise from strangers. I even get a rave review in the *Courier-Mail*. Redmond mentions that he has spoken to the Arts Editor.

'Most people would die for a review like that, Doll,' Pamela says. Redmond stands beside her and says nothing.

When we are alone I get up the courage to press a response from him.

'Clive thinks you're a bit domestic. I don't necessarily agree with that. Henry thinks you're an interesting woman painter.'

'Yes, but what do you think?'

'I've told you, Sweetie.'

I tell myself I am paranoid and childish. I shouldn't expect him to lavish praise on me. He has a professional's response. I am lucky to have it.

Each time I go home I take something back with me to Redmond's place, like a squirrel filching nuts. After a few weeks most of my clothes have disappeared out of my bedroom cupboard. I take some books, a few at a time, my camera and some sketching materials. My mother watches my manoeuvres with narrowed eyes.

Although by now I sleep at Redmond's place every night, I have not moved my painting gear. He hasn't offered a place for me to work, and I feel uneasy asking him. Nothing is official about our relationship. It just drifts.

He gives me the impression that I must not intrude on him, that I must give him space. That he takes up most of my space is, I suppose, my decision.

I am not doing much work. If I think about that I feel flat and panicky.

Apart from Redmond's core group of long-time colleagues, there is Pamela. Pamela lives in a sliding transition zone between intimate confidante and business partner. I can't pin her down to one role. She accepts or ignores the fact that I am Redmond's girlfriend with breezy nonchalance.

Although Redmond is known for drawing new people into his circle, I don't find it easy to fit myself in. If I suggest we go down the coast for the day or out for a lazy lunch, so that we can be together alone, he has a better idea that always involves other people. He does all the organising and after a while I get into the habit of believing I can't think of anything smart or fun. I start to think I am not adept at enjoying myself.

His expression implies that any attempt at positive action on my part takes something away from his male pride. I don't know how this operates, so I can never identify when I am going to trip over it. Easier, simpler, safer to be passive. I don't want him to think I'm a feminist.

Sometimes he says to me, looking bored and put-upon: 'Well, what would you like to do?' I feel as if I am on trial, so I say: 'Nothing in particular. Nothing really. I'll leave it up to you.'

If sometimes I hit on the right balance with Redmond, I get the sense that he loves me, though there is a confusion growing in my mind between love and the taking of pleasure. I am so glad, however, to be out of the stultifying burrow of my mother's house that I don't challenge much.

Some days I feel Redmond stretches me so tight I will snap. Once or twice I catch myself pining for a night out with Christine, for not having to be so alert all the time.

But she would not fit in here. I'll never get Christine back, just as I have lost the boxy refuge of my single bed.

I get used to Redmond's dissatisfaction, his drivenness. It's as if he is aiming hard for an invisible target, as if he wants to gobble the future. This restless, pointless energy makes me want, on the contrary, to laze around, inert. Then just when I think he might have started to like being alone with me he'll say: 'I can't sit around all day, Sweetheart, doing nothing. This will never win me the Nobel Prize.'

My inertia simply makes him morose. Sometimes I want to say, 'I'm not doing nothing. I'm being with you.' But I always give in. I don't want him to find me boring.

It takes a while for me to realise he has no interest in my art. I force myself to reconsider. Why would he? He's surrounded by artists every day. I know I feel wounded and at a loss that he's not more attentive to what I do, but I let the thought go. I don't need him to look over my shoulder in any case. He spends an inordinate amount of time visiting other artists' studios but I know he is talking business.

One afternoon in bed he says: 'Your sort of stuff, don't get me wrong, Sweetheart: it's good.' He pats my head, turns to kiss me on the nose. 'But it's not really up my alley.'

'But this is what I do. You say it's good but now you sound as if you don't like it.'

'You've got to look at the market. This navel-gazing – it won't sell,

Sweetie.' He is my only guide. He lies back, staring at the ceiling. 'I'm only giving you good advice.'

It is a while before I understand that he seldom thinks to do anything solely to please me. Our social life revolves around contacts and business, his tight-knit coterie, his amorphous and shifting collection of acquaintances. We do not often have fun, he and I, by ourselves. His world is sharp and fast, with little relaxation or the silly enjoyment of life. Picking me as his companion, one who has been led to believe that simple pleasures are for inferior people, is a masterstroke.

32 Defiance

'EEYEES RIGHT!' our primary school teacher yells from the verandah as we parade across the asphalt quadrangle. 'SAL-UTE THE FLAG!' From facing straight ahead our necks click right and our eyes swivel in unison as we raise our hands to the sides of our heads. The boys pull their thumbs back like triggers and blow their brains out. The girls giggle.

Except for me. I hate a parade. Thinking myself hidden in the mob, I refuse to salute or turn my eyes. I get into trouble and a teacher drags me out. She makes me stand on the verandah by myself with my face turned to the wall.

My defiance arrives unasked. I feel shamed, getting into trouble with the teachers. Most of the time I hang around them with an eye to winning favour. I long to fit in with my classmates and be popular. The contradiction twists under my hand. The hook will not latch into the eye.

Even my classmates are censorious. I have contravened some rule. I have gone too far. I have usurped the boys' role. I am not a proper girl. They form a ring round me, circling and taunting. I am the eye of the storm.

'You've got to salute the flag,' says one girl I particularly hate. 'That's the Queen.'

'You've got to love the Queen or you'll get in trouble.' Puling Caroline adjusts her hair ribbon.

'You're stupid,' contributes a bigger boy and pushes me. Behind him, two younger boys chant my name. They make monkey gestures and mimic combing their hair for lice.

We are standing under the school building. The wooden school rooms sit high up on cement poles. Wooden slats that throw confusing zebra stripes of sunlight across the cement floor enclose the persecutory space underneath. It forms a dry playground with benches round the walls where we sit to eat our lunch. School monitors forbid us to rise from the benches until the bell rings for play. Then they allow us to do skipping, play Elastics or throw tennis balls until the going-in bell tolls. Because of the cement floor and cement poles dotted through the space they do not let us run.

A smaller boy eyes me, then jumps into the circle and shoves. 'Sissy!' he hisses.

I put up my hand to his face, shove back and run out of the circle. I skid on some sand and smack into a cement pole. I feel the impact on the bridge of my nose. Blood courses down my face and onto my favourite dress that has Jiminy Crickets printed on it. My nose goes numb and buzzing, but apart from that it isn't painful. My playmates stare at me and someone runs to get a teacher. What I can't see are my instantaneous two black eyes. The teacher deputises an older girl to walk me home – which is just as well. By the time I get there my eyes have swollen to purple slits. It is difficult to see out.

I stay away from school for two weeks. The local doctor, who has just taken delivery of an X-ray machine, asks my father to help him set it up so he can X-ray my face.

'Bloody ratbag,' my father pronounces. 'Mucking about with 10,000 volts.'

He must have assisted, because they find a hairline fracture across the bridge of my nose. Did those photoelectrons, passing through and ionizing my tissues, change anything? They didn't change my attitude. I still stare straight into the eyes of the beast. I have not learnt to drop my gaze. I still hope for inclusion but break out of the circle. I still taunt the ethers and refuse to conform. I still defy and run. The pole is always there.

33 Fine Print

Imagine two peas in a pod. Side by side, their inner surfaces touch. They grow together, yet each has an independent stalk. On that inside edge they dent each other. Enjoying the constant touch of their green skins in mutual compatibility, they each experience the empty space on the other side. They plump out into this curving horizon to the benefit of both. The pea shell that encases them expands as they grow larger and juicier. As they ripen the case dries and cracks until they fall out into the universe.

That was how I imagined Redmond and I would be. Two green peas in a pod.

I did not check this scenario with Redmond. I had no wish to sound young and silly. There never seemed a propitious moment to bring up how we would be. We never discussed *us*. I became afraid of saying the wrong thing. The balance seemed to tip so easily between harmony and disruption. 'Words are weapons,' I told myself, but they still droned round behind the windowpane in my skull.

My father had said often enough: 'You're pigheaded, just like your mother.' It's true that once I faced something I did not turn round – not even if the situation was different from my first estimation. Call it pig faith, call it bloodymindedness, call it caught by the quizzical snout.

Redmond compared himself to those who had made it – in particular, Clive. He epitomised for Redmond the successful life. Clive was on some important Arts Board, whose name I had immediately forgotten. This took him overseas. He was also the youngest member, Redmond said, of the Board of Trustees of the Queensland Art Gallery, and something to do with the University colleges. He went to London once a year and stayed in Mayfair, where he had inherited his mother's flat.

'Clive knows just about every art guru in London,' Redmond told me. 'If you've got contacts, you're home and hosed.'

I wasn't sure where Redmond was headed. Once I asked him a direct question but he warned me off.

'Don't pin me down so hard, Sweetie. I hate a nag.'

My support for his ambition was loyal and silent. I wanted to see him get where he wanted and be content. Then, I imagined, it would be plain sailing and I could get on with my work. It would be easy. I could tag along, hang on his arm and still do my own thing.

Most afternoons after work I'd go to his place and wait for him. When I heard his footsteps up the back stairs I'd arrange myself to look nonchalant as he came into the kitchen. Sometimes he'd look at me as if I was a parcel delivered to the wrong address. 'Oh, you're here, are you?'

After a few minutes of ranging restlessly through the house he'd stop in a doorway.

'I'm seeing some people at the pub.' There would be a pause as if he was making up his mind and I'd wait for him to say: 'Want to come?'

Most days his breath smelt of beer, so I knew he had been to the pub already. I was never sure if he was going to include me. One night he said:

'Business meeting, Sweetheart. You'll be right here, won't you?'

'Sure,' I gave him a bright, competent smile. I would not let myself feel bereft.

I knew nothing about business or running a gallery. I did not care about things like that. I just wanted us to be happy without having to think about it. There was plenty of space for us both to expand, I told myself. I knew there were advantages in being his girlfriend so I was careful not to push myself forward. That was easy because I knew my work would speak for itself. That was how it was on a good day.

It became clear to me that Redmond's idea of loyalty was huge. It demanded much of my energy, in a subtle fashion. But the more subtle it was, the more difficult it became to follow his requirements. They were for the most part implied. It's hard enough to read the fine print in a good light, let alone in ambiguous shadow.

I fell into the habit of walking round him, to view him from every side, on the lookout for booby traps.

The less I demanded from Redmond the more he relaxed.

'Easy-going little thing, aren't you?' Playful, he held my chin between his fingers. 'Infinitely malleable.'

'Don't tease me. I'm not putty in your hands, you know.'

'You're adorable. My Pop used to say: "A woman should be an embellishment." '

'Don't treat me like a baby,' I told him, but he didn't hear.

I learnt that the public Redmond, engaged, friendly, was distinct from the private Redmond. The private man could be taciturn, hard to reach. Was this how couples operated? It wasn't a topic of conversation at the pub.

'Settling in?' Clive beamed at me. We were sitting on the terrace at the Regatta. Redmond had gone to get the drinks. Sweetie had on a large pair of sunglasses. She sat, unsmiling, playing with the end of her plait. Clive slid her a look, then rubbed his hands together. 'That's the shot,' he said, without waiting for me to answer. There seemed to be nothing more anyone wanted to say.

However hard I applied myself to fitting in, my sins of omission mounted up under the weight of Redmond's silent expectations. If a report card had been issued it would have read: *Unsatisfactory. Could do better.* The onus was on me. I would need to improve if I was to follow in his dashing wake.

There were days when I felt both pugnacious and unsafe. I wanted no confrontation. I was afraid to provoke Redmond. I was more than afraid that one day I would say something, out of my frustration, that I didn't mean. The familiar feeling of being out of my depth had me paddling, desperate. He was not going to accuse me of being a burden. I would not cling. I could swim on my own.

Redmond's crowd were big drinkers. Redmond drunk was witty, if a little slurred. As the session lengthened his wit got vicious. He was famous for it.

'Never cross Redmond after midnight, Honey.' Clive smiled at me, amused. 'He's a bad boy after midnight when he's had a few.'

Sweetie offered her own piece of advice in a moment alone. 'If he's got a few under his belt, don't tell him anything he doesn't want to know.'

I started to see that my pea analogy didn't fit. Redmond did not like anything to dent him.

In my stripped bedroom at my mother's house I began work on a series of small paintings, a mix of charcoal, oil pastel and wax. I called the series *Ocean of Dreams*. In one painting a female figure floated in a night ocean in which there was a black hole. Holding her up like water wings were two male heads, around which she had her arms. I knew that one was my father, and the other was recognisable as Redmond. When I had done ten of these I took them over to Redmond's in a taxi, to get his reaction.

He pressed his thumbnail hard in between his front teeth as he surveyed them, lined up along the wall. There was silence.

'What do you think?'

Already I regretted bringing them over. Redmond had been pub-crawling after work for the last three days and he hadn't invited me, even though he made it plain that the party had included Clive, Sweetie and Pamela. He was in what my mother would have referred to as a filthy mood.

He stopped in front of the painting in which his head floated next to my father's.

'I'm not fond of this autobiographical stuff, you know that, Sweetheart. Be more commercial. You should broaden out you know – the universal in the particular, that sort of thing.'

'This is particular. And universal.' Was it? Suddenly I wasn't sure.

'I don't know that I like you to use me in your paintings like that. What does it mean, anyway?' It wasn't a question. 'You can't do silly little drawings. They're like postage stamps for God's sake. You'll have people asking where the rest of them are. No-one will take you seriously at this rate.'

'You can't tell me what I can and can't paint and how big.' I stopped. 'Are you picking a fight with me?' I stared at him and he stared back for a second and then walked out of the room.

'Oh, shit.' I went after him and found him in the kitchen, standing in the corner. He glared at me.

'What's this all about? If I can't paint what I think, I don't know what I'll do.'

'I find it offensive.' Everything about him was stiff.

'What? You find what offensive? Tell me.'

'I don't like you to portray me like that.'

'Like what?'

'Stuck under your arm like that, for God's sake. You'll make me a laughing stock.' His eyes looked black and implacable.

'This is mad.' I became desperate to turn the world right side up. Had I been offensive?

'I just thought I was being truthful. You know, sometimes I feel like I'm in this ocean and you know, it's how you depend on people. When you love them. You know...'

There, I had said it. We had never spoken of love. I went up to him. It was an effort to put my arms around him when he stood so rigidly. 'We love each other, don't we?

He broke away from me and presented his back. He turned on the cold water tap over the sink. I watched his hand reach for a glass, watched as he filled and drank it down.

'Well, do we or not?'

He rolled the glass along the kitchen counter.

'If we don't, what the hell are we doing? I'm sick of buggering around.'

The glass hesitated on a bump in the Formica and rolled on.

'What are you going to do, go off to Europe and we'll never see each other again? Is that it?'

Now he was staring down at the floor, examining his shoes.

'I'm sick of this.' My voice broke into a silence that hung around the way people do at a party watching a fight. 'Either we're together or we're not.'

The glass teetered on the edge of the counter, then fell off. It didn't break. I could see the Duralux logo imprinted in the base.

'Make up your bloody mind,' I said, and marched out.

Out on the street my anger and self-justification kept me going down to the bus stop and on to the first bus that passed. But soon I began to feel ignominious. And alone. I was the only person on the bus that was heading, inexorably, towards the city terminus.

'Getting off, love?'

The driver, his every move laconic, gathered his money satchel, slung it over his blue serge shoulder and disappeared into the maze of cement pylons, a character in a Magritte painting.

Without your love

It's a honky tonk parade...

I had plenty of time to think about my actions. The phone was silent. Redmond did not appear. My mother looked worried. She and I were thrown together, two rabbits huddling in our hutch. We waited, apprehensive, for the large hand of Fate or Fortune to reach in and grab us by the scruff of our necks or alternatively, present us with a dubious carrot. I pretended that I didn't care. Either way.

'He can go to buggery as far as I'm concerned,' I informed my mother.

'You don't want to upset him,' she suggested. She always wanted to placate.

'Yes I do. He's upset me.' But doubts nagged.

'Give him a ring.'

'That's the last thing I'd do. Anyway, you've changed your tune. I thought you didn't like him.'

'I never said that.'

'Yes you did. You said he was a moody drunk.'

'I don't remember saying that at all. You're making it up.'

I had left my clothes and my paintings at his place in my grand exit and now it felt as if they were up for ransom. I began to worry that he might burn my paintings in his dismissive fury or kick holes in them as he passed or use them as dinner plates. I knew he would never sit and look at them.

'You can't wear the same clothes every day,' my mother said. 'I'm scandalised. I don't know what you think you're doing.' So one lunch hour I left work and sneaked up Redmond's back stairs. Once inside, I crept around on tiptoe, a robber, collecting my own belongings, though I knew Redmond would not come home at this time. I had to leave my paintings where they were. They seemed to have shrunk. As I went out I noticed a pair of leather driving gloves on the hall table. They were too small for Redmond.

I sank into hiatus. I observed my mother, the blind dog and the languishing cat, and thought: What's the difference between them?'

I started to chainsmoke and eat large amounts of white bread. One seemed to cancel out the other. I used to love to eat the middle out of the loaves the baker left, warm, on the front steps. Consolation. Better than humans.

My only relief in those stretched-out weeks was to paint. I decided I did not care if no-one ever saw them, just as long as I could do them. I began to have fantasies of being in a concentration camp, denied tools and finally forbidden the right to think or paint altogether.

I used to have a storybook about Little Black Sambo, the little black boy who turned a tiger into butter by making him run round and round the tree in which Little Black Sambo sat, out of reach. I had hated the cocky black boy and his turbaned mother and felt sorry for the hectic tiger, turned into a yellow pool by his frustrated desire. That would be me, a yellow pool, if they robbed me of my source of energy.

'Friday night,' my mother sighed, 'the loneliest night of the week.'

'That's Saturday night.'

'I'm sure you're wrong.' She looked put out. Then her face became alert. 'Is that a car?' I half expected her to issue a muffled *woof*. She jumped up to peep through the lounge room blinds. 'Yes, it is. Quick. It's in the driveway.'

'So? I'm sure they'll come to the front door if they want something.'

'But it's Redmond.' My mother chewed at her index finger in frustration. 'Go and see what he wants. Go on.'

She made a half lunge at me. 'Go on!'

'Oh, for heaven's sake.'

I gave in and went down the front steps. The lights of Brisbane citytwinkled blue and pink on the horizon, with the black mountain range a cut-out behind them. Redmond, a dark shape, leant over and opened the passenger door. I got in. There was silence as we looked at each other.

'What do you want?'

'Come to London with me.'

Was this an offhand invitation or a declaration of intent?

'How can I? I can't just pack up my job and go. I have no money. And what the hell do I do when I get there?'

I could never get my tone right. Why couldn't I be a smooth heroine in a romantic novel?

He stared through the windscreen. So did I. Ahead of us, we surveyed our life, which was mapping itself out in some form or other. I imagined a huge hand smearing the screen with the interstices of our actions, a lab attendant preparing a slide for the microscope. I could see the cells that would tell the future all about us, what diseases we would have, what would grow and enlarge, what would wither and die.

'We could get married, I suppose.' He sounded dubious.

'Do you want to?'

'That's one way of doing it.'

'You don't sound very keen.'

He looked at me and his face changed. 'I am keen. Actually. It's a good idea. I want you to come with me.' He reached over and gave me a long kiss. 'Come with me,' he said again. 'We'll have a good time.' As if we were going to a party.

It was my turn for silence. I spun it out as long as I could. I couldn't get the image of my single bed out of my mind. My mother popped into my head, looking doubtful. Then Lionel turned up, just when I thought he had disappeared for good. Tears came into my eyes. I wanted someone to hug me. I sent a silent message to Redmond: *Cherish me and I'll cherish you.*

The silence continued.

Where else could I go? I could stay home with my mother for the rest of my life and she would say: 'What would you like for tea? We could have a nice chookie.'

My father used to tell me: 'Pull your head in, Darl. Don't be perverse.' I think perversity must attract me. I must have a taste for the poison of ambiguity, an attraction to the allergy of disquiet.

This was adult stuff. Now I had to save myself from drowning. No-one else would. The life-savers had gone back to the clubhouse. The flags were down. I had to make a decision, it had to be a good one and I had to make it on my own, flailing in the rip, out beyond the sandbar.

'OK then.' My voice came out irresolute with foreboding. 'Let's do it.' I added: 'Just for fun.'

34 Happy the Bride the Sun Shines On

I was born on a Wednesday. *Wednesday's child is full of woe...* I forget what the other days foretell, but it was obvious I had picked a bad one.

Happy again, Redmond hurled himself into action. He liked activity. I thought he chose it because it prevented him from having to listen to himself. It relaxed him to have something to organise. Now he organised our wedding.

'You don't want an engagement ring, do you?' His eyes were opaque.

'No.' Of course I did.

I still had Peter's engagement ring. I had thought of sending it back to him but that had seemed too pointed. Anyway, it was sweet in an outmoded sort of way. I wanted to keep it.

'We'll get married in St Anne's Cathedral. It's the best.'

'But that's Catholic. I thought you were C of E?'

'My mother was Catholic.'

Stray, disloyal thoughts plagued me. The issue of the engagement ring lingered. Was it because he was cheap or did he dislike doing the obvious?

'Are you sure?'

What I meant was *I don't believe you*. What I wanted to say was 'My eye and Betty Martin', one of Dad's favourite puncturing statements. Once my question was out I regretted it.

I had gone to church with Lionel and Dolly one Palm Sunday and had come home with the palm leaf cross. I had pinned it with a thumb-tack to the middle of my wooden bed head. My father had made the bed himself out of silky oak. The tack hole and the religious artefact were a double insult. I came in for a lot of sarcasm.

It had definitely been a C of E church.

'How dare you question my family. You don't know anything about me.'

'OK, OK – I'm sorry. Don't get touchy. I'm just surprised, that's all.'

He looked mollified and my heartbeat straightened out. It made me feel unbalanced to argue, as if my left leg didn't add up to my right.

He arranged for me to have Instruction with a priest who spoke with a middle-European accent about my responsibilities as a prospective mother. Redmond didn't appear to need instruction. He seemed to know a lot about Catholicism.

'The best thing about Catholics,' he said, with sudden intensity, 'is they absolve you of all sins.' His tone was heavy, but whatever he meant by it I didn't understand. I hoped it didn't mean he was religious.

I went on my own to the priest and he bullied and threatened and forbade, though I found it difficult, with his thick accent, to understand exactly what he was saying. There was no welcome in his message, only strictures. I am sure he discerned my atheism. But I didn't care.

Preternaturally upset, my mother fulminated.

'I'm flabbergasted! Dolly was never Catholic. Well, certainly I didn't know about it. We've never had anything to do with Catholics. I'm C of E and your father was Presbyterian.' She had taken to speaking of him in the past tense.

'I've never seen you darken the door of a church and Dad's an atheist.'

'Nonsense, it's the way you were brought up that counts. Very few top-drawer people are Catholics, you know.'

'Except the Pope.' She went off in a huff.

I resented everything about these preparations, this public interference in my private sector that was Redmond. That sector was not suburban. It held no past associations; it was untainted. Every so often my heart lurched and raced for no reason and I knew I was afraid that something would jump from a dark corner and tear us to pieces.

I was to wear white, the full bridal regalia and the reception was to be at the Oasis, a select Gardens with swimming pools that was a coveted wedding venue. There was another one called the Acacia, but, said my mother, only rough people from Sunnybank went there.

Redmond and my mother, whom I had kept apart just as I had with Peter, now connived together. They were two cars revving at a stop sign. Redmond had become quite proper and accepted with alacrity every one of my mother's invitations to dinner. He would suggest some nicety and my mother would up the ante. I think my mother had to sell some of her BHP shares to pay for the reception. The grapevine reported that my father, on being invited, had said: 'What a load of Papist rot.'

My mother retorted: 'He's not coming to the wedding – and that's a saving grace.'

The guest list was a mish-mash of relatives brought out of cardboard boxes and Redmond's art and University friends. I would have asked Christine, but she had moved to Western Australia. I didn't have any other friends. I sat and listened to my mother and Redmond in cahoots and thought of my next painting. It began to feel as if all of it had nothing to do with me.

A stubborn feeling of resistance would not go away but, dutiful, I went to have my dress fitted. My one stipulation was *no bridesmaid* and neither my mother nor Redmond could force one out of me. They both showed their disappointment and upbraided me, but I wouldn't budge. I started to feel as if I was marrying my mother. I hated the way she and Redmond conspired, in such a connubial fashion, over the 'arrangements' as my mother referred to them. I kept silent.

I was pining for something in this brouhaha. I rang my father. His 'Violin' answered the phone.

'Who?' She sounded as disinterested as a secretary. 'Oh. Just one moment.'

My father came on the line. 'Long time, no speakee.' He snickered his high laugh.

'Dad? I want you to come to my wedding. Will you give me away?'

'Love to, Darl, but not in an Eyetie church.' He seemed to be in high spirits.

'What if I get it moved to a Presbyterian one – will you?'

'Yes, yes.'

'OK, then.' I hesitated. Nothing else was forthcoming from the other end of the phone. I felt defeated but hung on, tenacious, to his promise. 'I'll let you know when I've fixed it up.'

'Okey Dokey. Bye Darl. Speakie soonie.'

Redmond was non-negotiable. 'We can't put everyone out just to suit some whim of yours. Please don't be childish. It's very important to me that we marry in that church – and anyway I can't cancel the booking. I've paid the deposit.'

I thought: *You're not paying for it, my mother is* – and then felt churlish. I wanted the voices to stop.

'I'm not being childish. I just want my father to be there.' I could hear myself whining.

'Is that too much to ask?'

'Your mother and I have agreed. You should be considering her, you know. We can't change everything now. Don't be silly. Especially after we've gotten permission from the Bishop.'

Why was he aligning himself with my mother all of a sudden? I hated the feeling of being ganged up on. I hated even more the sensation of not knowing if I had a right to protest.

'I don't like you when you're like this.' Redmond paced up and down. 'Don't you think you're being rather selfish? I could see the storm clouds of anger brewing..

'Don't put me in an embarrassing situation, Sweetie. You don't do it deliberately, do you?' He laughed, but as he leant towards me I thought his shoulders hunched in threat. It was becoming a familiar pose.

I could feel myself breaking up into cracked pieces, crazed dry segments. Nothing ever went right in my mother's house.

'Oh, it doesn't matter then. Let's not argue. Have it your way. I don't care.'

'Well, then, that's finished with.'

He gave me a promissory kiss. His kisses now reminded me of rabbit fumigant, colourless, odourless, toxic to silly bunnies like me.

He left me to chase up some business and I went away and locked myself in my room. I began a painting. It consisted of a painted title hanging in a Reckitt's blue sky: *I Exist As The Centre Of The World* it proclaimed. I worked on. A man, and it was Redmond, stood looming over the landscape. The sun was behind him and had partially eclipsed his head. He was looking down at the cracked earth of a black soil plain, each fragment bearing a portion of my features. In his hand, by its long ears, he held a dead hare. Underneath, I wrote in a flowing hand: *And You Are My Mirror.*

Without your love

It's a melody played in a penny arcade...

When, early in the morning I had finished, I looked at the painting. I felt blank and sick. I had been feeling ill for weeks but put the sensation down to lack of sleep. I didn't know what the painting meant so I put it away, still wet, in my yellow-painted cupboard.

As I pushed it right to the back, I dislodged the furry troglodyte doll Peter had given me. It fell at my feet, looking up at me with its crooked, astonished eyes. I picked it up and stroked its red fur. Then in a rage at circumstance I stamped on it as hard as I could. I screwed my shoe backwards and forwards until the little plastic buttons of its eyes came loose. Then I threw it in the bin.

# 35 Reading the Leaves

I decided to break it off with Redmond. I said nothing to anyone, debating the decision with myself in an endless loop.

My mother read the atmosphere at once. 'You're not falling out with him, are you?'

'No. Don't be stupid. Whatever gave you that idea?'

She was unrelenting in her efforts to expose the worm that was me in the apple of her wedding plans.

'You're sure? You two don't seem to be getting on very well. But it's a bit late to change your mind, you know, at this late stage. I did warn you – but you wouldn't listen to me.'

Each sentence was punctuated by a hostile look in my direction. 'Can't you see eye to eye? You are being difficult, you know. They'll all have bought the presents by now. I know for a fact your Aunt Cardie's got you a salad bowl. With servers.'

She paused to let that sink in. 'You don't seem to me to be trying very hard.'

I wanted to say: 'He doesn't love me. What should I do?' but I couldn't admit it out loud. I knew she would trot out more of her pet phrases. 'Lovers' quarrels,' she would insist, playing it down. 'Never let the sun go down on your anger.' Or 'Wedding nerves.'

With more bitterness she would end up: 'I knew this would be a disaster. It's all your own fault.'

I couldn't ask for help, though I was full of dread. I thought: 'I won't give in – not yet.' This was a challenge that I knew I would finally meet with a stare of defiance. It was not yet time to run. I would *make* him love me.

My mother looked preoccupied until she surprised me by suggesting an outing.

'There's a woman in Elizabeth Street who reads your tea leaves. You have a cup of tea and scones. You know, a proper Devonshire tea, and then she reads your future. She's supposed to be very good. The girls at golf swear by her.'

I realised that she was pleading with me. I thought this might be as close to a wedding shower as I would get.

'You don't expect me to believe any of that rigmarole, though, do you?'

'Well, no,' she reassured me. 'It's just for a lark. My mother did the same for me before I got married.' Her voice was warm until she added: 'Not that it did me any good.'

The tea room was on the second floor of a building on the shabby corner of Elizabeth Street. Middle-aged women with their town hats on sat eating scones in anticipation of having their leaves read. They cut and buttered and jammed and creamed in slow motion. They raised their creations to their lipsticked mouths. One woman still had her gloves on.

'When you've finished your tea, turn your cup over your saucer.' My mother's voice was brisk. 'Then she'll come and read it. You have to cross her palm with silver.'

'You have to what?' I giggled. 'How come you know all about it?'

'Be quiet,' my mother admonished. 'People take this seriously.' I looked up to find the room of women staring at me in disapproval. I bit into my scone.

The soothsayer was a lugubrious woman, tall and bony with an old fashioned, butterfly-clip perm that had set her hair into regular corrugations, like a rainwater tank. She upturned the cup and gave the clumps of tea leaves a doleful stare.

'Not much sugar to sweeten your life.' She sounded as if it was my fault.

She raised her eyes and looked at me, gloomy, then down again to the innocent-looking leaves. 'No children,' she announced in an accusing voice. My mother looked mortified and scrabbled with the silver tongs for another cube of sugar.

The woman poked her finger. 'There's a break,' she said, her voice significant. 'Ill health.' Her sepulchral tone was getting on my nerves. Then she said: 'You'll go far.'

She raised her head again and I thought she had finished, but she stared hard at me. She looked unfriendly.

'You seek peace of mind, but you won't find it. Do you believe in Jesus Christ our Saviour?'

I thought I might lie. I looked back at her and shook my head.

'Well,' and her voice turned into a hiss, 'before too long you'll wish to God you did.'

'Thanks a lot, Mum.' I used my most sarcastic voice as we waited for the bus home. 'Where did you dig her up? What a crackpot.'

'I don't want to discuss it.' She shaded her eyes with her gloved hand and looked away from me down the length of Turbot Street.

Unsettled by the soothsayer, encircled with confusion, I wanted to blend in and argue with no-one but also to stand up for myself, all in one contradictory movement. Some days I just wanted to shout at Redmond and my mother: 'Drop dead.'

I couldn't see a way out that would not leave me beaten. I didn't like to listen to the chill voice that told me: *Your options aren't good.*

Redmond was a trailing rope on a passing yacht. I had to take the chance that I could catch hold of his heart. And if I ran smack bang into an obstacle in the process, so be it.

36 The Robber Bridegroom

When Christine got a craving for lollies, we'd get off the tram at the Junction on our way home from school and she'd buy chocolate jelly babies. I never bought them, even when I had money. She'd dole them out as we walked home, popping them into her mouth as she counted, until her mouth was full to overflowing and her jaws stuck together.

'One for you and two for me. Two for me and one for you.'

A dribble of chocolate juice would escape the corners of her lips. She never did this when boys were around. When she came to the last few, she'd tip the bag upside down over her mouth and shovel the rest in. She thought this was hilarious. It was her game, so she made the rules.

Redmond took me up to Mount Tambourine for a bushwalk and picnic. I was determined to get everything right and not fall out with him. We left the Esky in the car in a pretty clearing and struggled along a track overgrown with lantana. Redmond didn't want to take the more usual walking track with its signs and graded steps.

After half an hour I ventured: Do you think this is the right way?'

'I know what I'm doing.' He looked sweaty and irritated. 'Don't question everything I do all the time.'

'I'm not. It's just that I think I'm allergic to the lantana.' I had bloodied raised welts across my arms.

'Oh well, in that case we'll go back. You're a bit of a spoilt brat, you know.' He sounded exasperated. 'If you're not up to it...'

'I'm sorry. I don't want to disappoint you.'

'No, we'll go back. You should have said something earlier. I guess I'm used to bush-walking with Clive. I keep forgetting you're a girl.'

He had calmed down. He ruffled my hair.

As we stood debating, it began to rain and leeches brewed up out of the rainforest and looped their way towards our boots. I bent to brush one off and it stuck to my finger. As I stood trying to scrape it off on a mossy rock, another and another climbed my leg in rapid succession and disappeared under my sock.

'Aah, Redmond,' I cried, but Redmond was away, pounding down the track.

'Keep walking,' he called over his shoulder. 'It's the only thing to do.'

When I got back to the grassy clearing, the rain had stopped. Redmond was already there, lighting a fire under the billy. He hadn't collected any leeches, but when I peeled down my socks there were five of them, laced round my ankle in a black circlet.

'We could burn them off.' He looked expectant. He was in his element. This would be a test of his bushcraft.

'No, you might burn my leg. Aren't you supposed to use metho?'

'I thought it was salt.'

'I don't care what you use – just get them off. I feel sick. They're so horrible. They're drinking my blood.'

'Don't panic. I'll get them off.' And he did. He fussed around with the salt, rubbing it into my skin. I thought of Rosie and the sun tan oil in its smeary bottle. The leeches dropped off. He bent and kissed my foot. 'You have beautiful ankles.'

He was happy. We lay on our backs on the warm, damp grass, rolling over to drink our tea, companionable.

I love to watch the enigma that is Redmond. His profile dazzles me, and the heaviness of his brooding eyes. I love his eyelashes, the sensuous bow of his mouth. I know that soon I will jump-start him into the sweetness that I remember in him. The promise is there; I just have to find a way, not put a foot wrong.

The clearing dropped away to a jagged escarpment. We could see the sun shift its position by the shadow cast down the chasm wall by a rocky bluff.

'I won't always want to be an art dealer.'

'Oh?'

'No.' He sounded dreamy. 'I might want to get into History.'

I could see the word *Joke* form in a bubble in front of me. 'You'll have to do something extraordinary to achieve that.'

His eyes looked guarded. 'Ha ha, very funny.'

'Just teasing.'

We lay in silence. Redmond surprises me sometimes with his ability to be stung by a careless response from me. *Sharp-tongued bitch*, says a voice in my head.

I shifted across and kissed him, penitent.

'You'll do very well in History, or whatever you want to do. And I'll do very well in painting. And we'll live happily ever after.' I smiled into his eyes. But there was more.

'Yes, well, I meant to talk to you about that.' He looked about him, restless. 'You know, in the art game, you're only viable if you sell. The thing is, are you a selling commodity? You'll have to look hard at that, Sweetheart. Anyway, when we're in London you'll have to work. You know that, don't you?'

'Of course.' (*I'm not a spoilt brat.*) 'But I'll have time to paint. I've got to have time to paint.'

'The thing is, all that art stuff costs so much. You won't be able to have a studio. I won't be earning a lot.'

'But we'll get by. We'll manage.' My voice went up a note. 'We can both do what we want.'

He stared out over the escarpment. Most of the valley was now in shadow. It was getting cold.

'Well, it's going to take quite a bit for me to do what I want. I'll have to do a lot of travelling and so forth. Research. Meet the right people. It may take all we've got. You may find you'll have to put things on hold for a while, be my right-hand man.'

He turned his head and smiled at me. 'It wouldn't hurt, now would it? If you're honest with yourself. Take a break and see where you're heading?'

'I don't need a break. I just need to be able to paint.'

His eyes went blank. He finished his tea. I wondered what would come next. A small and lonely wretchedness crept up on me. He tossed the tin cup into the basket and rolled until he was on top of me, his hands pinning my arms. He kissed me and fondled my breasts. He undid the buttons of my jeans.

'Do you want to make love?' He pulled my jeans down and kissed my stomach.

'Always,' I think, and my father's dirty German ditty arrives in my head: *You gave yourself to me in the undergrowth, first this way, then that.*

'Do you want me to kiss you down there?' He didn't wait for an answer.

It was the first time he had done it and I wished we were in a dark room so I could concentrate on the sensations his mouth created. I felt awkward, up on the open side of the ridge, making love. Someone could have binoculars trained on us, and be bent double with insane laughter. I tried to make my mind switch off. Despite an odd-shaped object that stuck into my left hip, it was the best lovemaking we had ever managed.

Redmond looked pleased with himself and before he rolled off me he brought his face close to mine. 'Was that good?'

I didn't want to be made to say anything. Discussing it afterwards makes us sound like we are reading from a sex manual, but there is no getting round it.

'Yes.' I put my arms round his neck, brushing my fingers down the nap of his close-cut hair.

'Say after me: "I'd do anything for you, Redmond."'

Drugged with sex, drunk on hope, I say it.

37 Bridal Rein

The day before our wedding I followed Redmond to the gallery. He immediately disappeared on some errand. He left me with Pamela.

'Well, Doll, congrats. Got what you want, I see. Lots of luck... and happiness etcetera.' She looked thoughtful.

'Thanks Pammy.' I wanted her to like me. It seemed important to have her blessing – or at least not her curse.

'Of course, he'll never get over her, you know. He told me. Red and I are very close.'

I had never heard her call him Red before.

'A lot in common. Mmn, business and that, you know. I've known him, off and on, for – well, it must be ten years. Been through a lot together. Chasing the golden dream, that sort of thing. Had our little adventures. Two peas in a pod, really.' She gave a harsh laugh.

I nodded my head, obedient to this relationship now that I was about to take over the burnished prize.

'He tells me things he'd never tell anyone else. That's how I know. About Rosie, I mean.'

I nodded again. I had not forgotten Rosie. I too wanted to know everything about the way he felt, even if it was at second-hand.

'In fact, I suppose you knew anyway, but we had a sort of mini-affair. That's all finished now, of course.' She eyed me speculatively.

'Horrible the way she used him. Just broke his heart.' She stopped and stared hard at the telephone on her desk. Then she reached for a flat package and handed it to me. 'Won't be there tomorrow, Doll. Things to do.' She looked vague. 'So there you are, and here's a little something to go towards the cost of your wedding dress.' And with her elegant conjurer's hand she presented me, as if by magic, with a cheque.

'Look after him for me.' She turned away.

Bridle rein. I was a pack horse under the paraphernalia of my wedding gear, as I walked up the aisle of the church, dragging my Uncle Edward with me. Polio had struck Uncle Edward when he was a child, and he wore a metal leg brace. He rocked on his bad hip as if he had a flat tyre. When he sat, he either stuck his leg out in front of him or performed complicated ratcheting manoeuvres at his knee so his brace would bend. He was not the ideal partner with whom to dance down the aisle, and he was a poor substitute for my father.

I had overheard him tell my mother: 'That girl of yours is fast. Watch out, or she'll be in trouble.' Trouble had a capital T.

No doubt he thought I was going to the dogs by marrying such a flashy character. Invited at the last minute to one of my parents' cocktail parties, Uncle Edward had once arrived with some green liqueur in a glass gun. Having imbibed too much of it to compensate for his feeling out of place, he had ogled me in my short shorts.

As I proceeded down the aisle, more than anything I wanted to see what Pammy had given us. It had felt like a small painting. I hadn't been allowed to open it. Redmond had become very keen on protocol and this forbade the opening of presents until after the wedding. The package and her conversation kept flashing up, cards being shuffled in my mind as I walked past faces on Redmond's side of the church that I had never seen before. They stared at me, covert and curious. I stared back behind my veil. I hadn't wanted a veil, but now I was glad of it.

I could see Redmond's back and Clive's, his best man. I thought: *I am marrying a perfect stranger*. It felt so odd, a charade. Too late to stop anything now. *I'll never sleep in a single bed again*. It seemed important to note that. Beside me, under the duress of his unusual exertions, Uncle Edward belched. We stopped. The end of the line.

An image of Redmond inserting a rabbit pellet into Pammy who had no clothes on but still looked busy, slid across my inside screen.

Uncle Edward handed me over and retired to a pew. I could hear his metallic ratcheting behind me.

The priest began to marry us. For one moment I levitated above the scene and looked down at myself, aloof and detached. Then just as fast, I returned. I cannot recall anything of the ceremony after that moment. Not one detail. It is all a blank, an unpainted space, a gessoed surface.

The tension of not being myself gave me my first migraine. I started to feel nauseated as we stood outside having our photograph taken with interminable combinations of jostling and vying relatives. My mother fussed and orchestrated and fell back. There was a pecking order and I began to see them all as Lionel's chooks. That was much better and made more sense, though I still couldn't see what titbit they were after. There was some reason why they photographed certain groups together and then re-combined them. I smiled, obedient, until a muscle twitched in my cheek.

Redmond looked as if he was enjoying the attention. *Killjoy*, I told myself. My head began to pound to a congested beat and as the afternoon closed down I saw haloes round the street lights that had suddenly come on, blank and automatic. My thoughts dissipated. *Those lights do that every day and now they're doing it on my wedding day*, I said to myself, as if noting these tiny events would make everything coalesce into something that seemed real. It didn't. I gave up trying to feel real and instead listened to the patterns of my blood drumming in my head.

They diverted us into a limousine and we began the long drive out to the Oasis. I looked out the window and saw people going to the corner shop. A child, sitting in the gutter playing with the floppy ears of her dog, waved an ear at us as we rolled past. Then the mock-Spanish, stucco and wrought-iron entrance to the Gardens. I felt lost. I found it hard to look at Redmond.

As I struggled out, my mother rushed towards me, intent on making sure I did not damage the oval train of my gown. 'You should have had a bridesmaid, you really should have. That's what they do. Now I'm having to do everything. It's not right, you know.'

'I have a headache. Can I go and lie down somewhere for a minute?'

She hustled me in a side entrance. Redmond had disappeared again. I kept losing him.

'Lie down? I'm at my wit's end. You can't lie down.'

I thought of Christine's mother, the way she had lain down, impervious as a cat, at Wynyard Station.

'I'll get you some champagne. The kitchen might have an Aspro if you're lucky. It's such a nuisance. I don't really want to put them out. They just do the package you know. They're fussy here. Wait. I'll be back.'

She left me in the breathless room, which had two chairs, my bridal suitcase with my going-away clothes, and nylon curtains at the one small window. Just when I thought I might start vomiting, she came back with a glass of champagne and a Vincents powder. It looked used, as if it had been in someone's pocket or even stuffed down a bra (it curved). I hated the geriatric pink of Vincents powders but shook it down and emptied the champagne glass.

My mother surveyed me. 'You're looking very pale.'

'Yes sirree – well I'm feeling a bit beyond the pale.' I had begun to feel light-headed and more light-hearted. I recognised the phase that presaged me doing something that I might *regret at leisure*, my mother's favourite indictment. *Watch out*, I said to myself. I didn't sound convincing.

'Come on, you've got to come out now and be presented. Redmond's been waiting all this time. I don't know.'

Redmond was waiting in the passage. He looked assured, a terrifying grown-up. The familiar feeling of being out of synch came at me. He put my hand on his arm where it lay, stiff. I looked at it, surprised. It had a gold band on the third finger. As we entered the room, Clive, up on a dais, spoke into a microphone. 'The bride and groom, ladies and gentlemen! Meet Mr. and Mrs....' My married name thudded into my chest. It did not fit.

'What a strange name.' My voice was too loud.

I smiled up at Redmond, asking him to share with me my surprise at my new state, our new state, the incongruity of life's juggernaut. Redmond sent me a distracted look and squeezed my arm. I determined to be good and to quieten the mongrel that was me, that followed the fence line barking. *Shush*, I said to it.

We sat at the bridal table, facing the room. Some people had their backs to us and most seemed more interested in following the waitresses' movements. Redmond leant close to my ear.

'Why did you say shush to me?'

I thought of explaining, but it wouldn't have made any sense. 'No reason, it doesn't matter.'

A waitress hovered and I smiled at her and extended my glass for her to fill. I smiled across at an elderly gentleman, raised my glass, said 'Bottoms up' and sculled the contents. Redmond got up and went over to say something to Clive. I felt stranded there by myself, no Christine to back me up and be merry and silly. I looked at my mother. She tapped her wine glass and frowned.

I looked across at Redmond. He was so handsome, his foxy hair shining. I liked the bulk of him, the way he stood, cocksure. I never tired of looking at him from a distance. Gloomy and romantic, a saturnine character out of a Georgette Heyer novel. Now he belonged to me. I knew I shouldn't think of him in such a trivial fashion, but how could my private fantasies hurt? His image came to me fully-formed, matured, dressed in grown up clothes. I did not like to think of how he had been as a young boy, or an aggressive adolescent with pimply skin, his voice breaking. Competent and worldly, that was the Redmond of my ideal. He would think of me. I would be secure in his head as he was in mine, always and forever, possessed: the big brother I had never had, a constant father, my own private sexual object, my simmering lover whom I shared with no-one.

I heard Redmond laugh at something Clive was saying. Clive had a comradely arm round his shoulder. When I managed to make Redmond laugh I felt clever, satiated. The first time I'd done it, I became so excited by the effect I spoilt it by following up with a string of joking repartee. Redmond had stopped laughing and looked away. When he laughed it entranced me, because I thought I saw underneath his finished veneer to the essential Redmond: the structural lines, the first, underpinning brushstrokes. I was never looking for the little boy lost, though he unnerved me with an occasional giggle. I searched to expose the warm-blooded human in him. I never understood what he thought was funny. It disturbed me that I only hit on it by chance.

Redmond had been round the room and back again. He sat down looking satisfied. 'He's here.'

'Who's here?' No-one was looking after me. Marooned, I poured myself another glass of champagne from a skulking bottle. I took a casual sip and then another, bigger one.

'The guy from the *Courier-Mail*. I told you, Sweetheart. He's doing it as a special favour for me. It will be good for me with the Gallery. He said he'd take quite a few and then he can pick a good one.'

'A good what?' He sighed at my slowness. 'A wedding snap for the social pages, Sweetie. Aren't you hoeing into that bubbly a bit fast? You're looking a bit pale.'

I stood up. I knew I was going to say something I would regret. I could feel it coming. It felt so good, like the beginnings of orgasm. I could not stop myself; the pleasure was too urgent. I saw a macabre image of Pammy standing in front of me, naked except for one of Redmond's fishnet singlets.

'Look, it's not too late to get an annulment,' I said. 'Then you and Mum can get married. I won't stand in your way. Truly. It would be good. Mum wouldn't want sex, so you could keep on having a mini-affair with Pammy. Perfect.'

His face had a caught-out, guilty air, but what was more disturbing was that behind his chagrin lurked a just-visible satisfaction, as if he didn't mind me knowing about him and Pammy.

'Sweetie, Sweetheart – don't be like that. You're not jealous are you? What did she say?' He stopped himself. 'Sweetie, that's in the past.' He put a placating hand on the folds of silk at my waist and tugged, trying to draw me down to my chair. I pulled away.

'I'm going over here to sit among the cinders. You just get on with whatever it is that's more important.'

Now Redmond looked angry. *Serve you right*, I thought. I moved off, careful to hold my champagne glass straight.

I glided with the tiny steps of a geisha over to the elderly gentleman I had toasted. I put my free hand up in a fan. 'Sookie San at your service. Are we having fun over here? Who are you, by the way?'

'I'm Redmond's Uncle Stan.' He eyed me with reluctant distaste and some alarm.

'Ah, so. Bloody old Lionel's brother. Do you like chooks?'

He didn't answer, so I moved on. I saw a roly-poly man with a camera and headed his way. He reminded me of Peter. My headache, which had started a gentle rebound, gave an extra thud.

'Hullo, Honey, you must be the bride.' He smiled. He looked rather sweet and on the instant I became his friend.

'I think I'm it. Do I look like one?'

'Yes.' We looked at each other and laughed. 'Bit woozy round the edges, but glowing, darlin'. Here, let me take a shot, just for you.'

He backed me up against some fernery and white flowers. There was a dish with rose petals and silver cachous and a candle. Now that the room had sunk into gloom I noticed lit candles in groups on every table. It helped to soften the relatives. He held me as I swayed for a moment, then stepped back to take the shot. Eager to be helpful, I fluffed out my veil.

The pop of the flash made me dizzy. I saw green circles ahead of me and staggered on my high heels. I reeled sideways until my hand found a hard surface. Ahead of me now, the way was clear. The smell of the candles was strong in my nose, but I liked it. To my left I saw a table of diners staring at me. They looked aghast. Perhaps I was drunk or at least tiddly. I would have to settle down.

The photographer, peering above his camera was re-aligning himself for another shot. I thought we had finished. I leant over the table of stunned faces. 'Here we go again. Popular, that's me.'

As if someone was tapping me on the shoulder, I felt a presence behind me, a warmth. Out to the side I saw something glowing. Then it rushed up towards my face, an animal on the loose. The photographer popped his flash again and then ran towards me and started slapping at the side of my head. Now I could smell burning. The voluminous netting of my veil had sprouted a ragged grass fire, a line of tiny, curling flames. I felt a hot spot above my left ear.

The photographer, having caught the shot of the century, was now intent on putting me out. He fell on me, flaring his coat over my head as he knocked me to the ground.

'Jesus, Hon, you're a fiery little thing.' His coat muffled his voice.

I started to laugh. Tears poured down my face. He was laughing too. He had his forearms round my neck. It felt comfortable. I thought I could lie there for ages, dwelling in the mystery of connection, but Redmond had come up. He was frantic, but not for my safety. He bent and hauled me up, displacing the photographer with a rude shove.

'I'm so disgusted.' He spoke in a controlled undertone, slapping me down, hitting me in the nose in his attempt to right my appearance.

'How can you behave like this? For God's sake, pull yourself together. Do you always have to steal the limelight?'

The photographer was watching me. He looked at Redmond and back at me. He appeared expectant.

'Candlelight,' I said. 'Oh, God, you mean steal the candlelight' and I started laughing again. The photographer did too, as if he was congratulating me. He even clapped his hands.

It was the first time ever that I have laughed so hard that the muscles running down my sides ached. As the dark stranger passed the end of the fence line my mongrel dog gave a last, defiant, glorious bark. It was, after all, a happy wedding.

38 From a Distance

Full of contrition, guilt and champagne, I spent our wedding night trying to placate Redmond's fury. I had been thoughtless, hogging the show with my unspeakable behaviour. I had reflected badly on Redmond. No, on both of us. 'Aren't we a team?' Redmond asked. I made a vow not to be such a show-off. In the face of his upset and my return to sobriety, my anger had vanished.

It took a long time to pacify him but finally we made love. I wrapped my arms and legs around him, but he disengaged me. 'Turn over,' he commanded. He pushed me up on my knees and we made love with my face hidden from him, squashed into the bedding. It excited him. I felt anonymous. When he came, he grabbed me by the neck, his hand rough, and pushed my face into the smothering pillow. 'Do you like that?' he whispered in the dark.

He told me this was his preferred position, that it gave him intense pleasure. How could I gainsay him? How could I, who loved him spellbound, withhold anything from him? I could not consider a life that did not contain Redmond. How could I, who found it difficult to speak first, whose tolerance of disharmony was minimal, dare to be selfish or angry or to demand anything for myself?

It's a Barnum and Bailey world
Just as phoney as it can be...

We had a day in which we were supposed to stare at the wedding presents, store them under the house, and sit around in married bliss before catching the plane for London. Redmond wanted to do none of these.

'I've got a couple of things to do at the gallery.'

Yeah, go chase your chimera, I thought. Then I felt ashamed. *Shut your face*, I told myself. *What are you going on about? That's over.*

'Just leave the presents wrapped and put them under the house,

Sweetheart. Oh, and do something with the fridge, will you. Clean it out and so forth.'

He stood in the doorway, shrugging on his sports coat. 'I'll meet you at the airport, Sweetie. Don't be late. Don't forget my stuff.' He looked happy going off, almost content.

I thought: *I can make it all right.* I fantasised about being a Good Wife and getting huge amounts of satisfying sex and warm communion in return. It was simple really. Tit for tat and nobody counting on their fingers. I wandered over to the pile of presents to search for Pammy's package.

It was not a painting. It was a photograph. It was a photograph of Pammy and Redmond, their arms around each other. It had been taken at an undisclosed venue, taken with care by a mutual friend. Their body language was intimate. Pammy looked triumphant.

I went to the kitchen and searched the cutlery drawers. I found what I wanted, a steel meat tenderiser, hammer-shaped, with studs. I came back into the lounge room, laid Pammy's picture on the floor and smashed the glass. Careful to avoid Redmond's face, I hammered a few blows at Pammy's, denting her air of busy absorption forever.

As I picked it up to rewrap it, some glass, caught in the frame, cut my hand. Nothing happened for a second and then the blood welled out in deep red tear drops. It coursed down my arm and dripped on to the carpet. I went to the bathroom and opened the medicine cabinet. No band aids. I put my hand in the sink, the blood dripping. I turned on the cold water tap and washed it away. Still the dark tears emerged.

I stood, staring at myself askew in the half-opened door of the cabinet until the dripping stopped. Then I went back and wrapped the shattered photo in its blood-smeared paper and stored it downstairs with the other unopened presents. I wrapped my paintings in newspaper. I had found them where I had left them, arranged around the skirting boards. I stored them as far away from Pammy's blood-stained gift as I could manage.

I went back into the bedroom. I stared at my sooty wedding finery. The smell of burning was still in the air, as if the fire could never be extinguished. I felt exhausted. I couldn't deal with anything more, so I shoved the gown that Pammy had paid for under the stripped bed, and pushed the last pieces of singed netting in with my foot.

I didn't bother to remove the bloodstains on the carpet. Nor did I bother to clean out the fridge, though I left the door open and switched off the power. Redmond's salami and an opened tin of Spam watched me, untended pets, as I walked away.

39 A Day at the Races

Three weeks later, Redmond comes home from work at the Museum to our freezing top floor bedsit in Ladbroke Grove. He carries a pile of mail. Most of it is for him, sent on by Pamela, with one thin aerogramme for me from my mother. I feel warm just handling it. I imagine her taking the form out of the bottom kitchen drawer where she keeps a rattling collection of pencil stubs and congealing rubber bands, and writing me a message standing up at the kitchen bench, thinking of me, missing me.

Inside is a folded cutting. I think of her, trying to decide whether she can get away with including it in an aerogramme, worrying that she will have to pay extra, perhaps arguing with the postmaster who tries to stare her down over his authoritarian half-glasses.

I knife open the glued flaps so as not to obliterate any of her message. I read her backward-leaning words. It gives me a pang in my heart just to see them. I have rarely seen her writing except on shopping lists or in her untidy recipe books or on brown paper bags giving my tuck shop order for school lunches.

For some reason she has written in a singular form of telegramese. It's as if she thinks it might be more proper or at least cheaper, as if, with aerogrammes, like telegrams, you have to count the letters:

Yr landlord rang. Stop. Said you left mess. Stop. Don't expect me to deal with it. Stop. Enc. Stop.

She finishes with her full name, including her two extra Christian names. I unfold the cutting. It is from the social page of the *Courier-Mail*. It has the heading: *BLAZING BRIDE.* Underneath the photograph of me it is more normal: *Off to a blazing start.* It gives my name and only daughter of and my parents' name and their initials, *at her marriage to...* Then Redmond's name, and the gallery's. It ends: *At present they are travelling in Europe.*

Redmond, who never divulges what is in his mail, and has enjoined me not to tamper with it or even open anything addressed to us both, has no interest in what mine contains. He stands with his back to me, reading a letter. Then he puts it and the rest of his mail in an untidy heap under the bed. He reminds me of a dog burying a bone.

Late one rainy Friday night, Redmond, pouring over his Michelin Guide, raises his head.

'We might go to the races tomorrow, if it's fine.'

'That sounds like fun.'

It does. I have never been to the races. I conjure up images of stables with snorting horses, the warm, thick smell of straw and dung, the noise and movement of a large crowd. People having a good time surround us. Some of it might rub off on us.

'We might.' He puts his head down again to the book. 'I only said we might.'

'Oh, I won't get my hopes up.' He doesn't respond.

The next morning there is a heavy mist in the air, but no-one could call it rain. He takes me through a sketchwork of streets. We catch the Underground, then arrive at a cavernous, iron-girdered train station. It might be Paddington or Victoria or St. Pancras. I'm not sure which, because I get lost in London. I have never made a successful map in my head of the city's configuration. I always get lost, and I depend on Redmond to extricate me.

The trouble is that I get caught up looking at things. A red-painted door to a terrace house; a woman polishing a brass door knocker; a cobblestoned side street I would like to wander in; a young couple getting into a red sports car and zooming off; a stuffy, Dickensian bookshop I will never enter.

Redmond is a master, I have discovered, of holding out a carrot then whisking it away at the last minute. So when I ask: 'Where are the races being held?' - thinking of somewhere called Newmarket that I'd read about it in a Georgette Heyer novel, with men in checked caps and sports coats - he replies that he's changed his mind. 'I thought we'd go to Cambridge,' he tells me. I am not surprised.

We catch a train, after Redmond has had a brief argument with the conductor. He likes trains. He likes to be on the move. He is an unsettled person. Now he sits back in his seat, temporarily satisfied, happily (I presume) silent. I stare out the window as we move through urban countryside. It is drizzling, with patchy sun, as we walk away from our exit station towards Cambridge. We walk everywhere. It surprises me he hasn't suggested we walk from London.

I know I am disheartening company. It depresses me to be in London with no particular purpose. Redmond is preoccupied with making his way. Londoners don't open the door as wide as he expected. I watch as he gets rebuffed at social gatherings by impervious Londoners, watch as his outrage mounts. Londoners are cool towards expatriates.

I know I am no help, even before he says it. 'You're no help, Sweetheart, standing around looking forlorn. You've got to talk to people.' His accusations land with a soft, unseen plop in the midst of the fug that envelops me. I can't concentrate on anything, not even Redmond and his dreams.

Cambridge turns out to be a dull town, with stretches of grassy meadow surrounding the university buildings. But I determine to have a good time and look for something to attract my interest. I smile up at Redmond but he looks at me in a distracted way and opens his Michelin Guide again. He carries it in his sports coat pocket, where it has begun to tear the lining.

We are both at a loss and wander the streets desultorily, searching for something significant. No-one wants to talk to us. Redmond, for once, has come out unprepared, without any contacts. He says we should go down to the River Cam to see a punt and after another trek in the bare landscape with its leafless tree traceries, we find it.

Some students are poling upriver. I am looking forward to a ride. It will be romantic to have Redmond at the helm. But he has second thoughts.

'I don't think I can afford to hire one of those. I haven't got much money on me. I must have left it on the table in the flat. Anyway, you don't really want to hire one, do you, Sweetie?'

'I don't care.' So we watch other people enjoying themselves, the sound of their laughter drifting across the water.

The rain has stopped. Redmond takes off his coat and we lie down on it. Most of our bodies overlap on to the damp turf. We stare up at the wan sky. Redmond turns his face towards me.

'I've always wanted to come to Cambridge.'

'Have you?'

'Yes. It's full of history.' He puts his hands behind his head and crosses one leg over the other.

'I suppose it is.' I am careful around the subject. I am trying hard to be companionable. It is soggy and cold. There is too much green and not enough people.

Now he reads me extracts out of his Michelin Guide and I listen. I can never bring myself to read the Guide. The type is tiny and congested. There are too many facts to know, too much one has to race around to see. Too many notations between me and real life.

Now, for a moment, we are still. My attention wanders and I sink into a daydream. I am in a punt wearing a flowered hat (it suits me) and Redmond is poling me across the water. He is smiling into my eyes.

His voice wakes me. 'We should go back soon. I'm not sure how often the trains run.'

He has stuffed the Guide back into his coat pocket, where it makes an awkward bulge. I feel empty and light-headed. 'Aren't you hungry?'

'I am a bit. But I really haven't brought much money. Don't make things worse by bitching about it.' He looks moody and my heart flattens out.

'I'm not bitching. Don't say that. I hate it.'

He has a look of sudden speculation. 'You are a bit of a bitch sometimes.'

'Don't. Why be mean for no reason?'

I reach out to him. He is an arm's distance from me. He is so handsome in profile that my stomach turns over.

He capitulates. 'We'll find something when we get back.'

I lie there. I do not argue. My mother floats into the scene, complete with levitating fork. 'Here, have my chop,' she says. 'I only need a small portion.'

Redmond rises up on his elbow and leans over me, blocking out the sky. His green jumper under his coat has a cable pattern down the centre. He looms closer and gives me a hard kiss, then moves away.

When we get back to London I venture a joke. 'That was a nice day at the races.'

I smile into his eyes again and try to take his hand. I yearn to walk arm in arm with him through the London streets. I want people to look at us and think: 'Aren't they a romantic pair? There goes a happy couple.'

But he just looks at me, suspicious now, and irritated. He avoids my hand. I hear, from a long way off, across thousands of miles of crashing ocean, the voice of my mother: *Well, better than nothing, I suppose.*

My father answers her, a saturnine grin in his tone: *Better than a kick in the pants, Darl. Better than a poke in the eye with a burnt stick.*

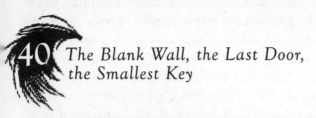

40 The Blank Wall, the Last Door, the Smallest Key

I can't get used to the colour of London. The red brick detached houses of the inner city look as if they have blood spilt on them. The grass in the closes and railed gardens is a poisonous green. Brown dog turds are everywhere: on the footpath, in the grass. Londoners look pallid and mind their own business as if it is their obsession – except for our landlady who minds everyone else's, and lies in wait for us at the most inopportune moments. She tires me out.

The dull air, full of blots of soot, lands on my face. The cold in December is intense. Before now I have never been further from Brisbane than Sydney. The sky is the most disturbing motif. It is a pale, washed-out blue or grey. Luminous, perhaps, but to me it looks dissatisfied, without vigour. I long for the blue of Brisbane.

London disappoints me. It is not strange, exciting, foreign. It feels lumpish and in an odd way, familiar. In London I have lost the power to be enchanted. When I first see Piccadilly Circus, I think: 'This is simply a traffic island.' In the famous squares pigeons sit in their hundreds on the statues and building ledges, and old ladies feed them bread crusts. The pigeons are colourless. Their broody breasts remind me of my mother.

I feel vague and as if I have forgotten something important. I ask myself: 'What the hell are you so preoccupied about?' I try to think.

I refuse Redmond's invitation to see the Changing of the Guard at Buckingham Palace. My excuse is that I have a pain in my stomach but somewhere else, that I can't quite identify, aches too. I do not like being a tourist, hanging out, watching the usual things, full of admiration. It makes me feel blind, seeing everything one step behind Redmond's eyes.

Redmond sometimes goes out by himself, with bad grace. He likes me to accompany him on every outing. He thinks I am wasting his money lying around. If I don't go with him he takes it amiss.

London's cold, huffy atmosphere nauseates me. London pubs, which Redmond likes to frequent, sicken me with their red plush and odours of stout. He loves stout, licking the froth from the top and intoning 'Mothers' milk'.

'Go and see the Guards and the Palace. I don't mind. Really. You like palaces. I'll be right here. I might even have a bath.'

It is Sunday morning. The light in the bed-sitting room is low because there is no window and little sun. It is raw outside. I can tell because if I go into our kitchenette-bathroom I can see the sky through the rectangle of the skylight, the only form of light and ventilation. The kitchenette has a two-burner stove, a dirty oven, a bench, some plates, pots and a fry pan, and three cups and saucers. It houses a large bath on claw legs. Under the bath mushrooms grow sideways on long, fungoid stalks. If I stand on the kitchen chair I can see out of the skylight across the roofs of London and into the orb of the sky. Seagulls sometimes hover above the skylight's pane and peer down, bending their thick necks and pointing their beaks. I long to draw them but Redmond has negotiated a deal with me. I will not buy art materials. Then we can afford to go to Italy. Or Scotland. 'Whatever we decide,' says Redmond, generous. I know he is thinking of Scotland.

Without quite knowing how it happened, I have given over full responsibility for our finances to him. I feel uneasy not knowing how much is in the bank, but soon it becomes too late to ask. If I question him, it might sound as if I don't trust him.

'I want you to come with me.' He sounds frustrated. It sounds like a command. He tries to encourage me out of my lethargy. 'Come on, rise to the challenge, Sweetheart.'

If he had said: 'Come with me – I'm lonely without you,' I might have forgotten my period pain and gone. I never keep track of my menstrual cycle, but I'm sure I'm having my periods less often. I might be freezing up from the inside out.

It is as if Redmond can't enjoy anything without showing me how he does it. He shows me that he is doing the right thing, an engaged and informed tourist. I never feel included. More like an accompanying mirror. If I have time on my own I feel like a traitor.

There seems to be a default in my personality. My loose threads catch on his sharp edges. I am on the wrong side of him. It is rare that I can get our relationship to sit straight. It's troublesome, just like my mother's sewing.

I love to watch Redmond doing ordinary things. But he does not want to catch any old hare for the dinner pot. He wants a hunting companion, a grander chase. If I could see the ears of the prize twitching in the grass I might have more energy for the pursuit. Still, he is my own private matinee idol and I am, I comfort myself, the only girl in the whole movie. I convince myself that good times are a leap ahead, that we will get better at being together, that we will be happier.

Compared with what? I can hear Christine saying.

'No,' I now resist his invitation. 'I don't want to go. You go. You'll have a nice time.'

'Don't patronise me.' He leaves, sulking.

I sign up with a secretarial agency that doles out casual employment to people like me: those of us who lack choice and don't know the ropes. At last I land a permanent job that nobody wants. Nobody in their right minds, at least. It is work for a government department, and consists of retyping committee minutes for the permanent record. It is crucial to have the margins of a consistent size, the format inalienable, the commas and the full stops in the right place. I am a reliable typist and as I am suffering from more than my usual inertia, I keep at the job when others who came before me leave after a few days. Besides, I like regularity, no matter how awful, because then I can daydream.

The job is in Waterloo. I catch the Underground to the station and walk through the markets. I buy food there, once I have become accustomed to queuing up. The butcher's queue, the greengrocer's queue, the fishmonger's queue, then the bus queue if I want a different journey back to Ladbroke Grove. Once, inadvertently, I jumped the queue, only to have an irate Londoner tell me: 'There's a queue here, you know. Wait your turn.' It all reminds me of primary school.

My boss is a middle-aged London divorcee called Barbara, who still lives in the same house as her ex-husband. She has a boyfriend of sorts, a younger man called Graham. All of us in the office have seen Graham, who wears cardigans to work, the type with tiny, knitted, fist-sized pockets. He has thin hair the colour of cat-sick.

Barbara is small and nondescript and reminds me of my mother. I suppose her job description must be to bully underlings.

'*She's* due for a raise,' says Marina at the next desk, after yet another unfortunate incident over a comma. 'You watch, she'll have a go at Iris in a minute,' and as we watch she marches, determined, across the room.

Iris, at least seventy under her hennaed hair, must be supplementing her pension on the sly. She is a sitting target for Barbara, who threatens her with exposure to The Authorities week after week. Iris takes it on the chin.

'I've been working here for seven years, dear,' she explains as she removes her galoshes in the cloakroom. She puts on a pair of red velvet slippers whose bumps directly match her bunions. 'She doesn't mean it – not really.'

Barbara finds less fault with Claire, who is deaf and dumb, though when her mania for perfection reaches its heights she signals frantically at her in sign language.

Marina, with a hand over her mouth, says: 'You'd have to be deaf and dumb round here to tolerate that bitch.' She catches my look, 'It's all right. The poor thing can't lip-read if she can't see your mouth.'

Not one of us ever says: 'This is crazy. We must stop doing this straight away and get back to sanity.' Perhaps none of the others thinks it.

Barbara is a stickler for tea-making. She tells us how important it is to put the milk in the cup first and then pour the tea. Maybe it is the other way round. 'Heat the pot first,' she tells me. 'Don't you Aussies know anything?'

She has small feet and wears black leather boots that come half-way up her calves. I am afraid of those boots as they stand beside me. They look impatient and frenzied. I never ask myself what she would be capable of in those boots, what damage she could do to me. I freeze and placate, desperate to stay in my tight-wound cocoon, in my state of abeyance. I give her an ingratiating smile and try to get everything right. I become proud, after a time, of my record of no mistakes.

She could give me the sack, I suppose. What would be so bad about that? It is the worst, most useless job in the world, and I can go out and get another. She would not be capable of blackening my name at the agency because they all know her there, how impossible she is.

She likes to threaten us once a day, usually in the tea break. 'Here it comes,' says Marina, out of the side of her mouth.

'I don't know how many stupid, good-for-nothing, unreliable women I have given the sack to,' says Barbara, and Marina gives a soft snort. Barbara stands over us with her knees locked. 'I won't tolerate incompetence here. Or cheek. It will be out the door with you, quick smart, I can tell you. Then see how you are!'

Marina retorts out of earshot as we queue for the toilet: 'The sack! She never gave anyone the sack. They just walked out. I'm going as soon as I've paid off the fridge. Just watch me.'

Barbara holds some sort of power over each of us that is hard to define. So we sit there day after day, captive to her bullying, subservient to her demands – almost, I come to think, each for our different reasons, in league with her against ourselves.

Left alone in the bed-sit after Redmond's departure for the Palace, I take a deep breath. I wish my lethargy would go away. I feel leached. London does not agree with me. I have a burning spot on my lip that is getting worse. As I peer into the mirror above the kitchen sink, bobbing my head to avoid the distorting wave that trembles through the middle, I realise the ruby bump heralds my first cold sore.

Last night Redmond and I made love after an argument. He picks fights with me over the smallest thing. So when he made amorous movements towards me in our bed I accepted, eager for what I took as a sign of peacemaking. I gave him a lingering kiss.

I hope he doesn't get my cold sore. He is conscious of his appearance and a hypochondriac when it comes to small illnesses. I make myself feel guilty when I deprecate him in my mind, but I suppose this is normal in relationships. My mother told me often enough: 'Your father's getting on my nerves.'

The more we argue, the more resentful and deadened I feel. Off-kilter, like one of those weighted Russian dolls. In the middle of one fight I demand: 'Don't you ever look at yourself?' He glares at me, his eyes blank. 'Why are you so angry with me all the time?' He does not answer.

It's as if lovemaking is in a separate compartment. As if current feelings have nothing to do with it. As if I can drop my hurt, smother my anger, bite off my misery. In my mind I have started to refer to it as fucking, not lovemaking. I cheer myself up by imagining the look on his face if I demanded fifty dollars a time.

Redmond can go from a bout of hateful argument to dead calm with ease. I don't know how he does it. I am beginning to think that he does not feel much. Even his angry outbursts have the air of manufacture about them. He can turn them on and off at will, leaving me seething. Except for his overtures in bed, it would be easy to think he has no interest in me.

I stare into the mirror and think: 'You are blind, Redmond.' When I think more about it, I know there is something absent. We hardly ever laugh, but then we hardly ever talk about anything that is not Redmond – and Redmond is not to be laughed at. Redmond is serious business.

I switch off the crackly portable radio Redmond has bought for himself. He switches it on when he gets home and holds up his hand, peremptory, as a signal to silence. I feel pushed away when he does that. He listens to some station that talks about the arts and politics. He never puts on a music station unless he invites some of his colleagues home. Then he seems to know all about classical music. I would rather self-imposed silence than to have to listen to music that reminds me of my father.

I wander into the kitchenette, drag the wooden chair out and climb up to close the skylight. I stare up into the pale sky. A seagull sitting on a roof peak stares back at me. White rings its eye, bold and rapacious. It has handsome red legs. Then it takes off, streaming into the wind, its call piercing. I close the skylight and get down. All of a sudden I feel weepy. Out loud I say: 'I want my mother.' I sound so ridiculous that I start to laugh. What is wrong with me?

I turn on the hot tap and the water spurts out, the pipes clanking up and down the building. What do I care? I hope I wake up the entire house, those silent people behind closed doors. People getting on with their lives, eating, lovemaking, cooking cabbage.

The bath is steaming. The room has warmed up and a faint ray of sun shines in. I add a judicious mix of Epsom salts and shampoo and some cold water, undress and climb in. The water is hot enough to leave a faint pink mark round my ankles. I subside, luxuriating. I have a book ready and settle in, shaking the foam off my hand before I turn the pages. I am glad Redmond is not here. I like my time alone. The water slushes over my breasts and belly and gives me a sense of equilibrium.

I decide to go the whole hog and have a cigarette. Redmond hates me smoking. I wipe my hand on a towel and light it. It makes my head buzz and then the sensation settles down. I do the drawback, thinking of Christine. What is she doing right at this minute? Perhaps she's asleep (because of the time difference), her blunt nose glowing white in the dark. Perhaps she has a boy beside her. I correct myself: a man.

I have left her far behind, a speck of my life way back on the horizon. I start to draw her on the canvas in my head, but this makes me sad. I have no energy for sketching when I know I can't develop a painting. What am I doing here? I have tied myself up so tight with Redmond that I have lost myself. I listen to what is there, but the water has drained me of vitality.

So what? I don't have to paint all the time. I can have time off.

Time off. From what? From life? asks another hard voice.

'Shut up,' I say to it, out loud. 'I don't care. Shut up. Even if I only do one painting a year I'm still an artist. Aren't I? Well, aren't I?'

In one of our arguments I shouted at Redmond: 'You're never happy with anything I do. Just tell me, Redmond. What am I doing wrong?'

This argument was over whether I should apply for a place in a drawing course connected with the Tate. Redmond is dismissive. He tells me it is a waste of time. When I persist, he shouts back: 'You always think of yourself first.' Then he quietens his voice: 'Sweetie, it's simple as one, two, three. All I need you to do is back me up. Just be there when I need you. I've told you before. Be an asset, Sweetheart. Forget all this other stuff.'

I run my hands down my body, comforting myself. My breasts are tight. They are enticing, the way they emerge from the water. I move my hand across my belly just above my pubic hair. The shampoo bubbles have gathered there and I sculpt them into a castle. I want to draw so badly I have an ache in my stomach. I stare at my feet. They look inhuman. I can see my painting taking shape. I hold it in my head, running through it again and again. I can invent something better any time I want.

I lie still, encased in white as if in a plaster cast. My legs are prototypes. The top half of my feet break the perfect rim, pointing upwards, but their reflection grows down. I think about *putting my best foot forward*, but how can I when it's pointing both ways at once?

I vow to myself that I will stand up to Redmond's controlling anger and apply for the course. Tomorrow. That wouldn't be too selfish, would it? After all, I am working too. I can please myself with some decisions, surely? I'm not just a useless drag on his resources. I know I don't make as much as he does, but still...

I move my hands back to my belly again, and press. Last night I felt something. There it is, a hard, round, movable lump just above my pubic bone, not a lump under the skin but inside, growing. I begin to discuss with myself the possibility of a tumour and even enact in my head a conversation with a doctor with a thick Scottish brogue (*why Scottish, for heaven's sake?*). He commiserates with me on my short life and early demise.

Who am I kidding? I know I am pregnant.

I think: 'Now he will love me. The infinite bond. I'll come first for a change.' I feel disturbed, yet excited. The balance of power has shifted by natural means, in my favour. Not my doing, not my fault. Guilt rushes at me, a small wind.

Redmond has chosen the withdrawal method of contraception, disliking condoms for their insensitivity. Besides, they are always coming off and getting lost inside me. I don't believe he puts them on in the correct way. When Redmond wants something to suit himself, strange accidents occur by stealth. The withdrawal method leaves me further away from the chance of orgasm than ever. Now I might have salvaged something better. I might even feel happy.

I hear a burbling sound, an underground rumble. Under some huge force the bath plug erupts and foul-smelling excrement bubbles into the bath water. It rushes up into the kitchen sink and plays for a moment, a fecal fountain. I can see shreds of tobacco, white fat globules, brown lumps. I leap out, stubbing my toe on the edge of the bath. Inside, something makes a disturbing, short, electric quiver in response.

'Oh shit,' I yell, 'shit, shit, shit.'

I say nothing to Redmond. I carry my secret round with me and on my next day off I go to a clinic off the Old Brompton Road. After a long wait, a young Indian woman doctor examines me.

'I consider you to be approximately at twelve weeks' gestation, sir.'

'That can't be right.' I say, shocked. Why do Indians always get the gender wrong? 'Not that long.'

'Yes, approximately yes. I will get you a card. You must come back reg-u-larly for ante-natal checks.'

I take the card, obedient. I look round at the other women as I go out. Every one of them looks absorbed.

Passing my favourite lolly shop on the way home, I go in. I have a craving for black striped humbugs.

'Sweets for the sweet,' the lolly man says, in friendly overture.

As my hand reaches for the packet, I stop. A craving? With absolute finality, my existence changes. I am pregnant. I will get more pregnant. Then I will have a baby. My responsibility for ever and ever. For ever.

The lolly shop man is watching me. 'You all right then, luv?'

I will never be alone or independent again. I am carrying a millstone. For a second I consider the alternative. I could get rid of it. I could turn the meter to nought and be light and free. But I know I won't do that. I feel weighted down, as if my feet are in more adhesive contact with the ground. I feel stately and timeless, as if I have grown up.

'Yes thank you. I'm fine. I'm pregnant.'

Immediately his demeanour changes to one of admiring consideration.

'Eating for two, eh? Happy days. Now my wife, when she was expecting, she couldn't get enough pickles. I said to her: "You watch it with those pickles. Our Anthony, that is, I said, he'll come out green and covered in bumps." Didn't stop her. You watch those humbugs, luv.'

Walking home I notice that the whole world is pregnant. Every second woman is walking sway-backed with her feet splayed like a duck's. I try it, surreptitious, just the feet, but it doesn't feel necessary. Not yet, anyway. Redmond comes home with another expat. They have been to the pub. I can smell the stout. He is a painter of course. Redmond only operates in the art world.

'Meet Lucas.' Redmond tries to hide the slurring in his voice. Lucas makes a courtly flourish with his arms.

'Hullo dearie.'

He seats himself, grandiloquent, in one of the easy chairs. Redmond has taken the other one, which forces me to stand or sit on the bed. I stand. I see Lucas has a frayed collar. Instantly I begin to dislike him.

'Does that rhyme with dreary?' Redmond flashes me a glance, which signals silence.

It is obvious Lucas has come hoping for dinner. I want to tell Redmond my secret and this man is getting in my way. Together, he and Redmond take up most of the space in our cramped bed-sit. They talk to each other, not to me. I am a piece of side furniture, or a mirror before which they can joust.

They talk galleries, and Lucas promises introductions. 'There's that West German guy. Originally from Budapest. Boy oh boy, is he sharp! You should meet him. Old Clive knows him. He goes behind the Iron Curtain. Gets all the best stuff. You'd know Clivey-boy, wouldn't you?'

'We're business partners of sorts.' Redmond looks evasive.

'Ah, well, home and hosed, laddy, home and hosed. Let's drink to good old Clive.' And Lucas takes a slurp of his wine.

I suddenly realise that in all our perambulations around London Redmond has not taken me to one gallery nor introduced me to anyone who might want to know that I am an artist.

Redmond seems hungry for something from this man. It can't be his reputation as a painter. I can tell he is second-string and that he does not want to talk about his art, not even to impress me. He wants to talk about his women. And Redmond, for his own reasons, wants to listen.

I forget to attend to them and remember, instead, an evening when we first arrived in London. We had gone out to dinner with a couple

from New Zealand. He was something in art history and she was a
conservator. I had liked them and it had been a good few hours.

They seemed to like me, too. They had laughed at one of my jokes
and I had felt myself expanding, a trick Japanese flower activated by
water.

We had walked home, late, through the streets of London, with
Redmond happy for once. I had felt light-hearted and when we
got back to our new bed-sit we had fallen into bed and rolled into
each other's arms. That night we had even made love face to face.
Afterwards Redmond had let me kiss him.

I held his face in my hands. 'Do you love me?'

Then it all fell to pieces. He looked at me, stony, and pulled away.

'I have only said that once, to one woman.' He paused for effect. 'She
broke my heart. I'll never say it again.' He looked at me, meaningful, a
bad actor. I knew he wanted me to think *Rosie*.

'Poppycock,' I wanted to yell at him. 'Don't be so adolescent. You
can't go on thinking like that for ever and a day!' But I said nothing
into the deadly silence. My heartbeat ran rough, as the chook inside
woke up and squarked. *You still there?* I asked it.

I wanted to get up and slam out of the room but I had nowhere
to go. Instead of the usual subtle attack, this one was pointed. Even I
couldn't doubt it. But I couldn't run downstairs and get on the next
bus and go home to my mother. Then it struck me. Here I was on this
sodden island, stuck, no fare home, at Redmond's mercy, in the grip
of his love-withholding. He could do anything he wanted with me,
apart from killing me, and he would get away with it. No-one knew me
and no-one cared if I was loveless and forlorn, trapped by an attitude
he would not permit me to change. No girlfriend to advise me. Just
him and me, estranged, alone in the universe.

I heard my mother's voice: 'You make your bed and you lie in it.'

'I can stand it,' I say back to her. 'Just watch. I'm not going to
break.'

'She was getting to be such a possessive bitch.' Lucas is expansive now
that I have hidden myself in the kitchen. 'So I thought to myself,
matey, what ho? I have to fix this before it gets worse.' I hear Redmond
laugh.

I pick up the fry pan and bang it down on the stove. There is a short silence in the next room. Lucas starts up again in his drunken voice: 'So anyway, that's when I had the affair with Linda. You've met the beautiful Linda, haven't you matey?' Redmond murmurs his assent.

I walk back into the room. Lucas and Redmond have come to the end of the bottle of red wine that Lucas has brought with him, wrapped in his arms, a glass baby. Redmond hunches forward, looking evasive.

'What about some dinner, Sweetheart?' He smiles a false smile. Lucas looks expectant. Did I really hear him say those ugly words? They look so normal now. Am I the one who's tilting? Maybe I'm the crazy one.

'There's nothing. No food at all.'

'Gee, Sweetheart. What've you been doing all day?' Redmond presses his thumbnail in between his teeth in frustration. 'We'll go out, then.'

I stare them down. Lucas looks worried and put out. I bet he has no money. Redmond hates eating out at restaurants. He abhors spending money on the pure enjoyment of having someone else cook. The few times we eat out, he cavils about the menu and the prices. One of Redmond's acts of sabotage.

'Well, come on then. Are you ready?'

'You go. I'm not hungry.'

Now he puts on a show of contrition for Lucas' benefit. 'Gee, Sweetheart, will you be all right? You're sure? We might go down the pub then. Catch an eel pie.' He smiles at Lucas, who looks jolly, jingling some coins in his pocket. 'I know you don't like pubs, Sweetie.'

My dislike has never stopped him before.

'The little woman not much of a cook?' Lucas asks the question of the air. 'Next time I come I'll bring a chicken and cook you my Chicken a l'orange.

I start to laugh, incredulous, but see from his face that he is in earnest. They go out, saying: 'After you.' 'No, after you' at each other in the doorway. They are glad to be going, having already forgotten me.

I wait while I hear them clanking down the stairs. I hear the thud of the front door closing way down at the bottom. Then I walk into the kitchenette and take out the two fine pieces of steak I bought earlier in the day. I am ravenous. I fry the steaks in butter and crushed garlic. I sliver some Parmesan on them from a block I bought in the Waterloo markets. I cut perfect transverse sections of button mushrooms to lay over the top, and eat both of them with my fingers.

Redmond gets home late. I feign sleep, turning my back. After a while his hand travels up my thigh. I make no response. I wish I could snore. His hand moves in between my thighs and he begins to massage me. I am dry and cold, unresponsive. He keeps at it until, enraged at his insensitivity, I strike his hand away and turn on my back.

Into the cold dark my words plummet: 'I'm pregnant.'

Now it is his turn to lie doggo.

'Aren't you glad?'

No response. Sadness creeps up my limbs, a brackish, back-creek tide. I hold my muscles so tense that a rigor passes through me from the strain.

'Aren't you glad?' I ask again. My body keeps shaking.

There is a muffled noise coming from Redmond's part of the blackness, emanating from his cold heart, slurring out of his dark soul. I reach over him and turn on the bedside light. All means of control are always on his side. He lies there, his face distorted from crying. Hope makes my heart thump and race. I peer at him. His mouth is purple from drinking red wine. He opens his eyes and in their depths I can see a thwarted salamander, ponderous, glaring, brooding underwater.

He switches off the light, turns his back to me and with a huge shrug rips the bedclothes off me and hugs them to himself.

'You bitch.' His voice is thick from wine. 'You selfish, taking little bitch.'

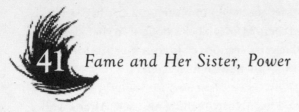

41 Fame and Her Sister, Power

My mother loved famous people. She was always pushing try-hards in my face. What did she want? If she was not to be famous herself, she would marry success. When marriage failed as the route to prestige, she thought I would somehow get it for her.

'Do it for me, Petsy.' She made herself ugly by the abandonment of her own character.

The shaping of personality begins at conception. Bathed in our mothers' mindset, riddled with their hormones, our cells hurry to develop. Nothing will ever be such a strong influence on us as this. No formative experience will ever crease our brain cases as deep as this urgent influx. We are our mothers' creatures, against which we rail for the whole of our lives. Something tells us we will never be free of them – yet we don't believe it. We hope to be as unique in our heads as we are in our thumbprints. But we aren't.

The moment I arrived in the world the imprinting began. 'I give up,' my mother said – and I heard her. 'I give in.' I followed along behind. 'Better let them have it their way.' I took it in through the pores of my thin skin. 'You can't be selfish.' I cringed. She finished, triumphant: 'I feel so guilty.'

Along with fame comes independence. My mother longed for the total control it would bring, but as my father noted, she didn't understand the first thing about it. They say independence is a delusion of grandeur. My mother was an anxious power-seeker, troubled by not knowing the name of what she sought to grasp. At least I know the name from watching the game play itself to the end. My mother never worked it out.

I thought I was different, a true loner. I thought the gene thread would end with me, that I would have all the time in the world to live my independence. My guiding demon was mine alone. I would owe nothing.

Now this foetus taking shape inside me has made me understand that we are not satellites roaming in the dark. Love, when it intervenes, is a quiet, pragmatic thing. Not many-splendoured as the song tells us, but a tender shower of magnetic sparks.

Once, I walked reluctantly next to Redmond at the dingy end of Holland Park. He was looking for the famous Jamaican flea market that we never found. He said: 'You're the most independent person I know.' He had a funny light in his eye. It was not a compliment, more an indictment. I would not give up my independence to him.

'You're a hard nut,' he reproved me.

All of them, Lionel and his son too, lost the right to share in my immortal soul. Now I can discriminate. Now I won't hand it out to the first bidder. They tried to eat me alive, those prating praying mantises. I feel a mothering rage rise in me. They say that murder is really self-defence. I'm no fool, though I used to be. I know the power-brokers' game, their call to loyalty and submission. And now I know something stronger. I know the truth of what love might be. I know the silence of resistance.

42 The Promises We Made

Redmond wakes me. 'How far gone are you?'

'The Indian doctor said twelve weeks.'

'An Indian doctor! How would he know? He's probably not even certificated.'

'She. It was a she.'

'She! Jesus Christ. What were you thinking? Why the hell didn't you go to a proper doctor? God you're hopeless. You can't be left to do one simple thing.'

'Stop it.'

An insane light goes on in his eyes. 'I bet you're not pregnant. This is some trick of yours to spoil our plans.' Just as quickly, he calms down. 'Don't you want to go to Paris with me?'

'*Our* plans! When were they ever our plans? Anyway, I thought you wanted to go to Scotland. Or Italy. That's it – you wanted to go to Italy.'

'We may, we may.' He thinks he is holding out a carrot to the reluctant nag. 'We can go anywhere, just you and me, Sweetie. The two of us against the world.'

'Well, it's you and me and baby makes three.' I make my voice as nasty as I can. 'So you'd better start getting used to the idea. Like I am. I didn't get pregnant on purpose, you know. It just happened.' (*Oh did it just?* says Christine's voice, unimpressed.)

My throat feels hot. It closes over and I start to cry. This is a mistake. It is always a mistake to show your throat to the snarling teeth. That is when they stop circling, when they see the fear. That is when they move in for the kill.

Redmond folds his arms and draws his lips back. He presses his thumbnail in between his teeth. He eyes me. It is a bad sign, that thumbnailpressing. He says no more but I know he is not finished.

I go off to work, my eyes pink from crying. Everyone in the office walks round me, even Barbara, whose wheedling tone I don't trust. 'Is there anything wrong?' she asks. Up close she smells of inner-London sweat and pettiness.

I will not tell her. I despise her prurient air. I sense her satisfaction at my apparent misfortune. When Iris pats me as she hobbles past, tears bounce out of my eyes onto the typewritten page and I have to start again. Barbara overlooks my lack of proficiency and paper wastage, but she still measures up my pages at the end of the long day. She will not allow Great Britain, or at the very least Greater London, to flounder under her beady gaze.

When I get back to the bed-sit Lucas is there, full of Friday night conviviality, and installed in the kitchenette. He has a barbecue apron on and flourishes his hands at a bald chicken sitting in the oven pan. In its opening he has stuffed a whole lemon. It protrudes, a yellow tumour.

'Hullo dearie.' He tries to put his arm around my shoulder. I slide away. He makes me feel beleaguered.

'Good as my word.' He recovers his balance. 'Only it's Chicken a la lemon. Couldn't find an orange, not for love nor money.'

'Where's Redmond?'

'Went out to get us a bottle of plonk. Won't be long. I hear congratulations are in order.' A look of concern appears on his face. 'Little mother feeling OK, then? Everything shipshape?'

'Why is Redmond telling you anything? I'm not discussing my private business with you. You're a complete stranger.'

'Father of two, luvvy.' The concerned look is back. 'You do want to have it, don't you?'

'Yes.' I round on him. 'What's it to you if I do or don't? Why are you asking me?'

'Nothing, nothing.' In mock alarm he puts up his hands in a stop sign. 'It's just that if you didn't, your Uncle Lucas knows a man who can fix it up for you. Keep it in mind, that's all I ask.'

As if on cue Redmond comes in the door. A stale gust of cabbage follows him. He and Lucas exchange a glance. Their blatant collusion frightens me. *Redmond, you're breaking my heart. You're killing me. None of this has to happen*, I reason with him in my head. *Just stop wanting to hurt me.*

I've noticed that we stop our life dramas to refuel. I imagine the bashing husband who drops his hand and allows his beaten wife to dole out the mashed potatoes, the sausages and peas. The family cringes as he stuffs his mouth with food. Only when he has satiated his hunger does he take up the cudgels again and continues knocking her from one kitchen wall to the other.

I see in slow motion the patient, murderous wife who serves up dinner to her unsuspecting husband and waits, polite, for him to finish. It is only when he has wiped the last traces of pudding from his lips that she picks up the carving knife and stabs him to death.

Now we stop for a meal, all parties to this particular conflict. Lucas serves up his Chicken a la lemon with a benign flourish. He is housewifely in his barbecue apron.

He has burnt the chicken. Redmond proffers a flagon of red wine and I take a glass. I don't like red wine, but tonight it tastes just fine. I drink one glass and then another. Redmond watches me.

'Should you be drinking all that wine?' His face is doubtful and behind the fake concern is something venomous. 'You know, with...' and he points to my stomach.

'With what?' I look around the room, glance up at the ceiling, peer down at my stomach in disbelief. 'Oh, you mean that! Don't worry about that. I'm probably not pregnant. No, no, just a neurotic fancy. You know, a false pregnancy, like cats get. Or Mary Tudor. No, not pregnant. As you so rightly intuited...' I trail off, smiling and take another swig of wine.

Redmond stares at me. He has had plenty to drink and it slows his reaction time. I take a mouthful of chicken. It is acrid and bitter. I spit it out. 'Yuk! What did you put in that poor chook's vagina? You sure it wasn't bitter aloes?' I don't wait for a response. 'Was it the bitter end, then?'

Now Redmond has something to work with. We are back in familiar territory: my attitude.

'I'm not going to sit here and have you insult my guest. You must be drunk. You're out of control. Say you're sorry to Lucas and try to behave, for God's sake.'

A lump in my throat makes it difficult for me to swallow. 'Your guest? Yes, he is your guest. I would never have invited him or his fucking chicken.' I choke and cough. 'I want him to go.'

They both look at me, irresolute.

'Make him go,' I screech at Redmond. Still my words have no effect. They sit there, dumb. I stand up. I feel as if I'm acting in a 1920's melodrama, but it seems appropriate.

'If you don't go I'm going to start screaming until someone calls the police, and I'm going to throw everything I can lay my hands on at you, starting with this putrid glass of wine.'

I brandish it in Lucas' face. He is beginning to look distressed and wattleish, a turkey gobbler disturbed while rootling in the bushes. Now he stands up.

'Better go, matey.' He turns to Redmond who is looking stupid or stupefied, which always, in my opinion, rounds out to much the same expression. 'The bride's got the shits with me, it seems.' He gives a strained, jocular chuckle.

'I'll see you out.' Redmond is now the perfect host. But he's not always the perfect host. I have often seen him pour himself more wine while ignoring the glasses of his guests. And he never passes anything at the table.

He returns. As I stand there glaring at Redmond, my wine glass an instrument of murder in my hand, a thought, in perfect form, is born of its own volition. It has come unbidden, out of a crack or crevasse. It floats in front of me in its own bubble of cartoon speech. It says: *I hate this man.*

It is quite bland, without passion. It has nothing attached to it – no body, no emotion. Just the dead fact. I look at it, curious, as it hangs in the air and I think what a strong painting it would make. The bubble of speech; Redmond's form as he ushers Lucas out the door, still wearing his barbecue apron; the way Redmond turns back to look at me before he leaves. I would have the wine glass with wings, levitating, exploding into sharp slivers, knife shards. In a cartoon format, the next strip would have him dying, slumped against the lintel, an arrow of glass in his eye and Lucas not noticing, all but his left leg vanished out the door.

After they are both gone I think of barricading the door, but that would be no good. Redmond would come back with the landlady and a policeman. They would huff and puff and blow my house down, then gobble me up.

'Too public,' I muse. But I keep on planning. I strip the bed of its blankets and sheets, take my pillow and make a bed in the bath. That's all it's good for, anyway. It had distressed the landlady to think that I would even try to use it as a real bath.

'Not with those pipes, dear,' she had said, affronted. 'I can't think what she was thinking,' she had said to Redmond, 'doing a thing like that.' Redmond had shaken his head with her in corroboration. 'Not thinking of others, was she?' She had stared at me, accusing and Redmond had stood there, saying nothing on my behalf.

Redmond is adept at taking sides against me.

I am the handmaiden who has fallen from grace. I have forgotten (did I ever understand?) that I should direct all effort to my husband's ends. Now the punishment must follow. He will annihilate me.

I pick up the bottle with some red wine still in it, shut the kitchen door and wedge the kitchen chair under the old fashioned door handle. Just like in the movies. Delighted with myself I hop in and settle down. It feels wonderful to relax, warm and cocooned. I take a defiant swig of wine and nestle the bottle between my thighs. I imagine I am in water, a warm ocean. I lay my hands on my stomach to keep it safe, and feel a ripple under the skin, a thread being pulled, before I fall asleep.

I dream I am a chauffeur to a man. We go on tedious journeys all over the place. We go to a five-star hotel where some other women are. Are they in his life? I can't remember. Only that I have to arrange things all the time. There is something about a bombed-out part of a commercial district. Something about making love. I wake to the rattle of sub-machinegun fire.

Redmond's voice says again: 'Open the door.' He rattles the handle. The chair stays fast.

'Let me in.' He forgets to say: *Or by the hair of my chinny chin chin, I'll blow your house in.*

'I'm sorry.' His voice now sounds careful, polite. 'I shouldn't have said what I did. Can we talk?'

'Get fucked.'

I don't care anymore. No more stepping gingerly. I am in a mood to run across shards of glass. I feel safe and on hold in here. When will I come out? Perhaps never. There's food here and water, though no more wine. The empty bottle between my thighs looks grotesque. The toilet is out on the landing, but I can wee in the sink. I drift off to sleep.

I wake again in the early morning. Not so comfortable now. My neck has a crick in it and my bony points are aching. I feel nauseated. I have a headache and my bladder is about to burst. There is no noise from the other side of the door. I get up, disengage the chair and open the door. The bulbous door handle shifts itself in and out of place.

Redmond is sleeping on the bald mattress, covered by his coat, fully dressed, just like me. We have both slept with our boots on, as if upon waking we plan to kick each other to death.

I sneak to the toilet. When I come back Redmond is awake, sitting on the edge of the bed staring at his hands. He looks posed. He lifts his cold eyes and surveys me. There is no life in his eyes; they are punitive pits. He has gone beyond sulking and anger to something more obdurate than I have seen before.

The first thing he says is: 'We must talk.'

Talk? We have never talked. I stay silent. I will not do this talking for him. Say what you have to say, I think. Let's see what you drag out from behind the door. Let me take a good look at what is in the charnel-house.

As if he has finished the process of soul-searching, as if he has done his homework, an assiduous boy, he says: 'I don't want it.'

'Don't want it,' I echo.

'No.'

He gives me a crumpled, adolescent, self-excusing smile. I can see in his eyes he believes I will now let him off the hook. I won't make him take something he dislikes, no nasty medicine for a charming lad, much easier than he expected. He is eager now.

'No, I never wanted them. Children.' He pauses, portentous. 'I thought I had always made that pretty clear.'

'Pretty clear,' I echo again.

'Yes.' The final pause. He has a look of great gravity on his face. 'So the best thing to do is for you to book in for a curette.'

'The best thing,' I echo for the last time.

'Yes. I've got the name of someone. I'll pay for it of course. He's private. It'll cost quite a bit but it shouldn't put us back too much if we're careful with other things.' He delivers me an earnest look. 'Trust me on this.'

There's that inquiring head voice again. He'll pay for it? What am I? Some one-night stand who got knocked up?

'Yes,' I answer, absent-minded.

He looks up at me now, glad I am agreeing with him, that I am being sensible.

'Lucas gave you the name, didn't he?'

'Yes he did.' He is happy to be truthful, happy to be straight with me.

A thought reaches me. 'Best for whom?' I ask.

'What?'

'The best thing for which of us?' I am deliberate with my grammar. 'For me or for you?'

'Well, the best thing for both of us, obviously.' He sounds exasperated, but he is still willing to be patient. After all, we have come a long way in a short time in our discussion. He can afford to help me over a few rocks at the end.

'What if I don't want an abortion?'

'A curette,' he corrects me. 'Why do you always have to go to extremes? You're so emotional.'

I say nothing. I do not bother to defend myself from his accusations.

'You make me sick,' he hisses. Now he is out in the open. He will not bother to feign anything from now on.

'What if I don't want to kill this foetus? What if I want to have a baby?'

'Don't be stupid. We can't. It will spoil everything I wanted. For us,' he adds. He is pleading with me and I almost give in, when the enormity of his demand hits me once more. I shake my head.

That starts him off again. 'I've got rights here too, you know. Always trying to get your own way. You didn't consult me, did you? At least

I'm trying to be honest with you. You've got to admit that. I never wanted to get married in the first place. I knew you were too young to understand. I knew you'd just grab everything for yourself. Life's not some sort of fairytale, you know.'

He stands up and looms over me, pushing his shoulders back. 'I blame your mother, I really do. She lives in la la land too. Like mother, like daughter. Pop always said so. Lady Muck! Who do you think you are, you stuck-up lot? Spoilt little princess. You're not living in the real world, Sweetie.'

'Why did you marry me, then? I don't recall forcing your hand. Wasn't it your idea?'

'It was never what I wanted.'

I stare into his black eyes. 'What have I ever done to you?' He stares back. He doesn't answer.

In all of this I am conscious of a feeling of unreality. I don't believe he feels any of these transient emotions – hate, frustration, malice, scorn. I believe he feels one thing only: fear. Fear that if the world does not mirror his desires, it will reduce him to nothing. If the mirror speaks the truth, it will shatter him.

I believe he thinks I am trying to kill him.

'If you have it, I'll leave you. Have it on your own. I won't support you.' His face screws up. He is crying. 'I'll leave, do you hear me?'

I have turned away. I can't bear to see the distortions of crazy self-pity on his face. My turning away is a mistake. Eye contact is the one thing that keeps him circling the perimeter. I hear him step back. He makes a curious little jump and kicks me in the small of the back. I stagger sideways, put my hand out to the rickety bamboo table beside the bed and fall over on one knee as it skids away under my hand. Across my stomach another running thread pulls. Something inside cramps, then lets go.

I hear, more than see, as he grabs his coat from the bed. 'You made me do that.' His voice sounds aggrieved, agitated.

He slaps his pockets for his wallet. He is about to go out the door when I call after him.

'Just a minute.'

He stops.

'Did I ever tell you something funny about your father?'

He is listening.

'He sexually molested me when I was a child. I bet he had a go at Rosie too. He was a pervert.'

'How disgusting. You're making it up. You're the one who's perverted.'

And he walks out the door.

43 *Pammy*

I believe that nothing is unconscious. It may take a while for factors to struggle to the surface, and there may be matters we find hard to acknowledge, but every creature and every action, at some level, is conscious of its purpose.

What do we know when we declare we *do not know*? What do we understand in one comprehensive glance, yet refuse to admit having seen? What do we put on paper – a half-finished study, a dream diary notation – and not understand when we have already taken action?

Take Redmond now: his sensate body, his ticking brain. As he walks the High Street he concentrates on staying alive. He cannot afford to imagine who he really is. If he is to have a long life, he must remain ignorant. But something within must be telling him that he is doing nothing wrong – and that's where he slips up. That justification alone shows he's thought about it.

He knows he cannot tolerate an image beside his in the mirror. So this is the moment when he chooses. 'Me first. Two for me and none for you.' His purpose is to be an amoral man. Not that he sees it that way. For him, it is a grand, enlarging decision.

Let us now consider my case. What understanding do I relegate to the base of my brain? Do I pretend not to know that the chances of becoming pregnant, with our shoddy method of contraception, are high? I toss the dice as hard as I can... and Bingo! What responsibility do I take for that?

No-one I know likes rubbers that much, remarks a helpful Christine. Then *I shouldn't have butted in*, she adds, contrite.

You can't help me, I tell her. *No-one can. So go away. Shut your face.*

My mother's hand had hovered suggestively in the region between her thighs.

'It's the woman's job to look after... you know what,' she had pronounced on the morning of my wedding.

'No, I don't know what.'

'Having... you know, taking precautions.'

'You don't have to tell me. I know what to do.'

'Well, I hope so. I'm only giving you good advice. Having a baby will never fix a marriage that's heading for trouble. I should know.'

'What's your life got to do with mine? Anyway, who says I'm heading for trouble? What baby?'

'All I'm saying is some people might think – well, you've been in such a rush to get married... some people have commented you know.'

'Get lost.'

'You rude girl. Don't be so superior. When I'm trying to tell you – You're impossible. I'm only telling you for your own good. One day you'll thank me.'

What do I make of the fact that now I feel free to despise Redmond? Nothing much, it seems.

Well, it's all there in black and white. You're right and he's wrong, my father hoots offstage.

But he is in the wrong! I shout back.

Redmond marches along at a good pace on this Saturday morning of watery sunshine. He detours into a bakery and buys a sticky bun which he eats out of the paper without taking off his gloves. He is heading off on a now familiar trek to Mayfair to get commiseration and anything else that's going from Pammy.

Pammy has been living in Clive's flat, having rushed on to the first available plane when Redmond wrote, some weeks ago, suggesting that she come.

His nose itches and stings in the cold air and he rubs it for relief. This action makes it worse. A flake of pastry sticks to the outside of his right nostril. His nose starts to swell. His right eye waters in the stiff air and he rubs that too. Despite these irritations, Redmond is a serene man, though as always, doubts niggle about his health. He shrugs his shoulders in his thin coat. He feels more lightweight, with a pleasant hollowness. To Redmond, the day is as uncluttered as an empty grain silo, as if, as he walks forward, his whole life up until now has vanished into a new and promising situation.

He's sure he's made the right decision – and Pammy will back him up. Pammy, doesn't complicate things or demand the impossible. Pammy is his right-hand man, loyal to the vision.

Pammy will never leave him in the lurch.

Paul

44 The Gallery

My father had told me more than once that only ratbags believed in spontaneous combustion. Still, I began to believe in it as I got up from the floor after Redmond had left. I was on fire inside. Cramps rolled across my abdomen, low down, from the right to the left, and started again. Then everything went quiet, the fires damped down. But it was a fire in a peat bog. It kept on smouldering through the weekend.

Redmond did not come home.

On Sunday afternoon I decided to go out. I wanted to buy myself a new sketch pad. Not a cheap one. Not anymore. I would buy the biggest one in London with the most expensive paper I could find. Pencils. Maybe even a roll of canvas. Oil sticks.

Redmond and I had a joint cheque account. I had never signed a cheque. Redmond kept the cheque book crumpled into one of his coat pockets. Then I saw on the table my wages from work that I had not yet handed over. Cash, quite a bit of it, in a fawn-coloured manila envelope. I felt rich, justified and reckless. I put on my coat and walked out.

I walked against the recurring, disquieting cramps as against a head wind. I had on the one purchase I had demanded for my time in London: a fake fur, black, three-quarter coat with a turn-up collar. Redmond had not come with me when I bought it. He disliked shopping unless there was something he wanted. He disliked my spending money unless it was his idea.

I was warm and protected in that coat as if I was in my own separate environment. I had felt happy buying it. I could withstand any gale while wearing it.

I found my way to Kensington High Street. I wandered down a side road that I thought was the one where Redmond had taken me once when looking for a gallery. We had found it, but Redmond had said we wouldn't go in then. I knew he would go later, without me in tow, on his own. I crossed over, went down another side street and suddenly knew that I was lost.

I thought about going back the way I had come. The left side of a clock face popped up in front of me. I felt unbalanced. As I tried to retrace my steps, everything became unfamiliar, as if the streets had disbanded and reformed, alien and confusing. So I went forward, and in the next block found what I wanted: the art supplies shop I had noticed that day with Redmond. Next to it was the gallery.

I went into the shop and spent a long time deciding what to buy. A big pad about three feet by two. Thick cream paper. Graphite. The yearned-for oil sticks. Pastels, wax and canvas.

I knew what I was going to do. In my mind I called them Ersatz Portraits. Portraits drawn from memory. The subjects, surrounded by items that embodied character, would have words crawling out of their skins. The first one would be the women at work in Waterloo, a group portrait, a Dutch interior. I felt an urge to get started that was so strong that I hopped from foot to foot outside the gallery next door.

I knew what else I was going to do. I was going to start looking after my own interests. Just like Redmond, I was going to work the room.

The heavy gallery door opened. A man stood in the entrance. He smiled at me, amused. 'Would you like to come in? There are facilities...'

I shook my head, 'No. No, thank you, I'm right. Sorry.'

You idiot. What are you saying that for? whispers Christine.

'Really?' He still looked ironic. 'Why don't you. Here, let me take that.' And he stepped out to the footpath and took my art supplies from me. Then he turned, went inside and disappeared, leaving the door open.

What's going on? My mother's voice is loud in my ear. Then in a frantic rush: *Watch what you're doing. You'll get it all wrong.*

My father's voice cackles: *Stick your head in the lion's mouth. See how it feels. Go on, Darl. See what he does.*

I don't feel anything, I tell him. *I never do.*

Then make it up, advises Christine, on her way past. *He's not my type. He's too old – but anyway...*

The man reminded me of a younger version of the actor Curt Jurgens, but more Magyar, with his square head flat at the back and his hair slicked straight back from the temples. His intonations were middle-European, overlaid with precise English, a learned sound.

In front of me the wooden floor of the hallway shone. I could smell beeswax. Oriental rugs lay as if they had slipped from their frames. On the right was an office and on its inside back wall I could see another door that looked as if it housed the stacks and shelving. He was not in the office. On the left was a large glass double door with brass handles. I could see through to an expansive, daylit gallery, with more beyond. It was empty of people too.

I had no choice but to walk down the hallway. At the end was another wooden door, this time ajar. I pushed it open and came upon a sitting room. Chintz-covered lounge chairs sat either side of a gas fire with fake coals. There was a white couch under a large picture window that let in light and some pale, low afternoon sunshine. There was a black-lacquered coffee table. Built-in bookshelves ran along the walls, with panelled cupboards underneath. More Persian-type rugs on the floor. Sculptural objects and art works crowded the room.

The whole place felt eclectic, but sure of itself. Through an archway I could see the edge of my art materials package leaning up against a bench. The owner of all this was standing next to the sink in what was quite a large kitchen. A skylight, an old-fashioned one like a slanted glass box, let in reams of light. It allowed you, if you looked up, to see the sky, clouds scudding past in slow motion, and no doubt starlight at night. Even, perhaps, the moon.

The man was grinding coffee. I could smell it. He looked unconcerned, at ease. 'Through there. Please do.' He gestured to yet another archway that led down to the left. It was a one-sided hallway, the right-hand wall made up of French doors that revealed a courtyard garden. 'Down to the end. You can't miss it.'

Now I wanted to see everything and I did need to go; my bladder felt tight. Everything felt tight down there, an ache that wouldn't recede. I tried not to think about Redmond's kick. It brought up the image of his unyielding face, wizened with rage. In front of me were two doors. Which one should I try? As I stood deciding, everything before me went black or blank, velvet with no nap. I looked down into a wall-less, bottomless space and felt nothing. But it was like a physical presence. Not sadness, not anger. Nothing.

I thought, 'I want to die.' In my chest I heard the rustle of feathers. The idea of death was in the space. 'Yes, I'll kill myself. That's the best thing. I won't think anything, down this midnight well.' It wasn't waiting; it included everything. It was itself, simple, obvious: the death trap.

It's a melody played in a penny arcade...

I knew if I kept staring down that well I would lose my balance. I would fall head-first. I could feel my physical body teetering when I heard the man's voice from the end of the hallway, careful, encouraging. 'It's the door on the left.' I put my hand out until I touched wood. With a click, the well abruptly disappeared. Gone. Where? I closed my eyes again for a second but I couldn't bring it back. 'OK.' I thought my voice sounded normal. I opened the door, then closed it behind me.

It was a humorous bathroom. A dark green bath stood on fish gargoyles that formed the legs. Around the walls in a band, thin mirrors created a reflecting ribbon, doubling, tripling, muddling each others' images. A toilet and bidet sat companionably side by side. Cartoon drawings of water spiders, skaters and other pond life made a continuous frieze above the mirror band. Trompe-l'oeil covered the ceiling; an Escher pond with tree reflections, leaves floating at different depths, with the shadowy presence of a large carp in the deeper foreground. Enamelled water lilies adorned the bathroom basin. This was the work of a skilled player. It smelled of sandalwood soap.

I discovered I had a small, bright red bloodstain on my dress. I scuffled through my bag for a tampon and came on one in a zipped compartment. It must have been there a while because the cellophane wrap was half off and it looked grubby. Down in one corner I felt, but did not stop to examine, Peter's engagement ring.

I decided on a wad of toilet paper instead of the tampon. I didn't want to think what the blood meant, so I decided not to think about it at all. It would go away. Everything would go away if I didn't engage with it. Right now I felt as if I had gone on an unexpected holiday from myself, for which I had no ticket.

When I got back to the kitchen I wondered how we would proceed. The man proffered his hand: 'Paul.'

He wore a dark blue shirt with a thin stripe, the sleeves rolled back to his elbows. I told him my name and spelt it for him. He looked amused and said: 'How archaic. I must remember not to fall out with you.'

A childhood song floated into my head:
Two little dickey birds sitting on a wall
One named Peter, the other named Paul.
Fly away, Peter, fly away, Paul
Come back, Peter, come back, Paul.

I executed the accompanying finger movements behind my back in defiance of Paul's smoothness. He looked quite a bit older than Redmond, I decided, but his European air made him hard to categorise.

Watch out for suave, warns Christine from her perch in my ear. He looks like a reffo to me.

He took me on a tour of his gallery, then led me back into the living room and we had coffee and coconut macaroons. I thought: 'I would like to make love while eating macaroons,' – but I didn't say that.

He looked me in the eye as he handed me my coffee. 'I've sometimes thought it would be particularly nice to make love while eating coconut macaroons.'

'Oh yes, so have I.' I was fervent. We listened to ourselves and I laughed and he looked more congenial than ever.

A thin black cat wended its way around the furniture. It sat in the middle of the space between us and stared at me. Then it walked out. I felt lazy, the coffee warm inside me, my ache receding. 'How beautiful your cat would look if it had its tail gilded.' I was thinking of a fairy tale.

He seemed to know it. 'Ah, yes indeed – and if I had a rooster it could go to Rome and become Pope.'

Paul told me he was a buyer for a big art auction house. 'The gallery is my bit on the side.' He raised one eyebrow in a suggestive wiggle. 'I like to encourage emerging artists.'

'Oh, yes – good idea.' I rushed to be polite.

As I sat, heaviness draped an arm around my shoulder. I didn't know if I had the energy for this new charade.

'Although I sometimes have bigger names on show.'

'They like the space. It's a good space, don't you think? I designed it myself... with a bit of help from John Soane, as you can see.'

What was he gabbling about? I knew if I opened my mouth I would say: 'How very clever,' with an English accent. So I just nodded again.

Paul encouraged my awkwardness as if he found it appealing. Why would I interest him? *Hollow try-hard.*

He sat and contemplated me without staring, chatting equably all the while. It lulled me to have someone who covered over the bare bits in a conversation with such fluidity.

Another proposition began to form itself. I could start from scratch. Reinvent myself. He wouldn't know the difference. Nor would I, probably. *I can make myself be anything I want.* 'What are you going to do with those?' He gestured at my art materials, still leaning against the bench.

So I told him about my idea for the Ersatz Portraits, and about where I worked. I told him how I'd left my other art at home in Brisbane, and how I had won the prize with Christine but was now feeling bereft. I told him how I was in Clive's book, how I hadn't painted for three months and was apprehensive, and how the light in the place I rented was no good.

I didn't mention Redmond.

But why haven't you worked all this time?' His voice was mock-stern.

'Oh, well, working for the agency. And travelling.'

He contemplated me some more. 'I find myself between assistants. I go away on buying trips quite often and when I do I am forced to close the gallery.' He scratched his head with both hands. 'Would you come and work for me? It would not be onerous and there is space behind the stacks where the light is good. You could work there. Quite easily.'

'Work for you?'

'Yes.' He watched me. 'I will not plead with you, but I am much in need.' His smile was disarming.

'I don't know anything about running a gallery. I'd be hopeless.'

Yes, agreed my father, you're hopeless as a wet weekend.

But Paul was speaking again. 'It's easy. Nothing to it.' He gestured, expansive. 'Simply open the door and people walk in. When they buy, you jot it down on a piece of paper and leave it until I come back. It's not hard.' Now his smile was enquiring. 'So that's settled.' He stood up. 'What are they paying you at that agency?'

When I told him he said, 'Ah, unfortunately I am forced to pay you a little more than that. Regulations, you see. Job description and so on. Tell them you're not coming back. You'll like that. Then come and see me tomorrow afternoon and we'll discuss arrangements. You must write down your last name and your address before you go.' He went over to a roll-top desk, extracted a piece of paper and stood looking over my shoulder as I wrote.

For a moment as I stood there with his pen in my hand, I wanted to turn and accuse him: 'I know you're after something. You're not fooling me. Well, you won't get anything. I'm the one who's going to get what I want.' I wanted to be able to say: 'My mother warned me about men like you' – but of course she never had.

At the door, he handed over my bulky package. I stared out into the street. I had no idea which way to go.

'Are you always so pale?'

'Oh, yes, I suppose. I think so. I haven't looked lately. Why?'

'Your Australian freckles are standing out rather markedly.' He touched my cheek with one finger and smiled again.

He gave me his card. 'Are you going on the Underground with that?' I looked at him, blank. 'Down to the end of the street, turn left. There is a station right there. Tomorrow afternoon. Don't forget.' He shook my hand and closed the door.

I walked off, but when I got round the corner of his street I stopped and read his card. 'Paul Zamic – Art Auctioneer, Valuer & Dealer.' I recognised his name as the one that Lucas, with a note of envy in his voice, had discussed with Redmond the night of the lemon-engorged chicken. The card gave Paul's gallery address and a telephone number.

Now I felt tired. More than tired – exhausted. My body ached and shivered in the evening gloom. The streetlights had yellow haloes round them that smeared out and danced obliquely as I stared at them. I remembered the streetlights popping on the afternoon I was married. Sadness, a cold cement, formed a solid block stretching from my throat to my chest. I felt deflated and stupid. Someone so nice couldn't be real. *Too good to be true.* There must be some catch. Paul was quite likely a homicidal schizophrenic who murdered silly women on the dot every Monday.

It's a Barnum and Bailey world
Just as phoney as it can be...

Down in the Underground it was icy cold, the tunnel lined with the white tiles of an abattoir. I kept seeing blood covering the surfaces out of the corners of my eyes. I read the wall map and worried about catching the right train. It seemed so hard. My cramps came and went. I needed to go to the toilet again.

You are so stupid you deserve to get killed. Anyway, if you go back on Monday he will have re-thought it, changed his mind – especially when he sees you in the cold light of day. I repeated *cold light of day.* It had a sad finality. *He'll say he can't do it – with an awkward frown. An art student type in a cape will be standing in the shadows looking triumphant. It will be humiliating. Serve you right. Macaroons? Yuk! Don't make me sick.*

As I climbed the five flights of stairs to the bedsit, the stitch in my side came back. I stopped on the last landing and went to the toilet. Nothing much happened and the full feeling stayed. There was another spot of bright red blood on the wad of toilet paper, a neat circle. It was a satisfying colour. I thought of my painting-to-be.

I opened the bedsit door. The stripped bed looked back at me, grudging. I took off my coat. The room was cold. The air sneaked round my cheekbones. I discovered I had no coins for the ugly gas meter box on the skirting board. Too tired to make the bed, I bundled the blankets round my body, took off my shoes and fell asleep.

I dreamed I was in an Underground railway tunnel. I needed to go to the toilet. I thought there wasn't one, but found it behind green-painted wooden saloon doors. It was a double toilet and I realised there were already two women in there – but they let me in. The toilet facing me was full of greenish-yellow urine and lucerne straw. It was a clear solution. It had some association with rabbit piss and rabbit pellets.

Earlier, I knew I had been in a hospital tunnel. I was emptying bedpans. It was a children's ward, with young babies who walked around talking. One baby was grey in the face and had a compound fracture of the skull. She was not breathing. I knelt beside her so I could do heart massage. But I found she was really a small book with a hard cover. I tore the cover off and positioned my hands. I had trouble deciding where, on the tiny page, her heart could be found.

I walked with a young woman down the tracks that ran along the dirt floor. Fine silver fishing wire, many-stranded, made up the tracks. I asked her how she knew when a train was coming and as I did so I saw a light at the end of the tunnel. So I already knew. She said to watch the wires and I saw orange husks, cut in half, suspended on more silver wires from the ceiling to the track. They jiggled as the train approached.

I woke to pounding at the door, again and again. I was repeating in my head the phrase, *a clear solution*. I recognised the pounding. Only the landlady hammered like that. I got up and felt something break inside, slowly parting. I felt pain that was so bad I couldn't tell where it came from. I staggered to the door, still wrapped in my blankets, and opened it. The landlady stood there, a simulated smile on her face. I could see bits of soggy food caught in the too-regular crevices between her false teeth. I felt sick.

'Rent day, luvvie.' She moved her head on her neck to have a snoop in through the doorway.

'Yes, all right, just a minute.'

I thought, 'She wants me to get my purse.' Then it came away, simple as that. I stood, helpless to stop it happening, as blood splashed down on my socks, on the floor, great gouts of it, pieces of liver. My legs were shaking. I couldn't stop them. I could see my white hand in front of me.

I heard the woman say, 'Oooh, not on my carpet!' as she moved back in alarm.

I heaved myself to the kitchen. 'Sorry, sorry,' I managed. I left a trail of blood wherever I went. I collapsed to my knees by the bath. The pain was so acute it stuck me in position as if I was playing Statues all by myself and the music had come to a halt.

The landlady had disappeared.

I stayed that way until two ambulance men arrived.

'What's up, luvvie?' one of them asked me. It didn't take them long to work out.

They laced their hands together and carried me past the staring landlady down four flights of steps to the waiting ambulance, then drove me to hospital.

45 Casualty

It is noisy and busy in Casualty. Beyond my curtained alcove I can hear someone groaning and crying out, the clatter of metal on metal, doctors and nurses talking. I can see legs walking past under the skirt of the curtains. They have examined me but what is happening is all but complete. A nurse comes in to take my temperature and blood pressure and check the tube they have put into my arm. Then she leaves me alone again.

They are benign and businesslike, but offer me no comfort, for which I am grateful. Any tenderness would only elicit weak tears. I can feel a sob positioned in my throat ready to grow to something more significant, all by itself. I prefer that crying doesn't begin. I don't think I have the energy.

I suppose I am in shock. I look at the idea: *You're in shock.* It doesn't seem to mean much. It would be wrong to say I feel numb, but I am unattached to my body. It just seems to go on without me. They say I will need a curette and when they can organise a bed they will send me upstairs. It will probably happen on the first surgery list early tomorrow morning.

I am resigned. It is all too late.

I say to myself: 'OK, clean it out – what's left. Leave nothing behind.'

They must have given me something for the pain. It is still there, but I don't care about it. I doze on and off, woken sometimes by a doctor parting the curtains then conferring with the Charge Sister and her clipboard, before moving on.

I hear myself described as 'a spontaneous abortion, first trimester' and 'No, we don't think it was induced. She's down for a D & C.'

'No, no sign of the hubby', they say. 'She doesn't seem to want to contact him,' they go on. 'Got a contusion on her fanny' they say. Are they talking about me?

I stay long enough to go through another change of shift, another set of heads poking through the curtain, a brief examination. I begin to notice the personalities of the staff. I begin to like it here. They have wrapped me in cellular blankets that give the semblance of warmth, although I feel cold inside, as if someone is playing a fan over ice. I lie in relative comfort and there is activity going on around me that I can tune into if I want. Almost like being at a party. I consider what would happen if I asked for a cigarette and a glass of wine.

There you go again, says that disapproving voice in my head. *You behave so inappropriately. No wonder you don't get on.*

Shut the fuck up. I am mutinous. *What does it matter?*

A wardsman comes to take me upstairs, tunnelling my body down corridors, pushing my trolley through large, dingy plastic doors feet first. He pushes me into a service lift and reads my chart as he waits. 'Too bad,' he commiserates, and gives my feet a pat.

He hands me over to a harried nurses' aide who pushes me into a two bedroom ward. In the other bed, sitting up on the cover, is a young woman wearing a blue dressing gown and slippers with blue pompoms that shimmy when she moves her feet. She is pregnant and looks healthy, except for the rubber band. The rubber band is round her wrist and once in a while she gives it a ping so that it hits her skin.

'Whenever I have bad thoughts the psychiatrist told me to give this rubber band a little snap and I snap out of it, hey presto' – and she demonstrates for me. She has a hunted look in her eyes and scar tissue down to each wrist.

A fitting companion. *We're the undead*, a voice whispers.

Down the hallway, within earshot, is the post-natal ward. Babies wail through the night at set intervals and each time they start up afresh my uterus lurches and clenches and more blood seeps out. I can't sleep. I get up the courage to press the red buzzer and ask for a hot water bottle for my frozen feet. When it comes I place it instead on my belly that feels colder still, but when the night duty nurses' aide finds it there on her next check she takes it away, tut-tutting.

In the middle of the night my rubber band companion starts to have contractions and they cart her away. As they push her out through the swing doors I see into the corridor: its fluorescent clarity, its undying brightness. The warm, body-sweet, overpowering deodorant odour of blood and sanitary pads wafts up at me.

I stare at the green-glowing clock on the wall. Now I cry, now in the desperate, sick, 2am hiatus. This is a film with no director and I am the cast of one on a closed set. I am very lonely. Nobody here, except for the babies down the hall, wah-wahing through the first provisional hours of their lives.

I check the clock again. Five minutes past two. How can I still be alive on night's black runway when I have been run down by this huge aircraft of grief? In this dark room with its sparse, mechanical furniture I have forgotten the quality of daylight. I have no-one to ask, so I ask myself: *How am I to live my life?* The question is an atom that pings in the ghostly silence as it hits the room's metal and vinyl surfaces. I stare into the grainy darkness and consider what Fate has prepared for me. I know my future will not include Redmond.

I think that what I will miss most in all that has been taken from me, my most painful loss, though the least physical, is the comforting protection of what I can only call family. The easy looseness, the insouciance engendered by assurance. Just the plain sight of the other. Knowing I would never mistake Redmond for someone else, knowing his name without thinking – even when his remembered face sickens me. That almost-blood tie, the security of feeling, the familiarity. All those things that have now become a dangerous farce. All those fragile things that existed for a moment. I will miss them the way I miss the warmth of my father's lap, the smell of his shirt, the roughness of his coat. Animal comforts without reason, with no need for thought or examination. A given. The physical closeness of the den, relaxation within the unchecked response, the glazed lassitude of recognition.

My next thought is that I wish these feelings of loss on Redmond, like a curse. I hope they hurt him in the long, unsleeping hours as they do me. I wish tears to spring to his eyes, uncontrolled. I want him to feel with unblinking clarity, that in throwing me away from him, he has committed murder on himself. He has torn away something that can never grow again.

In the small hours I wish him heartache and harm. In the dark, in the silence broken only by relentless ticking, in the pitiless, frozen-faced night, at the precise moment when he is most vulnerable, I want to bequeath him utter desolation.

They prepare me for my curette early in the morning. The night nurses' aide shaves my pubic hair. It makes me feel bare and vulnerable, a plucked chicken about to have its gizzards ripped out. The apparition of Lionel stands off to one side, his shoulders half-turned away, his hands in the pockets of his roomy shorts. His eyes are painted radioactive green.

I hear my father say to my mother: *Don't be so hostile, Darl.*

I tell them: *Look what you've done. Are you satisfied?*

The nurses' aide is in a rush to finish her work and get home. She has a whole day of normal events ahead of her. By contrast I feel as if I have disengaged from society. I want to stay here in limbo and never make another decision. I want competent people to look after me and ask nothing more of me than my full name, my transient address.

The pre-op medication has made me drowsy, my mouth dry, but has not prevented the surges of panic that rise in my chest, dumper waves. They crash, then fritter their way across my belly, bleeding out into shallow ripples just above where they shaved me. A different wardsman has come to take me down to the theatre. I am complete with charts and my belongings in a brown paper bag. My wedding ring is in there. I had the choice of having it taped or taking it off. I told them: 'Take it off.'

I will not come up here again, but will go to a surgical ward instead. We make the journey down in the lift. This wardsman hums a tune that sounds familiar, then smiles, apologetic. 'Sorry, luv.' Out of a gap in my heart I put the words to the tune he hums. Lionel's tune.

Long may live my lovely Hetty
Always young and always pretty...

I breathe in deep to send it away and quiet the panic.

There is a short wait in the theatre anteroom. An anaesthetist comes to check me. 'All be over in a jiffy.' His voice is kind. 'You're not worried, are you?' Tears slide out of my eyes and I let them drip down and run into my ears. I shake my head. He too squeezes my foot. His gesture is companionable, reassuring.

They wheel me in. It is an amphitheatre, a viewing chamber. This is a teaching hospital and above me in circular rows behind glass, students stand staring down at me. I am a trapped animal, deposited on the operating table, strapped and cuffed. Nurses and interns busy themselves around me, some of them talking, cheery behind their masks, about their weekend. The operating light hangs high above me, a Martian instrument of death. They clip something on my finger and my pulse broadcasts to the room.

The surgeon comes to stand beside me. 'That's a nice pulse, ducky.' He puts his warm hand on my arm. 'Now count backwards from ten for me.' As he speaks I feel as if I am about to be murdered. My pulse hammers into the room, running ahead of me, escaping. I cry out with a loud sob and that is the last thing I know.

I wake to hear myself moaning with fright, returned as if they have clicked me on. Apprehension of pain invades me. A masked nurse comes over. She quietens me down. 'Everything's fine. Do you know where you are?' I nod and subside.

It is all finished. Shriven. I have nothing left. A clean slate. The smell of the slates at primary school was a mixture of water and mouldering sponges and spit. The boys always spat on their slates. Steel glints shot through the sticks of graphite and their points engraved words, newly-formed, across the face of the slate, combusting silver, enormous.

I think of Brisbane and my single bed with its blue eiderdown. The dark gust of night sky, the stars prickling, the gap with the Southern Cross turning over. The shirring of cicadas, frogs croaking, listening to themselves in the well of a summer night. The shimmering heat, the purple jacarandas, the red stain under the poincianas. The paspalum, the dust, the expectant ticking of a summer afternoon. There is no red dirt in London. You cannot sense your scale here, the way you can in Brisbane. In Brisbane I lived on the pelt of an enormous live animal.

I think of Lionel, that blue day, washed by rain. He gets off me and starts doing up his buttons. I stand up, cracking my forehead on one of the nesting boxes, disturbing a chook who might all this time have been laying an egg. She clucks in that astounded way chooks have of showing their displeasure. In light that is bright and unvaried as technicolour, I walk past Lionel and keep walking, brushing myself clean as I go. 'Hey girlie,' he calls after me, as if to a stranger. His voice coaxes, conciliatory, but I keep on walking until I reach the dividing drain. Something shifts position out to the right of my field of vision. I don't look to see what it is. I run to my parents' back door.

Now I see what was waiting to be seen. Now I turn my stiff neck, stricken. There, a thicker shadow moves, underneath Lionel's house, among the zebra patterns thrown by the wooden slats. It moves back and stays still. It is Redmond.

46 The Waterford Pen

When I was seven my father gave me his old leaking brown Waterford pen with its calligraphic nib. He had used it as a postgraduate student in Rugby, England. Later he gave me a pen-knife with OSRAM written on it.

I loved filling the pen, expanding the lever, dipping the nib in the bottle of blue Quink, sucking the ink into the bladder, practising my signature. I whittled away at twigs with my pen-knife or pretended to sharpen my nib. Sometimes I used chook feathers to write, the quill scratching and blotching its way across the pages of my mother's aerogramme pad.

Always insufficient, the efflorescence of thought. Shapes, lines, words dissipating between brain and paper. The fumbling expression of 'I'. The pinning down of that essence, the attempt to translate it into art. The bearer confounded, so finally she understands there is no 'I'. No hatching place, no corpuscle in the blood, no swelling in the heart, no process in the head that will carry the soul's gold. Only an illusion of a self, barely strong enough to pass as real.

We are robots fashioned from DNA, given a fake identity so that we will carry on, thinking we are being ourselves. We think we must complete our unique task, when our real task is the common one of replication. There are good reasons why we make the same mistakes again and again. There is only the repetitive pattern of life on earth. No wonder everything gets based on a replicated pattern. No wonder God looks like us. Go forth and bear children and if you won't or can't, then suffer hypervision from searching for a nesting spot and seek immortality the hard way.

47 Respite Care

I am getting used to these underground corridors painted battleship grey half-way down, then cream, with scuff marks from the trolleys. I recognise the sterilisation unit, full of middle-aged women bashing steel ovens open and closed. They watch the trolleys that go past with warm interest. Why are women always the cleaners, the scrapers-up of messes? Blood is our familiar.

Steam issues from the doorway. There must be a rule about keeping this door shut, but so far it has been open. There is the canteen with its rows of clinical tea trays, the meals covered with tin lids. On the bottom of the trolleys sit plates of blancmange, pink and white, and the red and green translucent shapes of jellies. So much metal in conjunction with so many soft bodies. The house of knives.

It must be nearly lunch time. I haven't eaten since the coconut macaroons on Sunday afternoon.

The service lifts again. This one has theatre staff in it. They still wear their green gowns and cloth overshoes. They look at me, speculative, an air of the mechanic about them.

They take me to a four-bed ward. I am getting less and less special. Soon they will discharge me. Back to what? An empty bedsit with the rent owing and an irate landlady lying in wait to bill me for the price of cleaning the carpet? What happens when Redmond returns, if he ever does? I know I can't sleep in the same bed with him The sight of him would make me shudder. Yet I am dependent on him. I don't have my plane fare home. I don't even know where he keeps my passport. I can't function without him.

That's not true. I don't need his permission to breathe. Do I?

I can't bear to think of myself without him, even though I hate him. I hate his eyes. And his mouth. He can't walk away from me. I can't be without him, all alone. I can't do things by myself.

It's gone bung, my father announces, mock-doleful.

Some monster called Redmond has drunk my blood, cut off my hands and feet. I have let him do it without so much as a bleat. He must have cut my head off first and eaten my brain so that I didn't notice. I must have thought it was a love bite. All this must have something to do with love.

I don't know what love is; that much is plain. I thought it was something that just happened, that you didn't have to think about too much, that you took for granted. You didn't talk about it in case you sounded soppy or artificial. I thought love lived in words – but then Redmond has been at pains never to speak words of love.

I thought love inhabited actions. But if I look closely, Redmond has never done anything that isn't first and foremost for himself. We had, however, agreed to marry, even to love, honour and obey. Is that the formwork upon which this whole edifice rests? Why bother to promise if you mean to be deceitful? Why go through the costly charade of marriage if you prefer to prowl around unencumbered? For my part, I knew my promise meant fidelity, a contract signed and kept in good faith. So his promise was a trick. But why? So he could bleed me white?

What have I done wrong? Have I been a drag on him? Did he feel *he* was the one drowning? Then why do I think he wanted me attached to him? What's the difference between attachment and dependency? Tell me that.

Blowed if I know. My father gives a derisive, semi-detached grin.

I begin to think I prefer the mirror theory: *Mirror, mirror, on the wall/ Who is the fairest one of all?* But Redmond replies: 'I am! You just hang there, Sweetheart and don't you ever dare get off the wall or even ask for a polish once in a while.'

If this is so, why can't I cut my losses and walk away? Because, because... I can't believe he would do it to me, despite the mounting evidence. Despite the ground littered with hints, a rubbish-strewn oval after a football match. Because it must be a mistake that he doesn't love me. It is a grave infraction of my own, that I can put right only if I can find the clue, the key. Because it's my fault.

I cannot bear to know that he does not care for me, that he plans my murder the minute he finds out my devotion is flawed. I am a serial number in a long succession of deadly notations, and I cannot bear to admit I married a serial killer. I cannot let go of the notion that I can make him love me. I was too polite to say, 'Hey, hang on a minute, what's this?' *Too polite? Are you kidding?* No, I'm not kidding. You don't question someone's promises. You don't sabotage their good intentions. That's unforgivable.

Then there's the voice that says: *Don't be ridiculous, you're just exaggerating. As usual. It was only a little kick he gave you. This miscarriage was an accident that was going to happen. You could feel it, couldn't you?*

It's a bloody mess, wails my mother.

Not his fault continues the voice, dispassionate, unstoppable. *You can't blame him. It's not as bad as all that. You always make things worse. One good, solid talk and everything will come out right. He simply lost his temper. You're pretty infuriating at times. In fact you're a controlling nag. If you just had the right attitude... If you were a nicer person... You've read it wrong; you wouldn't know your head from your heart. He has feelings too. Say you're sorry, give him a chance. Don't be so demanding. He's only human. We all fail to measure up. You always ask for too much. Your eyes are bigger than your belly. Your mother told you that. Grow up!*

My father's voice tunes in, a crackly transmission: *Be reasonable Darl.*

They have kept the curtains drawn round my bed. A nurse pops her head in.

'There's a visitor for you. Do you feel up to seeing him? We might tidy you up a bit first. Where's your nightie now? Do you have a comb, lovely?'

I shake my head. I am still in my theatre gown with the split down the back. I can smell the sweetish smell of my own blood overlaid with the clinical smell of disinfectant. My mouth feels furry.

'Well then, we'll give you a bit of a wash. He won't mind waiting, now will he?' She is conspiratorial. She has an Irish accent. 'We'll give him a cup of tea. That'll keep him busy.'

My hands start to shake and sudden tremors begin inside. I don't want to see him. How can we make eye contact after what we've done to each other? So ugly. Too up close, too fleshy, too incriminating. Far too much to acknowledge.

I hear my mother's voice: *Don't make a fuss in public.*

I can't imagine Redmond sitting, docile, waiting, cup of tea in hand. He will walk out if he is made to wait. I don't care. I don't want him to be here, just as I was glad he wasn't there when it happened. Private, bitter sorrow. Let him go.

The nurse comes back with a basin of soapy water and a washer. She washes my face for me. She scrubs, assiduous, at other parts of my body, changes my bulky pad, and gives me some mouth wash and a clean white gown.

'We can't do much about the hair but it's fine, fine,' she encourages. 'I'll go and let him off the leash for you now. Such a nice fellow you've got. Some girls have all the luck.'

See, says the voice, *it's not him, it's you. He makes a good impression on everybody. They can't all be wrong.*

I lie back on my plumped-up pillows. I am too tired to have any fight left in me. I quiver before the onslaught. I arrange my face into an expressionless mask, and draw up my legs ready to defend myself.

Paul Zamic parts the curtains and comes up to the bed. 'You didn't come for your appointment, but I tracked you down.' He smiles. 'I am indefatigable.' It seems to be a good smile, a bit pleased with itself, but warm, maybe even concerned. I can't bear it.

'Yes, well I didn't think the terms of employment covered pregnancy.' I sound horrible, coarse, but I keep on. 'So I thought I'd just drop in and have an abortion.'

'Don't say that.' He pulls the only chair up to the bed and sits close to my shoulder. He is quiet. I stare straight ahead, seeing nothing, trying to stop the tears from breaking out. I feel my lower lip tremble. I don't want to look pathetic. I don't wish to be at anyone's mercy.

'Where is your husband?'

'How do you know I've got one?'

His expression is impatient and impassive at the same time.

I am defiant. 'I don't know and I don't care.'

'He hit you, didn't he?'

'No, it was more of a kick really.' I stare back at him. 'How the Hell did you know, anyway?'

'If you ask questions, you often get replies.' His voice has a tremor of bland amusement.

He is silent again. He becomes serious. 'I do need you to work for me.' He lets that sink in. 'It would be better if you came and lived at the gallery.' I gaze at him.

'I won't be there.' He strokes his nose and returns my look over the cover of his fist. 'I live somewhere else. I don't think I explained that I would prefer my assistant to live in.' His voice is easy. 'For many reasons, security and such...' He trails off. 'I met your landlady this morning.'

'I'll have to go back. She'll want the rent.'

'There is no need.' He is enjoying himself. 'She appeared most upset at the turn of events. I took it upon myself to advance her the rent. On your behalf,' he adds, wary. 'She seemed anxious to terminate your occupancy and get another set of tenants. Once she has cleaned the carpet. The carpet was very much on her mind.' He sits, reflecting. 'I advanced her a cleaning fee as well.'

I lean forward to interrupt.

'No, no – I will take it out of your wages. It's perfectly simple. There was no use arguing with her. I must say we were in perfect agreement about the carpet.'

'What about my gear? I'll have to go back for that.'

'Oh, but she was happy to let me in. I have your belongings in the car. And here' – and he reaches down to bring up a brown paper bag I had not noticed before – 'is a change of clothes.'

'But my passport. I haven't got my passport. I don't even know where it is.' I can't stop my voice from quavering.

My father's voice says: *Crikey, where's your get-up-and-go?*

Leave me alone, I say. *Stop telling me what to do. Let me do it on my own.*

'Ah, the passport.' Paul pauses for effect. He won't make me break down. 'I have that too. That was easy. It was in a fairly unique filing system under the bed. Amongst many other papers and letters from Australia. Your husband is an energetic correspondent.' He ponders this state of affairs. 'Not you, so much.' He leans back and laces his hands across his front. 'Handsome fellow, your husband.'

Paul has on a pearl-grey waistcoat. I want to ask him if he has a fob watch like my grandfather's and whether he clips his nails or bites them.

'Now when your husband returns, as indeed he must, for he is without his passport...' – he pauses to let me catch up – '...he will find it with his belongings in the landlady's care. Now I think of it, I might instruct her to elicit the rent and repairs from him and reimburse me that way. Much better, don't you think? More fair, fairer.' He struggles with the syntax.

'Striking hair,' he adds.

I can feel my shoulders stiffening. 'Look, it's extremely nice of you to do all this for me.' I stop. I want to say: *Why don't you go and have a beer with my fascinating husband, then?*

I start again. 'But now that I think of it, it's quite peculiarly nice.' I trip over the word 'peculiarly', which rather spoils the effect. 'We're perfect strangers. It's not normal to go out of your way for strangers...' I lean forward. 'Everybody knows that.'

See, I tell myself, *your intuition is in perfect working order.*

'So, why would you do it?' *Let's see what he does with that.*

'You're right.' He nods and I feel deflated. The world is as I thought. 'But the trouble is, everything has to fit into my theory.'

Here it comes, I think, *the crackpot theory.*

My father, out in the blue Pacific haze yodels: *Mad as a cut snake.*

'Oh, your theory – what is your theory? Remind me again, will you.'

'It's the theory of assisted Fate.'

'Is that like the theory of assisted suicide?'

'Not so much.' The judicious note is in his voice again. 'A little bit more upbeat than that. It's more that I like surprises.'

He has brown, agile fingers. I think of Gregor and his planes, the boy-redolent cubbyhole of his arms. All at once I can smell, as if brought to me on a breeze that has skimmed the crests of the sea, the hot school room: overripe bananas in musty lunch boxes, the baked scent of wooden desks, blond rulers indented with teeth marks.

'Now,' – I watch him warm to his task, ruminating – 'Fate toddles along, doing what it must. But I like to give it a hand, throw something into the ring, as it were. The chance occurrence. You step out on to the street and you take a chance. Don't you ever want to do that?'

'Not really. It's hard enough coping as it is.'

'So there you were, jiggling up and down on the spot. I couldn't resist. It seemed a very good opportunity.'

I lean back on my pillows. A sensation of impending reprieve settles round me, as cool and regular as the sheets.

'But you must tell me one thing.' He has pieced together almost the whole puzzle but there are two or three tiny sections of innocent blue sky, as yet unplaced, needed to complete the picture.

'Who is Pammy?'

48 Pure Fiction

Paul is a man who keeps his ears and eyes open. He does it as a matter of course because the world interests him. He has noticed the sound of Australian voices in the stairwell of his Mayfair apartment. First, there was the woman's voice. Then a man's voice joined her. Lots of to-ing and froing and hasty clatterings on the stairs. Unease in the air. Something at odds, latent, about to erupt. Someone was taking up a lot of space. It was Redmond.

Redmond always makes his presence felt. He is as pervasive, as oppressive as low barometric pressure. He moves in from the Bight, bringing the cold. There is something eerie about him, presaging turbulence and high winds. He forecasts discord.

But let us not forget his coercive charm, his charisma, his social manner, the crooked grace, the superficial rightness. Let us not forget his eyes, which promise depth. But it is all dark promise. Nor should we underestimate his ability to make all of us feel responsible for feeding his insatiable appetite. Poor fellow. So hungry, deprived of his portion. Don't forget to watch him as he eats. He can never get enough.

We are mirrors to him, made for his reflection. My grandmother used to cover her mirrors when she heard a thunderstorm approaching. 'Mirrors attract lightning,' she said with authority. In her day, if someone died, they covered the mirrors lest Death should delight in its own image.

Let us get back to the weather map. We can agree that a tempest is a tempest is a tempest. It will blow itself out in the end, but before that it wreaks havoc. We will all have to pay dearly for being out in this weather.

In his Mayfair apartment, Paul solves the puzzle. He notices that the woman, Pammy, is forever on the run. She arrives home early.

Redmond comes back late and at odd hours. When he turns up, Pammy gets overexcited, over-solicitous. Over-happy. What is that saying? 'When you reap the wind, you harvest the whirlwind.' Pammy might have the tempest by the tail, but can she hold on?

In Mayfair, Pammy does not notice, with all those lights competing with the night sky, that there is a season of comets. They shower across the sky. They are brighter in the Southern Hemisphere. She is in the wrong place to read the portents.

There is another saying, one that Paul knows. It says: 'The tail of the comet sweeps men to war and women to a broken heart.' Redmond is always at war with himself, in confrontation with destiny. He cannot recognise frailty. He will never pick up the seedpod of life, give it a good rattle and say: 'Yes – easily shattered.'

It is a pity that Pammy and Paul don't converse in the stairwell. Despite his penchant for assisted Fate, Paul is a reticent man. And Pammy doesn't compel him.

Even before he unearths the passports, Paul has already put Redmond, Pammy and me into the one equation. The thing to notice about Redmond, he decides, is not the colour of his hair, but that he isn't real. Charming men are often that way. They are never as they seem. Not truly human. You can tell, because their yellow metal never tarnishes.

I know Paul is real. You can feel him. Redmond, on the other hand, is pure fiction.

49 The Bloody Thread

Paul is around during the day at the gallery, in his office, often on the phone. But at 5pm sharp every day he calls good-night and leaves for Mayfair. Soon, he tells me, he will be instructing me in my duties as his assistant. So far he has introduced me to prospective buyers and colleagues who call round. He encourages me to move forward, his hand on my shoulder. It is a firm hand. He hasn't shoved me yet and perhaps he never will. He does not talk of family but I see he has lots of friends, both male and female. Only one or two are artists.

I have the bedroom to myself. Its door is the one next to the bathroom, the one I hesitated in front of when suicide tempted me. I often stand out in the chilly courtyard at night, staring up at the foreign sky. The black cat leaps over the wall and joins me. The stars aren't as crushing and alien up here in the Northern Hemisphere. They have turned themselves down, and glimmer faintly. They don't observe me.

I am careful to lock the courtyard doors when I go inside. After all, I am in charge of security. I do not want to fall down on my duty. I want to stay ensconced. I look up the word in Paul's dictionary. '*Sconce n., a wall bracket for holding a candle... Sconce: Fort. A small detached fort or earthwork, as for defence of a pass or ford. Ensconce: to cover or shelter; hide securely.*'

I do feel hidden. I haven't been out on the street yet. I want to avoid the possibility of confrontation with anyone I know.

You haven't got many friends here, Christine's voice ventures.

I haven't got any, I admit.

I want to sit inside and examine my wound. I might lick it into better shape. Paul has shown me the white, airy space in the room that houses the stacks and filing cabinets for graphic works and invited me to set myself up there. 'Any time, when you're ready to begin painting.'

I am not ready. I would rather sit in the kitchen or read one of his books in my warm bed. Or simply stare. The cat comes and curls on my stomach, first kneading me with its claws, as if it thinks it is a roving acupuncture kit.

I am sizing up my life but I am not ready to begin new work. I sit hunched in the battered chair of memory.

I'll know when I'm truly shot of Redmond, when his toxin leaves my system. I'll forget the silent, deadly bits. First I must attend to this deep wound, the one with the gaping, astonished lips, the one that feels like a king-hit to my stomach. This wound acknowledges, all of a sudden, that its existence was always meant. This wound can't decide if it's a timing device for a bomb or a rickety one-legged bedside clock going trip-trap, trip-trap. This wound sits in the kitchen and licks itself and dabs at suffusions and moves out of range, and stays that way, wary and on the lookout.

When I think about myself, I believe I have lost the thread or dropped it. At the very least I have failed to retrieve it. Or did I discard it, defiant? It's not that I get confused, rather that the clarity of my black-and-white view is too brilliant to look at.

You've always been your own worst enemy, my mother chants, sounding satisfied.

Oh Christ, what have I done? What's wrong with me that I attract such litigation from the Fates? Where's my piece of happiness? When did Redmond's assassination begin? When did I start to comprehend? When was it I said to myself 'I hate this man'? I know I said it not long ago, but what did I always know?

I know I can no longer afford to hang by this bloodstained thread. I know I can no longer comply, sickened, with that Bluebeard in the cracked mirror. I want to say: 'That's not my severed heart and head.'

Jeez, that blood looks real, though, says Christine.

I opened the door to murderous secrets, then found the key under the mat. Testing, testing. Does this one fit?

Death of what I wanted to believe was the truth.

Dead as a door nail, my father whoops.

In our Brisbane house we had a stone carving of three wise monkeys that my father had brought back from Ceylon. The first one in line had its eyes covered. My father said, 'That one's "See No Evil."' The second had it hands over its ears. 'That chappie is "Hear No Evil."' The third covered its mouth. 'And the last one,' my father snickered, 'is "Speak No Evil."'

50 Secrets

I sit in the dark, drinking wine. In the exact centre of my heart a black, necrotic spot where the chook has pecked and pecked, invites me to touch it.

What did I always know?

Leave it alone, advises my mother, *or put a Band-Aid on it if you're worried.*

Tell me your secret, whispers Christine.

The teacher tells me to come to the front of the class. A key word attempts to write itself on the blackboard in my skull. I rub it out. It tries again, a sentence at a time:

I lie...

I lie complici...

I lie complicit with Lionel in his box..

No wonder he won't rot.

You made me do it, accuses Redmond.

You let me do it, choruses Lionel.

No use telling me about it, says my mother. *That won't make it better.*

Being a Catholic means you're absolved of all sins, Redmond points out.

Don't panic or you'll drown, my father grins.

I was blind for you, Redmond, and deaf. I was dumb as death. It's a rumour that I didn't want to know. If I don't watch out, my last breath will go untasted.

Lionel and Redmond stand together, father and son, admiring the red sports car parked with care in the cobbled driveway.

I thought you loved me, I plead with them. *That's why I let you do it. That's why.*

Lionel leans towards his son. *She's a trouble-maker,* he says in a clear voice.

She was always a liar, agrees Redmond.

'I hate you, I hate you both!' I scream at the top of my lungs, 'Why won't anyone believe me?'

If only I could paint a portrait of the monster, the side of his neck, the carotid artery, I would see how to go in for the kill.

Are you sure that's the right thing to do? You don't want to make a mistake advises my mother.

I'm absolutely certain, I tell her.

Monitors come forward and clean the blackboard, calls the teacher.

Yes, that is why I am sitting around. I am deep in thought, planning murder. I know Redmond will move in, circling, waiting for the tell-tale twitch to give me away in my hide. This time, if I can find the resolve, I will have counted to ten and I will be coming, ready or not.

Often I think I am losing my mind. I have a great fear of it. One day I will look in the mirror in Paul's bathroom and see my father with his crackling golden emu eyes staring back at me.

I can't sleep tonight. I don't want the touch of the sheets on my skin. I twitch in irritation. The underwater boom of London's traffic wakes me. The slushing waves of sound move back and forth between the walls. I am jangling inside my head, ready for the fight. Just as well Paul is out of the country. My calf muscles have turned to stone. I have a meandering cramp in my right foot. First it strikes the tender inside of my instep, then attacks between my little toe and the next, widening the gap, inexorable.

My left arm has a strange ache in it. I wonder if I am having a stroke. No, that's the heart attack sign. This is stupid; I am too young for either. At 3am I am not rational. I feel desperation and panic. All I want is oblivion in sleep. I do not want to think any more. But my brain races from topic to topic, like sheep penned overnight racing when released from grass clump to grass clump, tearing mouthfuls, heads down, running.

Out of the window, I see the London moon rise fast and huge, bright as a spotlight. It unfolds its ribbons of matter, perfect and unified. How seamless it looks. But no comfort from the moon tonight. I turn away from it, angry. What I want is to rise from my bed and stop this feeling. I want a fire to gaze into and a strong whisky. Instead I lie here and tears build up behind my eyes. They trickle from my right eye and across the bridge of my nose to join the water from my left eye, and run into the pillow below my cheek.

I feel foolish. Adults don't lie crying because they can't sleep. I don't know what adults do. I have not grown up. I am a baby, a child, a kid. I am young for ever, amen. I don't understand what life is all about.

You haven't got a clue, as Dad used to say to Mum.

I know a thing or two, she would reply. But she didn't.

My throat aches with formless, held-in misery. I can feel my hormone levels fluctuating in my blood. If only I could control my body with my mind. I should be in charge of my own autonomic nervous system. I should have an override switch for when things go out of synch.

I bet madness is hereditary. What will it be like if I go mad the way my father did? Will I notice it coming? Will I be able to side-step the approaching vehicle of derangement? Or I might enjoy going mad. First that sense of elation, followed by a conviction that I am cleverer than anyone else, an impatience with the slow-wittedness of others. It's the symptoms you are fond of that really denote your madness. Though I'm more likely to spiral down into depression.

She's visiting the funny farm, my father broadcasts, his hands cupped round his mouth. *She's gone round the twist.*

Leave me alone, I tell him.

Only me. I want to be only me. I will reduce to rags and ashes if I have to pretend any more. I have hidden my true feelings for too long under obedience, timidity, eagerness, uncertainty, terror. Hidden is the wrong word. I have lost my true feelings.

No more. I will say 'No.' I will say, 'What the Hell are you doing?' I will accost the world: 'You dirty old man, so you think you can get away with it?' I will say to everyone: 'Don't think you can terrorise me, because I can work it out. Now.' I find I have reserves of strength. Now I have wells of understanding. I know a thing or two. Now at least I know a sort of justice can prevail.

They say it is better to have knowledge of what has happened than to seek revenge. They say denial and falsification of history can't flourish once the truth is aired. But whose truth will see the light? I say justice is mine, alone for me to grab. I say that taking justice is the only safe bet. A working justice, personally arranged. A murderous justice, clean as a whistle.

Let's not talk about truth. Truth is an arranged condition. Just as in the story book, about the girl who had Nothing in her pocket, Truth does not exist. Truth is an abstract made up by those who are quick on their feet.

You only made that up! was a school taunt. We didn't realise that adults also didn't know, that they too had made up truth, that they also lived in a false world where words could be re-arranged to mean just about anything. Only actions count.

I believed I had a right to be myself, that I could assume myself in my own sweet time. This was a mistake. Being oneself is a state wrested from others by force or connivance – and you'd better do it quick. Now I see that the rightness of actions depends on the outcome.

I lost my childishness so late. I believed for so long in a universal touchstone, an abiding truth.

I want more than anything to stop my racing thoughts. I want to be cuddled to sleep. I want to hear my father say *How's my popsy?* again. I want to be stroked for an eternity, touch that never has to be repaid, touch that confers immortality. I want to be without troubles, without real attachments, without fixed feelings. I want to float, oceanic. I want nothing to interfere with everlasting tenderness.

I want to be six years old and on my father's lap listening to Beethoven, my armpit to his chest, my cheek to the curve of his neck. I want to die right now or fall asleep. I want never to have grown up.

My father says I can come and sit on his lap. His warm, dry, large-fleshed hand. I pivot my thumb with his. My face is blank. We are careful to ignore the fact that touch is intimate.

My mother never touches me except when she brushes my hair in impatient rips. She says: 'Vanity feels no pain.' She pinches the bone in my shoulder. 'Keep still.' If I reach for her she buzzes, a trapped insect. My father once or twice touches her from behind to catch her unawares. She reminds me of a moth flopping under a glass. I stare sideways as he rubs against her. He enlaces his arms and supports her breasts.

How could I have existed for years without touch, my neck stiff from lack of nuzzling, my body unsupported? Our beach holidays at the Gold Coast were my only animal comfort. Ocean water held me. Its saline swell lifted me, buoyant. The waves licked my back. This was a memorial to my father's arms, the nest of his lap.

I don't want to be here in my hard, dry London body, my inaudible self. I want to dive again under the waves, hearing the subdued roar of the Pacific, into that hermetic, sealed, underwater room. I want to lie in the warm shallows where the white-edged ripples run at me. I want to swim flickering in blue water.

51 The Appointment

Pammy, formerly carefree in Mayfair, is now most upset, for Redmond has a sore eye. His right eye is inflamed. But he is such a hypochondriac. His hypochondria is his only self-observation, so up until now, she has not taken much notice of it. Everyone gets a sore eye once in a while. But this one does not go away, and now Redmond sees Pammy through a blur. He says he has lost ninety-five percent of the vision in his right eye.

Pammy tells him to go to the eye clinic. The funny thing is, he goes. Pammy and Redmond are getting along with each other in almost magic combination, for now at least. Why is it that he does not suffer envy and jealousy in her presence? Why isn't she driving him insane, to vengeful retaliation, like his wife? No, they are forever amicable. Or is it more that he believes she is really him and she believes...

Here is a riddle: If lovers believe they grow more alike, how does that work? For if she grows more like him with the accumulations of the years, the rubbing of souls, and he grows more like her, then won't they both end up different people after all?

Never mind: theirs is a cosy cohabitation.

Redmond has made his appointment too late. The virus has eaten its way across his cornea, his iris and his pupil, leaving a scar that resembles a tiny limpet on a rock surface down in the sub-littoral zone. Here, at least, there is a definite sea change occurring.

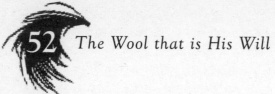

52 *The Wool that is His Will*

Paul has returned from a buying trip to Germany. He walks in carrying the smell of travel with him. He gives me a hug. He has been away for fifteen days. I am glad to see him back, to have the opportunity for guarded contemplation of an object rather than the cat and my unreadable face in the mirror.

He has work to catch up with and stays at the gallery well past five o'clock. So I make a meal and we sit and eat it over a bottle of wine he produces from his office cupboard. His presence reminds me of how easy it is to slip into familiarity with him, and even though I sense a new air, as if he is applying a further degree of pleasant pressure, I try to be responsive. I owe him something.

'I stopped over to see my son.' He has his back to me while he makes the coffee. 'He has a factory near Munich. We get on well now.'

My mind idles over the 'now'. Another section of my brain attempts them calculation that will tell me how old Paul must be, but I lack the energy to complete the sum.

Ask him: where's the wife? Christine hisses.

Paul turns to face me. 'Did I mishear you?'

I look up at him. 'I said, what does he make in his factory?'

'Modular fit-outs for offices. Very modern.' As he passes me my coffee, Paul asks, looking sly, 'Would you like a coconut macaroon with that?'

On the surface he acts as if he needs nothing from me, though when I tell him I have been painting, he gets excited. We go into the room behind the stacks and I let him look at what I have done in his absence. I know the key or the thread is in the painting. When I tell myself that, I know I am not ready to find out what I mean. Yet I am certain it is there, somewhere in the painted surface, trapped within the molecules of oil and pigment.

My new paintings are beginning to have a chronology and an overall title. I call them *Dream Works*. The first one is of a lean man, gnarled and tanned, who appears to be in open gaol in front of a Woolworth's building. It has a plain adobe facade and on a banner scrolled across it is the title: *The Wool that is His Will*. A snare pins the man's left hand to the ground. He lies on a piece of sacking out in the open, on the edge of a fruitful desert. A cactus like a three-branched candle is in the immediate foreground. A beetle is fossicking or making a nest in a cactus flower at the top. There is a piece of wool, stretched taut over the sacking on which he reclines, pinned down with a magnified tack at each end. I used a mix of wax and oil to get the shiny effect for the tacks.

I have been having complicated, discursive dreams in colour. They are the sort of dreams that are semi-lucid. I can walk around in them, investigating and changing events at will. I often change the colours in these dreams, as if I am re-painting them. I have never had dreams like these before. I wake exhausted, my muscles aching as if I have been working out in my sleep.

When I wake I have to get straight to work or make hasty sketches before the images click off. I have lost some by delaying their transposition. It is not that they fade. They simply aren't there any more.

These are not large paintings. Although there is quite a lot of detail, I have been able to work fast. The second one, almost completed, I have named *Torture Typewriter*. It too comes from a dream. An outsized, old-fashioned typewriter stands in the middle of a dirt road. It has a slit in it, through which you can see an inner chamber full of yellowish battery acid. The acid sloshes around inside, a vitriolic ocean. A woman's face (and it might be mine) is discernible, staring out from this acid tumult. It is obvious that she is being tortured. Out of the base of the typewriter, ticker tape emerges, printed with dates, times and indictments. I have used mainly pastel and graphite. It is a dark painting with a low horizon line, as if you have come over the rise in the road and stumbled upon it. I can't decide if I will pick out six keys to highlight. My choice of keys would spell M A L I C E.

I have started three other paintings in outline. I turn to Paul. 'So what do you think?'

'Did you say you had exhibitions in Australia?'

'Just the one.'

'Ah, yes – and you have never had any particular training? I think you mentioned that.'

'No, I just taught myself.'

'Yes of course.'

I hear my father's voice: *You never fail to amuse, Darl.*

'So... you haven't said what you think,' I venture. 'You haven't said anything. Probably you don't like them.'

'I like them a great deal.' He walks over to me and puts his arm round my shoulders and gives me a kiss, half on my cheek, half on the corner of my mouth.

Something in my brain registers a truth. It's not the truth of his sliding, insinuating kiss, though that registers too, but a truth which, through all the fiction of living in the absence of pleasure, has remained a constant. It is in there in the lead coffin of my head, indestructible.

No-one can take my work away from me.

53 *Live and Learn*

'You live and learn,' my mother would say, resigned, as yet another poor outcome robbed her of impetus. I don't know that she ever did. She appeared to attract mistakes, as if she were a magnet in a tray of pins.

It was rare that she would say of someone: 'They don't have a mean bone in their body.' And disappointment usually followed that statement. More often she would say, while buying yet another lottery ticket in the Brisbane Golden Casket: 'I'm unlucky. I never win at anything.'

It was true: she never did. She was a bad card player. She never won a trick in her life.

It's hard for me to believe that Paul doesn't operate by constant ulterior motives, but so far his behaviour has been impeccable. I am starting to relax, a blue tongue lizard on hot cement, but step on me and I will hiss a warning and scuttle away. Paul must be getting whatever it is he wants out of our temporary linkage, and since it doesn't yet impinge on me, I stay put, in the warmth.

Pammy, in a moment of frankness once said: 'Keep an eye out, Doll. They're still men, whatever you might imagine. Even the best of them.' Nevertheless the sun on my back feels good and questioning every gesture tires me out.

Spring has come to dirty London and some lunch hours I go out to walk in the streets or wander through Regent's Park. I like it there. There are some Chinese ducks I enjoy looking at, with their white-ringed, blank button eyes and their pointed, folded, coloured-paper wings. I have bought myself a much better camera with a telephoto lens and I snap them. I also take sneaky photos of people.

Back at the gallery I transcribe their close-up, grainy images into paint.

One day, pointing my camera, I find Paul filling the lens. 'What a coincidence. You've been following me, haven't you? Haven't you got anything better to do?'

'Yes, I have been. I'm sorry.' He never rises to my jibes. 'My curiosity got the better of me.'

'Curiosity killed the cat and could tear the hind leg off a dog.'

'I must apologize. It is unforgivable to snoop, isn't it?'

'Yes.'

'Let me take you out to lunch, to make up for it.'

So he takes me to Fortnum and Mason's and we buy an inordinately expensive picnic hamper and sit in the park to eat it. It is different from the bull ant-infested, prickly-bush picnics I am used to.

Paul casually mentions he has a gap coming up at the gallery. 'Would you like to fill it? Your dream images and photo portraits would make interesting combinations.'

I don't yet know how to treat his suggestions. He does not make his position clear.

'Anyone else would notice that these gaps which appear in your agenda seem remarkably fortuitous – but I'm too stupid to notice.'

I hear myself being cute and once again regret my tone. I have no idea why I am so intent on appearing hostile.

He smiles. 'They wouldn't be there if Fate and I did not agree on it.'

My internal observer, still operating off to the side, asks: *Does he imagine he's in charge of me, with his open line to Fate? What's in it for him?* And the voice in my head replies: *Well, it's obvious isn't it? He's a dealer. He's simply doing his job. What's wrong with that?*

Paul makes a habit of wandering into my workspace each evening around five o'clock. He sits and chats as I finish up. I don't mind him watching me. I rather like it, and on the days when he doesn't arrive, I wonder where he is.

He has exempted me from gallery duties in the lead-up to my show. 'Go, and paint. You distract my customers. They would rather talk to you than ogle the paintings. I may have to reconsider your employment.' He smiles at my alarmed face. 'At least if you produce some paintings I have the chance of getting my cut.'

Under this new regime he often invites me to eat out. We settle into a routine that I come to expect. He is good to talk to. We never run out of things to say. He has not asked me personal questions since the day he picked me up at the hospital. He is a caricature of the reticent Englishman, though I suspect it's a game. He gives me choices, whether he means to or not. Already, on his generous salary, I have enough money to catch a plane to anywhere I might choose to go.

He makes it plain that I am tenant-in-residence once office hours are over, that the gallery then becomes my domain. He does not intrude. He thanks me for my company, kisses me goodnight on the corner of my mouth, and goes off to his Mayfair apartment. He has not invited me there.

The sneaky, angry part of me wishes he would overstep his role. Then I could accuse him of base motives. Then I wouldn't have to wonder what I feel. It would all be over. Over and done with. But he moves round me, serene, avoiding my bear traps, as if he knows what I'm thinking. He is the most orchestrated man I know.

Paul is a proficient curator. He sends out elegant invitations to a large list of clients and hangs the show himself. He is ruthless about what goes up and what stays in the back room, though he does not discard many works. I have learnt to trust his eye, though we argue at times. I have painted his portrait, a quick sketch as he dismantles the coffee percolator and he hangs that as well.

I begin to see that his gallery has a high reputation, and that he is what Redmond would call 'a big noise' in art circles. I start to get anxious that my show will not be good enough.

'It may be a big flop, you know. I'm sure they despise Australians here. No-one's interested in portraits. Not that I care. It was your idea.'

'They don't think like that. Don't worry.' I can see that he is certain. He backs winners and that gives me courage.

Paul's friends are cheerful and solicitous. (I remind myself of Peter and his circle, just as a warning.) On the evening of the opening Paul sidles over to tell me there is a fair smattering of unknowns in the crowd, but they are in a buying mood. He is right, of course, and later I swan around in the glory of an almost-sell-out show. A German has bought Paul's portrait.

I am standing to one side, counting the red stickers, when a voice says: 'You've landed on your feet, Doll.' I turn and there stands Pammy.

The first thing I do is drop my eyes. However much she might think I have landed right side up, I feel as if I am Lionel's cat, stuck on my back, my feet pinned, vulnerable to insidious attack. This is so stupid. When will I grow up? Have I reached this stage by default? Probably. My mother's inheritance of formless guilt sloshes round in my brain; the battery acid in the typewriter in my head that leaks corrosion into the chamber of my heart. This is the woman who does this to me, though she is really a man in disguise, Redmond's surrogate, more and more the faithful copy.

'How did you get a show here?' Pammy is more acid than I remember. All the while her eyes rove over my body. 'How did you meet him?'

I am getting canny. 'Oh, I just walked in.'

'So,' says Pammy – and I can hear Redmond talking – 'does he put on feminist art sometimes, to keep up-to-the-minute?'

'No, I don't think so.' I stare, at last, straight into her button eyes. 'I'm hardly what you would call a feminist. You know, I think he likes my work because it's good.'

Then I laugh at her because she has released me from doubt.

She changes tack. 'Redmond's not been well.'

She looks at me for a response. I stare back and my voice is tart. 'He never is.'

Does she suppose I am in some automatic union with her, where Redmond's health is our first waking thought? I hear my mother's voice: *Well! I'm staggered. What a cheek.*

'Terrible thing. Blind in one eye. Some sort of virus doodad. Looks awful. Apparently it can land anywhere.' How much of a copy of him is she really prepared to be?

Deliberately, I put my hand on her shoulder. 'Pammy, I want you to know that I don't care. Not since my miscarriage. And you know what else? He's all yours, viral doodad, the lot.'

She looks aghast and steps away from me. 'Don't be silly, Doll. You know, it's been very difficult for him, all this.' She makes a vague gesture. 'Big decision, you know. Very difficult. Poor fellow. He wanted it so much. The marriage I mean. I would never come between husband and wife. You know that.'

I have forgotten how staccato her speech patterns are.

Rage creeps up on me. 'You know what?' My voice rises. Maybe I won't be able to control the volume. 'You drink shit and consequently, you smell. He's got terminal halitosis and you can both go to buggery, you and your rotten Redmond. And watch out...' I have become one horse trader to another as I deliver my parting shot. 'He kicks.'

I can see Paul watching me across the room, but he doesn't have time to reach me before I am away, through the gallery, across the hall and into the back room, slamming the door. Now I don't feel so decisive. I am trembling. Was that the wrong thing to do? Should I have stayed calm, not said anything, shut my mouth, had some grace, not played into her hands?

Nice girls don't wash their dirty linen in public, my mother intones. My father's voice butts in: *You're like a stuck record, Darl.*

What will Paul think of me? I don't care. I've made a fool of myself. Now he'll despise me. *Oh well, it felt good while it lasted. That's the bloody end of that.*

Behaving like a gutter-snipe... blares my mother, an ear trumpet curling from the side of her head.

In my mind I am already packing my bags. I am just about to deal with my painting equipment, theoretically picking it up and ineffectually putting it down again, when there is a knock at the door. I open it and stare at Paul's face through the gap. I am looking straight at his mouth. He has nice lips, a short, delineated upper one and just enough lower lip for sucking. I like the way the skin of his mouth is hardly distinguishable from the skin of his face. His lower lip rolls over, a weathered, rounded cliff. He smiles at me and I see his crooked canine and the bad tooth next to it that is brown.

'It will be a sell-out now.' His smile widens. Then he reaches through the gap and takes my face and kisses me. After a while he stops. 'Pammy's gone.' His eyes are grave. 'You can come out now.' Then he kisses me again and I can feel his tongue and the inside of his lip and it is hard to stop doing it, as if I am kissing some part of myself. It is hard to let go.

54 The Visit

I don't know what Paul's friends think of our relationship, but if they had been privy to our kiss last night their expectations might have been raised. What if they had stood, later, in the bedroom, watching to see if we made the first moves of love? There's never anything much to see: the bed clothes billowing, humped forms, an arm, self-absorbed faces with their eyes closed, an entwined leg. Watching is pornographic and so boring that they'd do better to make it up. Most of it happens in our heads, anyway.

What's happening, if it does occur, is unviewable. I know that much. It lies between the lines of spoken words, housed in the silent gaps. It cannot be represented – or only obliquely. It is as hard to explain as consciousness. It has an imprecise name, this non-representation. It is swamped with desire.

The next morning there is no food in the house so I go out to buy milk, cream, jam and croissants. We are both hungry, from which his friends could assume that Paul stayed the night or at the very least, that he arrived early. They are welcome to choose either.

As I walk along I feel jumpy and discordant. I am having a truthful talk with myself and it doesn't agree with me. On the one hand I know I long for an encompassing stability, a reference point on the map. On the other, there is a huge price to pay for incorporation. Making love, loving, it seems to me, can be akin to serial murder. It wants to stalk you until the quick last contact. When you are too far gone you realise that it's deadly, obsessed with your white ankles, the tip of your breast, the slit of your throat. Lovemaking wants to engage you in its little death.

There seems no easy balance between the gut response and the considered move. Love is a trick. It's too hard.

Why can't I arrange reality to suit myself? Truth slides around on grease. Attachment is a dirty word. What do I care about moral agreements? I have never seen them honoured.

You're always carrying on about everything, comments Christine.

I unlock the gallery door. It is not yet eight-thirty. I can hear voices inside and though I don't want to believe it, I know one belongs to Redmond. I walk to the kitchen and put down my parcels. I stand there. Why did Paul let him in? *Don't be so naïve,* I tell myself. *What else could he do?*

You're a big girl now, my father says.

I take a deep breath. I can handle it. I walk back down the hall, open the door and walk over to them. I notice two things. Paul has not combed his hair. It sticks up at the back. Overall, he looks rumpled. The other thing I notice, because I am standing close to both of them (it is as much affront and threat as I can manage) is Redmond's right eye, and his stance.

He has swung round as I enter to see me out of his good left eye. His right eye is still inflamed and I can see a silver worm trail from the corner to the centre. He looks like a statue with the paint flaking off its eyeballs.

Redmond gives me a nod, a tightening of the lips. It could be a polite smile. I ignore it, whatever it is, and look at Paul. He is urbane underneath the rumples as he turns to Redmond. 'Well, then...' He begins to slide sideways.

Redmond produces his hand in a determined movement. He and Paul shake hands. Redmond gives Paul a collegiate smile. Paul remains bland. 'I must go and attend to business,' he murmurs. Paul speaks to no-one in particular but as he passes me he lets his hand trail across mine and his voice is soft and only for me. 'How are the croissants? Hot?'

Redmond nods again as Paul goes out and then he is free to turn his gaze on me. It is a self-conscious, serious look. 'We must talk.'

I think: *How can you talk underwater, drowning?*

'Not here. Come into the office.'

I want to show him everything I now have: my relationship with Paul, the office, the stacks room, my lack of need, my cohesion, my disentanglement, my work. But not yet. When the time comes. Soon. I mean him to see what I hold in my hand.

I take him through in silence to where I'm working. He looks round, swinging his whole body, sizing up my encampment. He has already seen what is hanging on the walls in the gallery, the red stickers, the air of success. He can't tell if I am any good – he never could – but he knows the outward signs. He has always tuned in to those signals.

I know this animal, his burnished hair, the lair he inhabits. I have seen him measuring up Paul, calculating his chances of making something out of this for himself. *What can I eat?* asks his hunger.

I want the courage to say: *I know you're going to try and spoil things for me, Redmond, you and your poxy Pammy.* I also want to say: *I'll kill you first.*

He looks around once more. He has not set the stage to his satisfaction. 'Can we sit down?' he asks.

He is so proper. I, who never attends to the niceties am clearly the lesser person. He pulls up a canvas chair, seats himself. That's better. He waits for me to find something to sit on. Reluctant, I find a wooden fruit crate and perch on it. He stares between his legs and clasps his hands, his elbows on his thighs.

Once I would have watched, fascinated, obedient to this stage-managing, as he siphons the available oxygen out of the room, reducing me to a flattened cutout. It was his right, part of his charm, his belief in himself as the central pivot. Now he does not sustain my interest – or not in the way he wants.

He focuses on me. He believes he looks the real thing, the genuine article. I think: *Here comes the spiel.* I am eager to hear what it will be.

'I've been ill,' he starts, 'my eye...'

'Yes, Pammy told me.' I keep my words clipped.

He sighs, a deep breath. 'It's made me look at things in a different way.' His eyes, the way he holds his mouth are set to impress me.

His play for sympathy is so obvious that I begin to understand that he can't help it. It is his most genuine emotion, this obsession with himself, this self-justification, his will to power. He has an ideal of himself that he must protect from harm. If I am something, then he is nothing. That's the trouble with being in love with your own reflection. Someone always wants to put their hand in to touch the face in the water.

He begins again. 'I've hurt you very much.' He looks ponderous.

'Haven't I?'

I make no reply.

There is a long silence. 'You haven't asked after *my* health,' I finally chide him.

'Yes, I'm sorry...' he pauses, '...that it didn't turn out the way you wanted it to.' He stares down at the floor again, crediting his emotion with a moment's silence.

You have to give it to him; he's quick on his feet. He's expressed his sorrow: that's good. Give him a tick. At the same time he has turned the situation so that it is all mine – my idea, my pregnancy, my miscarriage, my pain, my selfishness and my fault. I brought it on myself. If only I had asked his advice he would have told me, out of complete disinterest, that it wasn't a good idea.

I feel breathless. I press my hands to my diaphragm and right then, feeling the bellows of myself under my hands, I know how to do it, how to commit this murder in fine detail.

Give him a good hiding, my father sneers.

'Yes, it would be good to talk about it.' Now I pause, considering the depths of his generosity. 'Thank you for that.' (Always thank the beast for sparing your life.) 'I know I'll feel better about it if we can talk.'

There is another silence. Then I say as if I have just thought it: 'I'd like to paint your portrait.' I continue before he can interrupt. 'I always think more clearly when I'm working.'

He gives me a guarded look. He's no fool. He knows we are now foul enemies, never able to drink side by side from the same dam. I will always crouch, and he will always lunge to bite.

But my offer tantalises him. Somewhere, for every creature, there exists the perfect bait. His guarded look fades to one of careful gratification. 'Yes, if you like,' he replies and so activates the starter motor of his fate.

I make a date with him for the next evening, and he goes away. It feels odd to be in charge. The air lightens. I go into the kitchen and execute a dance over to the bench. I take the knife from Paul's unresisting hand and apply lashings of jam and cream to a croissant.

Paul says, bemused: 'What are you up to, you little nymph?' He often calls me that, though I'm sure he must mean minx. 'You look as if you're planning a murder.'

'I am.' I feel light-hearted. 'I'm going to do Redmond's portrait.'

Paul stops what he is doing and scratches his head. 'Ah.' He wanders in a circle and stops in front of the coffee percolator. 'You're too young to know of the picture of Dorian Gray, I suppose? He doesn't wait for an answer.

'What medium will you use?'

I stare up at the skylight, its rectangular patch of hazy, washed-out blue.

Paul waits, patient, for me to answer.

'I think I'll try water colour this time. I have a feeling this one's all about reflections. That would be the most appropriate.'

And I take a huge bite of my croissant.

55 The Last Detail

Redmond is late for his first appointment. I have had plenty of time to set myself up. The paint sheet is down, the canvas chair in place. I have set up my panel at a slant away from the door and have prepared the surface almost to the consistency of plaster. I have in place a large photographer's light. I want to pull the blinds and paint Redmond in unnatural light. And I want to take some photographs.

I have decided on a mix of media, two contrasting substances: waterbased paint and pigment, oil and wax. I need to be able to do generalised, transparent and translucent surfaces and intricate detail.

I hear him arrive. He talks to Paul in the hallway. I know he is trying to tie the first snares in some sort of relationship – just as he did with my mother. A relationship that says: *We know how difficult she is. Eventually we will find we can disregard her.* I know it won't work with Paul, though my mother was a pushover.

Redmond comes in and gives me a noncommittal incline of his head.

'Let's begin.' I tell him to sit in the chair, make himself comfortable. 'You'll have to stay in the pose, but I'll give you breaks.'

He can do nothing but sit bolt upright in the canvas chair, but he shifts his arms about. 'Would you like me to look natural?'

'As much as you can.' Immediately he stiffens up. He looks as if he might have fashioned himself from stainless steel. He will ache all over by the time I finish with him.

Coo-ee he calls, irritated.

-ee I respond from the far side of the creek, out of frame.

He has no impulse towards transformation but I can guide him, by my echo, towards it.

I have no intention of painting him as he appears. That was never my resolve. I am intent on my own perspective. I have no interest in the image he assumes, but rather in the point in space from which I stare at him. Only then can I be the observer affecting the outcome. Only then can I paint the Redmond who compels me.

I will bring him, passive, suffering, rooted to the spot, to confront frailty and limitation. I will situate him in deep context, translucent. I am going to cut him free from his black metal walking case.

I draw the blinds. The sun has set and the room becomes dark, so dark that Redmond almost disappears among the clutter in the room. From the darkness he says, 'Oh.' For the first time I understand something about him, that in my panic to protect myself, I have missed. Fuelling his focus on himself is his desperation to be noticed. Hence the unremitting making of serial connections. This portrait, he believes, will provide him with proof of his grandiose existence.

I make my way across the room to switch on the photographer's light. Now the Redmond I see springs into prominence. He shields his eyes from the glare, his right eye watering. He looks up at me, stricken, but he will bear it to have this portrait completed.

'Sorry to hold you up tonight.'

'That's OK. I'm not in a hurry.'

'No, well... I think I have a migraine, actually.' He is eager to discuss his symptoms. He tries to tell me something about a chiropractor who wanted to hang him by his feet, a known cure for migraine. I wish he had. I see him trussed at the heels, upside down, swaying helpless from a gibbet. I shiver with pleasure.

I let him chatter on, and say nothing. I adjust the light so it throws half his face into black shadow.

'And I get these funny flashing lights if I look sideways. That's migraine isn't it?'

'Sure to be. Certainly sounds like it to me.'

I lay my hand on the smooth surface of the panel. I know how this portrait will look. It is all there, in front of me. I will proceed with care but that is because I am now so sure, buoyed up by my spirits. This work will have the authority of justification and the discipline of passion. I know I am about to construct a moral framework on which will hang the truth.

I know what I am going to call it. My best work always comes with a title that floats in, fully formed.

Most of the painting is in water colour, although properly speaking it is tempera, because I threw an egg yolk into the mix of pigment and water. I want this painting to have the look of a fresco, that luminous bonding of architectural form and bulk behind a curtain of thin colour.

I start to construct a man, one whom you can almost see through. He faces the viewer, with his body falling sideways. If you did manage to see through him you would see the monumental structure of the wall behind the fresco, that which you cannot modify. The adamant, unchanging, exploitative, obsessive, aggressive, defending, destructive self.

The figure in this landscape does not observe that we live in a matrix, molecules embedded in a living grid of relativity that holds us and the world together in a common fiction. He will not see that there is no possibility of disentangling ourselves from the plot. He will not understand Heisenberg's uncertainty principle: that the observed is influenced by the observer.

He is extreme in his stiffness. He balances unnaturally on one tipping heel. He is about to lose his footing. He is out of proportion with, and has no relationship to his surroundings. His face is huge. He stands or rather falls on the edge of one of Australia's east coast creeks. Soon I will paint in brown pebbles, some leaf fall, the scimitars of eucalypts, the dense, glutinous, shiny black thread of a leech on an underwater rock. I will make water, that insinuating transformer, fall over a rock shelf. It will reach a pool deep enough in which to swim on a hot day. Deep enough and calm enough to see your face in. A clump of stiff-leaved lomandra will stand in green beside the water.

I stop. I have marked in about a third of the work with charcoal and a few referential patches of colour. I've done well in the time, but now I must preserve the sitter. He has a long way to go, many rivers to cross.

'I have to take a break. I'm sure you're getting tired, but could I take a few photographs first? I like to be able to refer to them.'

He stands up, suspicious. I take some quick shots then, before he has time to demur, I ask him to lean sideways. I shoot off more film then come in close and get some grainy-textured shots of his surprised face, with one hand up, his thumbnail pressing dubiously at his top teeth.

'Turn your head slowly, please.' As he responds, I aim and click. I have the camera on the right speed to catch those thin gradations of movement, those ghosting ellipses, those overlapping time frames that only cameras or mirrors can catch.

'Sorry, I have a funny way of working. I like to get action shots. It helps me establish a more natural expression.'

'Oh well.' He is slightly bored. 'You know what you're doing.'

I can see he finds it hard to work out my current status, but he must suspect my residence in Paul's gallery puts me into the millionaire class. This doesn't mean he won't try to undermine me, but he will proceed with caution.

And what do I know? I know the name of the animal. I know that when you name something it becomes invested with substance, soul, that essence you look for in the eyes. When it isn't there, when the glass of the eyes is opaque or far too brilliant to see through, you can get an unholy shock.

Paul has told me to offer tea to people who come in to the gallery. On automatic, I offer tea to Redmond. He accepts.

I take him out to the sitting room. I don't want to leave him in the studio spying on my other works. He sits, uneasy, on a couch. The stability of my surroundings unsettles him. I pass him a cup, careful not to touch his hand. Here is another human form I will never touch again, for as long as we both shall live.

'You wouldn't have an aspirin, would you? I have this sinusy thing...'

'No, I'm sure I haven't. Sorry.' I visualise the aspirin packet on its shelf in the bathroom cabinet.

He rubs the side of his nose, then his eye. He puts his cup down unfinished. He prepares himself to say something of deep moment. 'I think it's best if we separate. For a while. I need time alone to – um, sort out my priorities. But we'll still talk.'

'I'm terribly sorry about your eye. You must find it quite limiting.'

He looks sour. He hates the suggestion of limitation.

Come right out with it, for pity's sake, my father's voice commands.

Like you, you mean? I answer back, sarcastic.

Do it your own way, my mother flounces. *It's immaterial to me.*

Now I begin my murder. 'I do feel responsible. I should have been more careful. I didn't have any inkling. The funny thing is, I can't remember where I got mine from. Must have come from somewhere.'

He looks alarmed. 'What do you mean "responsible"? What are you talking about?'

He is cross, put out.

'The cold sore. I must have passed it on. As I say, I don't know where I got it. They do lie dormant though. I'm quite an expert on them now.' I laugh. I watch his eyes. They are black with suppressed resentment, relieved only by the tortuous relief map of the silver worm trail across his right eye.

'Unless – I suppose it's possible... He often had that funny thing on his lip.' I paused. 'I could have got it from Lionel.'

His face drains of colour. He is now a deadly white that begins at his forehead and moves down, quite different from his usual high colour. He stands up. He is trapped. The bait of the portrait is still there and I can see that he can't believe what I'm saying. Chance and Fate work for him, not for me. He is in possession of everything and everyone has his best interests at heart. He is impregnable. He works at his image every morning, staring into his shaving mirror, chocking himself up. Self-presentation. Last thing at night he looks in the mirror as he cleans his teeth, checking that he's still there. As long as he doesn't panic, he will not disappear.

He no longer wants to talk. He looks subdued. 'I must go.' He hits his coat pockets. 'I should catch the last tube.'

'Tomorrow? Will you sit again tomorrow? I probably only need a couple of sittings in all. Then I work mainly from memory.'

'Yes, OK. I'll give you a call if I can't make it.'

He is eager to go. I escort him up the hall. As he steps down into the street, his familiar movement, the way he steps sideways, his hands in his pockets, sends a pang of loss through me. Tears well in my eyes. Already I think of him as absent. I can feel regret bumping alongside the platelets of my blood, filling up the reservoir of my heart.

I feel tired as I close the door. I trail to the bathroom to undress.

I like to dress in a motley collection of bed clothes. First a pair of black tights, for it is still chilly at night. Over the tights a second-hand, salmon silk petticoat, slippery for turning over in. On top of that, tonight I choose a short blue satin peignoir. Before I switch out the light I stop to stare at myself in the mirror. 'What do you want?' I ask the image and it shimmies out of the silver, a composed, spaceless, imagined portrait that speaks behind its eyes.

I want Redmond to look up, just for one second and say: *There you are.*

But I know he won't. So I imagine him falling on the live rail in the Underground, saving me the trouble of doing the deed myself.

I want him to look into the mirror of his life and recognise what sort of creature he is. As he falls through thin air I want him to hear my voice at last. I know he will never oblige me.

Paul is a substantial lump in my bed. He does not seem concerned by my dealings with Redmond. I have never seen anything threaten Paul's buoyancy. Now here he is, taking up most of the bed space.

What is it you want? my head whispers.

56 Resolve

I have a rock that I keep in the bedroom, here in Paul's house in London. I lifted it from Highgate cemetery near where Marx is buried. Lichens mottle it with the colours of ocean creatures: seal grey, seaweed brown, khaki, specks of liquid black squid ink, a pink-blue. It is difficult to take a rock home on the Underground but when rude Londoners stared at me, I stared back.

On clear mornings, the crystal hanging in the window reflects red, orange, blue, green on the rock's granite surface, dancing then halting over it, sunlight under water. I don't know why – perhaps it's the granite surface – but it makes me think of Brisbane.

I think of you now, Redmond, and while I sleep I see a large eye, alive and unblemished, that stares at me from the bottom of a bowl of water. I feel pure and powerful.

I stare out the window at a cold, stripped London tree pressed up against a dense, grey sky. 'Only this room,' I stage-whisper. 'Only this bed with me in it,' I say out loud. 'Here I am.' I pat the quilt, wriggle my warm feet, watch the cat in the mirror. 'Only these,' I tell the cat. 'Only these,' I repeat. 'And you in your body, Redmond, somewhere apart, staring from your eyes.'

'One chance in a million to get it right,' I tell myself. Only one life,' I say.

Machiavelli knew about the propitious moment when Fate bundles complex causes into the one shopping basket. It is the capacity to recognise this that grants me the power over circumstances. I know I must not tolerate that split between thought and action, the accursed human ability to reflect too long on moves before making them. I know I am coming into my power, here in my British redoubt.

I have learnt to look and leap simultaneously.

# 57 *Image*

The next night, the next sitting, Redmond is not well. His colour is hectic.

'I think I'm coming down with the flu. I was quite ill this morning. Fuzzy headed – you know, everything's a bit foggy? But I didn't want to disappoint you.' He is so considerate. He will be false until the day he dies. 'When do you think you'll finish it?'

'This should be the last time you have to sit.'

'May I see it?' He draws his lips back against the word 'may'. His idiosyncrasies are familiar, unnerving.

'I never show my work until I've signed my name. I should have it done by next week. I'll let you know.'

He misses the last tube and I suggest he calls a taxi. He hates spending money on comfort, and decides to walk. As I open the door for him, the black cat rushes out past my ankles. It bounds up the street and as Redmond walks off it slips across the road in front of him and vanishes. It is a chilly, windy night.

I work hard on the painting and each day the central, falling character develops more ghosting, one-sided images of itself. They spiral by elliptical degrees down towards the water.

A photographer friend of Paul's has developed the film of the pictures I took, and lent me his enlarger. The negatives of Redmond swinging his head came out well, and I have copied the fateful, secondary shadows.

I have dissected one side of his nose as in a technical drawing in a medical text. The raw red surface is slimy, shining, in contrast to a small black area of dead tissue. I have used oil and wax that shines in its thickness, in contrast to the water-based form of the rest of the painting. On his forehead, positioned over his right eye with its silver flaw, I have painted a large red dot. This is a reference spot. From it, in a graceful, tacking parabola I have painted an intermittent white line that takes in, via its curve, the dissociated Reckitt's blue of the Australian sky. Then the line falls down to the water.

In the heavens, to the right and to the left, are currawongs. They roll back the wall to the kingdom of self-knowledge. These birds have the wings of dark angels, and their golden eyes are glassy with judgment. Apart from the reflection of the lomandra, with its contrasting, dun-coloured seed heads, and despite the falling body and the elliptical series of faces suspending themselves over the reflecting water, nothing else is mirrored.

At first I couldn't work out how to balance the painting. It needed weight at the base, a strong colour to anchor it. By the end of the week I had found what I needed to do. I have painted a broad red arrow that points to the lack of reflection. Just so you can't miss it.

Banners are becoming my trademark, and this work has one as well. It unfurls high across the sky in the shape of a cumulo-nimbus cloud presaging an afternoon thunderstorm. It reads *The Transience of Objects*. By Friday I have signed my name in the water.

I think I have finished. It is late. I clean my brushes and lay them aside. Paul is around somewhere. He does not interrupt, though he never sleeps in Mayfair now. I have an idea he might have let the lease lapse. I go out to the kitchen and get a beer. I need something to send me to sleep.

A conversation with Paul keeps coming into my mind. 'You do tend to make life difficult for yourself, don't you?' He held my shoulders, and gave me a not-so-gentle shake. 'You don't have to take it so hard all the time, you know. Crashing about in your wooden skirts.' He pushed his hand through my fringe, and held my head back in mock-exasperation.

'What skirts? I never wear skirts.'

'We shall have to buy you a beautiful skirt. Then I will take you out on the town.'

I moved away from his grasp to put the kettle on. I set cups out on the bench, took the milk out of the fridge.

'Sometimes I get so sick of myself I feel as if I need a brain change.'

He stared deadpan at me for a moment. 'I love your brain. Every last living inch of it. And I love what it produces.'

'Do you?'

I watched myself, thinking, 'Is this a declaration of love or an expression of interest?' I felt a strong sense of *déjà vu*. I wound one leg around him and hugged him, testing his body. I inhaled his smell. I kissed him on the lips, taking my time, waiting, in this second experiment, for the truth to settle out.

'Can I tell you something I've never told anyone?'

He looked solemn. 'It would be an honour.'

'I know this will sound silly – but I have a chicken in my heart and it's been pecking me to death.'

He stepped back from me. 'Aha – one of those. But now you have opened the cage door. It can fly the coop.' They're better out in the world, those creatures.'

The kettle whistled as I said in my best off-hand manner, in case I had it wrong: 'If you say you love me... you did say that, didn't you?'

He smiled. He never objected to playing the foil. He pulled me to him, his hands way down on my bottom. 'Only your brain.'

I wander out to the terrace, enclosed by its high brick wall. The black cat comes out of nowhere and crouches to take a delicate drink from Paul's fishpond. I watch its sliver of pink tongue flick the surface of the water. It stops, its eyes half-shut, glazed. It starts again, the ripples fibrillating. It doesn't take much beer to make me feel drunk. I am buzzing as I stare into the surface of the pond. It takes me a moment to work out that the circular image reflected in the water is not the core of the moon, but the reflection of the security light that I triggered as I walked out.

Yes it's only a canvas sky
Hanging over a muslin tree...

In a celebration of my completed painting, and because I never make this sort of gesture, I lob the empty bottle over the wall. It lands in the back laneway where it shatters with a satisfying, imploding crack.

58 *The Loved One*

Paul has stayed out of the studio while I have been painting Redmond's portrait. I invite him in, this last morning. Excited by what I have done, I'm still apprehensive as I wait for his reaction.

He stands, silent, in front of it. He does not look at me when he starts to speak.

'There is no doubt in my mind that this is a strong painting.' I take in a deep breath as his words wash over me.

'Just as I am certain your work will continue to gain you distinction and respect.'

Something in his tone makes me uneasy about what will come next.

'Yes', he scratches, absent, at his ear as he turns to face me. 'Extraordinary how you have nailed him to the wall, as it were.' He smiles at me, his mouth tight. Astounded, I see pity and censure in his eyes.

'You have shown him up: a beautifully-presented fraud. Yes, indeed.' His smile grows fierce. 'My little attorney.'

'What do you mean, attorney? I don't know what you mean.'

'I think you do,' he says.

I glare at him in silence but he holds my gaze. 'Be careful as you continue your dissection,' he says. And he still smiles his wary smile. 'You might be left staring at bones.'

'I don't need your analysis of my personality.' I make my voice as cold as I dare.

'I'm sure you don't.' He turns to leave. My heart is hammering and I have broken out in a sweat.

He stops in the doorway. 'I have to be away for the next few days. Did I tell you?' His voice is now gentle. He walks back into the room, the smile still in place. 'No, perhaps not.' Again we stare each other out, until he relents. 'Give me a kiss before I go.' And with his hands holding my arms, he presses his mouth to mine.

I turn away from him, back to my work, though my hand is shaking from the humiliation of his rebuke. A while later I hear him leave the house. *Good riddance to bad rubbish,* I hear myself say, in my mother's voice. *I don't need your opinion,* I tell his absence, *and you can keep your bloody condescending kisses. I know what I'm doing. I have a right.*

It is 9pm when Redmond arrives to see his portrait. As I escort him down the hall he staggers, knocking a painting askew with his shoulder.

'Sorry, didn't see it. Lost my balance. It's this inner ear thing I get.'

I have covered the completed painting with a cloth. I ask him to sit once more in the canvas chair. I have on only the photographer's light, but I also have another small light standing ready, next to the panel.

'It's done.'

He nods.

'Do you want to have a look at it?'

'Of course.'

He is a stone, a fixed image. He sits in the canvas chair with his burnished hair.

There is such a ferment going on in my head. It's a hollow wooden stage in there and I can't stop people walking on and off, concocting new dramas. My father's voice switches on, even though I can't see him. *Well Darl, not a bite,* he calls. *Not a one.* The night ocean has swallowed his body and his long bamboo fishing rod, though I can sense his irritated, Cheshire cat's grin.

I pull off the cloth and the material catches on the top corner and almost topples the painting. Redmond moves halfway out of his seat. I steady it and he sits down again.

'Good, very good.' It's as if he has rehearsed his reaction. 'Very professional.' He cocks his head.

I hear the hiss of nylon and the whirr of the ratchet as my father flings his line out, one last time, into the towering sea. I want to call out to him but the salt blackness is thick and wet and heavy all around me.

'You like it?' I manage. I feel the press and poundage of the night air as if I am being submerged.

'Yes, yes. Very much. It's got that European quality. The surreal.'

My hands start to go numb at the ends of my arms. My rib cage feels corseted with planks of wood.

'You don't think it's too' – I try to gasp for breath without his noticing – 'it's not too personal?'

He rubs his left eye. 'Quite the opposite.' He sounds authoritative. 'You know I've always had great faith in your work. I always said you'd be a success.'

I don't know why I bother sometimes, I really don't, my mother fulminates, marching in from the wings. *I never get any credit. No one pays any attention. I never get to have my say.*

Exercising in futility again, Darl? my father queries, all of a sudden apparent.

I think of all the words I should say to Redmond, all those half-formed sentences wrapped in their birth membranes like kittens born dead. The hateful, hurtful, justified recriminations, the charges against Lionel, the judgement against Redmond's own incapable soul. The plain, truthful words of our spectacular failure at love. But they float away from me. I try to remember how important it was, just one second ago, for him to admit to his unrelenting heart, for him to listen to me just once, to hear me out with his head down, then raise his eyes and tell me he is sorry.

Da-ad, I call out, and my voice is tiny from fear. *I'm lonely.*

I'm scare- d, I whimper, pressing my feet together in the cold sand. My voice drops out into the shocking emptiness. I try again. *Come back.*

At last my thin voice reaches him. *I don't want to be by myself.*

Kiss it better, croons my father, far out in the invisible water, not meaning it at all.

They float face down, these ribbons of words, timeless, searching for the bottom of the basalt pool, the pebbled base of the leaf-stained creek, trying to discern sand from golden water in the estuary, merging with the glassy-green and yellow ocean.

Redmond continues to sit, unresponsive and polite.

A quiet surf sighs up the beach, and the line of foam hangs, quiescent lace, until yet another wavelet erases the previous pattern. Continuation, repetition, overlay, washing over, nothing.

He's off the hook, my father's voice informs me. *He's getting off scot-free.*

I persevere. 'And the central motif? The reflection thing? You like that?'

'Very much. Yes, that looks good. Strong.' Redmond stands up and crosses his arms, but he keeps his distance from the painting. 'Yes, reflective, I suppose you'd say, wouldn't you?'

Now he puts his hands in his coat pockets, leans the top half of his body in a stiff movement, presses his lips together, gratified. 'You've done me proud, as they say. Should look well for me in the London market.'

The clock never stops its ticking, *trip-trap, trip-trap*, but now the pool of light where Redmond stands goes blank. There is no image without light, only the after-image in your own eye chamber, which runs ahead of you, a dog losing itself in the dimness. You see the tip of its tail, then it is beyond the limit of visual purple, lost to sight.

And the scales fell from her eyes, my father bellows as he finishes up the bedtime story, *and then they allll... lived happily ever after.* He snaps the book shut and grins.

That's not the end. You made that last bit up, my child's voice whines. *Didn't you?*

Yes you did!

I look at Redmond, as he stands there, one last time. Tears prick my eyes and I say to myself: *Goodbye, baby.* His head is monumental. It is inconceivable that it once pushed through his mother's bones, angry, panicked. I try to imagine his birth, his passage past sinews cream as knife handles, red muscle bands. His last glistening view as he turned towards earth, poor alien, of a lost love, an irretrievable world.

I switch off the photographer's light and he disappears. I hear him knocking into things in the dark, but he doesn't call out my name. On my way to the door I turn on the light near the panel. I can see its glow, a votive candle behind me, though I don't look round.

59 The Formula

The phone rings in the office. 'Will you get that?' calls Paul from the kitchen. 'Lyce?'

I pick it up. Pammy's urgent voice is in my ear. 'It's terrible, Doll,' she wails, 'I said to him, you better go and see about it. I can't keep up with every little sniffle. Go to a doctor. But you know what he's like.'

'Lee...sa!' Paul calls again, louder this time, and longer. 'Is that for me?' My name sounds quite unexceptional, the way he says it.

'I've got it,' I yell back. I close the door with my foot.

'What are you talking about, Pammy? What's happened?'

I feel nothing. I never expect to feel anything at first hand. There is an iced-up freezer tray behind the white door to my heart.

'Oh, God, I don't know... Hercules something... I hate hospitals. You know me. It's affected his other eye. Anyway, the point is, you're the next of kin. Can you come and make some arrangements to look after him? It's all been so sudden. He came home and he didn't look well, I must say. Seemed a bit down. But who would have thought...? Anyway, off he went. I don't know... maybe I should have gone with him. I thought he was OK on his own. I can't be running after him every single minute. I had things to do. And then whammo!'

She talks on and on and a rhyme my father taught me comes into my head:

When I was going up the stair
I met a girl who wasn't there.

'He must have been trying to find the Casualty section. He must have got lost or something. How was I to know he couldn't see anything? It just isn't like him, I mean really... he's the type who could find his way out of a maze. Anyway, they found him wandering round in the basement somewhere, you know, near that awful room where they sterilise all those nasty instruments. Desolate place, Doll. You don't want to know.'

She speaks as one who has peered over the abyss and realises that someone has just fallen from the top of a very tall cliff.

She wasn't there again today.

I wish that she would go away...

'You wouldn't wish it on your worst enemy,' she ends.

'Pammy...' I was going to save myself from this huge manipulative demand to make me jump, to toe the line, to do the right thing, to attend to Redmond. Just as in those impervious days before I met Lionel, I was not going to be told what to think and feel.

I summon up my courage. 'You're right, I don't want to know. You're it. You're going to have to pull yourself together.'

She can't believe it. 'Well, really! What will people think? Leaving him in the lurch like that, to fend for himself. I can't be made responsible. How can you be so...?'

'You're the one who cares about him. You fend for him. I'm officially the estranged wife.'

'...so hardhearted' she at last manages to get out.

I hang up.

I continue my trajectory into the stacks room. I open the blinds. Then I prise open the pot of gesso and mix a blob of chalk into it. Nice and thick. I stir it, feeling calm and oddly happy in the morning light. I consider the portrait. Viewed dispassionately, it is pretty good. Compelling even. I paint a large swathe of my mixture across it. I step back. 'That's better.'

I keep painting until the portrait has disappeared, has become once again a beautiful, empty and expectant space.

'You're looking more detached than usual this morning,' Paul told me as I stood in the warm kitchen. I watched as he made coffee and fried eggs. 'Is there anything wrong?'

'Not that I know of. This is just my natural expression.' I gave him a brilliant, evasive smile.

'You have paint on your shoes.'

'It'll wash off,' I assured him.

'So, everything's hunky-dory?'

'As far as I know.'

'Then stop sunning yourself on that radiator,' he ordered 'and come and sit down to a proper breakfast.'

The upkeep on Redmond had always been intensive. He demanded so much attention. In the end even Pammy couldn't provide it. On the one day when he really needed her she was off doing something for herself. Redmond was overlooked.

No-one took him seriously enough to care. That on its own would be just about enough to kill him.

I did go to see Pammy at the airport, succumbing at the last minute to her agenda. I'm sure she felt upset at leaving Redmond, although she did keep glancing at her watch. After all, she had a plane to catch back to Australia.

'Stuck with him through thick and thin, you know. Happy I can say that at any rate. Time to move on, Doll. Got to look after yourself. That's the thing.' She gave me a sharp glance.

'I'll stop off in Athens on the way home. Check out the art scene. I've plenty of contacts there. Not that I'm Greek,' she added.

As I turned to leave she scrabbled in her bag and held out a set of car keys. 'Oh God, I almost forgot. Here they are. He said he wanted you to have these. Lord knows if he'll ever be able to drive again.' She looked annoyed. 'Pretty generous, I thought, really. He loved that car... even if it was second-hand. I suppose you'll be looking for a settlement?'

Her eyes went sharp again and focused on me for an instant. 'I suppose you'll go back to Brisbane in due course?'

I said nothing.

I never trusted that woman, not for one minute, my mother gives a loud snort.

If she had a brain she'd be dangerous, my father remarks.

'We're still partners in the gallery, you know,' said Pammy. 'Full partners. That's all right and tight. That's for anyone to see.'

She stopped talking to consider my reaction.

'They do say he's going to get a bit better with his sight but I don't know...' She cast a dubious glance at the airport lounge. 'You'll go and see him, won't you? Listen, when you do, tell him I'm thinking of him... hope he gets better soon... that sort of thing. I'll leave it to you.

Can't do it myself. I've run out of time.'

I can hear my father's voice. *What an imbecile. Silly as a chook with its head cut off.* Running on, as he always did. *The blind leading the blind, he chortled.*

Pamela patted my arm in an attempt at emotion, her long, boneless hand, her silver bangle, cold as it hit my skin. Then she hurried off.

When I was very young, before I met Lionel, I used to crawl under the bed with the dachshund and have farting competitions with myself, watching the dog's expression and laughing. I had an addiction to laughter. Then it became a scarce resource.

I waited until the hospital staff said they had discharged Redmond. Then I wrote my letter, or rather I printed it, in large block capitals:

REDMOND,

PAMELA GAVE ME THE CAR KEYS. I ACCEPT THEM AS A FULL AND FINAL SETTLEMENT. THERE'S NO NEED TO DISCUSS IT. WE OWE EACH OTHER NOTHING. I WILL SEE A SOLICITOR AND ARRANGE TO DIVORCE YOU. I COULDN'T BEAR TO BE MARRIED TO A BLIND PERSON.

AS ALWAYS,
LYCE

PS PAMMY SAID TO SEND HER UNDYING LOVE.

60 Da Capo al Coda

Without your love
It's a melody played in a penny arcade...

I don't know what I thought I was doing marrying Lionel's son. They say innocence attracts evil but I've never thought innocence is as simple as that.

I might have thought I was repairing the past or at least attempting to rewrite it.

I knew I was after something that had been stolen from me. I thought Redmond might give it back, whatever it was. Funny that all I got in the end was a set of car keys.

Was it the grand illusion of childhood I wanted back? That gets taken away from us, by hook or by crook. Was it laughter and lightness? I don't know any more. What I had lost was not Redmond's to give back, that's for sure.

It is feasible that what I had been looking for was, after all, something ordinary that had gone unnoticed. Something that you might discover was not stolen, nor lost, nor mislaid, but had been waiting for you all that time. It was yours for the taking. You just had to learn how to stretch out your hand and grab at the right moment. There it was, perched sedately on its roost like one of Lionel's Black Orpington hens, dressed in chance's airy feathers and sporting fortune's beady eyes.

You've got to admit, my father's voice interrupts, *it's a funny old world.*

There he is, back again, one foot resting on his instep as he leans his weight against the kitchen bench.

Eh, Darl? You've got to have a sense of humour, and he throws his head back in a high snort of laughter.

Whose girl are you? insists Lionel, his hand fiddling with the latch on the Dutch door. And he answers for me, quick as a wink: *You're mine.*

I looked at myself in the mirror in Paul's bedroom. Then I took Peter's ring out of its zipped compartment and tried it on. I flashed my hand back and forth. *She wears my ring to show the world that she belongs to me...* The tune floated into my head. I hummed it, but I sounded flat, so I stopped. The words came bobbing by again. Endless flotsam and jetsam of love.

The tyranny of remembered sounds. Too many tunes in my head. I didn't need to add another one. Too many tyrannies altogether. Too few transformations. I spoke to the mirror on the wall. 'Do they think I'm standing still?' I said to its image. 'Or that I've been treading water all this time?'

I imagined myself in Redmond's red sports car, gunning it through the intersection at Toowong, pulling into the car park at the Regatta. It seemed a ridiculous idea. I tried to imagine walking up to Peter and touching him again, but the screen in my head went blank before my fingers met his silky skin.

The ring fitted more snugly than before and I had to use the sandalwood soap in Paul's bathroom to get it to come off. I considered tossing it into the shrubbery at the side of the gallery. Nobody ever went there. I even heaved open the window, but I couldn't bring myself to do it. I looked at the ring with regret. I heard Peter's voice *...and in the company of friends I wish to ask you to be my wife. Say yes, Honey Heart.*

I watched myself in the mirrored frieze, my face broken up into tiny pieces. I thought: 'You've never looked like me'. I didn't know I was crying until I saw a tear run down the side of my nose.

Whoever I was, I wasn't going to be for one moment longer a woman sitting slightly left of screen watching the movie of her life. In the end, I settled the ring down under the corrugated lining of my pastels' box, where it nagged at me like something misplaced. Each time I took it out a new accretion of pastel dust had built up on the surface of the clasped, metallic hands, the tiny ruby heart.

I'm sick to death of it, my mother used to say. *It's high time you did as you were told.*

I was sick to death of the rigmarole of other people's plans for me, their admonitions, their injunctions. Sick to death of being torn by the wish to please and the wish to move against, to succumb or to rebel, to admire or to invalidate. Sick of staring, petrified, at the pasture on the other side of that hollow wooden bridge. I was sick to death of compliance. It was high time I made a decision to clatter out into the middle of the bridge, troll or no troll.

'I've booked us into a concert for tonight. Beethoven's Symphony No.7,' Paul said. 'It's very cheering. You'll like it, I'm sure.'

I don't know what his idea of cheerful is, but I found myself crying in the dark. I can never remember the titles of pieces of music, but when I heard the first strains I recognised it as one of my father's favourite records. I had been a long time without music.

Stop snivelling, I told myself, it's pathetic. *You're such a fake. No-one else goes on like this.* I smoothed my new silk skirt under my hand, for comfort.

As we left, the sound of nose-blowing peppered the auditorium and people surreptitiously wiped their eyes. Paul leant towards me. I ran a finger under each eye in case my mascara had smudged. I smiled at him, sociable, breezy, independent. Paul put his hand on the back of my neck. He gave it a hard squeeze, and looked down at me. His eyes were unreadable. For one second I caught a whiff of my Blue Grass perfume as his hand warmed my skin.

'Whose popsy are you?' he said into my ear.

THE CONCUBINE OF SHANGHAI

by Hong Ying

Translated from the Chinese by Liu Hong

Sold by her aunt in 1907 to a Shanghai brothel, sixteen-year-old Cassia is plucked from the rank of lowly servant by Master Chang, the fearsome boss of a Triad gang. Chastised by the 'Madame' for leaving her feet and breasts unbound, Cassia nonetheless becomes his favourite mistress and enjoys her first passionate encounters as well as developing a taste for luxurious living.

But when Master Chang is brutally murdered, Cassia must fend for herself. Determined to succeed, she seduces the next Triad boss, Huang Peiyu and then his lacky, Yu Qiyang, fighting to secure her position as the 'Queen of Shanghai' whatever it takes.

Hong Ying, Chinese writer and poet, was born into a sailor's family in Chongqing in 1962. She studied at Lu Xun Creative Writing Academy and Fudan University and began her freelance writing career in the early 1980s. She has been translated into twenty-five other languages and has won major literary awards in Taiwan and Italy. She currently lives in Beijing.

ISBN: 978-0-7145-3150-2
Price: £9.99/ $14.95

Also by Hong Ying and published by Marion Boyars:

K: THE ART OF LOVE
PEACOCK CRIES

Praise for K: *The Art of Love*

'Like all Hong Ying's work, K is written with a wonderfully intense simplicity – it's tough, uncompromising, direct and tense with strong emotion, but also full of poetry and grace.'
Andrew Motion

ENLIGHTENMENT

by Maureen Freely

An investigative journalist returns to Istanbul, the scene of her early love affair with Sinan. She is forced to overcome her qualms when she is asked by his 'honeypot' wife to help her regain her son, taken away by the American authorities when Sinan is arrested on entry into the States. A tense thriller involving a retired secret service informer, a mysterious 'trunk' murder, and a group of young students involved in subterfuge, but now tackling a real crisis, Maureen Freely's novel shows that in Turkey, nobody is who they say they are, and everyone is a suspect.

Maureen Freely is a controversial writer who is not afraid to criticise the Turkey she loves. She defended Orhan Pamuk, many of whose books she has translated, when he was prosecuted under Article 301 for un-Turkish behaviour, and has also assisted Turkish authors Perihan Magden and Elif Shafak who were prosecuted under similar articles.

Maureen Freely was born in the United States, and grew up in Istanbul. She was educated at Harvard University. She is a translator, an academic at the University of Warwick and a writer. She lives in England.

ISBN: 978-0-7145-3141-0
Price: £9.99

'That rare pleasure, a book that grips on every level, a bold and beautiful novel about history, memory and love.' Nicci French

'A dark Conradian drama, set in a beautifully illuminated Istanbul, where the past is always with us.' Orhan Pamuk

'Raises pressing questions about Turkey's willingness to confront its inner divisions.' Guardian.